I0612422

The Feast of Tombola

Doug Booth

Copyright 2011 RD Booth
All Rights Reserved

For those who dream of paradise

The Feast of Tombola

Part One

One

On the fourth evening Aayla went to where Cassidy sat on the leeward beach, the mild sensation from the tincture warming her. They drank a few drops each evening, not more, spilling what remained in their cups into the sand. Not partaking in the festivities would be quickly noticed by her father or The Grand Guardian who alone abstained from the tincture, each man ensuring the continuance of the festive mood. No restriction was imposed on the village.

The week was one of merriment and celebration, first-coupling and joining, the willingness to give of oneself and spontaneous release. The villagers understood the importance of embracing the Twelve Scriptures, behaving wantonly from dawn to dusk and into the night. But her father couldn't be everywhere and the eldest son of the ancient Grand Guardian would be certainly bidding his father farewell, sharing their final words together.

That evening the village would be summoned to the gorge. None but the very young and feeble were ever excused. This would be Cassidy's fifth year at the Tombola Pole. Five years since he'd flung the merciful stone that killed his father, diminishing the Chief Counsellor's sense of duty and garnering his hate.

Not until the first day of The Seven Feasts did the village know who might be chosen to give of themselves.

From the year of their first-change friends and neighbours gathered at the pole, pushing and shoving to grab the first stones, though none but the Chief Counsellor would hurl the killing stone from his sling.

This year the ancient Grand Guardian himself was the one chosen.

Cassidy understood, as did his father and his father before him. Now Aayla understood that pretence would let them see what others could not. Amongst so many they were alone and, to Aayla, Cassidy was the wisest and most handsome of all the village men. Yet they didn't speak. Aayla was upset. She wanted to hurl her stone. She wanted the evening to end. She wanted to sleep with Cassidy on the cool sand and wake with him to swim in the blue water.

At half past the eleventh hour, according to time kept by The Grand Guardian, a thunderous reverberation shattered the gaiety along the shore. People stumbled to their feet; others waded from the water as the throng began a slow march to the gorge. Many stood naked but for scanty shields quickly pulled on, their bodies covered with festive pigments.

Cassidy walked in one direction, Aayla went in another.

The moonlit sea was calm; torches lined the high stone walls of the precipice that had split apart in an unrecorded epoch to form the gorge. Flames flickered erratically, revellers danced, eerie shadows painted those damp walls with distorted spectres appropriate to the night.

He sat at the threshold of his 100th year in shallow water, his frail body too weak to tremble, his mind densely fogged by the opium tainting his blood. He was no longer cognizant of his looming death, no longer chilled by fear as those who came to honour him gathered by his limp body at the sandy depression in the gorge.

In his final moments he appeared no different from the many others who'd gone before him. His thin legs were hidden by dark water, his veined hands tied to the Tombola Pole at his back. His eyes were sunken, glassy and red. His head, sparsely covered with strands of white hair, drooped into his chest and no one paused to consider what fear or joy might occupy his mind.

He was no longer fearful that life after death might exist solely in the ephemeral memories of the living, his private preoccupation since told by his son that he should prepare for his time at the Pole of Tombola

No preamble was expected. The eldest son simply sliced the air with his hand, carving an arc from where the village stood to his father. The youngest son was nowhere to be seen.

The village girls standing by the water's edge, their eyes brightly decorated, hurled their stones across the shortest distance, most missing the mark, some stones splashing into the low tide, others striking his legs or his chest. The boys' volley reached its mark with the fullest impact, each stone resounding in a macabre chorus according to its weight and dimension.

Cassidy stood amongst them, disguising his mood. The parents and neighbours behind him threw too high or too low. Not Shakkra who stood by her son, sharing his joy. She was sombre and sober, her aim precise. She was killing the man who had once killed her husband.

The Chief Counsellor, experienced with his leather sling, flung the last stone with speed and stoic efficiency. The thwack was loud, surrounded by deathly silence.

The Grand Guardian died at midnight as decreed by his Twelve Scriptures, his skin and his bones broken. He was gone, his lifeless body bloodied, discoloured with bruises. Death and peace everlasting his deserved recompense, they knew, for having tended to a flock that was no longer his.

The village filtered into the dark and the forest, toward the shore leaving him alone in the rising tide waters at the foot of the Tombola Pole. The dancing and festive mood wasn't yet over.

When they had gone the eldest son crossed the bridge and passed through the gate with Irene. He had much to consider, much to complete before the predawn when he would free the old man of his bonds and secrete his body into the sea. He was now The Grand Guardian, their mentor and saviour. He was more certain than ever before of his future, the future of Tombola and the future of his younger brother who would work in the field as any other, and pay homage as any other.

What had poisoned the old man's mind that he would believe a boy of seventeen and his scheming mother capable of governing Tombola?

Two

At the beach the village once again filled their cups. Aayla ignored them. She followed Cassidy into the darkness and far beyond the melee before running to grasp his hand and watch him gazing at the heavens. She wondered what he saw that others did not see. She wanted to see through his eyes. Nor was he any different when he looked at the blue water or the bright lines that crossed the blue sky from nowhere and soon disappeared.

When he looked at her, she wondered even more.

She wanted to talk, to tell him what she'd learned, however she knew his moods and didn't. He was remembering his father. Instead she lay by his side and soon fell asleep.

Not many hours later Cassidy awoke several miles to the south of the village. He lay on the white sands that framed the Isle of Tombola. Aayla was curled into his arms. The air was still, quiet. Palm leaves drooped, dormant, their recent dew glistening under a new sun. Her body felt cool to his touch.

He rose without disturbing her, studying her for long moments, mesmerized by her child-like innocence. He felt deep emotion for her, yet he couldn't act upon his emotion. Any such violation of the Twelve Scriptures would incur The Grand Guardian's wrath and Aayla would be lost to him forever. She was forbidden to him. She was promised to another.

Despite the decree, each knew the youthful texture of the other's skin, the taste of hunger on the other's lips. He knew the soft curves of her body, and she dreamt each night of the hard lines sculpted into his. They were seventeen. In a fleeting year Aayla would couple with the youngest brother of The Grand Guardian. She would join with him and begin The Seven Feasts together.

Cassidy ran to the sea to bathe, to strengthen his mind and weaken his body against the familiar urges rampant within him. When he was cleansed, the damp sand washed away, he swam into deeper water until he could swim no farther, kicking and waving his arms to stay afloat, seeing her and wanting her. Even from so far away she was beautiful to his eyes.

He swam with long, gentle strokes to the shore and went to her, not making a sound. He sat by her side, kneading her bare hip, his eyes searching the sea, the horizon and the sky. His mind was filled with questions. His eyes filled with wonder. He knew, as his father once knew, and the knowledge troubled him.

When Aayla awoke she stretched her taut body, her mind clear. He wondered whether her mind ever slept. She knelt and she kissed him. She let her eyes absorb him and she ran into the blue water up to her knees where she squatted to give herself privacy. Then she swam, Cassidy observing her every stroke, unconcerned. Of the two she was the better swimmer. Still, he was the man and he would protect her.

When she returned, she dropped to her knees in front of him, smiling. She was naked, save her brightly coloured maiden-shield crafted from soft leather. He wore the same. He wasn't tall, the way he held himself made him taller than he was, though he was muscular and sinewy. His hair was dark, his skin a dark amber and his teeth shone like stars when he smiled at her.

She was petite, smaller in stature, her body the colour of caramel sprinkled with cinnamon and perfectly proportioned. Her golden crimped hair resembled an impish crown, her blue eyes more crystal clear than the blue water at midday

She kissed him. It's all they could do when away from the eyes of the village and her father. Doing more would endanger them and his punishment wouldn't be one of willing sacrifice.

They picked wild berries for their breakfast. When they were satiated Aayla filled her hands once more and squeezed them together.

"Cassidy, I heard the old women of the village talking, the ones who gossip and cackle because their best days are forgotten. They thought I was not listening, when I was. They were telling of how girls can pretend never to have coupled, with wild berries mashed for their juices, or the blood of young goats. I feel deep emotion for you, Cassidy. And you do for me."

"No, Aayla. We must not. You know we must not. The danger is too great. Our futures are decreed. You will first couple with Dakota, not me. And you will join with him. Then you will be forbidden to me when he becomes The Grand Guardian in one year. As Irene, you will not share affection with others."

"You feel deep emotion for me. I know that you do. I see how you look upon me. I see how you must run to the blue water to escape what you feel. They know. They all know. And you know. Do not think to tell me untruths."

"I do. And he knows that I do. He waits for me to give him a reason, as he waited for my father."

"When the last moon was high he sat at the pole and was touched with a 101 stones, as was your father. My heart is happy for you, Cassidy, that you flung the stone after so many suns and moons of waiting. I am happy for Shakkra. I went to her but she wanted aloneness."

"But his youngest son is not dead; the one he decreed will couple and join with you during the next Seven Feasts."

"No, Cassidy. You will be my first-mate. I will couple with you, or no one."

"You cannot defy your father, Aayla, or The Grand Guardian. It will go badly for you. I know this."

"How can you know? What would they do to the daughter of The Chief Counsellor?"

"They would punish me instead." He forced a laugh. "I am already punished. They will join me with the fat one. When I couple with her, when I see her face so close, I will die from fright or be crushed by her weight when she rolls upon me. No one will find me. No one has seen her shield, Aayla. Her maiden is concealed by her heavy stomach." He put his hands to her face. "Is that what you want, for me to die under the fat one?"

"You will couple with me, Cassidy, not the ugly one. I will join with you or no one at all. I do not care that I will be Irene, the first-mate of The Grand Guardian. I will be your first-mate and you will never share affection during The Seven Feasts. I will be enough for you."

"And I..."

She waited, but he said nothing more.

"In the dark, Cassidy, he will never know. There are always goats and pigs to slaughter the day before. The blood would be clean. I know how. I have practiced, alone in my parents' hearth when you leave me to find your favourite tree; I have practiced with goat's milk tinted with berry juice. At first when I stood and walked I spilled a little. Now I do not. When I imagine we are together you are stained the way I will stain Dakota. Cassidy I have one year to practice more with only berries. Anyway, he will not care. He wants another." She grimaced. "I think the berries will be better. I will let you know tomorrow."

"Aayla, we cannot."

"We will."

"We will not. You do not know, Aayla. I do."

"What do you know?"

"I know you begin to practice tricking Dakota because in your mind you know what is decreed, even though you feel deep emotion for me. I know what we must do and what we cannot. I know that I wait to see you without your maiden-shield, and how I feel when I think of how you will look. I know when I do you will be joined with him, and me with the fat one whose maiden I will need help from the village to see. I know that what I want or feel does not matter. I feel hurt when I think of you. I know that not to think would be best." He shrugged. "I cannot help myself."

She glanced at his loin-shield, as though quite superior to him.

"Do you feel hurt now? Are you thinking of me without my maiden-shield right now, Cassidy? Or, if you are not, who? You are thinking of someone very beautiful and young. I can see that you are. Is there someone else you feel deep emotion for?"

"No, Aayla, I am thinking of you. But you know what will happen. You see what happens in the spring to all the women who are not cautious, and we lack the medicine used by the older ones. My mother has told me, when we speak in whispers because of him. It is decreed that women must be cautious unless they are newly joined and after their first child. That is why they act as they do during The Seven Feasts. I know this."

"Then you should go into the blue water to cool yourself and to change the shape of your loin-shield before the old women see you this way and believe you are searching for someone to pull you from your shield. I see the way they look upon you. They are eager to pull you from your shield. So go to them. I will go to my hearth to forget you and prepare for my joining with Dakota. I will use my berries and pretend I am with him."

"Yes, Aayla, you will go to your hearth, to dream of me," he smirked, "to stain with your berries whatever you use to replace me. I do not need old women."

She leapt onto him, smearing his face with the pulp in her hands. "I will not. I no longer feel deep emotion for you."

"You will, and when the moon is high you will tell me how good I was with you. Now get off of me."

"And how will you spend the day on your perch, Cassidy? Will you put raindrops into the forest today? And do not tell me untruths because I see you. I know where your tree is. I see with my eyes what you do."

She squeezed her legs tightly against him.

"What have you seen, Aayla? How many times have spied upon me?"

He was suddenly solemn. His body was tense, forcing her to release her tight grip. She eased onto the sand and stood, strangely uncertain what she should answer. She searched his piercing eyes. He was waiting for the truth.

"I have seen you thinking of me. I see you sitting alone, Cassidy. I see you making raindrops in the forest. I see the changes in your face and I know you are seeing me in your mind without my maiden-shield. I feel the same changes in my face when I am alone." She swallowed, wanting to touch him. "I go there when I know others cannot see me. I wait to go closer until you are sitting on your branch because the tree is where you find aloneness."

"What else, Aayla? And don't lie to me."

Her forehead crunched into thin lines. "What did you say, Cassidy? What words did you speak?"

"I am sorry. My mind was in another place... with you. I was thinking of lying with you. I wanted to say, do not tell

14

me untruths."

"I would never. I am sorry. From now I will give you aloneness."

"How many times have you followed me?"

"Many times," she sulked.

"Is that all you have seen, Aayla?"

"What else would I see? I see trees and grass, when I want to see you, when you are always so high that I cannot see what I want in my heart." She beamed, glancing at his leather shield. "I must be content to see you in my mind. Often when I see you I think you will pull it away from you so that you will not have to couple with me. Then I see your raindrops and I know I am wrong."

"Nothing more, you are certain?"

"Yes, I am certain."

He smirked. "So, you spy on me so that you might see me and measure me against others?"

She didn't answer.

He wrapped his arms around her, pulled her close so that she could wrestle free and ran with her to the ocean where he didn't stop until she floated in his arms. Then he pushed her away, laughing, watching her disappear behind a wall of hectic water. He stopped laughing when she surfaced, gasping, her hair twisted in all directions, the festive pigment on her eyes smudged into blotches the more she rubbed.

"Aayla, the greatest mermaid…you look like a drowned sea urchin to me."

"I want to be a woman for you, and you treat me like a child before her first-change. I no longer feel deep emotion for you. And I hope your face stays red forever. I am not a little girl and each time you see your red face in the reflection plate you will remember the first time you saw me without this." He didn't understand her rapid movements beneath the surface, until her wet shield whipped across his face. "Stay here if you want, Cassidy. You can die in the blue water. I do not care."

"Aayla…"

She strode towards the shore, waiting to twirl until her feet touched the dry sand. From where he stood he couldn't tell. He was afraid to move, clenching the tiny shield in his hands. The village women he'd seen naked and painted were joined, from one year to many years older than him until they remained in their villas to sleep or to remember better years when they, too, were pursued by young men.

Aayla was his age with pure skin, her body unpainted, moulded to perfection. Now she was naked, her body taunting him, every inch of her glistening. He knew his nights and days without her would forever be a torment.

He went to her, not surprised by her snub. She was Aayla. He followed her towards the trees, knowing she would glance over her shoulders, letting him close the distance between them. When he came to her she let him see all of her, easing onto her knees, stretching forward and lying facedown, nestling her body into the heated sand and resting her head on her folded arms.

"Do not look upon me."

"You are forcing me to look upon you. And you tell me not to? Do you know how beautiful you are to me, Aayla?"

"Yes, I do, and I am not forcing you. Forcing is a bad word. You will not couple with me, and now I must force you to look upon me. Go away from me. "

"No, Aayla. My heart is bursting with deep emotion for you. You know of my feelings and how I have waited my entire life to see you this way."

She turned her head. "But you wait for another to see me unclothed and to couple with me."

Cassidy swung around. He stamped one foot into the sand, then the other. Would she always be this difficult? He hoped so. She was Aayla, his, perfect in every way and he

16

would not chance to tell her. The danger was too great. He snorted. She wouldn't believe him.

"No other will see you this way, if I must take you from Tombola."

She raised her head. "Will you float in the sky, Cassidy, like a bird, and hold me in your talons until you drop me to the sand or into the blue water. Do you want to lose me and forget me?"

"You are laughing at me."

"No, I am not. You know we are safe here. You know that we are, and what is past the blue water that we cannot see? You have heard the stories. This is our home. Who do you know who has left? The ancient Grand Guardian and his eldest son alone travel across the blue water before the early sun so that they might see yet not be seen. Not even my father has the courage to leave." She stood, unashamed, dusting the sand from her body with leisurely sweeps of her hands. "Now you do not have to imagine how I am without my maiden-shield when you are in your secret tree filling the air with raindrops, Cassidy."

She kissed him and stepped back, her arms by her side, wanting him to see all of her.

"This is not the best way for me to cool myself, Aayla. And, yes, I will make raindrops in the forest today, and tomorrow, because of you. Now we must go. We must return to the village before we are missed and you will never come to my tree again."

She creased her brow. "Why? Why can we not go together? I can climb as well as you. I can climb better. Why must we be apart to do alone what we can do together?"

"Please, Aayla, come."

He held out his hand.

"Go without me, Cassidy. Nothing is written in the Twelve Scriptures to prevent me from having aloneness and walking without my maiden-shield when none can see me or none wants to."

"Aayla, I feel so much emotion for you. What I see is a mermaid, unclothed and beautiful to my eyes. I have never seen anyone as perfect. Why do you not approach The Grand Guardian for permission to stone me instead? The result will be no different. And now we must leave, so that we might be together from the early moon to the early sun."

"No, Cassidy. Go to your favourite tree and pretend I am with you. Leave me to pretend you are with me…and leave me my shield."

"Aayla…"

"Go, Cassidy. I want aloneness from you. I want to swim and bathe without you. Maybe I will come to you at the early moon. I do not know. Maybe I will stay in my parents' hearth alone."

He left, disheartened. He went into the tropical forest, his bare feet cushioned by soft grass, fallen leaves and vines, the weight of one footfall concealed before another was made. He knelt into the yielding floor, brushing away the camouflage from an iron chest once buried by his great-grandfather. He raised the lid, reached for his favourite book and climbed to his perch.

He hated himself for making Aayla sad, not eager to spend his day without her. Neither was he anxious for darkness that would bring sleepless privation. In his villa, more humble than hers, he could no longer read by the flickering light of his bed lamp because of the man.

Books were unknown. The village had no need of books or knowledge beyond the cultivation of their fields and the wisdom of The Grand Guardian and the guidance of the Chief Counsellor. They were born, nurtured until their first-change when they would toil with the others in the fields. In their eighteenth year they coupled and joined and became like all others before them.

Most who first came of their free will to Tombola were dead. Those who were not, he supposed, chose to forget while others possessed no memory at all.

Soon he would have his own villa and give children to a woman for whom he felt no emotion while, in his heart, he wanted Aayla more than his freedom. While in his troubled young mind he knew he must have both. Without one, he would never have the other.

He read until the dim light filtering through the tall trees strained his eyes, his mind filled with his newest images of Aayla. He clambered from his perch, buried his book and went to the beach to rid his mind of confusion.

No work was done during The Seven Feasts, a time of celebration and joy, a time of random affection between neighbours and raucous abandon. One year from then Cassidy would see Aayla together with Dakota and know they had coupled.

Images of their bodies pressed together tortured his mind, and would until the day he would sit at the pole. He wondered when that day would come. He thought very soon, once they discovered what he had done. He wondered whether he would be as brave as his father who hadn't taken the tincture, whose cheeks weren't filled with figs to dull his senses.

He remembered his father who hadn't cried out, the look in his father's eyes that retold his every word. He remembered vivid tales of his great-grandfather, a man of strong will and well-versed, one of the first arrived on the island to escape the hangman's knot. He remembered his father's determination, his every secret lesson and how he, his father's son, had dropped his stone defiantly into the water five years before.

Neither The Grand Guardian nor his sons had liked Cassidy for how he was different, he knew. He was curious, and silent. He wanted to know more than he should about

Tombolina and what he would see from atop the twin cliffs. Often they would see him standing at the gorge before and after The Seven Feasts when he wasn't allowed, looking across the bridge and peering towards the precipice.

The Chief Counsellor saw in the boy's eyes what he could not read in his mind. Tombolina was forbidden to all, with the exception of those who The Grand Guardian and Irene sought to comfort and make ready in the Sacred Pond.

Jealousy or envy didn't exist amongst them, love was unknown. Nothing was owned so that nothing would be coveted as decreed in the Twelve Scriptures.

The Chief Counsellor often saw Cassidy talking with his daughter. He was anxious to one day cast that last stone above all others. He didn't like the boy. He scarcely liked his daughter, whether she was his or not.

His daughter would join with the half brother of the Grand Guardian. That he was expelled from his father's hearth with his mother who was, until that moment, Irene didn't matter. One day he who was now the guardian of the island would die or sit at the pole. His half-brother would take his place, Aayla would govern by Dakota's side and. he, as her father, would do well.

Three

Cassidy passed the day alone in his tree, watching for her, choosing not to read. What was decreed would not be undone. Aayla was dreaming of the impossible. She would join with Dakota; he would spend what remained of his life with a horrible creature and nothing would amend what was written.

He knew so much he couldn't tell her, that he wanted to share with her. He knew of the hidden channel on Tombolina. He'd swum the full length and had put his hand to the smooth hull of what he knew was a magnificent yacht not made of wood. He knew of the Sacred Pond and had swum in its warm, shallow water. He knew how the precipice stood high above the smaller and secret isle. He'd seen its sheer wall more than once. He'd seen from afar the fine hearth painted the colour of gold, the high doors the colour of his great-grandfather's watch, the colour of its windows glittering like mirrors where The Grand Guardian lived with Irene by a crystal pool and amidst lush gardens. He saw the bright lights within, much brighter than his lantern or any other, as bright as day. He'd heard the dull roar emanating from the small hut far to the side and hidden in a grove, and he knew what was there.

He knew what flew across the skies, leaving white lines, and he wanted to tell her, knowing full well she wouldn't believe him. Who in the village would? He knew from his father where Tombola rose from the sea and what lay to the east and to the west of the isle. He knew what snow was in the cold north, snow he would never feel. He knew of arid desert sands. He knew that he missed his father and gave him thanks each night for the secrets they once shared. What he didn't know was how to escape.

He knew what he asked of Aayla was wrong. He was untruthful to her, and would be again.

He couldn't confess to her. Her knowledge would make her complicit. He dreamed of being her first-mate. He wanted no one else. No one on the Isle of Tombola was more beautiful and he loathed the thought of Aayla joining with Dakota.

Aayla knew each time The Grand Guardian was gone from the island with his eldest son onboard the yacht or in the whirring machine he knew was a helicopter. She would overhear her parents talking in their villa. They had no reason not to. Soon she would join with Dakota who would take his brother's place to govern with Irene who was his mother, until Aayla was ready. Until then Aayla would live with them on Tombolina and her family would prosper.

She didn't know.

Cassidy's mood was so sombre that he barely managed to slide from the tree. He called her name in a loud whisper, not trusting her impish behaviour. How many times did he deceive her and misuse her? How would he dare to tell her that he had, and for what purpose?

He decided he wouldn't, because he loved her. She wouldn't understand. She wouldn't believe him, as much as he loved her and longed to tell her the word she didn't know. He knew that with love would come jealousy and envy, and with those, his father once told him, coveting and greed.

One day he would absently utter similar wrong words to another not as distracted as Aayla and expose himself for what he'd done and what he knew. Then she would be lost to him. His one way to have her and to keep her was to deceive her. He would sleep with her twice more on the beach. From then on, until she was joined, he would see her when their work in the field was done, when men would attend to the repairs of their hearths and women would work to prepare the evening meals.

She would run to the beach as before, to swim and bathe and wait to sit with him in the sand and the late-day heat of the sun. And now that she knew of his tree she would imagine false thoughts and not want to wait alone. Now when would he read?

He went to the greeting area where he poured a large measure of tincture into his cup under the watchful and approving eyes of painted women recently joined and others much older, all sharing affection, friends sharing first-mates without inhibition, neighbours unabashedly caressing painted neighbours.

He went to the shore where Aayla waited and passed behind her, whispering her name. She lingered as long she could before she followed, emptying her cup into the sand and taking his hand.

They walked for what he thought must be an hour, two miles at least, though she didn't know time or distance. Nor did she care. She knew the rising and setting sun, she knew the quarter, half and full moons and she knew she was with the one man for whom she would ever feel deep emotion.

She would not lose him. She was the daughter of the Chief Counsellor. They would never stone her. Neither would they stone Cassidy. She would hurl herself from the precipice if they killed him. She would find a way onto Tombolina and throw herself from the towering cliff into the violence of the surging waters of the gorge.

"Cassidy, the berries are the better way. They do not fall out and the skins are so fine that he will easily mash them inside me." She waited. "Did you hear me, Cassidy? He will easily mash them inside me. He will see me unclothed and know what I am like."

He maintained his stride, making her struggle to stay close. "Yes, I know," he called out, his head tilted slightly. "But I will not hear your screams of pleasure from the underside of the fat one. So what does it matter, Aayla? You will not hear my last breath and I will not hear the sounds of your mashing."

"You belong in the pen with the pigs and the goats."

"I am cleaner than a pig and smell better than a goat in his rutting season," he pivoted, letting her crash into him. "You should know that, Aayla. And if you do not, you will wait less than a year to discover the difference. I am convinced he will enjoy what is under the silky blonde hair of his doe. I know he will see that colour in the dark, if not the mashed skins of wild berries."

Her eyes opened wide, her mouth wider, and he waited until the last moment to grasp her fist in mid-air. He swung her over his shoulder, gripping one wrist, letting the other attack his back, his other hand pinning her legs to his chest. When he was waist-high he unloaded her weight into the sea.

He waited.

"You are a captivating mermaid, a siren of the sea swimming in my heart, yet you want to swim with a pig that smells like a goat."

"Do not make words as we make food in the fields, as you catch fish in the blue water. I do not understand you. I do not want to swim. I want to couple with you. I am a woman, Cassidy. We do not need the medicine used by the older women if you are quick and your mind is not trapped inside me."

"It is not my mind that would be trapped inside your blonde curls, Aayla. I could never be that quick to leave you whenever we first couple, or when we have a last time to sleep together. The more you weaken me, the stronger I must be...for you as much as for me."

"You would rather play with me as a child."

"And you would rather spy upon me, as a child, as I sit in my tree."

He looked away.

"Cassidy, what is wrong? Why are we speaking words we do not mean?"

"Because I know what you do not."

"They all know you are different. You pretend to be quiet, when they see in your eyes that you are beyond even the oldest and the wisest of our village. I watch you, Cassidy, when you toil in the field and throw your net into the blue water, but you are not in the fields or the water. You are somewhere beyond where the blue water flows into the sky. I see how you stare where I see nothing. I see you. You are no different when you are with me." She paused. "Will you tell me before too many suns what you know? Will I know soon what you keep from me?"

"What I keep from you, Aayla, I cannot explain. What I know is that to couple with you will weaken me, when I must be strong for you."

She twisted in the water and went to the shore. Ignoring him she stepped from her shield and returned to the sea to swim away from him.

He watched her closely, matching each of her strokes with twice as many strides, closing the distance between them. She'd drunk only a small quantity of tincture but he didn't trust the state of her mind.

He grabbed her foot, dragged her into his arms and held her in place. He carried her to shore and laid her onto the sand before the day's warmth dissipated into the night air. He listened to her cry and stared out to sea, waiting for sleep to overtake her. When he was certain, he squirmed from his shield and curled against her.

When she woke she felt a familiar weight pressing into the arch at the small of her back. She felt his warmth. She raised herself onto her elbows and gazed out to sea. Her temples tingled from the night before.

"Cassidy, are your eyes open? You are not facing the blue water."

"I am facing the most beautiful knolls instead, Aayla. They are smooth. They have no trees to climb and are too small to walk upon, heated with the morning sun and soft to my lingering touch."

"Cassidy, again I do not understand what you say. What strange words are you speaking?"

She tried to roll against his weight and the pressure of his hands. He fondled one side, then the other and she lowered her head onto her folded arms.

She giggled. "Are my mounds better to squeeze unclothed, Cassidy?"

"I have squeezed them many times before in the blue water."

"But never without my maiden-shield. Tell me."

"I like what I see. I am content to stay as I am, Aayla, until we must leave. I did not sleep well."

"You cannot live without me, Cassidy, and all you can say is that you like them. I see how the other boys look upon me when I wait for you, and the other girls who are not as beautiful." She wriggled. "Let me stand."

"I cannot."

"Let me stand, Cassidy. The river beneath your head wants to flow."

He jumped up, reached for his shield that lay in the sand and ran to the sea. She barely had time to absorb what she was seeing, what so quickly disappeared from her sight.

Her shield remained in the sand and she went to him as a mother about to scold a child.

"You did not squat to let out your water, Aayla."

"We do not have to squat. We can do everything that you do." She glared at him. "You slept unclothed with me. You lay by my side. You knew what I did not."

"You would not have slept. Your head is filled with thoughts of coupling. I wanted to dry my loin-shield. Mine is not as fine as yours, daughter of the Chief Counsellor."

"Your mother made my shield." She grabbed at him beneath the water. "And now you wear yours in the water where I cannot see you. Why do you not want me, Cassidy? What have I done to you that you hide from me in the forest and feel shame in front of me? You know we are meant to share a hearth. Your mother feels deep emotion for me, why not her son?"

"She feels emotion for you as a daughter."

"In my heart she is my mother. Her emotion for me is deep. She is happy when she is with me in the water. We are like sisters. She is warm and soft. You are a goatskin satchel filled with stones. "

"She cries when the rest of the village sleeps. In bed she whispers to my father."

"I feel sorrow in my heart for her. Often she speaks of him. I also remember him."

"Soon I will tell you more of my father, Aayla. You will know more of me and all of what I know. He was a wise man and taught me many important lessons. He wanted me to possess what he could not. He wanted me to know so that I, too, would be wise one day."

Her brow creased. "In those lessons, did he teach you strange words?"

He nodded. "Yes, words passed to him from his father and his father's father. He wanted me to have what he could not give me. Yet he showed me how."

"I do not understand."

"You have no need."

"You will not couple with me?"

27

"I will not."

"Will you swim with me and play with me unclothed in the water? Will you let me see you one time, as I do in my dreams? "

"Will you promise to never again tempt me? Will you promise never again to doubt my emotion for you?"

"We have two more moons to sleep in the sand, this sun and one more to wake and run to the water. Until the third sun when we work in the field I will sleep with my maiden-shield in the sand and come to you in the blue water unclothed. I like how you look upon me differently. I will do what I can to change you and make you weak. And I will tell you something that I know. I feel happiness that you are tempted." She faced the shore. "Cassidy, do you believe the emotion you feel for me is what a boy feels for a sister. Or do you feel shame that you will not reach as far as Dakota when he mashes the berries inside me."

"You are not my sister and Dakota's shield is empty." His bravado failed. "And what do you know that I do not? You are a girl."

She ignored him and waded to the shore. She sat in the sand with her knees pressed tightly against her breasts, waiting. She knew what she would say, which wasn't what puzzled her.

"Will you sleep with me unclothed when the moon is high and the sky is dark?"

"Yes, I will, once you are taken by your dreams. And do not think to trick me and wait to take my strength that comes to me with the moons. I will wake and drag you to the blue water to cool you."

They sat quietly. Cassidy gazed at the early moon, Aayla at the sand.

"The Grand Guardian will leave Tombola tomorrow with Irene, Cassidy," she whispered. "They will not return until the fourth high sun."

Four full days, he thought, and that many nights.

"He will leave when the late sun and the early moon are together in the sky, for what is left to see of The Seven Feasts."

"No, he will leave before the early sun."

"And when he is gone your father will take you through the gate at the arch to play for the first time on the forbidden shore and your head will grow as large as the silver disk in the sky."

She looked at him strangely. "No one is allowed. My father is not allowed. It is decreed. Not even if when he is older Dakota becomes The Grand Guardian and I am Irene, when I am old and the skin on my face and my breasts sag and feel like the leather of your loin-shield. You will also be old, and will not care. I see the old men. I see how their shields swing against their knees when they walk and how they hang when they work in the field."

"What do you mean when you say, if when he is older? He will be The Grand Guardian with his mother by the next Seven Feasts. Until then his brother will teach him and guide him to make him ready."

"No, Cassidy. His brother sent him from Tombolina in shame with Irene. Now he is the true guardian until his last breath and Forrest is Irene."

Cassidy hid his surprise. He hunched his shoulders and took a deep breath.

"What is the difference whether one is the guardian of the island, or the other? They are brothers."

"They share half the ancient's blood. They are not true brothers."

"Nothing is changed. He will join with you, as the ancient decreed."

"No, I will not. You will see, Cassidy. My son will be yours."

"You are certain of what you have heard?"

29

"Dakota will not be our guardian. I will not be Irene."

"And his brother, you are certain of when he will leave?"

Aayla never misled him with her surreptitious information.

"Yes, I am certain." She searched his eyes. "Why must you know each time? Why is he more important to you than me? We have two moons and two suns before we must work again in the field. I do not want aloneness from you until the late sun. You will stay with me and we will return to the village once at each late sun before the moon for our cups of tincture."

"No, Aayla. We will not. We will leave each early sun. I cannot remain with you for two moons and two suns while you are naked. I know what is in your mind. I know what would happen between us."

"What is naked? Is that one word taught by your father?"

"Yes, and you must tell no one. They would not understand." He paused. "It means that you are unclothed. Now come, naked one. We must leave. Be content that when the moon is high I will not sleep because of you."

"Will you look upon me and put your head upon me when you are also… naked?"

"Yes, I will."

"Will you teach me the words you know, words I do not know? Will tell me what is in your mind when you look to where the blue water ends and you see what I cannot?"

"Yes, I will, and very soon. I promise you."

"I am not ready to leave." She stretched forward into the sand. "We will go when the sun chases the moon."

He chose not to argue. "I will sit here to think and to gaze upon you."

"I know, Cassidy. You will think of the time you will not share with me."

Aayla gazed across to where the blue water became the sky; Cassidy looked out to sea toward the horizon.

Before the left they bathed together and splashed. She jumped onto him, clinging to his neck, her legs wrapped tightly around him. She put her lips against his. She was his one temptation. She made his life unbearable when she was away from him, each gentle touch relived in the fields, his tree and his bed, which was the most tormenting.

He reached out to her and brought her to the shore. Together they strolled along the beach, releasing their hands not far from the village where naked and painted bodies lay strewn, some spent from the night before while others frolicked or bathed in the sea.

She went to her villa which was one of the two largest and most decorated in the village, where she had nothing to do but dream. She didn't want the warmth of the blue water or to lie under the sun amongst so many who cared nothing about her misery.

Four

She spent her day in her parents' villa. She had no desire to see young and old playing in the water and the sand. She knew other boys would come to her with silly grins on their faces, wanting to walk with her, their eyes wide with craving, wanting to play with her in deep water. They always did. And when she would tell Cassidy, wanting to see his emotion, he would twirl her around, laugh and shrug.

Cassidy spent the day in his tree reading his books. He was excited, though often his mind wandered to Aayla. Even if he could pilot the yacht, The Grand Guardian would know by the sound of the engines and search for him in the helicopter.

He put down the book, one of fifty hidden in his strongbox beneath a cushion of grass. He'd read each one twice, books filled with wonder, books of the world, the sea and the air, of sailors and soldiers and men long since dead. He thought of the yacht and the helicopter.

The villagers knew of both. They believed the ancient Grand Guardian was divine. They believed he and his sons alone could soar like birds and float upon the blue water like a giant fish. Cassidy knew the guardians past and present were mortal men who could read. Dakota could also read.

At night, when he was young, his father would teach him. By day they would write in the sand. Now his father was gone, as was Jacob and Jon Clayton before him, whose one photograph was yellowed and cracked with age. Reading the letters Jonathon had written decades before in the dark by a dimly lit lantern, Cassidy knew why Jonathon was never sat at the pole, why he was found dead on the sandy beach, his leg ripped from its torso by a shark and not a huge sea creature. His strongbox was never found. Nor would the strongbox ever be found, Cassidy once pledged to his father.

He knew of Dickens and Doyle, Hemingway and Maugham. He knew of planes and boats, motors and wings. He knew that to fly or to motor a yacht one first had to read, to know the stars and the wind, the currents and the tides.

He was exhilarated. The next day was the last of The Seven Feasts. The finest banquet of the seven suns would be held and the village would awake the morning after to work in the fields, their bodies depleted, their heads swimming in fog and in the spring many mothers would nurse while as many fathers would wonder. He didn't care.

He leapt to the ground to uncover the iron chest whose lock had rusted years before he was born. He looked at the pocket watch that he wound once each day. He secured the timepiece with a vine to the inside of his shield and hoped she wouldn't tease him. He was certain he would need to measure his time.

No one had ever crossed the bridge or passed the gate into the darkness behind the bars.

He dropped the lid and folded the grassy cover in place. The sun was low in the sky, behind the trees. She'd be angry with him, though she wouldn't know how to express what she felt. Hate was unknown to them. They either felt emotion or did not. Hate was a function of envy and greed and neither element existed.

He left his lush retreat and walked the half-mile to where the tall palm trees ended at the edge of the white sandy beach. He stopped abruptly, cursing himself, ashamed of the way he'd treated her when, all the while, he should have known. He hated himself. He would make her a promise, now no less essential to his existence than the final words he'd spoken to his father. And, if his destiny was to fail his father and sit at the pole, she would be left with his most precious gift to her.

He ate without sitting or tasting the food, so anxious was he to see her. He filled his cup and went to the water. He crossed in front of her and paid her no attention. Within minutes and well beyond eyes blurred with tincture, she held his hand.

"I no longer feel emotion for you, Cassidy."

"Yes, you do."

"No, I do not."

They walked a while longer.

"Aayla..."

"Aayla, Aayla, always Aayla. Do you...?"

"Do you ever shut up?"

She tripped him and jumped onto his back. "What is shut up? And why are you talking to me with these strange words I do not know? What do you know, Cassidy? Tell me"

"I will tell you when the late sun is gone and the moon begins to turn the blue water to silver. Now, get off me. You remind of the fat one."

She punched his stomach. "Now I do not feel emotion for you."

He stood, bringing her into his arms.

"Aayla, I know that you feel deep emotion for me, as deep as mine for you. I know so much that you do not, so much I am afraid to share with you."

"Why, Cassidy? How can you know more than me?"

"I am afraid because of my emotion for you. That will soon change. Later, at the early moon, I will tell you a little of what is in my mind. You will be as happy as you will be sad."

"I do not understand."

"You will. And why have you not removed your maiden-shield? Have you begun your bleeding?"

"No, I have not."

"No one is near us to see."

She stopped. "Cassidy, you want to see what my maiden-shield covers, yet you keep what is hidden beneath yours a secret to me. No," she insisted, "I will not."

"Seeing you naked is to see the sun and the moon, the blue water and white sand for the first time."

"I do not understand."

"My words are not strange."

"I do not understand you. I do not know what you want?"

"I want you, Aayla." He paused, looking ahead to where they would spend the night. "Our hearts are intended for each other. What the ancient Grand Guardian and your father planned for you is wrong. What they are doing is also wrong for me and for Dakota. He feels no emotion for you, as I do. And when we are bathed you will begin to know me. All I ask is that you be patient with me and spend one more sun without me"

"No."

"You must."

"Why? So that you can climb your tree to make raindrops where I cannot see you, when I am here and can stay with you? I will not. My father is right to believe something is not right with you. Do you know how Dakota plays with the girl he cannot live without? She told me. When they are in the forest he takes away her maiden-shield and covers her with his hands to make her feel good, the way she does in her dark hearth when she dreams of coupling with him and joining with him. They same way I do when I am alone. And she knows him as well. Often she sees what will never be hers to keep. You do not do that for me. You make sounds like the birds, you wait for the dark to touch what everyone sees of me and you hide yourself from me as though you are not a complete man. When I know that you are. Everyone knows. The other girls and the women talk of the small the shield you wear. At first my heart swelled with happiness because I knew what was in their minds. Now my heart is empty."

To her absolute surprise, he pushed his shield to the sand in a single fluid motion and faced her, careful to conceal the timepiece from her.

"Now you see what they can only imagine."

She gaped. "Cassidy, the other girls and the old women are right to chase you with their eyes when you are at the sand." She pushed her shield to the sand, stepping from the tiny bundle, covering her tiny patch of blonde with a delicate hand. "Do not make me cry when we couple under the high moon."

He breathed deeply. "No, Aayla. We will not couple, not under any moon. Now, shut up and walk. Be content with what you see."

"What is shut up?"

He grinned. "Not to hear your sweet voice once more until we bathe. Let me think of what I will tell you and what I cannot."

She fell silent, feeling good by his side. She wanted to run with him, to play with him in the water and to enjoy her recent discovery of him, held in check by his slow stride. They were unclothed and, in her mind, first-mates already coupled and joined the way she wanted. She would weaken him. She would weaken his mind and his body would consume her. They would not sleep through the last moon of The Seven Feasts. Instead he would consume her. If he did not, she would take his moon strength and would not

36

separate from him until the tall trees changed from black to greens and the long shadows yielded to the penetrating warmth of the sun on the sand.

When they arrived at the small alcove of trees they'd made their own, they went into the sea to bathe. Cassidy was content that the ocean had cooled, Aayla wasn't and worked all the harder at her mischievousness, content when he slung her over his shoulder and carried her to shore, a single firm hand securing her snugly against his cheek.

He eased her to her feet, pressing the length of her body against his. When he released her he sat silently, pensive. She paced to and fro, watching him closely, wanting him to watch her, wondering what was in his head if not her.

"Cassidy, what use is the biggest tree in the forest if it is dead or pulled from the earth?"

He followed her gaze.

"Aayla, sit with me."

"I do not want to sit. I want to lay with you and couple with you. This is the last moon of The Seven Feasts. If not now, when can we?"

She looked down.

"Nothing is dead on me, Aayla. Soon you will test the strength of the tree you long to climb and rest upon. I promise. Now you must listen to me and believe that what I am saying is true." He patted the sand. "Sit, Aayla. When we are finished talking we will swim and we will sleep. But now is your time to listen. I have been there, Aayla, with my father and alone."

She sat. "Where, Cassidy?"

"To the other side of the gate, beyond the gorge and the bridge. I have seen Tombolina as most others have not."

Her eyes opened wide.

"What you are saying is not possible. Do not tell me untruths. No one is allowed on Tombolina. The sands beyond the gorge are forbidden to us. We have all heard the stories of what will come to pass."

He put up his hand.

"You know that is not true. You know of the women not yet old who have lost their mates to the pole. You know he bathes with them in the Sacred Pond to comfort them. You know young girls go to be cleansed by him and made ready for coupling? If I am not your first, neither will Dakota be. His brother will know the feel of your soft curls before him, after Irene has painted you with her old hands. You will bathe naked with a man the age of your father, as your mother and mine bathed with the ancient." He grinned. "I saw my mother's eyes when she hurled her stone against his head. My father's strength was in her arm."

"I am not my mother. No. I will not. I will die in the water."

"Before the next early sun, we will return to where the trees conceal the village. You will stay alone and I will go north to Tombolina."

He pointed. She didn't know what was north. She knew where the sun rose and where the sun set.

"I will swim across the gorge and walk to where I know the girls and the women go to find his Sacred Pond. He lives in a magnificent mansion. He has electricity powered by a generator; I have seen his lights glowing brighter than the high sun."

What he saw in her eyes was fascination or fear. He couldn't tell. What he knew was that she wouldn't betray him. She loved him.

"Aayla, on the windward shore, where the bad water is agitated and always angry, not far from his mansion, is another channel that is much wider and deeper. In that channel I have touched the beautiful yacht that carries him across the ocean. Now that he will pass four moons away from the island I will see inside his house and know what he hides from us and what his father once hid from us. I will see the helicopter. That is why you have listened to your father for me and you must tell no one."

He touched her hair.

"What are you saying? What are these words I do not know? You are not right to say these words."

"My words will not seem strange much longer, Aayla. Soon you will understand, as I do. You must believe me. I do not spend my time, when my work is finished, making raindrops in the forest when I am alone. I read and I learn from many books. I study the ancient maps of my great-grandfather, Jonathon Clayton. And I think of many things. I think of you."

She didn't smile.

"You do make raindrops, because you feel deep emotion for me. I see you. You must not do this, Cassidy. It is decreed that no one must go onto the small island. You will sit at the pole."

"I will go tomorrow as I have done before, when your father has known of his absence. I will remain past the high moon and I will return with each late sun, each evening, when my work in the field is done. I promised my father I would take my mother from this place, and I will when I am certain of what I must do. That is what I will discover, and then you will come with me."

"No one leaves here, Cassidy."

"He does...in his helicopter, his whirring machine, which is better, I think, than the one I have seen in my books. My books are old. The pages are beginning to yellow and tear."

Aayla began sobbing. "I do not understand your words. I do not know you."

"You will. You will soon understand days and months and years. You will know time and what is a mile, the way he does...and I do. His knowledge comes from books. He reads, Aayla. So does Dakota. As do I, taught by my father.

That is what they know about me. That is why you will join with Dakota, because they know what I know."

"What, Cassidy?"

"That I have knowledge. I know how to put my words on paper so that others can see my words when I am not there or wish not to speak." He put a forefinger into the sand and drew. "This is your name, Aayla. This is how I write your name. And this is mine."

She watched his finger disturb the sand, studying the scrawls.

"I do not feel well, Cassidy."

"Soon you will. I will show you my books and teach you to read. We will sit in the sand and I will teach you to write. When we talk we will use words you do not yet know and then you will understand."

"What will I understand?"

"That we must leave this place. The blue water is the ocean, Aayla. The water does not flow into the sky. All the water you see flows from this ocean into another and another. The water you see is not the water you will see tomorrow, the next early sun. The water has no end, Aayla. And in the water are many places like Tombola, and much bigger, with villages of..." He pointed to the sky. "Aayla, what we see is not a star falling across the sky from the far darkness behind the sun. It is a plane. Inside are people like you and me. They are looking down at us. They can see us and everything we cannot. That is how they travel from one place to another, and they speak the words you think are strange."

He stood.

"Come, we will wash your face in the sea, before the blue water turns to silver."

"I am afraid, Cassidy. You must not go. You will not come back. I remember the stories." She lay on her side and huddled into her knees. "Do not go. We will not leave

Tombola. I will join with Dakota and you with another, as The Grand Guardian has decreed."

Seeing her in the sand, so despondent and desperate to understand, he took a deep breath and left her to swim in the sea. When he returned she was purring softly in her sleep.

Five

In the penumbra of early morning, she rubbed the dried tears from her eyes. She lay still, listening for his breathing. She was ready. She would ease her body over his and he would awaken too late to prevent her. Anyway, he'd made her a promise and she knew his body.

She knew of his moon strength. She'd watched him so many times as he slept, gaining his strength beneath his shield before he would weaken, each time becoming strong once again.

This early sun would be different. He was unclothed and she would see. She would turn and she would wait. Then she gasped.

He wasn't there. Neither was his shield. She leapt to her feet, searching the sand as far as she could see, and the dark water. She didn't see him. She ran to the shore, straining her eyes to see across the water, yelling his name. When he didn't reply she searched again to the north and to the south and ran along the shore.

She sprang into the water, frantic, not knowing in what direction to swim first. He would never think to leave without waking her. He felt deep emotion for her and would never leave her unprotected. She sank to her knees and wailed, pounding the shallow water with her fists.

She heard the shrill sound piercing the morning stillness. She saw Cassidy strolling towards her, swinging her maiden-shield in circles around his forefinger, singing like

42

the birds she once chased as a child. He wasn't dead.

She ran to him. She wrapped her arms around him, buried her face against his chest and looked up to see his stupid smirk.

"I saw you in the moonlight. I saw on your face what you were thinking," he pointed to the trees, "from the tallest tree. He has gone, Aayla. I heard the noise of his motors, like the sound in your stomach when you are hungry. I saw the red portside light of the yacht. He leaves when the tide is high and this time he travels to the west." He pointed. "The time is safe for me to go, before the sun is high."

She waited a moment, so that he might understand what she was thinking. She punched him in the face, knocking him backwards.

"I did think to take away your moon strength, Cassidy. I would never tell you an untruth." She tore her shield from his dangling hand. "Instead you took away my emotion for you. Do not follow me."

He stood his ground and smiled.

"Aayla, be patient with me. Spend your day without me until the late sun."

"No."

"You know that you must."

"No. You promised me."

"I will keep my word to you, when I believe the time is right. They would soon see your round belly if we do not separate in time…and I know you will not. I know you." He stroked her cheek. "I am no stronger. When the time is right we will couple, not before. I promise you that also. You are the daughter of the Chief Counsellor and are promised to The Grand Guardian's brother. Your life would be difficult in the village." He chortled. "And you would never know where my broken bones would lie beneath the earth. That is the one way most of village leaves this island, Aayla. And we do not know where they lie, or even if they do. Why is that? Why do I not know where my father lies or his father before him? That is the reason you must leave me."

"What are you saying? They are gone, returned to the soil. They are hidden from our eyes so that we might honour them as one. They are one with Tombola and give their goodness to the soil so that our crops may be plentiful. The ancient guardian now gives his goodness to the soil?"

"We killed an old man, whose son will continue his rule over us, the son who now travels across the blue water as he once did, to the west, to whatever he will do. I know where he goes."

"You cannot."

"I do. And I must discover more if I am to honour my promise to my father."

"Your father is in the soil. He does not care of your promise to him. What of your promise to me?"

"Aayla…"

"Aayla, Aayla, always Aayla with nothing more to say. Go, Cassidy, if I cannot stop you." She put a small hand hard against his chest. "I will leave here before you. I do not want to see you leave and do not look upon me. I went unclothed with you because I wanted to feel deep emotion for you and wanted you to couple with me. Now I do not. And at the next Seven Feasts, when I am joined, if I am not Irene, I will not share affection with you."

She left without saying another word, her shoulders slumped, tears in her eyes, wanting to escape him before she cried aloud.

Cassidy watched her until he could barely discern her, straining to see her slip into her shield from so far away. He was certain she would glance over her shoulders. She didn't, not once.

Soon she melded with the sand, invisible to his eyes.

Six

She would forgive him. He inhaled. Her intoxicating scent lingered on his fingertips, the silkiness of her soft curls he'd never before touched and her moan when he pressed into her yielding flesh lingered in his mind.

He'd told her more than he should. She was afraid. She didn't understand, yet. Soon she would and with understanding would come forgiveness. She was fire; he was water. She was the heat of a hot summer's day; he was the cool reprieve of the tall forest.

She was gone from sight when he crossed the main path from the beach to the village. Those who lay along the beach sharing affection with their neighbours paid no attention to him on their last day before once again toiling in the fields. Others slept.

He walked to the north, crossing the gorge with ease. At the far side he stopped, studying the Tombola Pole. She was wrong, yet she didn't know. He harboured no doubt. To couple with the daughter of the Chief Counsellor would put him at the pole. He would follow his father, not to enrich the soil, rather to the end his young life with a crushed skull.

He walked on, close to the tree line and unafraid. The channel water was high. At the secluded pond the water was warm and deep. When he'd swum as far as he could he paddled to the shore with one hand beneath him. Once there he lay motionless. He listened for the slightest sound, searching for the slightest movement, his watch tightly held in his fist. He waited an hour, his heart more relaxed than past times.

Aayla was right. No one was permitted on the island. The Grand Guardian and Irene dwelled alone in their newly inherited fine home, when Dakota was the rightful occupant of Tombolina. Some of the village knew what had happened to the boy and his mother, Aayla told him, most didn't, their minds too saturated with tincture to care.

He lay in the Sacred Pond where The Grand Guardian would continue to comfort young widows and prepare young girls for what they must do. His kindness was decreed. And, Cassidy thought, what man wouldn't want to bathe and make ready a new herd of virgins each year? He waited one hour more.

He rose from the water at eight. The hour was well past the time when villagers would gather for their morning meal, eager not to miss a moment of the final day that would end with a great feast.

He shivered and stepped into deeper water, removing and rinsing his loin-shield that had filled with fine sand. When he was done he strode onto dry sand and onto a path of flagstones that brought him to the gold-coloured home where he dressed. He crossed to one side, then the other. He circled the house and counted 400 paces from where he began.

Mirrored glass covered the many windows, not like the wooden slats of his villa. They shone like silver. The construction was of concrete with wrought iron railings leading to the door that faced a pool of clear water. On either side pillars reached to the second floor balcony and to an overhanging roof made of tiles.

The door was unlocked. No door on the island was barred. On Tombolina the one lock was at the gate between the bridge and the arch. Any other existed solely in the collective minds of the village. He felt no need to knock. If anyone was inside no one else would ever know what he'd done. They wouldn't wait for the pole. They would punish him as any imperfect baby, a sickly man or woman or those who'd lost their minds. They would take him away. And he didn't agree with Aayla in that regard. He believed they went to the sea.

He didn't tell Aayla everything. If she wanted to believe she no longer loved him, he knew differently. Often, when his mother and her second-mate slept in separate rooms, he would creep from the villa and go to the gorge. Once there he would swim to the windward shore where he would gaze at the moon, fall asleep on the rocks and wake to let the early morning current sweep him to where he began.

Many times, late at night, he would hear voices. He would bury himself into the wide cracks carved by the wind and sea into the stone wall. Or he would crouch behind huge boulders made smooth by the same raging water to listen. Often he would see the green, red and white lights of the yacht far out to sea, or skimming close to the shore from the north.

Though many times he would wait too long to swim with the current to where the gentle tidal water from the leeward shore swirled against the angrier windward water under the bridge and by the pole, scarcely returning to his hearth before the early sun.

He knew they would take him away sooner or later, preferring the latter if he was unable to take himself away.

He'd made a promise to his father, and now he would know more. He went in and was instantly chilled, the early morning heat sucked from his skin. He crept from the kitchen to the dining room, to the parlour and saw things he could never imagine, things even he didn't know.

He examined the kitchen, puzzled. Much of what he saw on the counters was unknown to him. He'd never seen those pictures in his books. He saw what he knew was an icebox, yet when he opened the door he saw no ice. Yet the meats were frozen and burned his fingers. Everything else was cold. He saw what he knew was a stove, but the surface was flat with the look and feel of glass. At the sink he turned a tap and he saw water flow, not like his own sink where his mother pumped water from the small reservoir captured rainwater on their roof.

In the room where they ate he saw a table made of stone and of glass. Behind the glass doors of a cabinet he saw plates with elaborate designs and glasses made from crystal as fine as a flower's petals. He saw liquor, though the many bottles meant nothing to him.

In the parlour carpets he'd never before seen or touched covered the parts of the floor, soft to his feet. On the walls he saw paintings of women, all of them young, all of them naked, not one as beautiful as Aayla or his mother. He saw statues, some made of white and grey stone, while others were metallic, the colour of copper pennies, some not as high as his waist, some as high as his knees. He touched each one, all of them women, standing, kneeling or sleeping, all of them naked. They were cold to his touch.

He saw chesterfields made of leather and large, heavy chairs quite exaggerated from the ones he'd seen in his books. They were brightly coloured and covered with soft cushions. He saw a mirror of dark glass framed in a box that sparkled like black coral under the sea, with wires protruding from the back and a pile of silver disks. Beside them was another black box that was shiny, a dull red light glowing from inside, more silver disks whose purpose was a mystery to him and yet another box inside a cabinet.

He saw lamps with wires that went into the same wall that he knew, lamps he'd seen in his books. He saw magazines. He flipped through the pages of one whose cover showed a young woman squatting in her maiden-shield. On some pages men shared affection with women, on others women tried to share affection with women. He wondered how. He wondered at the thing that looked like him but was much bigger and blue. One day soon he would know.

The pages and covers were smooth and shiny. On the second cover another woman seemed naked. He looked closer. She wasn't naked. She was wrapped in tight clothing from her shoulders to her feet, like a statue. Her hair glistened with strands of sapphire beads that were the colour of her eyes.

He replaced them as they were and went to the stairs. The door on one side opened to a closet filled with clothes and hats that were bulky and heavy and, he thought, must be uncomfortable to wear. Behind the second door were grey steel boxes attached to the wall, a miniature universe of blinking reds, greens, blues and whites, more wires than he'd ever seen and another door. He ignored what he knew was beyond his ability to understand and went to the stairs.

They spiralled. The first marble step was cold to his feet after the warmth of the carpet. He rested a hand on the polished rail and climbed. He stopped at the top, when he'd counted sixty-two, anxious to see behind the five doors.

In the first he saw bath, a toilet, a sink and a shower, like nothing he could have imagined. He sat in the bath and stood in the shower. He sat on the toilet and ran his hands over the smooth contours of the sink. The room was larger than his mother's entire villa. Behind the second door was a bed, wider than his body was long and twice his height in length. He saw tables and chairs with more cushions, another chesterfield and another dark mirror in a black frame. He saw many more magazines with pages of naked women, more silver disks and things he didn't know.

In a smaller room with no door he fell back against the wall in disbelief. He saw pants and shirts and ties all hanging in a row, and fedoras he'd seen in his books. He opened the drawers saw shorts made of soft fabrics, not loin-cloths, and he saw socks and shoes. He saw rings and watches and belts and thought of the photograph left in the strongbox by Jonathon Clayton.

On the other side hung dresses and skirts, blouses and fine robes, flat shoes with feathers and shoes that seemed impossible to wear: Irene's. He opened her drawers and saw things he didn't understand. He saw maiden-shields that were smooth, soft to his touch, and a hundred different colours, wondering what use they would be to her if anyone could see through them.

He saw things that looked like soft cups with straps that could serve no purpose. He saw more straps and strings he didn't understand, all brightly coloured. He saw tiny bottles and opened them, recoiling from the pungent scent. He saw boxes he was afraid to open. In the corner he saw their guardian robes trimmed with gold for him and silver for her.

He touched them and smelled them. They hadn't yet been worn.

His mind was racing.

In the third room he stopped at the door. Against one wall were two desks, each one with a flat silver box. One was open. Inside was another dark mirror, smaller than what he'd seen in the bedroom and parlour. The buttons with letters and numbers were similar to the ones on the typewriters in his books, but this wasn't one. When he tapped them nothing happened

He saw more many more silver disks, this time in clear boxes. So many lights were blinking in the greens and reds of the yacht. He saw machines with paper stacked inside, another filed with bits of paper impossible to read. He touched chairs covered in soft material and when he thought to sit behind the biggest desk he fell over onto the floor.

Afraid, thinking someone might have heard.

He left.

The fourth room was a bedroom. He stood in the doorway thinking. He was looking into Dakota's room. He went in. Large photographs of cities he didn't know covered the walls, cities he might never know. One showed what he knew was the world from what he imagined must be the far end of the universe. Two others showed young girls in colourful shields at the beach with patches of material on their breasts, all of them smiling, none of them as beautiful as Aayla.

The closet was filled with fine clothes. When he closed his eyes he could scarcely feel the fabric. By the bed was a lamp. Under the lamp was a book. Another wall had shelves with many books. In the dresser he saw more clothes. He looked down to his leather shield and felt sick.

The bed was perfectly made. What Aayla had told him was true. Dakota was gone, sent to live with his mother in the eldest son's old villa across from hers.

He saw a soft bag with a dozen zippers. Inside he saw another silver box, a much smaller one wrapped with wires and a passport. He knew about passports. He had Jonathon's. Dakota also had a recent driver's permit issued by the State of Florida, though his was rigid. Jonathon's was now a scrap of weathered and yellow paper. He saw money and more rigid cards that looked like the driver's permit, yet different.

Dakota had left the house with the tunics on his back.

Cassidy closed the door.

At the fifth room he stood in amazement. He'd never imagined so many books. He'd read of libraries and his father once told him what his father had told him, but never did he imagine. He looked at his watch. Ten o'clock. He was hungry and went to the kitchen.

In the cupboards he saw cans he couldn't open. In the

fridge saw jars of fruits he'd never seen, floating in juices, meats he'd never seen, that he read were packaged, and brown crystals that tasted like sand and threatened to close his throat. He read the label. Even with spiced water, who would want such a taste in their mouth?

The water was stored in small, soft bottles, not like the clay jugs used by the village. He reached for one, pulling at the top before pausing to consider the dilemma. He twisted the bottle one way, the top the other, drenching himself with spray before dropping the bottle from his hands. He looked at the floor and the walls, alarmed. Water was everywhere. He'd never seen water explode.

Calming himself he reached to the floor. The water would evaporate before their return; the bottle he would take with him to bury in the sand.

Intrigued by the room filled with books, anxious to see more, he gulped water from the spout in the sink and left. He ran up the stairs and stood in the middle of the room, fascinated. He saw pens and pencils, paper and another basket filled with what he thought must be a million pieces of paper. And books. So many books.

He sat carefully at a dark, heavy desk trimmed with the colour of gold, not trusting the chair. The leather was cold against his legs, his buttocks and his back. He felt small. He shivered.

All that he saw on the desk was more paper, elaborate pens and a glass half-filled with amber liquid that was familiar to his nose, what Jonathon had once written was rum laced with opium: the tincture.

To either side of him and behind him were three walls lined with books from corner to corner and from the height of his hip to the ceiling. He'd read fifty books in his short life. Now he was seeing a hundred times more. At each wall wooden ladders the colour of the desk were attached to the floor and the ceiling. He went to the one that first caught his attention.

He was in a wonderland. His only reasons not to die happily at that moment, he mused, were Shakkra and Aayla.

Encyclopaedias, dictionaries, novels written by authors not yet alive when Jonathon came to the islands, an atlas that kept his attention until he almost slipped, and books about people he'd never known.

His journey across the room on the rungs of the second ladder was no less enthralling. Tall books, thin and thick books, black, gold, brown and red books, green and yellow books lined the walls. History books of bygone eras and travel books. He flipped through a few, a message to himself forming in his mind. He was seeing books on yachting, seamanship and flying.

He stepped onto the third ladder to see books on art and fine cuisine he knew nothing about. He saw books on wine and liquor, cars and mechanics. He saw books for someone who was a dummy, others on finance and investment. He saw much older books, covered in leather and embossed with gold, like his own. They looked older and smelled older, many layered with dust. They were the hardest to reach and, he thought, had been on the shelf the longest, left unread for many years.

From the second highest rung he barely saw the upper portion of the brown leather spine and the clean white pages behind the others. He climbed to the highest rung and reached in behind the uneven façade, the side of his head pressed hard against the ceiling. He gripped the book and brought it out cautiously.

He sucked in a burst of air that stole his breath rather than give it. The book hadn't fallen behind the others. He was certain. He stared at the cover. The book was not meant to be found. The leather spine wasn't embossed with gold and the jacket wasn't worn with time. The leather was smooth and smelled of newness. On the cover was written by hand and in black ink: The Journal of Wendell Parkens. Tucked under the cover was a letter folded in three.

His mind was blank or racing, he didn't know. His hands moved, beyond his control. He was afraid, yet he wasn't. This was the moment he'd longed for, the moment he'd once pledged to his father would happen.

He scrambled to the floor and ran to the desk. With the paper unfolded precisely, so that he would know how to replace the seams, he leaned forward and read.

*

I lament that I am no longer The Grand Guardian of this paradise we call Tombola, once known throughout my formative years, and until I journeyed to this place, this secluded isle of my paternal forefathers, as Wendell Parkens.

I was, four nights past, in a state of considerable disbelief, for I am clear of mind and able-bodied for a man at the threshold of his 100th year. I feel at this moment that I might live forever, though I am informed by my eldest son that I will not.

I confess, on this the eve of my prescribed passing, that I am at once apprehensive and timorous, uncertain of what awaits me at the precipice of my private abyss.

My first-born son shall guide me into the shallow gorge. You, my youngest, shall be of great comfort to me and my Chief Counsellor shall honour me with the swiftness of his arm and the precision of his eye.

These simple words I write are the postscript of my years, the preface of my life story and that of the ancients who came before me as written in the Ancestral Tomes. Together they are the history of Tombola. Yet much is left to be written by you.

I write these words for, you, my youngest son, so that you might remember my words to you this very day and know what is right and what is wrong. You must one day defy and expel your half-brother who harbours ill-will against you and me, he who usurps you, as I once exiled him from this paradise he now seeks to ruin.

I write them for my deserved atonement as I approach the closing minutes of my eleventh hour. I write them so that I might know who shall rightfully wear my ring. I have written where my greatest symbol is perforce secreted. I dared not speak the words this day for fear my words would be heard by means of his covert deception.

The three together are the path to your future and deserved devotion of your flock.

I shall not hear your brother's knock upon my door, or be cognizant of our cherished minions who congregate before me, for I have drunk the ancient tincture without refrain and shall very soon be in a state of preparedness. Trust him not one moment of your life.

I begin to feel consumed by lassitude and lay my pen and parchment aside, for I have previously written in detail and humility, and without the slightest doubt or misconception regarding the passage of my life, all that I have done.

I am left with nothing more to declare for, truth be told, I am my father's son.

This date is July 03rd on the centenary of my birth and the eve of my murder.

*

Cassidy convulsed. He folded and replaced the letter into the book the way he removed it. He slammed the cover shut, terrified. Before him was the life story of The Grand Guardian whose eldest son had taken his place, stolen from the youngest son who would soon take Aayla for his first-mate.

He looked at his watch, a full day remained. His mother was accustomed to his wandering ways and seldom filled his plate before he walked through the door. Today he would test her kind nature to the fullest.

He stared at the journal, for a short while unmindful of what he'd told Aayla of The Grand Guardians, the father now dead, the son his successor. They were men, not divine, men who had knowledge from books.

This was the journal of he ancient Grand Guardian now dead. He put a hand to the cover and leaned forward. Careful to leave the letter untouched, he turned to the first page and held his breath.

Seven

I was born in 1910 to Mr. and Mrs. Aristotle Parkens. Father was an investment banker of some renown, the president of the Mortgage & Loan. Mother was primarily disposed to spending his money and planning social events when she was not instructing or correcting the domestic staff.

At the beginning I saw her most everyday, though I suppose I thought very little of our encounters and took her love for granted, nestled in her warmth and comforted by the soft purr of her lullabies. And for the first four years of my life I called her Nanna because speech did not come easily to me and calling her the way father did was needlessly difficult.

At the age of five I was given no choice at all, when throughout my life I had never been refused, summarily sent away one day at a time "to lessen the eventual possibility of one day becoming a disappointment" father had said. And for the first three years of my formal education I exceeded all expectations. Of course, by then I had come to realize that I did, in fact, have two mothers: Nanna to care for me and dress me, and the real Mrs. Parkens to pay for that care and show me off to her friends, which would often require that I perform in some uncharacteristic way.

One loved me, the other, most assuredly did not. Although not until much later in my life did I discover her reason.

I was born into an age of greatness, beginning with the Great War, the war to end all wars, which the world would soon learn was a terrible lie. That war ended when I was eight and, to me, the worst tragedy of the war was my personal loss. One cold November evening, not many days subsequent to the end of hostilities, Nanna made me hot cocoa and was in my room helping me with my lessons when I asked her why father was a coward. I knew the word. I was not stupid to that degree. I sat at the front of the class and always raised my hand, the first to answer any question. Sadly, I do not remember her expression, not after all these years. However I do remember what she said and how she wiped my eyes and pressed a warm hand to my cheek.

The other boys at school, some of them bigger than me, the ones who never wore new clothes and came to class with meagre sandwiches of white bread coated with butter and coarse sugar, or bologna and HP sauce, had blocked my path, yelling at me, calling me Wendy, so that Driver, fearing possible injuries to my person, pushed his way through instructing them to be quiet.

One of the older boys had begun the ruckus by shouting "coward, coward, your father's a bloody coward, Wendy. And you'll be one too." Another joined in, adding "he's right, Wendy. Your pa's a bloody coward. At least you have one, eh? Mine's not coming home. He's dead somewhere over there because of your pa and others like him." Another cried out, "My ma says it's true, Wendy. Your old man should have done right."

Nanna let me talk as she held me close. When I was done she sighed deeply and told me what was more important was that I become the finest man I could possibly be, to stand tall and not cower in the face of adversity and hardship. I remember stealing from under the quilted cover of my bed after she closed the door behind her, wanting to look up the words to make certain I had not misunderstood. I had not. The next morning at breakfast Cook was solemn, mother appeared flustered and father said not a single word. Not until sometime later did mother tell me how Nanna had left me to care for another, less obtuse child.

Sometime later that same day Maid slipped me a note, a special note from Nanna, and I knew mother was a horrible liar.

By the time I entered the secondary phase of my education father's craven lack of courage was forgotten, as was my secondary and demeaning appellation, largely because many of the boys had left school to support their desperate families, and I was pursuing my studies with as much ardour as I was the attention of Pricilla Bumsby.

The recitals had stopped, my compulsion for soft, nubile breasts had taken over and I quickly discovered that many of the poorer girls would gladly barter theirs for a ride in a grand limousine.

The world was changing, though, of greater importance, having emerged from a family of enviable social standing, and fast becoming a man of letters, I had the pick of the proverbial litter.

Pricilla was fourteen; I was fifteen, when she decided to inform me of her condition. She cried pitifully throughout her entire loquacious confession as though I'd let her down, as though she had not allowed our one experience together to end so tragically. I hated her instantly, almost as much as the incident itself when we were not at all certain as to whether or not we should undress. So we did not.

Quickly, amidst a cluster of trees at the back of the schoolyard, she waited for me to achieve a state of readiness: a strangely surreal, tactile experience, my preparedness judged and agreed upon by both of us. I remember her amazed expression moments before she pulled her long straight dress to her hips and jumped upon me, eagerly, forcing me backward against the rough bark, reaching under her school frock to do what I could not.

The effort to hold her in place and balance myself required the highest degree of concentration, forcing me to believe that our supposed passion was more likely a question of her not wanting to stab herself to death and me not wanting to become the unfortunate victim of her increasingly precarious weight.

When at first she screamed, she had buried her face into the crook of my neck, banging her head against the tree. Then something happened to me and she became all the more excited. Then nothing. All was said and done. Though, in truth, nothing was said and we were not quite sure what we had done. Not until she eased away, causing me great personal discomfort due to my person's necessary forward attitude, her clumsiness at dismounting and the unforgiving edging of her underwear which were the colour of hotel sheets and of similar quality, did we see.

Together we stood in awe, staring down...at me, at my blood-smeared, yet proud appendage which, I believed at the time, was swollen to inhuman proportions. That impression is my one valued memory of her. I never saw her naked. She wore soft-soled Oxfords, white ankles socks and I cannot recall her breasts which remained covered throughout the event and inaccessible to any part of me. I have no recollection of how she felt to me or smelled and, after her family sent her away, I never saw her again.

Though forever etched in my memory, and due in large part to her, is my earliest encounter with father's ire, a rare recognition of me, and the welt borne of that recognition that never completely faded. I wear the scar with pride to this day, for I did not cower in the face of adversity.

Mother's contribution to my condemnation was to lament for weeks that her son had fornicated with a trollop of the lowest common denominator. Worse, father saw fit to reward the girl with special care beyond the means or dreams of her ne'er-do-well and ill-intentioned parents.

At seventeen, with secondary completed, university loomed days ahead of me and Edna Wainwright had lured me into her arms. She was eighteen, a flapper, and precocious beyond decent norms. She was the daughter of father's premier client. She loved to dance in crowded jazz bars and wear short dresses with layered fringes that showed off the most private part of her endless legs, I remember.

She taught me the Charleston. She let me see the tops of her stockings at the dance hall and soon she began letting me touch her and kiss her. She wore her hair cropped, with bright red lipstick on her lips and she smoked. When other women chose to flatten their breasts, Edna did not. They were as full as they were soft and warm. One afternoon she had managed to siphon several ounces of her father's favourite elixir into a thermos and invited me to a picnic behind her home.

The end of summer was mocking us with a cooler day and light winds; Edna was mocking me with being too lovely to refuse. Beside her I was clumsy, telling myself I was anxious, not afraid, when, in truth, I was very nervous. I wanted her, not so much for my wife, rather for her body. I had never seen a girl naked, my previous experiences subsequent to Pricilla preferring that I prod them in the dark or in their clothes. My time had come to right the wrong, though I had no way of knowing how I should begin.

Happily, as I recall the day's events with absolute clarity, Edna foresaw the dilemma, or so I believed at the time. In retrospect, I submit that she possessed more experience than foresight. The whiskey, brandy or whatever liquid she'd siphoned from her father's stock barely began warming me superficially from within, fortifying me for the assault, before Edna's heat assailed me unashamedly from all quarters. She was determined and insatiable, a magnificent lover, a divine nude with contours my hands greedily carved into my mind.

After my first exploration of her I was left with no clear indication to me that I had been, in fact, her first, which by no means lessened the pleasure of my second. By our third and mutual assault I was accustomed to her many proclivities. We lay depleted and naked in the grass, our clothes hanging from branches or strewn across the grass. My fourth and most arduous emission into her went astray, interrupted by unexpected rumblings in the driveway.

We were discovered under the tree, with our books. My jacket hung from a branch, my shoes stood on their own by my stocking feet. Edna sat beside me, naked under her dress, our underclothes entwined between her damp legs.

A month later father's phone rang in his study. The next day Mr. Wainwright closed his account at the Mortgage & Loan, Edna went away and father's threat to me was real. Not that he'd become courageous; he was not, not at all. I was seventeen; he was fifty-six, he owned me and for the second time in as many years the silver and ruby insignia of his alma mater collided viciously with my wide-eyed expression.

He scarcely spoke another word to me throughout the rest of his life, such a disappointment was I, and to this present moment I believe a minute part of me remained embedded in the setting until the day he, for once, confronted his reality. Or, possibly, the day reality chose to confront father. However, I would not discover the timing of his introspection for many years.

From mother's perspective, the Wainwrights were never quite like the rest of us.

I left home several days later without the fanfare of parental pride, the fear of new frontiers or the grief of knowing I would be alone. I left with a letter of credit from the Mortgage & Loan, an invitation to return home at Christmas and the revelation that, from then on, I was expected to earn my keep as a junior clerk at the bank each subsequent summer until graduation.

My first weeks were uncertain. I lacked the distinction of being driven, of Driver opening my door and no one cared in the least that my clothes were of a finer quality or that I had learned to fold and unfold them on my own. We were equals: peers sent out in search of knowledge. The poor had no place in the halls of higher learning. For what good was knowledge without social standing?

My first Christmas as a freshman came and went, and with it the names of so many I do not recall. Nor, I am quite certain, did they ever recall me throughout their lives. They were easy evaluations and calculations, conveniences and achievements, as was I to them, which made the subsequent summer of '28 interminable. Father's threat had not diminished and I was not yet ready to be cast out.

While others summered at the ocean or by the lakeshore, I would not until August. Until then I would be indentured, made to work a six-day week for a paltry fifteen dollars, stripped of family privilege while he and mother spent their weekends by the lakeshore.

The elevator operator enjoyed a status greater than my own and I often suspected that he luxuriated in my malaise. He had a uniform to wear, supplied by father, and he earned a dollar more than me. Yet, despite the covert superiority he clearly cherished, I cherished the fifteen minutes each day when I would stand in for him during his lunch period and the ten minutes each morning and afternoon when he would leave his station at precisely the same time for tea.

I enjoyed no such luxury. I ate at my desk, from a brown bag which Cook prepared; I worked during tea-time when I was not running errands in the heat or the rain and at day's end I would stand at the tram stop with them: the workers. I was set apart, superior to them through no fault of my own and they spurned me. Worse, each Saturday at five, as I stood in line to meet the paymaster prior to boarding the streetcar for the long and uncomfortable journey home, my pay envelope was the thinnest

Though, to his credit, I must admit father did condescend that I might accompany Driver in the front seat to an agreeable location each weekday morning where I was let out several blocks from the bank. The walk, even on the worst days, was preferable to what I knew they were all thinking. Sundays, however, were mine.

Then came August, when we travelled as a family to the seashore. By eighteen I was an accomplished yachtsman, despite being prohibited from cruising alone aboard our forty-foot flush deck cruiser: a magnificent yacht which was, of course, as I later discovered, owned by the bank.

It's where I spent my evenings, soothed by the gentle swaying, content that I would no longer have to endure the rigors of my forced and servile existence. The day I stepped from the boat that summer was the day I left for school and the next two years were no different: Christmas, Easter, the bank and August. One year followed the other, father never asked and I never told him. Otherwise I would have lied. We were not close, not by the simplest of interpretation of the expression. As for mother, she always worried and I secretly derived a great deal of pleasure from her discomfiture.

I was twenty at the beginning of my fourth year and graduated at twenty-one, during which time I met Charlotte. She was in most of my classes and by our first Christmas she was a frequent visitor to my bed. She was attractive, strangely so, with deep red curls, perfectly white skin and the most admirable breasts I'd seen thus far. More importantly, in carnal matters, she was undeniably and incomparably voracious.

By Easter we agreed: My parents would be the first to know, upon our respective graduations, which I did with honours. Not so Charlotte, who had spent the better part of her collegiate career grading her professors more than the inverse. Many had failed in her evaluation of them, I suspect, based strictly on the never-ending source. In short: Everyone wanted Charlotte, and Charlotte acquiesced due in equal parts to her nature and her lack of academic ability which was intertwined with her phobic need to please her papa.

And, in this, papa would not be pleased. Charlotte barely managed to scrape through, due in large part to my obstruction of the professorial queue. She was pregnant and I was about to embark on a career with my laced boot barely planted on the bottom rung of the bank's corporate ladder. The elevator operator had been sent home and father saw no need to favour me, his only son.

And so began my life...as did what was to become the Great Depression: the very fountain of my personal and good fortune.

Eight

Cassidy glanced at his watch. He did not know whether to laugh or cry. The Grand Guardian was not only a man of flesh and blood; he grew into manhood as a privileged child who coupled for the first time long before the proper age. Then with many more girls he didn't love. And he was a yachtsman, which answered yet another question.

Cassidy knew of the Great War and the Great depression, but what of Charlotte? She was a woman given to lewd behaviour. She slept with her teachers, trading her body for good marks so that she might please her father. Yet her father wouldn't be pleased that she'd coupled with Wendell Parkens to give him a child. Cassidy searched his mind for the word, nodding. Charlotte was a whore. And, he assumed, the mother of the eldest son who was now The Grand Guardian.

He thought of The Seven Feasts. He'd promised Aayla he would couple with her one day, and he would. She'd promised never to share her affection with any other, before her girlish behaviour when she tried to infuse him with jealousy she didn't know. Anyway, Irene was not allowed to share affection and who could be certain of Dakota's future.

He smiled, remembering the sadness in her eyes. She would forgive him. He was certain her mood had more to do with her next bleeding than with his painful procrastination. She always forgave him.

He turned the page.

*

Outwardly father listened with calm detachment; inwardly he was seething. He was furious. His eyes never once acknowledged my bride. Mother sat tearfully. To her dismay the epoch was becoming increasingly difficult, social events infrequent occasions. I had robbed her of her finest hour, yet I felt not the slightest sympathy for her.

Charlotte and I thought it best to stand before a justice of the peace as neither one of us was particularly given to supplicating ourselves before the earthly envoy of her parents' parish. Indeed, we would arrive home as man and wife, unapologetic and unremorseful, for I had forgiven her past indiscretions and we began to love one another.

Father stood from his armchair. He asked that I follow him to his study and we left the women alone. Hundreds of men lost their jobs each day, yet father's idea of a dram remained a precise half snifter of the finest cognac. He extended a lesser measure to me and instructed me to take my seat.

"I was anticipating a tertiary blow to my pride from your prized ring, father, not your prized elixir."

"I've sent two away for you already, boy. I won't send a third. This one is squarely on you. She's your responsibility or burden, whichever description suits your view of things as they stand. I won't see my home transformed into a nursery."

"Father, with all due respect, I won't have you referring to my wife, your and mother's daughter-in-law, with such contempt. I expect your acceptance and your compassion for what lies ahead. She's family."

"Not mine, not your mother's and I won't have her in my house longer than I need to empty this glass. You've exceeded yourself beyond imagination. You'll do as I say and get the woman from my house or you'll find yourself without a home. I'll put you up at the Regency this one night. Take her, if you will. That's your choice, not mine. However tomorrow you'll return her to her parents. If you persist in this foolishness, Driver will take you to find other accommodations better suited to your present and future acquisitions, and in keeping with your position at the bank. You'll be docked a day's pay for your time and his."

"Very well, father. Might I expect Driver to take us with our luggage to the DeWitt residence or would you have us travel by tram to explain our situation to her father, who I'm certain will receive us with more civility than we see here?" I remember his expression as though he were glaring at me this very moment. "Yes, father, Conrad DeWitt of DeWitt Iron Ore."

"There's no situation other than promiscuity to explain. I know of the man. He won't regard the matter any differently."

I put down the glass. "Good afternoon, father. We shall be ready for Driver whenever he arrives at the hotel."

I walked out.

In the parlour mother was seated across from Charlotte. Maid had served tea and the women sat quietly swirling the steam in their cups. Charlotte stood, taking my hand. I bid my mother good day without emotion, not knowing what else to say, and we left. In the meantime Driver brought the car around to the front and loaded our bags into the storage compartment.

The fact that my wife was the heiress to the DeWitt family fortune, which was well-known throughout financial circles, had no influence on my decision to propose marriage. I did so out of love, or in the knowledge that I would one day love her. She glowed. She was becoming a mother, and she knew her papa would never abandon her.

The DeWitt home appeared more as an indomitable fortress behind wrought iron gates, high fences and steep granite steps leading to huge, twin doors of solid mahogany decorated with matching gargoyle knockers cast from solid bronze. The three-storey brickwork was reddish-brown; the shutters were bright white and the glass between glistened in the early evening sun. Driver pulled to the curb.

Despite Charlotte's smile, happy voice and reassuring words, I felt like an indigent put out from one kitchen and made to travel to another to beg for scraps. Secretly, what I felt was fear. I was an elevator operator about to meet one of the wealthiest men in the city and I had married his daughter for reasons he'd be inclined to dismiss.

Father was manicured, his demeanour haughty most times. His hair was never mussed, with or without his hat, he was never seen without his suit jacket, his pants always pressed to razor-sharp creases and he never did for himself what others could or should do for him.

Mr. DeWitt on the other hand came to the door himself with his sleeves rolled up, his pants attached to wide braces that disappeared over broad shoulders and his hair flowed in unkempt waves from front to back covering his ears and his collar. His hands were massive paws, his voice was gruff and he'd worn the beleaguered look etched into his face for a while, no less grim than the faces of the men standing forlorn in endless food lines. There was no happiness in his eyes, though he could not disguise his joy at seeing his daughter.

Seen from a distance, his wife, my mother-in-law, might have been a fine porcelain sculpture poised in an elegant art store. She was petite, soft-spoken; she stood perfectly still and she knew immediately. She appeared as though she would shatter into countless pieces. My fault, she knew. Charlotte simply stood silent and cried, not helping matters in the least.

Mr. DeWitt, a man accustomed to adversity, simply pointed and I preceded him to his study, a mongrel dog without a leash, passing through an open door when instructed, standing in the centre of the room, waiting for further instructions, permission to be seated. The conversation was difficult at best. My throat was parched; his was moistened with the finest scotch. No man, particularly a wealthy man, wants to know his daughter was ravaged by a penniless fellow whose immediate prospects are seriously in doubt, let alone being cajoled into marrying said failure.

No one was hiring and I had relied more heavily than I should on family, not expecting that father would rob me so cruelly of my rightful place at the family bank.

"None of what you propose will happen. Let me be clear, sir. My daughter's first choice will be one of annulment, at my insistence."

"On what grounds, sir, may I ask?"

"Theft, Mr. Parkens."

"Might I ask that you be more precise in your accusation, sir? What I've stolen is your daughter's heart, nothing more."

"Her inheritance…more precisely."

"Sir, I don't follow you."

"Charlotte stands to become a wealthy woman when my time comes. Until then I intend for her to live well. What I do not intend is to support someone whose idea of success is providing the well-to-do clients of his father's bank a smooth ride to the sixth floor. He did not disappoint you, sir. You, in fact, are the disappointment. I would have expected you, as would your father, to argue for what you have studied these past four years at his entire expense. On that point, neither do I intend for you to enjoy Charlotte's eventual inheritance at mine."

"You insult me. I've given you no reason to think the worst of me and my position at the bank is temporary."

He ignored me.

"Her second choice will be to give up whatever child she produces. I won't see her character tainted by innuendo and damaging gossip."

"We're legally wed."

"A mockery in my eyes, a lark in yours. You contrived an easy way out from a difficult circumstance. You know as well as I that you would not have married her had you not first enjoyed obvious privileges." He took a deep swallow of his scotch. "The choice is hers, of course."

"She'll refuse you."

"Then she'll live a different life. We raised and educated her to be well-rounded amongst the society she knows, not to labour. She has no such ethic, for better or worse. Were she a man I would think of differently of her, of course. As it is she'll be a wife and a mother one day, just not yours."

"Your low opinion of me is not warranted. I have ambition."

"You do not. We're not handed success and I am quite certain you're no source of pride to your father. I know the man's reputation. You've enjoyed a gilded life for too long and, from what I see, you're not prone to aspiration of any kind. A man of ambition would have argued his worth. That you did not speaks ill of you. I see nothing wrong with starting at the bottom. I did, as my father did before me. You chose to leave your father's home like a chided boy and arrived here in his chauffeured car rather than on your own two feet."

"Your daughter believes you will take us in, until such time as we find our way. We have only just returned."

"She's half right. She'll live here until the paperwork is done. Then she'll vacation abroad, a reward for succeeding in her studies. By the time she returns her tryst will be forgotten, if you comprehend my meaning."

"I do, as will your daughter whom I have no doubt will choose to stand by her husband. The thought of giving her child to another is abominable."

"Her child, you say." Mr. DeWitt drained his glass. "In the event she refuses me, she'll be disinherited. And need I remind you of the economic crisis enveloping us?" He stood. "I see by your expression that you have yet to discover the seriousness of our times. Good day, sir. Further conversation between us will serve no purpose."

He led me to the main doors and left me without a word. I strained to hear the slightest sound, a whisper, a mournful sob or her papa's harsh rebuke. I heard nothing at all. My pocket watch showed fifteen past the hour, then five minutes before, when finally I heard the dull thuds of Mr. DeWitt's heavy footfalls and the quicker tempo of his wife's clicking slippers.

They passed me by without the slightest formality to climb a winding staircase beyond my sight. I waited, afraid to move. I wanted to go to her, unable to move. I remained frozen in place until Charlotte stepped from the parlour and slumped against the wall. I was not welcome. Her father wanted me gone.

I had a slim and solitary chance at redemption, one chance to wed her and be a father to our child.

My journey to the Regency was worse than any I had experienced in summers past, possibly caused by my defeat or the burden of my luggage. I remained standing with little choice to do otherwise despite my encumbrances, the others clearly unaware of common decency. I stared beyond the windows, ignoring them, lost in thought. I would not acknowledge them. I knew what they were thinking.

The night alone was miserable, made all the worse by Mr. DeWitt's ultimatum to Charlotte. I looked at the phone for the longest time, searching for the words I knew would fail me. I would meet father at the bank at the opening of business the following day and, if my timing suited him, I would appreciate time off in order to find a home for my wife and future child. I would make up the time as quickly as possible.

He agreed with a discernible lack of interest. When I was done I placed the phone into the cradle and soothed my distress to the extent that befitted my mood.

The next day I arrived at the bank on my own, without Driver, and was made to wait in the lobby. When father believed I'd waited sufficiently long with my hat in hand he summoned me. For the first time I was not seeing father; I was meeting with Aristotle Parkens.

To my absolute surprise the meeting went well, concluding more to my satisfaction than not. I was not prepared to one day remember the commencement of my career from the perspective of an elevator operator, I insisted. Nor should he want his son regarded by others in the bank as the lowliest amongst their ranks. He could just as easily dismiss a bookkeeper as the operator and with very little debate he concurred.

The woman was sent home at the end of her workday with an extra twenty dollars in her envelope and a letter from father describing her ten years of service as exemplary, by which time I managed to locate the least uncomfortable lodging within my new budget.

I moved in immediately to begin my independence, regarding father and father-in-law with equal disdain.

That evening, weary and looking quite haggard, if not downtrodden, I rode the tram to the DeWitt residence where the master of the house once again answered the door after the gargoyle's single, loud bark. He said nothing, waiting, and before I spoke a single word I promised myself I would never feel small again.

I was a bookkeeper with a weekly wage of twenty dollars. I began without false pride or feigned humility that I had bettered myself. I had acquired a modest apartment that, until better times, would be a comfortable home. He said nothing. He nodded and walked away, leaving me perplexed and uncertain. Moments later Charlotte took my hand and led me into the empty parlour.

We left soon after in a taxi, neither of us chancing to glance over our shoulders at the empty windows behind us. Charlotte had packed her wardrobe and childhood possessions in steamer trunks, the smallest of which I helped the driver lash to the roof. The other jutted out from the rear compartment and when we arrived home Charlotte wailed through the night.

Our rooms at school, as austere as they were, were a simple convenience, a place to meet, study, and wake. This was our home and I answered each sob with a vow to one day have one as grand as the one she once knew.

How was a man expected to exist on barely one thousand dollars a year when his father owned a Cadillac worth three times that amount and lived in a mansion? Fine for the others, they possessed no barometer with which to judge their austere condition against such requisite creature comforts as were required by the more erudite and urbane of men. They knew no differently.

I would never have a car. We could scarcely buy one new piece of furniture at a time. No one was giving credit and the worst was yet to come. Winter was a wicked thing. The tram was never heated and often I would fall down the steps of our building for no better reason than the refusal of the indolent concierge to do a proper job. As well, the hallways were constantly cluttered with men's rubber boots, galoshes and the smells leaking through doors at dinnertime made our own simple meals tasteless.

Our daughter, Alice or Allison or some such pedestrian appellation, was born Christmas Eve 1931. I never came to know her, and forget her without remorse. I suspect she might possibly be dead by this late hour of my own life.

Her arrival was inconvenient, I remember. Father and

mother could not disregard their party guests and Mr. DeWitt showed no emotion at all during his brief visit to the clinic. Only Mrs. DeWitt was remotely pleased by the event and, suddenly, my weekly wage was divisible by three.

Father was adamant. Both the mother and daughter constituted indisputable mistakes: mine. Though in the spring he did agree that the Mortgage & Loan would grant me a mortgage without exemption from the usual terms and we moved into our new home by late summer with nothing set aside for a few days by the lakeshore. The seashore was beyond my means. The sacrifice was small in my view. In the eyes of Mr. DeWitt we were living beyond our means in uncertain times. Father had no opinion.

At Christmas of '32 the girl was a year old, my career was not advancing and Charlotte was much more a mother and much less a wife. At school I had been a banker's son and knew how to please her. Then, without reason, I was a bank clerk and could not please her at all. We visited the DeWitt's home on two occasions since my defeat and father's home on three. The last was the week before August when nothing was said.

Father, I recall, was visibly tired, quite ready for a month aboard the yacht at his precious seaside sanctuary. I believed he would invite us, if for no other reason than compensation for my meagre wages and long hours. He did not, and I believe that was when Charlotte began to loathe me completely. Further discussion was pointless. Father saw no reason. I was an employee and not entitled to more than a week each year until my sixth year. However, neither did he invite mother.

What I knew of my father was that I despised him, for his viciousness towards me, equally so for his indifference towards me. I was, I believe, his worst mistake. In truth, and in retrospect, I never knew him. Nor was I allowed. Neither mother nor I were privy to his business concerns, his late nights or his twice yearly business excursions on behalf of his investors and shareholders.

I knew nothing of his courtship with my mother; he never spoke of his life before her, nor did ever speak of his alma mater. He had no friendships or acquaintances that I was aware of from his school years. Nor was I even vaguely acquainted with the history of my paternal grandparents, other than they were dead. I never enquired, for which I blame him unequivocally for, throughout my life, I was afraid of him.

He told me briefly on one occasion prior to his departure, and quite matter-of-factly, that one day I would know his true nature, should I ever discover my own. I remember how he twirled his ring and made a fist so that the ruby sat like a trophy upon his clenched hand, his eyes fixed upon my scar, his lips curved into a curious snarl as though he sought to deride me one last time.

That day I hated father the most.

He returned looking no better and a month later he was dead. He was sixty-two and I forced myself to mourn, a shallow effort at best. The ruffians at school were right. Mother found him sitting in his study, facedown at his desk, the back of his head pasted to a work of art on the wall behind him.

The following day the bank closed and the workers were sent home. The day after I received his letters and that night my mother came to me for assistance. She no longer had a home to oversee.

I listened with Charlotte. I empathized with her. However what did she expect that I would do? Father, I reminded her, was miserly in his treatment of me and I sent her away after assuring her I would bury the man without any inconvenience to her. She received from me, at the end of our association, the rightful return on the investment she had made in me.

I never saw her again. I suspect no one did and I feel no regret for I read in father's secret missive to me that he had ensured her well-being. Not the first time mother was untruthful to me, nor the second, for when I asked her directly what she had done with his ring her expression was unconvincingly blank.

In his first letter father explained matter-of-factly, as though posting an entry in a journal such as this one you read, that he was the principal advisor at the bank. He trusted no one other than himself to care for the wealthiest of his clients, which I read as a point of fact and not a startling revelation. The depression, not yet labelled 'Great' was in its fourth year and increasingly they wanted their money back.

In truth, father was the wealthiest client of his own Mortgage & Loan. His instructions to me were emotionless, as though hearing his words, the final sentence a confession. He'd sold his home to the bank some years earlier along with the yacht and the oceanfront retreat without mother's knowledge and I stared at his signature in disbelief. He wanted me to remember him as Aristotle Parkens and not my father.

The following day I lost my home, Charlotte took the girl to live with her papa and I went to the address noted in father's second letter with the key he'd left me as my single remembrance of him. The Savings & Loan was on the other side of town and the letter was his permission for me to open the box belonging to the key.

Inside I discovered matching bundles neatly wrapped in brown paper and a large brown envelope. I knew what they were and touched them with curious reverence. The money was not mine, rightfully the property of the newly desperate...of which I was one, one of eighty-five thousand who'd fallen on hard times with no foreseeable future.

I counted through the piles suppressing my guilt as

much as my joy. One hundred thousand dollars, and in the large brown envelope were the deed and title to the Isle of Tombola.

Nine

Cassidy checked his watch, ignoring the rumblings in his stomach. Aayla would never believe him. Whether he would tell her was another matter. She already thought him insane.

He was sitting in The Grand Guardian's library surrounded by knowledge, books from the floor to the ceiling and across three of the four walls; spellbound by what he'd gleaned in such a short time.

He was well aware of the date, the current year, month and day. Neither his grandfather nor father had lost a day since Jonathon Clayton's gruesome shark attack, each day precisely noted on the inside covers of concealed books, on his father's bed and now on the chest. He felt a sense of achievement, not that he was certain.

He knew The Grand Guardian's first-born was not the eldest son, nor was the second. The two families were wealthy. DeWitt's from hard work, Parkens' from the hard work of others. The father was a banker who took his own life, leaving behind one hundred thousand dollars, the title and deed to the Isle of Tombola and his wife who was then abandoned by his son.

Cassidy knew of the four seasons, Christmas and Easter. He knew of guns, though he had never held one. He knew of dollars, paper money and coins, though he had touched neither until a few hours earlier and couldn't imagine how 100,000 of anything might look. He knew of good deeds and bad, he knew the titles of his books, yet he didn't understand what those words meant when their meaning included Tombola.

Once in his tree he would find them in his yellowed dictionary so that he would understand.

*

How could I demean myself, harbouring such glee? How could I return once more to where they loathed and despised me? I called Charlotte that evening, telling her I would travel the next day to another city to seek employment better suited to my nature and expressed my deep sadness at having disappointed her. She listened glumly, choosing not to reinforce the truth.

When our discourse concluded without spurious endearments, I went to the hotel dining room to order the finest champagne.

I read father's second letter like chapters of a novel, over and over again and woke with a terrible headache, not surprised that I'd learned nothing more about him. In the afternoon I booked passage by train to the shore, the gentle swaying reminiscent of my times aboard the yacht, my sleep undisturbed in my private berth. The next day my cabin onboard the liner was situated on the upper deck and not the lower.

I arrived in South Florida one week later and, once again, enjoyed the pick of the litter. Truth be told, I enjoyed a different one each night. I believed in my heart that being with one would be a blatant betrayal to my wife, whereas being with six would leave my conscience clear with nothing to explain or lament beyond my need for release.

I needed to forget that the reason I'd married Charlotte was now dead. I needed to expunge from my mind that Parkens was synonymous with cowardly.

On my first day I found a boatyard. I went to the chandlery for charts and I spoke with the harbourmaster to explain my needs, display my credentials from father's club and substantiate my abilities. When he was satisfied with my yachtsmanship, dare I say he was greatly impressed, I leased a cruiser similar in style and capability to father's and made the boatyard my temporary domicile.

By the evening of the second day I'd studied the tides and currents, plotted my course and went into town. Mutually satisfied, I sent her to wherever she would go as dawn's early light crept above the horizon. I was anxious to leave and saw no need for pretence.

I piloted the able craft with ease, grateful for my inherent inclination towards seamanship, not discounting the navigational training I acquired throughout the easier years of my youth. The twin engines brought me to the island in fewer than six exhilarating hours precisely positioned according to father's latitude and longitude and my acquired charts.

I circled once, twice and three times. I knew by previous study of the principal chart that the island was twenty-six miles in length, six miles across at its midway, shaped like a ferret on its side. Towards the south the topography was narrow, however not greatly so: the head of the ferret. The leeward shore, at equal distances from the southern and the northern tips, possessed a natural arc with several coves of decent dimension where the green hills appeared to descend into the sea, clearly visible from my position: the belly and paws of the ferret. The northern configuration, according to my chart, was the narrowest: the tail of the ferret.

From the most northerly point to the most southerly lay a high ridge, the island's spine, densely populated with glorious trees, descending gradually in a smooth line to the foothills which were at first difficult to discern. Closer to the north than the south was a magnificent precipice rising above the treetops, as would a fountain of ancient, molten rock.

From my more northerly vantage, well out to sea, the rocky summit appeared quite narrow and elevated above sea level to some 300 feet or more. I could not have been more inaccurate in my judgement.

The windward side of the slope was comprised of deep shades of green, not unlike a cluster of precious emeralds beyond one's reach, glistening under the sun; the leeward shore looked upon a slope coloured in shades of olives and limes.

Only upon much closer inspection did I determine that the towering precipice was, in fact, two natural structures and not one.

The Isle of Tombola was split in unequal halves as though with the sweep of a vicious and colossal Excalibur: the larger half residing on Tombola; the smaller standing indomitable on what father called Tombolina.

On the chart Tombolina did not exist, neither did Tombola. The gorge between them was narrow and dark, unmarked on my charts. I decided wisely to avoid unnecessary and unknown danger and proceeded to observe the remaining shoreline, which I determined could be easily explored on foot between the dawn and dusk of any fair day.

Indeed, I believed I was gazing upon the paradise of any sane man. My father's description was my one confirmation of any legal entitlement as not a single indication of his ownership was planted or elsewhere existed. Neither did a dock of any description exist on either shore of either island from which I might easily disembark.

The tide was passably high, allowing me decent depth, the water was crystal clear and the bottom was white with fine sand. Upon completion of my third circumnavigation I dropped the anchor off the leeward shore of the bigger island, confidant I'd made the boat secure before attending to the vessel's ladder.

My single protection was a flare pistol which I placed into the plastic bag twisted several times in the hope of keeping the weapon dry. I tied my belt tightly around my waist and jammed in the bag, standing at the bow and following the scope of laid out cable to the silver-grey shank of the anchor. The air was still, the sun was hot and prickled my skin. I was as anxious to feel the water as I was afraid to leave the safety of the boat. I was afraid, and I wondered whether I would always be afraid in my heart of hearts: a Parkens' legacy or a Parkens' curse.

How was I to know?

I leapt forward, my eyes shut tight, thrashing out against all that I imagined, surfacing as quickly as I could, frantically grabbing for the taut line. I was afraid, of course. I was alone in an endless sea, about to step upon an island, a foreign coast, without the least knowledge of what dangers awaited me.

I swam 100 feet or more, thankful when I could wade into the calm waters of the leeward shore. I called out, and waited. I called out again, this time louder, feeling my throat constrict, thinking myself a fool for not remaining aboard to communicate with any possible inhabitant by way of the ship's loud hailer.

I inched my way forward. My torso was dry, my swimming suit clung to me like a second skin and my feet were coated with a fine white dust. Perhaps I'd chosen the wrong point at which to begin my exploration. Father had not indicated.

I believed the windward side excessively violent for my purpose, the north too narrow in its available beach, its shore too high and rocky and the south appeared overrun with trees and peculiar vegetation which I had no desire to challenge.

From where I stood the beach was wide and long, 200 feet deep before a line of splendid palms and disappearing into infinity in either direction. I loosened my belt and freed the pistol from its wrapping. I first walked one way before reversing my direction and walking the other, this time somewhat closer to the trees, fully prepared and committed to killing any creature that might leap out at me. If encountered two, I would surely be the one killed. The one path I noticed near to the point at which I came ashore was overgrown and narrow. Going closer, cautiously, I could feel the dampness of the shade and was made to feel uneasy by the shadows and eerie stillness assailing my ears.

I was unprepared. I had no hatchet, no shoes and no clothing other than my swimming suit which left my arms bare as well as my legs below the knees. I lost all sense of time and the thought of warm flesh to explore was much more compelling to me than sleeping alone aboard a yacht moored to a sandy beach in the middle of nowhere and completely consumed by darkness. I would return the next day and I wrapped the pistol as tightly as possible.

Onboard the yacht I stripped away my suit. I dried myself under the sun and drank a cold beer. I stood awhile, the deck rocking gently beneath my feet, feeling as one with nature, as free and alive as I did small and vulnerable. I hauled in the anchor, the motors groaned in unison, the waters churned and I set a reciprocal course.

With my back to the helm I witnessed the two islands become one and fade to where my eyes played tricks on me, not at all certain what I would do with them or what Charlotte would think. What did one do with an island, or two?

I cruised into port in time for a mid-evening dinner. That particular one reminded me of Charlotte, which I thought was appropriate. Yet I sent her away at sunrise, to her dismay. She left wanting more, though to have acknowledged her, to have taken her with me for the day, would have meant another evening with her and that would not have been considerate of my wife.

Leaving her behind, I remember piloting the craft through the shallow swells with wild abandon, testing its limit, at once invigorated and uncertain, cutting the motors precisely where I had dropped anchor the previous day and swimming to the beach with a nylon cord attached to my waist.

The sensation of warm water flowing so intimately over my body for the first time remains indescribable. Previously I had restricted the complete nakedness of my person to my time spent perfunctorily in bed with Charlotte or once on the grass behind Edna's home. I tugged once on the line, causing the rubber box to fall from the bow. Inside were my clothes for the hours ahead, food, drink, a hatchet, a flashlight, a compass and camera I had purchased the night before, a length of braided rope, my watch and a real pistol.

Dressing was difficult, the salt and sand on my body fighting my every move. My objective was the path; my priority was conquering my fear. I decided I would hurry rather than walk deliberately, not venturing farther than the length of rope, believing I would lessen the chance of being mauled or pursued.

I tied the rope to a small and sturdy tree, and again to my waist. My pistol was strapped to my chest, the coiled rope held in one hand and the machete in the other. I read my compass. I was ready and I felt the need for someone to know. I yelled into the shadows that I was proceeding inward, and that I was armed.

Not ten feet later I looked back. I was engulfed by moist walls of green rubbing against me and I feared to look up. I hurried forward, hacking, chanting meaningless words because I heard no other sound. After twenty feet my progress slowed, if not my frantic swinging. After fifty, at the end of my rope, the path began to clear. The shadows were no longer frightful and the air was less humid, easier to breath.

I untied my rope. I searched for any landmark to remember and went farther with my compass in hand, attempting to walk a straight line and counting each step. I stopped at 300 paces and stared. Far to my left was a building, or the remnants of one that had once existed. Far to my right was an endless row of broken huts with sagging thatched roofs and doors strewn across the ground like roughly hewn mats.

The larger building had two floors, constructed of brick and mortar. Once a magnificent structure, I was certain, and of sufficient area to house a large family. The windows had no glass, nor lights or sources of electricity that I could determine and a single door hung at an angle from a rusted hinge. I shouted out, shivering at the disappearance of my voice into the silence and I gripped my pistol.

I went closer, calling out, taking several minutes to conclude that I was alone and that I should go inside. I thought to fire a warning shot, correcting myself upon the realization that I would then have one round less with which to defend myself. The place was barren, devoid of furniture. I determined that the bare walls had begun to crack apart untold years earlier.

The condition of the upper floor was no better. I decided that pirates had once ransacked the place, or a terrible storm. Parts of the ceiling opened to the sky and the bones of several birds lay scattered across the floors of each room. I needed to get out. I needed to see the ocean and the yacht.

Beyond the unanticipated thought of pirates fresh in my mind, I needed to consider what had been in father's mind. Why had he led me here? I understood his reasons for taking his life, he was a coward. However what had possessed him to buy such overgrown specks of land with nothing to offer beyond destruction and decay. And what good would my remaining ninety-eight thousand do to reverse the condition. I would be a king, a lord of some sort or a lone hermit without means. I would certainly be alone for Charlotte would never agree to a solitary life and I determined not to tell her. I cranked the anchor line through the hawsepipe, set my course and considered what I should do, one random thought usurping the other.

Late in the morning of the fifth day, after sending her away with the fondest of memories of me to see her through to her next dalliance or her wedding day, I met with the law firm who had prepared and witnessed the title deed. Upon producing my father's letter to me, and their subsequent verification of the deed, a senior barrister confirmed to me that I was in fact the owner, in spite of which I was firmly decided.

Unable to envision any viable use of the island, I signed with them an agreement which made them proprietary agents responsible for its sale at a time when no one was buying private islands. If anything, they were jumping from windows or in front of trains, whichever was convenient to their state of mind.

On the morning of my sixth day I lamented the need to leave her, explaining I would never forget her. I have no doubt she believed me, or my sad expression. When she was gone I undid my lines and spent the day at sea, meditating, planning what I would do or say in ten days time when I would see my beloved wife and dearest child.

That evening the moon was bright and the sea was calm. I was of two minds, debating, the weaker struggling to remain onboard, the stronger arguing my return to port and the discovery of appropriate venues to satisfy my hungers.

The feast was sumptuous, the company divine. I had certainly saved the best for last. We parted with mutual reluctance at noon, I suspect with distinctively different motives. Had I not been married, or had the island been a magnificent isle, I likely would have stayed longer with her.

Though I knew at the time why I would, and therein lay her trap: a snare not unlike Charlotte's.

She was younger than Charlotte by three years, eager to learn and please, though she sensed that I luxuriated in her youthful perfection, my pleasure impossible to disguise. Her parents had expired and she would have been a perfect mate. She was exquisite, though I could not trust her not to betray me as others had. And so I left her. What choice had I? With all I possessed, I would soon be a gentleman without means unless I returned home, secure in the knowledge she would soon find another ready to convince her of her beauty, her charms, and vow eternal love.

Ten

Cassidy's day was half over. Nightfall would come in six hours. He decided he would leave in the dark, certain the bright lights of the house would betray him. In a year's time he would live in his own villa and be a first-mate to the largest and homeliest girl in the entire village, afraid to imagine for a moment what his first-born might resemble, afraid the horrific image might invade his night time dreams of his mother and Aayla.

The girl had no buttocks, merely a split at the bottom of her back that drooped heavily on both sides. She seldom ran. When she did her breasts jerked violently in all directions. From a distance they looked like stale coconuts, streaked and brown and random hairs grew from her nipples .He'd never imagined her maiden, nor had he ever seen her shield or the leather strips encircling her hips. Her face was dotted with dark imperfections, several with thick stubble protruding at wild angles. The skin around her dull eyes was discoloured and loose. Her ears were thick, her lips had the appearance of being separately attached and her teeth jutted from her jaw like uneven shards.

Until then he would live in his mother's villa. He knew that his later than usual absence would concern her. She would scold him before she would embrace him and serve him a hot meal. Though he also knew that, if not for her worry, he would stay the night and each of the three nights ahead of him. What he was doing was crucial. He was in his sixth year.

Wendell Parkens came to the island from South Florida, travelling from somewhere to the north. Cassidy knew of Florida. He knew of Miami, the city where Jonathon Clayton first met Wendell Parkens, a name Cassidy knew from his great-grandfather's letters, a man Jon Clayton referred to in his first correspondences as learned. In his later writings, he believed the man was fast losing his mind.

Learned, Cassidy thought, and a coward who feared the fish that swim in the ocean and the birds that sing in the forest. The man came to the island with a gun, and still he yelled at the shadows, afraid to sleep at night for fear pirates might board his yacht and cut his throat.

Cassidy chortled to the point of giggling. The man really was Wendy.

Often, balanced on the favourite branch of his favourite tree he would read his favourite tale of buccaneers sailing the West Indies in centuries past, plundering Spanish galleons for gold to fill their purses and whores to bed. Wendell Parkens was no different. He took well-fed women to bed whenever he could, and sent them away before returning to the warmth of his hearth.

Cassidy scanned the walls. He would need years to read all the books, and thought he would count them before he left, wondering whether he could count to ninety-eight thousand.

He turned to the next page.

*

Father acquired the islands in 1906 and no evidence existed to prove or contradict whether he ever revisited his properties. He would never have tolerated the severe incommodities witnessed earlier by me. He would have arranged for more appropriate accommodations and, with that in mind, I spent what was left of my last day to appease my mounting curiosity.

In those early days, and particularly throughout those desperate times, men such as father stood apart from most others and fine hotels were few and far between: an extravagant comfort few others could afford. His name, I had no doubt, was filed away in some dreary back office or scrawled into a yellowing registry and I determined to visit the two of any possible consequence. One was in view of the other and I knew immediately my evaluation was not incorrect.

The first hotel of choice was the most elaborate, the most expensive and the dining room was predictably pretentious. Unquestionably an establishment father would have patronized. Why not, when others had paid his way? And I was quite correct in my assessment. He had stayed there, on countless occasions, each six months apart.

I thanked the concierge appropriately before spending what time was left to me in the majestic setting of the garden restaurant, musing. I would never know. How could I? Who would I ask? What had been in father's mind, possibly a dream or escape from me and mother, escape from mother who knew nothing of the isle, or escape from the pistol that ended his life.

Had he waited too long? And why had he thought to acknowledge me at death's door when he never had before? What did he know that I did not?

Strangely, father's unexpected death was my deliverance from the mediocrity he once forced upon me and I could envision him chortling in his grave at the irony, revelling in the narcissism he'd perfected in life. Or was I seeing him laughing at me? I never knew, not until the day I ceased to wonder.

That evening I boarded the liner, certain that Mr. DeWitt with his exaggerated and biased concept of integrity would soon have the authorities snapping at my heels were he to know of my unlikely windfall. And Charlotte, I knew, or suspected, would be the primary conduit to that intelligence.

For that reason I determined all the more not to share my newfound fortune with her, though she would benefit nonetheless. At week's end, boarding the train for yet another monotonous passage, my thoughts were essentially perfected. And, by the time I arrived in the city I always believed I would call home, they were.

I called Charlotte from my hotel room, prepared with a convincing fabrication regarding my delay, explaining that I would see her in three days time with the greatest news. She sounded despondent, regretful, surprised to hear my voice, and in the background I heard the girl crying. Not until years later did I imagine that she might not have expected my return, or had hoped for me not to. That day altered my life beyond imagination as you will soon discover in these pages, Dakota. I told her not to worry, that the world had become ours and that the opinions of Mr. DeWitt and his wife mattered not in the least to me.

On the third day I kept my word. I arrived at the residence in clothes not bought by father, at precisely eleven-thirty, and in my own custom roadster which was a 1930 Chrysler Imperial, so that my wife might accompany me to lunch in style.

The previous owner had paid close to what father had paid for the limousine and had barely enjoyed the wonderful ride. I relieved him of the luxurious burden for a quarter of the price and, therein, I knew, lay my future. I was quite dapper in my new three-piece suit, hat, and polished boots. Though I derived the greatest pleasure from Charlotte's shocked expression when she saw the diamond ring I could at last afford. Nor had I told her what to expect.

She was openly embarrassed by what she had chosen to wear. She believed our luncheon would take place in some mediocre diner and not the finest restaurant on the avenue whose establishments were understandably the privileged domain of the very well-heeled. Nor did she expect to sleep that night in her own bed, under her own roof in a bungalow I might not have afforded for years.

Truth be told, I enjoyed her discomfort: her just recompense for not standing by me during our short-lived strife which was not of my doing.

Throughout those three days I was the very antithesis of idle. The first phase of my plan was to visit the Savings & Loan to once again ensure the secrecy of my newly acquired property. With that task completed I met with the manager of the mortgage and forfeiture department, a humourless and narrow thinking man who readily supplied me with a list of homes which appeared to meet my quickly assembled criteria.

I was determined that if anyone was to benefit from the misfortune of destitute families losing their homes I would be the beneficiary and not the bank at my cost. One of his subordinates drove me to view three vacated homes, empty shells devoid of personality. I bought the nicest of the three for my own accommodation immediately upon returning to the Savings & Loan, not particularly mindful that I was acquiring some poor devil's home for mere pennies on the dollar.

That afternoon I bought my car and the following morning the other two dwellings at a fraction of the value. In the afternoon I went to a furniture and appliance store and by late evening all that was missing from the house were Charlotte and the girl.

On the morning of the fourth day we woke together and joined as man and wife should, albeit not as I'd hoped, and my thoughts quickly drifted to the sixth of the six women I'd taken to the boat. We would need time to rekindle our once heated passion which had quelled since that ruined Christmas and her instant inclination towards maternity, if not her disinclination towards me.

In truth, we never did. In the years following our copulation was pragmatic, a question of marital obligation concluding matter-of-factly and with mutual indifference once the need was met. At some point I decided we would never be more than each other's convenient and reciprocal release. At best she would evolve into the manager of my home and the girl. I would never be more than the guardian of their well-being. To that end I dedicated myself unashamedly and covertly to avarice

The first anniversary of father's death passed unnoticed, much as he had, primarily because many of the people he cast into poverty had decided to adjust their destinies to suit their then current situation without thinking beyond the final few moments of their lives: cowards all.

I once read that the beatitudes of the New Testament were somewhat paradoxical. The writer had been quite right and eloquent in his and my view.

Of what use were millennia-old promises when the meek were being blessed merely by an uncaring clergy, once in their coffins and at their graves? For they were not to inherit the earth; increasingly they were becoming part of it, which was quite a different matter. They were men of weak character, taken by a modern day plague brought on by destitution and hopelessness caused by men of a despicable nature such as my father.

My thoughts of that day remain clear to me, for how could I not remember? How many hours did I muse with sardonic satisfaction at knowing the answers. So dear father, so poor in spirit, is yours the kingdom of heaven, I questioned? Can you see me from on high? Can you? Shall mother, who possibly mourns you, be comforted? I think not. Truly, I do not.

Do the piteous who hunger and thirst care for righteousness in their lives? No, they do not, I submit. Their single contentment is in food and drink. And where do we go for mercy, when those who look down upon us are not merciful, such as you? And where is God when the pure of heart beseech Him each day for mercy to live another day, for food and for drink?

Are you by His side? I think not, for you were never pure of heart. Or do I hope that you are not? All these gentle people whose lives you have ruined, shall they sit by your side and forgive you in a kingdom deprived of their loved ones and dreams? Can you still dream, father, and, of greater importance, am I to one day be persecuted for the righteousness of what you have made me, of what I have become?

Is that what has happened with this recent awareness of my own death? Am I now to become a son of God, persecuted for my righteousness? Or shall this place, this isle, my kingdom, be my own, where I shall lay in peace throughout all my next life without the need to know or fear more? Tell me, father.

Businesses continued to crumple, food lines grew longer and many believed the worst was yet to come. Hope no longer existed. People were calling me daily, begging for one of my empty homes, and each day I would refuse them. Those who did work saw their wages steadily diminishing, thankful they were not the ones told not to come back on Monday. The price of homes was also plummeting: twenty-five percent in five years.

In that year I purchased five more empty homes from the bank at the same favourable rate. The banks were desperate for money, and I sold them for a third below fair market value for a total profit of 21,000 dollars. In '35 I bought twelve more, selling them by the onset of another winter. On those properties my profits amounted to not far from 35,000 dollars, fifty-six in under two years, plus my original investments and what remained of my inheritance.

I was twenty-five and on my way to being wealthy. Of

course, all Charlotte was required to know was that I was employed, that the house and car were paid for, and that I was doing well in real-estate, earning almost five thousand a year when our neighbours scarcely made two.

In '36 I went to the bank with a take-it-or leave-it proposition. I wanted first refusal on all their outstanding forfeitures. They agreed. With the coming of spring, and in the wake of several successful sales, I thought it wise to purchase a strongbox and take real possession of my increasing wealth in a currency I knew would never fail. I began not to trust the bank or their legal tender. I became suspicious of them. They wanted, without forewarning and without courteous preamble, to increase my preferential rate from ten to twenty percent. I declined, with good reason, and within a few months the Savings & Loan collapsed.

As rumour reported, the narrow-minded sparrow of a man was first to jump from his office window. He'd lost his own house and, by flailing himself downward onto the snow-covered sidewalk below, he'd simultaneously hurled his family into an even greater plight. Or so I assumed as I read his name amongst so many others.

That afternoon I went to another bank with terms more in keeping with my own interests and took over their list of vacant houses which were once the hearths of love, hope, and dreams.

The dead banker's self-inflicted misfortune ironically catapulted me into an era of even greater success, though I never thought to give him posthumous credit. What was done was done. My euphoria, however, was short-lived. Towards the autumn of '37 the girl attended her first day of school and by spring the following year the change in Charlotte was undeniable. Without the girl to occupy her time she had become idle and listless. I was not sufficient in her life. I was not for some time and she wanted more.

She'd been denied the benefits of her father's fortune

and reputation and she knew nothing of my own. She was betwixt the old and the new, and knew no better. We were wealthy, yet she believed herself poor despite lacking for nothing. I believe she grew to resent her father as much as she did me for my apparent lack of ambition, a situation she decided to worsen with herself entirely to blame for we had previously discussed the matter.

"Wendell, my dear, we are soon to have another child," she declared one evening after dinner when the girl at last had gone to her room to study.

"We simply can't afford another mouth to feed, Charlotte, not with your propensity for lavish living while others wallow in these difficult times. You have blatantly disobeyed me, choosing to go back on your promise to me. We agreed, didn't we?"

"We have little or no control over what is natural, and we didn't agree to anything. It's very clear to me that you want your freedom. You're never home, you never spend time with her, or me, and when you do it's to have your selfish urges satisfied."

I recall her caustic expression, the way she placed one hand deliberately over the other against her belly.

"This will be born of those selfish urges…sometime in the early spring."

"There's no room for another. This house wasn't meant for four. How do you propose a larger home? You see each day how I struggle to sell the few that I do, none of them as nice as this."

"Papa may help us. You can speak with him."

"Your father thinks me a failure and has yet to forgive me for the theft of your presumed innocence."

My intentional smirk caused her to lace her fingers, quite possibly to prevent her from assailing me with her cutlery.

"Imagine if he knew. What then, do you think? Might he

think differently of me? Might he think me the saviour of your reputation? You never did reveal to me the exact number of professors you delighted with your collegiate charms, Charlotte. Were I a man given to suspicion, which I am not, I might well ponder whether I was the one to satiate the insatiable. Can we ever truly change who we are?"

"The child is yours, and I wasn't your first. You have no need to act so superior."

"I've never doubted you, and I would hurl myself from a window before approaching your father for a single dime. Give a man what he expects and he'll always want more. Your father's no exception and he'll derive no such satisfaction from me. Don't be fooled by his easy manner and the painted smiles I've seen disappear often enough when he turns away."

"I'll find employment."

"Yes, of course you will, when all others are losing theirs. And what would you do? The one skill you once practiced with enviable dedication and inherent passion, which I would hardly expect you to capitalize on in your current condition, has since waned to the point of painful expectation. In short, Charlotte, your professors, and I as a student, were the beneficiaries of your finest years and single-mindedness. You have no marketable capabilities other than motherhood which, I hasten to add, I believe you might find somewhat burdensome when your domestic responsibilities are doubled."

"You have no right to bring up my past. Papa is right to despise you, and mother's opinion is no better. He believes you're dishonest. Why else would a man who sells houses require such a large strongbox in his own home?"

"My business affairs are not his to discuss with you or anyone else. He should praise me for the social embarrassment he was spared and for what I have accomplished in so little time. You see how our neighbours have fared. He has no possible reason to scorn me other than his feeble misgivings. And what your mother thinks of me is, likely as not, equal to my appraisal of her. DeWitt women aren't bred to work, dear Charlotte. Those were his words the night I took you to him. They are, however, entirely ready to enjoy the fruits of others' hard work."

I stood. Further conversation was futile. Charlotte would have her bigger home and nothing I could say or do would prevent its fourth occupant.

"We should never have married."

"Truer words…though had we not, what would have become of you? He would have sent you away. You would have lost the girl with nothing to remember her by but the scars she inflicted upon you and the downward slope of your once enviable breasts."

She pushed herself from the table.

"Other men find me attractive."

"Other men don't see you as I do. And what would any of them give you in exchange for a day or a lifetime?"

"A man."

I chortled. Had I struck her the repercussions would have been swift and severe and, without question, violent.

"A man provides for his family. I believe you meant to say 'a professor', distraught these past years by the abrupt cessation of your carnal studies."

"You were happy enough to take their place."

"I won't deny your appetite intrigued me, distracted into believing you'd never be so careless."

"You've never forgiven me."

"It's in the past, Charlotte, as I suspect we are. You'll have your bigger home and I'll have another mouth to feed, one whose arrival I've had no say in, not unlike the other. I have no doubt your mother will be alone in her joy."

"I've paid dearly for marrying you."

"Ah, the inheritance. Yes, well, in fact you've paid

nothing. Inheritances are of little value until such time as the benefactor expires and my challenge to my father the day we well remember negates your father's threat to you, though you'd be wise not to anticipate any large portion of his worth. You disappointed him, irrespective of my participation. You would have shown your true nature one day, Charlotte. Indeed, were it not for your preoccupation with the girl and her imprint upon you, I feel quite certain you would have disappointed me on one or many occasions. Once a whore, Charlotte, always a whore."

Charlotte winced, pained by her stinging slap against my face. I simply walked away, content to know what she did not.

Eleven

Cassidy was stunned. He felt as though his blood had congealed and ceased to flow. He'd known since his father first judged him old enough to keep the knowledge within his own mind that The Grand Guardian was Wendell Parkens, that Wendell Parkens was a man like any other.

There was one difference which made him the guardian while others on Tombola toiled in the fields and gave him adoration, all but the descendants of Jon Clayton and their women. He was educated, as were past generations of Claytons. The rest were not.

Cassidy's mother had no knowledge of where the strongbox lay concealed, nor did his grandmother or the wife of Jonathon Clayton who believed the information was potentially dangerous to them.

Wendell Parkens knew to mould those less strong around him. In the words he wrote of his father, there was no respect. He once sneered at a man who'd flung himself from a high window, in part from desperation, in part because of Wendell Parkens who believed the two girls given to him by Charlotte were fathered by others.

Cassidy thought for a moment of what might have happened to the girls, thinking they would be very old and feeble, if not dead. And if they were dead, were they at the threshold of darkness that followed life to greet him into eternity and abhor him as no one on Tombola could. He hoped so, for all that the man called Wendy Parkens had done. And with that hope flourished a wish he would harbour until he was ready to leave the house that night or the next. He wanted to find the Twelve Scriptures.

His hunger wasn't abating. He marked the open page with a pen he took from its cradle and went to the kitchen. The tiled floor hadn't dried and all he could find to eat was an apple, afraid to remove anything else for fear they would notice the loss and become suspicious.

He placed the core by the bottle and returned to the library. He had much more to read.

*

The second girl was delivered to us in April, the single reason I have to remember her name. I was in the second year of my relations with the Credit Union and exceeding any and all of my previous expectations despite housing prices which continued to plummet.

Charlotte was in her new home and we lived with civility rather than any facsimile of love. I rarely called upon her to play the adoring wife and I began to envision myself as a man with a more sophisticated palate, the man I had neglected for so long.

My wealth tripled, though much of that wealth was invested in hope. I began buying factories, vacant or equipped, that no one would buy. The world had spoken of war for months and such was my hope as much as my fear. I could not actively partake in a war that was not mine, for what good was wealth to a maimed or dead man?

By year's end my negotiations grew more complex, more demanding of my time. Sleep was an interruption to my success and often I would work through the night, forcing my hope to offset my fear. Not so Christmas Eve when the phone rang to ruin the day.

Mr. and Mrs. DeWitt had not come to the girl's party for he was feeling ill, which was no particular loss to me. Though giving the devil his due, telling Charlotte her father was dead was somewhat unpleasant.

We packaged the girls in a hurry and drove through a miserable storm to the gated home. He was dead on the floor, his mouth agape, his eyes staring dumbly from behind narrow slits, his scarred and thick fist clenching uselessly at his shirt, his pants stained with the embarrassment of recent wetness. Mr. DeWitt had passed on and had done so with an apparent understanding of the situation.

Mrs. DeWitt wept unstoppable tears more, I believe, for the inconvenience than the loss. He had been the man; she had been the wife, a status she could no longer maintain without him. So what was she to do? Like her daughter, she possessed no skill other than wifehood which had no measurable value.

The house was a cacophony of echoes. The women wailed throughout the night, the girl cried until she stopped to sleep, though her infant sibling knew no such limitation. The body was taken away later that morning, being that Christmas for many had become the worst day of the year and the coroner was a busy man.

We remained the entire day and on the 27th we went to the church to bid him farewell. Charlotte remained by her mother's side through to the New Year. I suppose having the girls to distract her helped the widowed woman. For my part, I welcomed in '39 with a smile. Not only did Mr. DeWitt depart to leave me in peace, I began selling my factories to the military for more than their worth and by September 03rd I had bought and sold a dozen more.

War was declared and I was a very rich man at the age of twenty-nine, my one failure the Isle of Tombola which was not yet sold, though I scarcely had time to think of the island or of father.

Had he not bought the islands, he likely would not have murdered himself in such a horrible way, mother might have been with her granddaughters for years to come and I might have been, at some point, a respectable banker with an indifferent yet dutiful wife. Nor would he have left me the key to my fortune. Indeed, how could I not be grateful that father was an unscrupulous rogue and thoughtless husband?

Food lines were becoming shorter. People once starving were standing in line to buy food, not begging for a spoonful more, buying groceries with money earned in factories once again alive with sounds of grinding wheels, spinning bobbins and metal stamping against metal. People were buying clothes and buying homes they could now afford, homes taken over by me from the bank and sold at full market value.

And the military needed more factories, with affordable homes near those factories. I wanted to build those homes, which I could not do with a bullet in my chest or marching on foreign soil for as long as the world required to put Germany in its place. Soon men would be coming home, with money to spend, and I would be the first to greet them.

Charlotte's inheritance was a pittance compared to what she wrongly or greedily anticipated, somewhere in the order of twenty-thousand dollars. Mrs. DeWitt refused to sell me her property. With what he bequeathed to her she had sufficient funds to live a long and comfortable life, though destiny preferred that she depart early be with her husband and within the first year of his death she lay beside him.

Another Christmas spoiled, though the first girl had quite forgotten her grandpapa and her presents soon took precedence over her recently deceased grandmother; the other possessed no memory at all of those who once cuddled her. As for Charlotte, she was her mother's sole beneficiary and believed she then had dominion over me. She did not, despite my acceptance to reside in a mansion which was entirely hers and where I was once loath to spend even the briefest time.

Winter, as the worst season is wont to do, took its time blossoming into spring. The war was in its seventh month and young men continued to believe themselves invincible, mostly those who still could not find work. I reflected for weeks on the need to tell her, since her mother's death and her immediate sense of independence which I interpreted as superiority.

Her newly found airs were vexing. I felt an unquenchable urge to diminish her. I remember seeing her reposed upon her récamier, fully cloaked in a satin robe. I had not seen her undressed in months. I sat on the edge of my bed: a personal possession deriving from mutual agreement. We were making new friends; I was too successful not to be noticed and enjoyed a seat of some importance at the Men's Club. Charlotte was becoming intimate with the wives of those men and divorce would be injurious to my plans and her developing status.

"Charlotte, dear, I would like a moment of your time."

She nodded. She knew by the tone of my voice to listen.

"I shall be leaving town at week's end. I shall be gone for a few weeks. Opportunities have presented themselves and to ignore them would be foolish in the extreme."

"The girls and I shall be quite safe here. Do what you feel is right."

Such was the extent of her emotion towards me.

"Thank you, and one more thing before I leave you to your thoughts, as I am expected at the club. I have decided to transfer the contents of my strongbox elsewhere to my advantage. To that end I have chosen several banks which performed well in previously difficult times. I believe this cursed depression has come to an end and I see no point in having my savings stagnate."

"Savings, Wendell, when all these years you've complained about my spending. Did you give each bank one dollar?"

I was feeling such elation, such overwhelming satisfaction, as though I was telling her father.

"No, Charlotte, not quite a dollar. I have given each bank a portion of my almost two and a half million. As your father was kind to you, so was mine to me; the essential difference being our basic natures."

"The basic nature of our fathers?"

Her retort was somewhat venomous, gratifying beyond any words I might imagine or create for affect.

"Yours was a thief. He stole two and a half million dollars, money which isn't yours. My father was honest; he ate with the lowliest of his workers and worked side by side with them. What he left me was honestly earned, by him as well as by me."

"Charlotte, earning implies working. Or must I remind you of a conversation not long ago regarding your capabilities? I tell you this because of the club. I cannot possibly disguise my success, and in order to achieve the goals I've set for myself I mustn't be diffident regarding my achievements. Such behaviour would be folly. Nor must we deprive ourselves or pretend frugality. We shall play our respective parts well and we shall deceive our friends."

"Pretend? Frugality? You have indeed played your part well. How long have you been this rich? Or dare I ask?"

"Very recently, though increasingly since I bought the first house. In that regard I must admit to a certain deceitfulness. I imagined your father intervening in my affairs. You know that he would, had he discovered the source of my windfall."

"He was right about you. You are your father's son."

"Glass houses, dear Charlotte. I've never questioned the paternity of your first daughter. Whose traits will she copy?"

"Not yours. I'll see to that."

"Though if they inherit yours I have no doubt they'll be

after my money soon enough, which they'll get the day I die and not a moment before. That will be the true test, Charlotte, for I have left everything to them and not you. More's the pity I won't be here to witness their kind affection towards you. So treat them well, Charlotte. I don't foresee the happy day arriving anytime soon. What I do expect is for two to become four and four to become eight and so on, without the need to put a bullet through my head."

I stood.

"Goodnight, Charlotte. I have nothing more to say."

I left the stately residence and went to the club. I consumed a late meal, drank a cognac or two while discussing the war with men equally interested in the subject. When they were gone I went to bed with an honest whore for the first time in my life. She was money well spent. When I arrived home Charlotte was asleep.

Friday I left in my car. Travelling by train would have been an unnecessary delay and possibly problematic in a way contrary to my objective. Stations across the country were the departure points for eager soldiers and weeping sweethearts and my attempts at purchasing any sort of accommodation aboard an ocean liner were futile. The few ships not commandeered by the War Department to serve as ambulance ships or troop transports were ordered decommissioned. I arrived in Florida the following Tuesday.

On Wednesday I went to the law office to discuss what might be done. Regrettably, in times of war islands were even less desirable than in times of impoverishment and I released them from their contract.

The harbour master remembered me without the need to question my seamanship a second time. What he questioned was what I was willing to pay and happily agreed. No one was sailing their yachts. The navy had purchased, rented or seized a number of his clients' boats, big or small, for use by the Coast Guard. His was spared patriotic service to his country and he needed the money more than a cruiser floating idle in his boathouse.

The Isle of Tombola was unchanged, not I. I came here to test my resolve not to fail. As I had done seven years earlier I circled the main island, uncertain, dropping anchor where I did once before.

I stripped away my clothes and sat naked with my legs dangling from the bow. I drank from the bottle, the cognac burning my throat. I was mesmerized, gazing in all directions. I hated the thought of moving, yet I did. I lowered the ladder and hurled myself over the gunwale, screaming, the aerated water attaching to my skin, each minute bubble bursting into thousands more. I was invigorated. I wanted to live. I wanted my freedom. I wanted never to go back to a woman who had learned from her parents to despise me.

In the distance, facing north, Tombolina was a greenish-grey shadow resting on a glittering palette of silver-white sand and metallic blue water. I pulled up the anchor and cruised a visual course to the farthest point which was flat and sandy, then to a point closest to Tombola which was no less sandy.

I'd never seen such an idyllic and glorious beach. The two islands were actually one, contrary to what I'd previously surmised, separated by a ravine that was not nearly as worrisome or dangerous to me as I had once imagined. The tide was at its lowest and I saw that one could easily swim from one shore to the other without fear of being pushed by the gentle current, a distance not exceeding 100 feet. I also determined that the highest tides would leave the thinnest ribbon of sand along each precipitous wall. Though I wisely elected not to drop anchor and returned to the beach I knew.

I had come prepared, curious to see what had changed and what had not. At the shore I dressed to protect myself against the vegetation and rough branches, not the humid heat. I went with my pistol and compass in hand, though not tethered to any rope. I remembered my way. At the clearing the thatched roofs of the huts had collapsed, the carpet of fallen doors splintered easily under my weight and the row of twisted walls had a comical, abstract appearance as though wanting to free themselves from the twine and the earth.

At the larger structure, the one made of brick and mortar, the door had dropped away from its hinge. Peering inside the condition had worsened. The stairway was somehow this time warning me away from the second storey and I heeded the portent fearing I might cause myself undo injury by falling or stepping upon a rusted nail. There was no smell, no colour: stark against the lush greens and glaring sun behind me.

Who had once lived there? Who had once been the master of those who dwelled in the row of huts? And how did they manage to survive until, finally, they had not? Or did they toil in misery and oppression until, finally, they did survive? What was the history of Tombola? What had father known? What had he not told me? And what part did he play in their abandonment or in their rescue? Was he a coward, I wondered? Or was I, in fact, the only son of their saviour?

I returned to the harbour master's boat, ill-equipped to undertake a night time voyage and, in point of fact, my intention was to spend the night at the island. I'd forewarned him that such might be the case and left him a promissory note for the full value of his yacht in the event that I would meet with some misadventure or decide to plot a one-way course from whatever I was leaving behind.

My dinner was simple: a plate of pork, beans and a slice

of buttered bread. My stomach too agitated to digest more and I began to feel the affects of the cognac which I'd reduced in volume to the final few drops. And just as well, for I believe I would have gone quite mad with the darkness and the quiet.

I lay on my back, staring at a universe that was equal in brilliance to the noontime sea. The sky was a veritable ceiling of silver, yet the darkness surrounding me was so complete that I could scarcely see my hands or my feet. I was alone in the world. I'd never experienced such blackness or such deprivation of my senses.

That night I slept on the afterdeck, huddled into a corner and covered by a single blanket against the evening dew, clutching my pistol, the running lights extinguished to conceal me from those who might do me harm. I woke countless times, or quite possibly I succumbed to my weary condition as many? Yet now I am fond of the darkness and the quiet and find solace in both, though that next morning I rejoiced at seeing the dull glow of the rising sun unveil Tombola with eerie slowness until rich greens contrasted with silver-white sand, lapping turquoise water, and the sun began to bake my skin and blind my eyes.

Then I happened to glance at my pistol and the joy that I felt disappeared.

I had no reason to revisit the island. What was of interest to me was Tombolina and the high tide which would allow me to navigate the narrow channel and cross between them without the slightest fear of running aground or causing irreparable damage to the propellers. I did not hesitate for fear I would change my mind. I was set in mind and body and would not falter.

Nearing the craggy shorelines I realized the gentle manner of the water had changed and steerage rapidly became more difficult. The current was not flowing through the shallow gorge; rather the violent water was coursing from the windward mouth with sufficient force to wet the foredeck. I pushed hard against the throttle to maintain my steerageway, distracted for the briefest moment, then another, forcing myself to look straight ahead once I was certain my eyes did not deceive me.

On the windward side I continued several hundred feet out to sea before feeling sufficiently secure to turn about and, from that position, with the sun higher in the sky and behind me, I could see the waves breaking, the water rushing through the gorge towards the leeward shore.

Cutting the engines I went for my charts and drank a cold beer. Within an hour I had circled Tombola and was back at the beach, wading to shore, at once intrigued and afraid, not pleased that I would spend one more night onboard. In truth, I had no choice. How else would I know? And how would I dare? After all, I was, was I not, a Parkens?

Subsequent to my lunch of bologna and bread which I washed down with beer, I swam to the shore feeling somewhat strange and vulnerable at being entirely naked. My torso and face were red from the wind and the sun, the rest of me adopting a peculiar and unfamiliar hue of pink. I strolled lazily in the surf, sometimes splashing, sometimes kicking at the foamy water while trailing the rubber box behind me which required not the slightest exertion.

At times I wanted to run, resisting the urge, believing I would feel ridiculous. I was not athletic and my anatomy was already experiencing sufficient novelty. Though I did glance over my shoulders often, alternating between the sea and the boat, searching for the tiniest reflection and prepared to run back, regretting I had not anchored closer to the gorge. After awhile the boat appeared no larger than a toy and soon after I stopped to shield my eyes and focus. In the other direction the better part of a mile remained for me to walk.

Earlier in the morning my passage through the shadowed gorge made my skin cold with gooseflesh. I felt small and at the mercy of the towering cliffs. Gazing upward the vertical walls appeared ancient and majestic to me. I felt safe, as though they would protect me, not hurt me, and I sank to the sand to watch the remaining water recede.

The beach had come to an end. That morning, traversing the gorge, I was concerned for my life and paid no attention to the distance travelled. Still, I knew what I had seen. Nor did I give any thought to extrapolating the distance from my charts, though I did believe my objective was located not far from the midway point.

I waited until the water's retreat weakened to a gentle current and the splashing sounds against the rock walls abated. I put the girl from my mind, any girl I might have brought with me to the isles to see her as naked as I. What might we have done? What a memorable adventure I would have given her. I chortled. Whoever she was, she would wait until the following night to hear what might have been.

My skin was hot to the touch, yet dry and stained with salt from the sea. I carried my box across the saturated sand, leaving behind an awkward line of footfalls. The air was abruptly damp and heavy. I dropped the box into the shallow water as soon as I could and performed a full circle, shivering, wrapping my arms tightly around me. My hot skin was cold, though my shoulders burned and my private parts shrivelled as though packed in dry ice.

I proceeded with caution, inching my way. When the warm water came to my waist I raised my hands to keep them dry. When it reached my chest I worried, for I could no longer see my feet and would have to swim. I glanced behind me at the box tilting this way and that, waiting indifferently for me to tug at it. When I kicked myself from the bottom I instantly felt its weight at my waist.

I thrashed more than I swam, afraid I suppose. I was nothing between those massive walls and the sea would care nothing about sucking me away. Then, without warning, my hands hit the bottom, then my chest and my knees. I scrambled to my feet and ran to the new shore, sinking, stumbling and falling. I was cloaked in sand, looking like a creature from some dark place. I loathed returning to the water, though I did. I sank to my knees and splashed myself clean. I dressed in my shorts and a long sleeve shirt, letting my feet dry atop the lid of the box before slipping into my socks and then my boots.

Then I strapped my pistol to my waist and walked towards the windward sea.

I was not wrong. Not 100 paces from where I stood to dress was the arch I had seen: a smooth and rounded doorway carved by nature or prehistoric man into the stone. I screamed out my presence, leaping backward, cringing and grabbing for my pistol, so loud and harsh was my echo. Beyond the aperture was darkness so complete that I feared to continue. My body twisted quickly around of its own volition, jerking me, my head looking up as though to snap its neck, certain my murder was imminent.

I took several deep breaths and hurried to the box. I gripped the flashlight and rushed with all speed to where I last stood, my mind frenzied, my heart racing, my blood chilled with adrenalin. What I did then surprises me even now. I clambered up the slippery slope, crashing once to my knees, once hard against my elbows, not once losing my tight grip on the light.

I hurried through the opening that was twice my height and three times the width of my shoulders. I screamed when the yellowish and foggy beam led me blindly into an unforgiving stone wall. I grunted and banged my head. The wall was wet and smooth for never having seen the light of day. The sensation was unpleasant. The floor was slippery and appeared like glass when I pointed the light at my feet. I peered through the arch, my back to the wall, fearing its wetness less than falling.

I had no idea why I was in that place, at the island, for what I had convinced myself to do I might have done anywhere, at anytime. That alone would have proven my conviction and courage; being alone in a dark cave was foolhardy beyond my ability to explain. I closed my eyes, adjusting to the darkness, and turned my head in the direction I shone the light.

Within arm's reach was a curvature in the wall and a space beyond which I could not discern. I inched myself forward, my extended hand squeezing the light, the other tightly gripping the pistol in its holster. I could feel myself easing around the gradual curve and chanced to look from whence I had come.

The portal was gone from sight and I promised myself not more than a dozen more paces. I began counting, under my breath, afraid to betray my presence. At twelve I stepped twice more and saw one more abyss. I went on, not knowing why. I counted to three and dropped the light. I scrambled clumsily forward, into the brightness of day, into my Garden of Eden, my paradise.

I was instantly warmed by sun. I'd never seen grass as green or trees as tall and full. Yellow and red flowers blossomed everywhere amongst lavender, pink, blue and orange. I walked freely, for I would never be lost, the precipice stood like a gatekeeper observing my every move, had I dared to pluck a mango, apple or succulent apricot from a tempting branch. And then I stopped.

Birds were chirping. The sound was foreign to me, calming. I ran to my left, towards the west, through luscious vegetation to a lagoon, my now Sacred Pond. Shallow swells rolled in from the shore. I ran in to my knees to where a thick awning of lush leaves and plants of indescribable beauty protected a natural channel. From there I ran to the ocean where I saw the tiny speck that was my boat and a more spectacular beach.

I ran back, kicking and splashing the warm water, stopping, spinning around several times, stopping when my body threatened to topple, staring up at the monolith in awe and wishing I had thought to bring my spyglass.

On Tombola's side of the gorge the summit was insurmountable, I believed; however on the islet side, Tombolina, I believed that one might successfully undertake such an excursion when well-equipped with a pickaxe and patience. The general terrain and condition of the surface, despite appearing suitable to a difficult journey, gave me reason to believe such a quest entirely plausible to consider. I felt myself equal to the challenge. What had I to lose, for, in my deepest and darkest thoughts, I knew why I had come?

I raced from the water through the foliage to a clearing and through more foliage to the east, to the windward shore, where I stood to witness the sea beginning to punish the rocky shoreline with increasingly harsh waves. I hurried back, elated. I centred myself in the clearing facing north. I walked slowly until reaching another wall of green spotted with nature's luxuriant richness.

I saw a path. I saw many paths. I elected the closest and walked for five minutes, possibly ten, stopping with my mouth agape.

At first I did not hear or I chose to disregard the sound of trickling water, growing louder, not unlike chimes made by strips of coloured glass teasing one another in a light breeze. The pool sparkled like a clear blue diamond; its bed was made of stones the size of my fist. The sides of the natural bowl were formed from layers of rock, one end providing for a smooth and natural place to sit. I shielded my eyes against the glare, searching for any movement from any living thing that might cause me harm.

I saw nothing. Again, I stripped away my clothes and jumped in from a height equal to my own.

My feet struck the bottom, my knees bent, and I soared to the surface. The floor was stony and smooth. I swam from one side to the other with ten strong strokes and the water was no deeper. The water was warm, at once invigorating and rejuvenating, more so than the sea, and when I was done I pulled myself out and lay as I was on a patch of moist grass until prompted by a spontaneous thought to bolt to my feet.

I dressed quickly and ran towards the gorge, to my great surprise, not the least apprehensive regarding the last several feet through the darkened tunnel. The water had not risen; I ripped off my clothes, stored them in the box with my pistol and swam with a purpose across the gorge to Tombola. Once there I ran with the box a safe distance, set it down in the sand and ran to the boat naked and free. I was elated.

The engines roared to life. I hoisted the anchor onto the deck, ignoring the hawespipe. I cruised along the shoreline to the box, dropping the anchor and flinging myself over the bow rail with a shriek. With the box onboard I sailed north along the leeward shore of Tombolina to a small cove where I stayed the night after a supper of chicken and potatoes.

Maid had never taught me anything worthwhile and Charlotte was better suited to idleness and shopping than cookery.

I wanted to watch as the islet melded with the dark universe. However I had much to do and when I peered out from the cabin nothing remained for me to see. Uncertain, I covered over the portholes not trusting the night. By daybreak I was ready, alone at the shore, my body refreshed, my mind alert, waiting for the first rays of warming light before putting my hand to the barrier of moist leaves blocking my way.

At the lagoon I laid down my burden, selected my tools and set off towards Tombolina's half of the severed summit.

From its base the climb appeared sufficiently facile, though I'd correctly foreseen the need to equip myself with a pick, water and sandwiches. The climb was not so deceptively difficult, the problem was me: my person was not at the time conditioned to exertion.

The ascent took ninety minutes along a trail previously marked with notches and crude wooden handles nailed into the trees. I was not the first to climb the rocky slope, at times on my hands and my knees, other times sideways, more than once losing my footing and painfully scraping my legs.

Achieving the pinnacle I fell backward, against a large tree. I closed my eyes, sweat oozing from every pore to moisten my skin and soak my clothing. When at last I caught my breath and opened my eyes I stood in complete disbelief of what I was seeing: the entire sea, the world and the Isle of Tombola from stem to stern, the greens of its rocky spine, the ruined encampment and a wilderness beyond my dreams.

I felt I could reach out and touch the sun.

I turned, bending to see between the trees and thought I must have died, transported to somewhere greatly superior to what some believe is heaven. I pinched my flesh. I had not died, nor would I anytime soon, though I was in that wondrous place and knew without question that one day I would return here, that one day I would die here. Then, overwhelmed by splendour, the wind and the sea, how was I to remotely envision my murder at the hands of your brother?

I lay on my front and inched my way to the precarious edge, the very fringe of my courage. Seeing the sister cliff so near, so imposing filled me with trepidation, yet I did not falter. I peered into the abyss. From the west the water flowed into the gorge unnoticed. From the east the surging current rushed in with vicious indifference, swirling, crashing against itself. The sound was a frightful opus, the sea rising up in anger against the uncaring monoliths, protesting their sudden restriction. The violence was unnerving and surprisingly silent, though I soon realized what was unnerving me the most was the sensation of being beckoned, lured into a perfect place forever.

I pushed myself away and onto my knees, not trusting my legs to support me, absorbing the view once more.

The descent took one third the time, thirty minutes, though with no fewer injuries incurred. At the lagoon I ate a breakfast of boiled eggs mashed onto buttered bread. I swam in the soothing water and relaxed under the sun while listening to chirping birds. I was unafraid. I was not in any way hesitant or uncertain. I was enjoying the peace and tranquility and, when I was ready, I sat with my legs stretched out.

I took the pistol from my belt and aimed the barrel one inch from the smallest digit of my left foot. If father could summon his one ounce of courage to blow away the larger part of his head, why could I not blow away the most useless of my appendages?

I knew I would scream, wrongly believing that my anticipation of pain far exceeded the damage I was about to inflict upon my person, and wisely thought to do so as a matter of pragmatism and fortitude before discharging the sidearm. The benefit of which remains a mystery to me. I shot twice, once to remove my toe and once into the air as I jerked backward.

I threw the pistol aside, fearful of compounding my injuries inadvertently, pounding the ground with my fists, grunting and squirming.

How I managed to hobble to my feet is a matter of supposition and not memory, my torment was that severe, though I do recall composing myself sufficiently to soak the bloody sore at the edge of the lagoon. The curative action took affect instantly, and I might well have lost consciousness with the searing pain, albeit a matter of irrelevant conjecture.

I dragged myself to the box and raised my foot to the lid, gritting my teeth until they ached as well, cursing aloud for not thinking to equip myself with any sort of tourniquet, pleased I had not chosen a larger target for surely I would have bled to death.

Gradually the pain subsided, as was expected. Although I was unaware of the exact moment of its disappearance, or when the bleeding was at last staunched by the angle of my foot and the scorching midday sun.

My trek to the boat was difficult, my torment returning upon introducing my foot to the seawater, my scream incredibly loud when I carelessly bumped the wound against the boat's ladder. The sole medicament available to me was the second bottle of cognac I had not touched the night before, which I decided was better taken internally as my wound was sufficiently healed.

I would return here, I knew, one day after the war. A man could easily disappear without a trace and Charlotte was amply independent in her papa's house and her mother's purse. She would have no need of my resources.

I chortled at the thought of leaving her, leaving them all. I circled the islands one last time, feeling lament as I idled awhile at the gorge. I had discovered what I had come here in search of and what I left behind was of no consequence other than the pistol at the lagoon that someone might see, or not. How else could I truly be certain?

I calculated my speed according to my course, the wind and sedative swell of the sea. My foot throbbed against the firm leather of my new shoe, though I had not a care in the world and halfway to port I thought myself sufficiently medicated.

I threw the bottle over the side. That night at the marina I bid farewell to the harbour master, declining his generosity. I required more comfort than a simple berth and a finer meal than hash mixed with peas or corn. I needed to dress my wound and find a woman who would not mind a man of my calibre with a bandaged foot.

Twelve

Cassidy scarcely believed what he was reading.

This story was far better than any of the Sherlock Holmes novels hidden from sight at the foot of his tree. Something else about The Grand Guardian that distinguished him from the village: his crippled foot.

The nine toes set him apart because imperfect children, as decreed in the Twelve Scriptures, were an unnatural blight on the village. They would be unable to play with other children, unable to toil in the fields or cast their nets and would grow to live solitary and unfulfilled lives. They would be undesirable as first-mates. To couple with them or to share affection with them during The Seven Feasts would bring more imperfect children to the island and, with them, eventual ruin

Therefore the Scriptures decreed that they would be taken away and cared for.

Cassidy stared at the page. The man shot off his toe. He was insane, a crazed coward, fearing he would fall into the sea. He pictured the twin precipices in his mind and looked at his watch. Ninety minutes, he scoffed, and thirty minutes to reach the ground. He would climb the cliff in a quarter of the time and reach the bottom before the sun set. Then he would bathe in the pond and compose the words he would write to Aayla.

*

My homeward journey was leisurely, made all the more so

with fine restaurants and little regard for the sanctity of Charlotte's marriage to me. I correctly assumed the whores would be busy with soldiers, sailors and airmen and my four selections were magnificent, once well-fed.

Despite my money being equally good and considerably more plentiful than what any would find in a soldier's thin pockets, I rationalized that decent women, much younger and prettier than those plying their trade, would certainly want the companionship of an educated man of means. I was not wrong and lingered each morning before sending them away. I arrived home on the fifth day, not yet accustomed to those cursed wrought iron gates.

On my desk in my office were letters she knew not to open, though one in particular was dated the day of my departure and lay atop the pile, no doubt her way of being snide with me. Someone in The War Department had decided I should be in Europe killing Germans, or being killed. I disagreed and when I removed my shoe with a smirk, she gasped as was her predictable way.

"I believe, Charlotte, someone else will have to kill my allotment of Nazis. As you can readily bear witness, while away on business, I was shot while defending myself."

"You shot off your own toe, Wendell. Not only are you despicable to me, you're cowardly as well. And why is your foot so brown, and your hands and your face?"

"My business was in the south. I went to enquire as to the possibility of procuring boats for the navy. These generals and admirals might well be men of war; they are, however, unskilled in finance. While there I had time each day to walk along the shore."

I took my foot from the desk.

"Had you not been so caustic in your mood that week, I might have taken you and the girls with me. I would have been less lonely. However I believed you to needed your time alone."

"And what will you do about them, while other men are volunteering by the score?"

"They volunteer for food and money. No one willingly stands in line to die, Charlotte. I will simply tell them the truth, with my receipts as my witness. In any event, regardless of what they might think of me, cripples aren't good foot soldiers. I believe the sea will make me sick and my poor eyesight would make me a danger in the air. Truth be told, my skills lie elsewhere."

"In lying to your wife without the slightest shame."

"I've never lied to you, not once. I believe you're referring to my money, which I was never required to disclose to you. I did so of my own accord."

"The girls would have lived a better life."

"One wouldn't know the difference and the oldest has done just fine. One day she'll make her own way in the world, as I have. More likely as you did, I imagine, and she certainly won't count you amongst her finest tutors, lest she marries a rich man."

"We should at least engage a cleaning woman and cook to ease my burden. This house is far too big to manage on my own. The other wives have begun hiring back their domestics."

"The other wives put their time to good use; some of them even work towards the household expenses. You don't. I daresay you'd drop dead at the thought, and your mother's gift to you won't last long when you start paying others to do your simple chores. These domestics are a responsibility, not unlike a family pet. Once brought in they must be trained; once trained they must be cared for."

"We'll soon be a laughing stock."

"Perhaps, one of us for reasons entirely different from what you imagine. Not I, and certainly not after I purchase the club, which I intend to acquire before the year is out."

She observed my foot.

"Was that part of your plan? You ruined your foot to avoid doing your duty so you could buy a club?"

"You know me so well, Charlotte. Yes, you're quite right. I'm a fiend, and very devious."

"I should report you."

"Then you would certainly suffer, along with the girls. I haven't yet made arrangements for your security in the event a tragedy befalls me and I would assuredly view your small opinion of me as a tragedy. And what would you say? Your purpose would be self-serving and your joy at seeing me humiliated short-lived. No, Charlotte. You've done well with and because of me. Be content in your contempt of me."

I took the letter in my hand.

"This was sent as a matter of course, most likely by some private, corporal, or female clerk anxious for all men to die alongside her husband. Do you suppose for a moment I would address my situation with anyone whose rank would deny him privileges at the club?"

"I want to sleep alone in my room tonight."

Charlotte did sleep alone. I told her the following morning of my meeting with the colonel. The man empathized with me, fully understanding my plight, nodding grimly as I explained how I'd purchased the pistol so that my wife might feel safe during my term of service overseas. I felt very much the fool, I told her, confessing to the man my maladroitness with the weapon during a recent attempted mugging in Florida while on a business trip.

However, I did neglect to tell her how he kindly accepted my invitation to dinner at the club, which I came to own by the first of January 1941. By then he was a general and very influential in many of my subsequent transactions.

Whether he ever believed my deception is of little importance. We satisfied each other's need and, at long last,

I transferred my entire office at home to my office at the club which boasted a comfortable en suite sleeping area where I would occasionally spend the night.

The arithmetic of my times that long year with Charlotte could be accomplished with the fingers of one hand, never satisfactory, perfunctory at best, though, unlike my journey home from Florida, local young and single women would eventually lead to my embarrassment. They have a way of attaching themselves and forsaking prudence in the heat of their lust, or using the guise of lust to fulfill a single-minded ambition common to all of them.

Married women of any description were verboten. They would be my downfall. The younger, prettier ones would tire of their husbands, spellbound by my demeanour and my wealth. The poorer ones would lack proper upbringing and soon see just my money. The older ones, my age and possibly a few years beyond, pretty or not, were out of the question. I harboured no predilection towards older women when so many others were available and willing to comfort me.

So what was I to do? Where was I to go for distraction? The obvious solution to my dilemma was the acquisition of discreet membership in another club, one of lesser reputation yet equally well attended as mine.

I laboured over the decision for weeks, at last succumbing to primal needs. They were unmarried women of a single description: very young and very beautiful with talent and desire to succeed at their chosen profession.

They all had names, possibly even their own, and knew me by whatever name I chose at the time. Of more interest to them was how much I would pay, an evaluation which at first was directly linked to my changing appetites and my frequency as a guest. Over time, however, both aspects became a constant and my billing was paid on the first of the month as a more privileged member. Indeed I must believe I was their most prized source of income, despite limiting my engagements to twice each week before returning to my office to sleep.

By the end of '42 I knew their bodies intimately, and their minds. Some were once orphans. A few were widows unable to find more conventional work, while others recognized their destinies, preferring to work in comfort with fine men and not on street corners or in loathsome boarding houses with men of ill-repute and unrefined intentions.

I thought of them as my girls, desiring some more than others, though never disappointing the rest and, to dwell on their relationships with me, I believe I might have come to love one or more of them had I known them longer.

My worth had also doubled to five million, exclusive of the club, and I never again discussed my private affairs with Charlotte.

At Christmas I sent them all lavish gifts and on New Year's Day, the day being one of their few holidays, I joined them all for dinner. Satiated and drunk, we slept that night wherever we saw fit, sat or closed our eyes, and in the morning I was gone before they awoke to small envelopes which I am certain caused exclamations of glee. They were, after all, my girls.

Midway through the summer of '43 the worst of all climatic conditions combined to make the day intolerable. Membership at the club was climbing nicely and each new member invariably wanted my counsel regarding my list of des res addresses. I had not taken a day's vacation to alleviate my stress in the ten years since father's death, discounting the forgotten few weeks which incorporated the loss of my toe.

That said, and much to my credit, I did send Charlotte and the girls to the country for two weeks each of the previous three years. Such separations gave them respite, and me the liberation I sought from the chains of my regret. I came to believe that I was complicit in the birth of neither girl; such was the domain of women and she had twice disheartened me.

The afternoon was dark and foreboding the day before her scheduled departure. The unseasonable cold chilled me to the bone. The winds were fierce, the sky a palette of charcoals and blacks. Explosions of deafening thunder shuddered through me, bolts of electric white made the street before me a canvas of glistening asphalt and chrome, a series of still lifes of people running frantically, their coattails flapping, their hands pressed hard upon their hats.

A night time sky was darker and my mood was equally sombre for no reason. I had spent the afternoon relaxing with two of my girls, one before the other. The thought had never occurred to me that I might enjoy them as one without engendering envy or jealousy between them.

My wealth had leapt to a staggering six million, I was known to anyone of importance and my calls were never refused. Yet, in my Bentley, the wipers slashing away unceasing droplets, I felt deep gloom, not contentment or satisfaction for all I had achieved in such a short time.

I had never walked or run in the rain, not even in my youth. I thought of Tombolina, when I ran naked and swam naked in the lagoon. So I did. I climbed from the car and walked with purposeful slowness, counting each step aloud, tapping small puddles with the soles of my shoes, leaping over the larger ones. I was soaked through by the time I reached the house, the cuffs of my trousers drenched beyond repair, rainwater dripping as much down my person as from my trench coat and hat. Not once in my life was I ever so utterly dishevelled and cold. Yet I felt good and alive, as I did on the island, to such an extent that I hated the thought of going in.

I was arriving home unusually early, I knew, though the

thought crossed my mind that the constable on patrol might ticket my car and, for the briefest moment, I considered running out without my coat or my hat. Then I considered the tempest swirling about me, as would the flatfooted cop, and I went in with no intentional stealth.

The older girl would not arrive home from her summer classes for an hour and I was thankful for whatever brief interlude her school day would provide me. Charlotte was adamant that the girl be well-rounded in social disciplines and I saw no need to object, my one contribution that of applause each Sunday afternoon, though neither dancing nor singing would see her through life.

The house was pleasantly warm, not damp at all. I chose not to call out Charlotte's name. At first I thought to go to our bedroom, to disrobe, to rid myself of my heavy and wet clothing as much as the disagreeable olfactory condition of my person. My second thought was to stop into my reading room for the pistol I'd purchased to properly substantiate my claim of being unfit.

I had discharged that single round into the air while driving home from Florida, my target a one dimensional man of considerable proportions sitting on a rock, presumably in Arizona or some such arid state, smoking a cigarette. Until this very day I'd forgotten him with no idea whether my bullet destroyed his billboard perfection or that of his horse. Five bullets remained.

I had harboured suspicions for a considerable time that I was not the only one from whom my dearest Charlotte sought pleasure, particularly since my abstinence of her. She was a woman, if not a good wife and, as such, required constant affirmation of her worth. And there she was, laying beneath him with her eyes squeezed shut, her lips so pursed that one painted sliver was barely discernible from the other.

I watched for some time, intrigued, somehow aroused.

Or was I amused, imagining myself with them? Above all I was prepared should they abruptly cease their gyrations and see me. She was quite responsive, more so than she ever was beneath me or beside me. I believe they would have gone on forever, mocking me. I coughed and wished her goodnight. He went first, as any gentleman worth the appellation would, his howl much less a surprise to me than Charlotte's. A perfect hole-in-one followed by a second between his raised shoulders to assuage his discomfort.

He thanked me with a grunt and sufficient displacement of his person to allow me to view my wife. What I did not contemplate in my haste to correct her adultery was that the missile would pass through its objective and enter Charlotte not far from where his nibs had.

As for Charlotte, her screams were ungodly, possibly imploring me to be merciful, to give her redemption. Her eyes had never opened as wide, either from pleasure or from fright. She was afraid, engulfed in fear for the first time, of the dead man, of touching her own private wound, of my smile and easy manner.

She had not much time left to her, nor did I. Neither could I think of what to say, her screams failing her, becoming frantic and breathless sobs. The job was half done; I could not leave her in such a damaged state. I believe she knew. I raised the pistol and leaned against the doorframe to study her. At that moment Charlotte understood the extent of her crime against me. She went next, his sordid vessel cleansed of her crime, the tiny and perfect hole in the centre of her head punctuating her final exclamation.

I harbour not the slightest uncertainty that she died as she would have wanted, under a man.

I stood, dripping wet, staring at naked and dead Charlotte pinned under her lover. The date was July 15th. The 16th was a Friday and the girls would expect to leave with their mother after breakfast. What was I to do? April was asleep in her bed and I slumped against the wall to consider my quandary.

The man would be easily dragged down the stairs to the kitchen, and Charlotte would pose no difficulty at all. My worry was for the girl, should I awaken her. And the oldest would soon interfere with any attempt to erase my actions.

I entertained no thought of surrender. She was wantonly unfaithful to me, freely so and without restraint, indisputably not coerced and undeniably delighting in the prelude to her final moments.

Regardless of the situation, who would believe that upon hearing her screams I had shot wildly in my delirious state? I snorted. After spending those thirteen years imprisoned with her, I would not spend one day longer incarcerated or possibly hang because of her. And what of the blood? His nibs and Charlotte were leaking profusely from their conjoined nether parts and he from the wound in his back.

The trail would be impossible to clean without the highest degree of diligence and the older girl had a relentless curiosity.

I extinguished the lights and went to the window. I tossed away my coat and raised the pane, letting the tempest into the room. The bedroom was over the garden, and by the garden was the parking space for my Bentley. Behind the house was a row of trees, grouped closely together and of sufficient height to provide privacy on summer days or when entertaining our guests.

The man, I observed, would best be freed from her by his ankles. His condition was despicable, having failed to retain himself. The sucking sound of their separation was gruesome and I'd been accurate in my assessment of his spillage. At the window I laid him face down to save the floor from further distress and sank to my knees. I forced my hands under his arms, heaving at once up and forward, my legs straddling the worst of him. I squirmed, struggling to manoeuvre him, ignoring the hole in his back and his stench.

Standing was difficult, pushing him forward into the opening much easier. My one concern was understandably the proximity of his natural and more recent exploded orifices against my person. He went out quickly, though I thought he might hesitate, not at all displeased that he proved me wrong.

"Once a whore always a whore, dearest Charlotte. We can't deny or alter what is naturally integral to us."

Charlotte was much less awkward. I said my farewell and gave her reassurances regarding the girls.

"Regards to your parents, Charlotte, if they knew nothing of your promiscuous ways before, they must certainly by now. And I will do what is necessary to care for your children. They, like you, will want for nothing."

I reached for her feet and pulled her to the edge of the bed where I sat her upright.

"I forgive you your sins against me, Charlotte. I harbour no doubt you shall require eternity to recount them."

I slipped one hand under her knees and placed my other under one of her arms before hauling her from the bed. She was heavy in my arms and the odour emanating from her ruined womb was sickening.

She slid feet first into the opening without hesitation, her torso quite another matter. Her buttocks were the first impediment, the weight of her lower extremities the second as I pushed her farther out. What I did not expect was her body rising up and her head crashing into the lower edge of the window, pinning her in place like a naked ragamuffin. I closed my eyes and grasped the sides of her head. I twisted once, disregarding her ghoulish retort and pushed her from sight.

I paid her no further attention. I closed the window.

I emptied my pockets, checking each one twice. I undressed with the door open, listening for the slightest sound and ran to the shower to cleanse myself of them. Dressed in a robe I remade the bed, adding the bloodied sheets to my bundle of clothes and, when the door downstairs opened, I closed the bedroom and went to greet the girl. As disconsolate as she would be, she would have to hear the news.

"Your mother was called upon, quite without warning, to assist a friend in need. The matter, brought to our attention within the past hour, is one of grave urgency. Your dear mother had no option. She left at once, of necessity."

I anticipated the sulky expression.

"Your vacation, however, will not be forfeited, merely delayed a very short while. We will not disappoint you or your sister in that regard, for we are as disheartened as you."

I suggested she prepare dinner to occupy her mind and allay her disappointment. After dinner she tended to her sister and when she was done she went to her bed. She was twelve and quite mature for her age. I felt no qualms at leaving her alone for an hour or more.

In my reading room I enjoyed an evening cognac before passing by their rooms to check on their condition. They were sleeping soundly and I set about my task. I placed my soiled clothes and his in a duffle bag with the sheets and the towels stained with their blood. I added a brick from the basement and dropped the bag from the bedroom window.

Outside the weather was not improved. I unlocked the gate and hurried to where I left my car. The constable had not passed by and the street was otherwise deserted. At the house I laboured with urgent desperation. The canvas bag laid atop my wife whose body, indecently exposed, had been washed clean by the rain, something she would never contemplate in life.

As for his nibs, he seemed somewhat uncomfortable and bewildered. His expression, I assumed at the time, not the one he'd been so ardently working to achieve.

Huddled together in the trunk of my car the couple seemed cozy, though I must confess I felt a mounting disquiet in my chest. I had no idea where to dispose of them other than the river. I went to the cellar perplexed by how I would throw them from a bridge with the extra burden of chain that would prevent any future ascent. I would be deprived of privacy and time, when the effort to conceal them in my car had already proven lengthy and demanding of my person.

The warmth of the furnace caused me to shiver and I dropped the chains to the floor, pausing a moment to consider. I smiled, thanking my wife for her thoughtfulness. Had she not wanted the house warmed against a damp chill, I would not have contemplated her suggestion to me.

I went to check on the girls. They were sleeping. I filled a snifter near to the top with cognac and returned to the cellar to further contemplate something I knew nothing about. Curious, I went to the kitchen for a pound of red meat. An hour later all that remained was the bone.

They left the trunk of my car with much less effort on my part than I anticipated. I dragged his nibs into the cellar by his ankles, facedown. He followed me with surprisingly little reluctance. I left him on the floor and went to retrieve Charlotte who came with me even more willingly. I laid her on her father's worktable to bind her legs and her arms to her torso to gain more rigidity. She smelled atrociously.

Being the smallest and most manageable she went in first, with no resistance and without her ring.

I was drenched and took a moment to consider my proposed management of his nibs while exorcising the deep chill from my bones with several sips of cognac. I left him as he was and went to the car.

Within the hour I was back and the canvas bag was buried deep between two shores.

The girls habitually awoke at seven. The current hour was ten and I determined to give the larger man two hours longer than Charlotte, whom I thought should be ready by one.

By midnight my clothes had partially dried, despite being somewhat stained. I swallowed what remained in my glass, not yet suitably fortified against task at hand for I could not in my mind design any pleasant manner in which to handle him. I went to the work table for thick leather gloves. I'd determined no advantage in manoeuvring him first onto the table or binding him. I would put him in directly.

On the hour I stood by the furnace, his nibs sprawled at my feet. I wondered how I would feel to see my wife's bones, deciding not to look. I opened the door and avoided her.

He was uncooperative in the extreme. To the extent that I could I heaved his person onto his knees, forcing him against the heated façade. With one arm I secured his upper portion by his neck, his lower with my gloved hand firmly gripping the tight space where his one leg joined with the other. He was firmly against me, my forearm painfully sore from the heat.

I strained, dreading the thought of what I must do should I be unable to insert his entirety into such a small space at once. Alas, he moved. With his head inside, his shoulders refused. I heaved him, feeling myself on the verge of regurgitation, his one leg over my shoulder his other secured by my arm.

I twisted him and shoved him, despising our intimacy, his second wound against my face.

His hair was aflame, the smell sickening. I twisted more, certain his face and neck were beginning to char. Never in my life had I been so determined, so in need of my strength and my strong will.

He began to inch his way in, the damaged condition of the skin and the flesh at his shoulders irrelevant to him. I disregarded Charlotte entirely, whether he might disturb her or not. I twisted him onto his front and manoeuvred myself between his legs, my gloved hands pushing violently against their apex and his carnage, my stomach in complete revolt.

With his ruptured aperture past the door I stepped away and retched. When I recovered I folded in one leg, then the other, I threw in his wallet and closed the door.

I undressed and went upstairs. I poured a substantial quantity of cognac and went outside to stand in the rain. I was exhilarated.

The older girl woke me at seven. When she was dressed she made breakfast and listened as I spoke.

"Your dear mother sends her fondest wishes. She called when you were asleep, pleased that you understood our predicament. She has entreated me to join her forthwith, for a short while, to comfort her as her friend's desperate condition continues to worsen."

She asked what was to become of her and her sister.

"Indeed, your mother's kind heart has put me in a difficult situation, for I know of no one with whom I might entrust your well-being. I deliberated well into the early hours in search of an agreeable solution."

She stood before me with little expression in her eyes, unless my memory fails me, for she was her mother's daughter and quite possibly not mine.

"You shall have an adventure, the two of you. For the brief duration of our absence you will stay in the care of the Sisters of the Holy Sacraments and, upon my return with your mother, we will have the most exciting vacation by the shore."

By noon the furnace was shut off for five hours and the girls went with me in the car. The youngest was unaffected; the oldest was predictably moody and self-centred. I explained to the mother superior that my wife and I would be gone for one month on urgent business which would be upsetting to the children. However we had no other choice. Their sensitivities apart, we must do what was best for them.

My instructions to the nuns were clear.

"In the unlikely event, Mother Superior, that my wife and I not return, I would ask that you and the sisters house and educate our girls until their respective ages of majority, releasing them from your care with sufficient skills to maintain good lives. I will, this very day, not foreseeing such an occurrence, though with their well-being at the forefront of my current preoccupations, arrange for the Sisters of the Holy Sacraments to receive generous dowries sufficient to last nine and eighteen years, respectively. However, when we return in a month's time and I have no reason at present to believe otherwise, my wife and I concur that you must consider the amount as a donation."

She blessed me and kissed the beads hanging from her neck, whispering a prayer which, I suspect, was to ensure my safe return. Alas, I had little comprehension of ancient beatitudes and simply nodded my recognition of the gratitude.

To the girls I left letters of instruction they would not read until their release, telling them of the lawyer they were to visit and the small fortunes I would place in trust for each one that very afternoon. My parting words were brief and reassuring. Their mother and I would return in four weeks or sooner, though I knew by that time April would not care and within a year neither would the other.

Each evening that week, once the sun had set, I heated the furnace to the highest possible degree and left the house.

By the following Saturday what remained of Charlotte and her lover was quickly vacuumed into non-existence by her most hated appliance. Her entire wardrobe I gave to the mission, her jewellery I gave to my girls at the club where I spent consecutive nights with each one without telling them why.

By the time I was ready at the end of the third week Charlotte's house was pristine, an empty and lifeless shell. I called a cartage company who performed with speed and efficiency to deliver all we owned to those more deserving. To our neighbours I explained very little beyond Charlotte's desire for fresh paint. My office at the club was barren with an empty desk and cabinets, which my secretary knew not to open. I would be gone for a month, I told her, joining my daughters and wife in the country for a well-deserved rest.

To our friends and the men at my club I said little more than my selfish pursuits must cease to deprive me of my family and, to five of them, I transferred the title and deed for a fraction of my cost. To my bankers I explained nothing at all, and in my new car, for which I paid cash, I drove south for five days with some gold, substantial packets of hundred-dollar bills and proof of several contributions to the Swiss banking system amounting to six million dollars…and a diamond wedding ring.

Thirteen

Cassidy thought what he was reading must be fiction. What sort of man would commit such crimes and put them to pen and paper for others to read? What man would ruin his foot as proof of his weakness? Even if he dared to show Aayla the words, she couldn't read them and she wouldn't believe him.

Wendell Parkens believed his wife was unfaithful, that his children weren't his, yet he saw no wrong in spreading his seed into so many strangers and the young whores at his brothel. He took her life and the man's when he found them in bed. Yet he decreed that all men and women of the village will share their affection for seven days and seven nights during The Seven Feasts and that all young girls will bathe with him in his Sacred Pond.

Unconsciously Cassidy creased his brow, his mind working hard to imagine a furnace so hot and so large that would turn flesh to powder. He knew the heat of campfires and of the wood stove in his villa. He knew what remained in the morning. What kind of evil man would give his daughters to strangers for nine and eighteen years?

He went to the window and peered towards the pool. Not far from the crystal water between the two shores was the helicopter. He imagined The Grand Guardian afraid to jump into the water, then removing his toe. He looked to the green grass below and imagined a black night filled with rain and brightened by lightning. He imagined Charlotte, naked and bleeding, the rain cleaning her.

In life she'd seduced many men and must have been endowed with beauty as well as charm, he thought. He imagined her framed by a window, covered with blood and how she fell to the wet ground. He went back to the desk.

For Cassidy, Christmas was reindeers in the snow by a cabin at the edge of a frozen lake, a painted postcard hidden in his strongbox and buried with Jonathon's letters which he would read again soon. He knew of snow, he remembered the stories passed down from Jonathon, though he had never felt its bite. He wanted to, but his father had on several occasions cautioned him against impatience.

He looked at his watch, his mind a whirlwind of confusion as though his head might explode and spray across the room like the water in the kitchen. How much more could he read with so little time?

After what he'd learned, how could he not read more? How could he not find the Twelve Scriptures and the Ancestral Tomes? How could he tell all that he knew to Aayla, and how could he not? How could he not climb to the very top of the world to gaze across the entire sea, to view the setting sun, the lush forests of Tombola to the north and the south and the village?

He would tell her. He would find the right words and he would make her believe.

He put his face close to the page. The sun was lower in the sky.

*

I spent a month at the seashore, clearing my mind, when not negotiating with banks of proven and stable reputation who, quite naturally, welcomed me with open arms and great affection upon hearing of my assets.

I found a woman for the first week whose charms were quite alluring and I believe our enjoyment was mutual; nevertheless I went without her to the boatyard where I met once again with the harbour master. We went to dinner and throughout our meal I explained my criteria to him. He could not believe his good fortune, for he was near destitution and agreed to act as my broker, containing himself with commendable effort and I believe at that very moment he thought me his saviour.

By the end of the second week he called me with the news of a yacht newly constructed. The next day we met for the sea trials. The magnificent vessel boasted fifty feet of LOA, a beam of seventeen, a steel hull, her decks constructed of teakwood, remarkable power with twin engines and the most modern of amenities in the cabin and at the helm.

I provisioned her with food and drink, tools, handguns and rifles and a new wardrobe to replace the one I'd discarded. Of greater importance were the planks of strong teakwood and steel tanks that would serve to construct my wharf, and a tent of the finest Egyptian cotton that would be my domicile on those interim nights too stormy with waves too high to remain onboard amidst the luxuries of Fortune.

I left port at first light without the first or subsequent three women whose warm bodies sustained me, for I was uncertain as to my future plans. I had a blueprint in my mind, a vague understanding of what I might do, secure in the knowledge that I was no longer a husband, nor a father, nor under any consideration for conscription. Beyond my signature at the banks, I did not exist to anyone and the harbour master had no reason to suspect that I was anything beyond a good friend and generous benefactor.

The southern summer was young, as was I, and I had much to contemplate. With Fortune burdened with its extraordinary payload my headway was slow, yet steady under fair skies and a calm sea. I would reach Tombola by mid-afternoon, my sincerest wish being that no one had taken my gun.

I would immediately set to work pitching my tent by the crystal pool where I would eat my midday meals, bathe at the end of each day and swim, though I would spend my first night onboard because conditions were favourable despite my distrust of the sea for fear of being marooned. In truth, having dismissed two beings from their incomplete existence and two others from my mind, I no longer felt afraid for my person. In fact I was anxious for night time, darkness and solitude to test my resolve. For the Isle of Tombola, I knew, was not my escape, rather my destiny.

I would begin my second day searching for another more inconspicuous and protected cove or inlet on Tombolina, where I would construct my wharf, an undertaking which I calculated would require the better part of a week. I cut all power, dropped the anchor and let go the helm. I was curious to see how the vessel would react to her freedom, letting her momentum swing me bow to stern so that her aft was facing the sandy shore of Tombolina.

Secure at the end of a taut length of scope, I stood before my refection in the starboard porthole and swore aloud that "I, Wendell Parkens, being of sound mind, do solemnly swear that I will never engage in conversation with myself for I have no desire to become insane."

Fourteen

"You were insane," Cassidy whispered. "Now I worry for my women. Your second son is no better than your first."

He stepped away from the book and ran from the room. He ran along the hall to the stairs, scarcely touching each step with his weight. At the bottom he went to the second closet, and reached to open the third door he'd seen. He stepped inside.

He saw handguns and rifles and others that he knew were guns but couldn't comprehend. He saw long red sticks and recognized what they were. He saw boxes of bullets, different from those he'd seen in his books. These were long and as round as when his thumb and forefinger were joined.

He saw a strange helmet with thick spectacles attached to the front that he put on his head. He brought the spectacles to his eyes with no difficulty at all and turned in the doorway to face the window. He let out a yelp and tore the thing from his head, certain he was blind.

He stood where he was and spoke to himself. He wasn't the son of a madman; he was the son of Zach, not a coward to scream like a frightened girl.

He stayed as he was, and soon the room became clear. He replaced the helmet and stepped back, staring into the closet. His mind flooded with questions. His heart filled with doubt, almost certain she would forgive him. How could she not? And suddenly he was afraid, for Aayla and his mother.

He closed the door and returned to the journal.

*

The sea was turquoise upon my third arrival; the ruffled edge of foam along the familiar shore was whiter than the sand that glared platinum under the sun. I stood in utter disbelief that this paradise, whose history you shall soon continue to author, was my home.

I stripped away my swimming suit and floated on my back, studying Fortune from a curious perspective. Her smooth lines made her appear much greater in length and sleeker from my vantage. I felt as though I owned the world.

My trek to the narrow channel leading to the lagoon was quickly done, my tent strapped to my back, other supplies dragging behind me in knee-deep water, for over the previous four weeks I had conditioned myself with arduous exercise and saw no purpose in challenging the gorge. The water in the sandy corridor was warm and clear and I felt my knees weaken at what I beheld at the clearing.

Before me and on both sides lay a vast, natural garden of colours one could not recreate in the most vivid mind. Behind me, whence I came, a wall of green from the calm, blue water to the pale blue of the sky. A place poor men would never know in their dreams, a Shangri-La the richest of men could never create.

What wondrous place was this Tombolina? I spun several times, elated at what I alone possessed.

I walked on, unashamed by overwhelming awe, wanting to shout, not from fear, from elation. I refrained, remembering my oath, seeing my weapon which lay untouched by my crippled foot, the bright chrome slightly dulled by weather, yet glistening. To me a surgeon's tool I would never use, a relic from a forgotten time: a keepsake.

My tent was erected with efficient ease and stocked with

provisions for my first dinner. I waded in the pool. I slept on the heated rocks and left as the sun disappeared behind swaying trees. In the morning I would initiate my search, though I woke with no memory of what might have taken place after I'd sealed myself into my cabin.

The next morning my mood was too agitated for inaction. Anxious for discovery, I ate a meagre breakfast of fruit and biscuits as I strode along the shore, a pistol strapped to my belt, my rifle slung from one shoulder, a well-honed machete from the other.

I looked out over the leeward shore to where the large and small islands met. The water in the gorge was at its highest. I began my search in the opposite direction, hoping for success. I wanted to find Fortune a good home, one befitting her proud lines. To leave her alone and subject to the swells of the sea was unthinkable. Without question I would certainly one day be the subject of idle curiosity or malicious envy.

I thought to provide myself with a satchel of sandwiches and beer, not certain where my search would lead or when I would, from necessity, retrace my footfalls disappointed.

I meandered along the entire length of beach to the north, at times along the edge of the sea, other times stooping to peer between the trunks of palm trees or sweep the sharp blade of my machete into the leaves of brightly coloured foliage and plants I had no idea about. Not far from where I was about to turn back, dejected, I came across a deep rivulet of water that disappeared into the foliage. I decided I would sit, waiting to see what would transpire once the water would cease to flow inward from the sea.

I was alone with no one to call upon should I be caught by a raging surge of incoming seawater, break a bone or somehow cause myself to stumble and lose my conscious mind. For no other reason did I resist the temptation to discover what lay beyond the foliage overhanging the channel well-worn by nature, if not by man. Men did once exist on my Isle of Tombola, men I did not know. Therefore what doubt could exist that I was not the sole creature in the universe to know of this Eden?

I spent those hours swimming, reposing under the sun and gazing at Fortune in the distance. What a fortunate man was I? Indeed, having gained so much by virtue of diligence and prudence, despite those who sought to undo me, to uncaringly and drastically alter my life for the worst.

So quietly and gently did the waters flood the channel that I failed to notice, so preoccupied was I with my thoughts and my dreams. I rose up, undressed, and without my weapons, my machete gripped tightly in my hand and tied to my wrist with a leather thong, I stepped into the channel. The water was as high as my chest, requiring that I push harder against the natural resistance as I neared the foliage, soon ducking my head so that my nose was often submerged, large green leaves and serpentine vines lapping my hair and my shoulders.

I proceeded, curious and unafraid, listening, halting abruptly where the thick and snarled ceiling thinned to open sky. What lay several hundred feet beyond was the blue sea at the most northerly tip of the island. To my right was a verdant mountain. I was truly disappointed. The width of the channel was too narrow to accommodate Fortune's beam. At low tide she would rest upon her port or starboard side in the soft sand, useless to me.

I swam the rest of the way, wading when I felt myself sufficiently exerted, my disappoint assuaged at seeing that my first evaluation of the northern tip was incorrect. The shore was not narrow and at low tide would be the island's crown. The rising slope was gentle and green, not nearly as unattainable as I'd previously believed.

I returned to gather my weapons. I spent the remainder

of the day consoled by what a few mere mortals had ever seen, determined I would succeed the next day, if not the day after.

I ate my evening meal onboard Fortune, anxious for a new day when I would explore the windward side that I knew was uneven and jagged in its topography. I toasted Aristotle Parkens with a plentiful cognac, as befit his characteristic disregard for moderation in most things, particularly in his disdain for his only son, for he made quite clear to me in his final missive that I was never again to refer to him as my father. He was, in truth, my redemption, which is not to say I would ever forgive him his trespasses against me.

My third day began with horrid humidity and a light rain that did not refresh me as I stood on the deck, crestfallen. Were I to proceed along the shore and through the gorge I would not regain my natural warmth. And I was uncomfortable at the thought of piloting Fortune through the narrow and fast-flowing passage, uncertain of the minimum depth.

Though the high water had not yet begun to ebb, her draft was much deeper than the harbour master's vessel and I was not prepared to endanger her. I shrugged; thankful I did not spend the night in my tent. I brought Fortune to life, the deep groan of her engines perfectly suited to my mood.

I proceeded north, past my recent discovery; my revolutions not much more than idle, scrutinizing every foot of shoreline through my binoculars, altering my course to northeast, then south and along the rocky shoreline of Tombolina's windward side. My expectations were not substantial.

The shoreline and tree line appeared as one to the eye. What little distance that did exist was strewn with huge rocks and monstrous boulders from another era. The seas were more agitated on the windward side, flowing over and receding from the rocky beach, my observations made more difficult as Fortune pitched and rolled with lazy confidence.

Not so her master. I was midway between the most northerly point and the gorge, nothing remotely resembling a suitable breakwater or hideaway disclosing itself to me. I felt that all was lost. Of what use to me was an island, if I could not protect and preserve the sole element that was my protection and my preservation? Had I come this far to fail, to once and for all show the world that Parkens was, indeed, synonymous with craven? That thought alone propelled me, for I was not craven.

We motored on, my thoughts and I, each one struggling against our shared despondency. Until, not a mile from the gorge, I spied what appeared as a black hole, as though half the bleak circumference lay in the dark waters of the sea, while the other half was carved into a foreboding façade of green leaves and tangled vines.

I brought Fortune to an idle state, at once curious and fearing that I had once been a Parkens. I wanted to leap for joy, instead I motored to the gorge noting my speed and my time, pleased that my estimation was correct. This place, whatever awaited me, was one half mile from Excalibur's split rock, my gorge and my once feared destiny.

I went to my icebox for a beer. The ice had melted into stagnant water and the beer was warm, though fresher than the air that was thick and without a breath of wind. Not much time remained to decide. Soon the tidal currents would reverse and, perhaps, close the dark void.

Still I waited. The sun had crossed its zenith and, were I to approach the shore, anchor and swim or wade the remaining distance, what time would remain for me to explore? I finished my beer, content to let Fortune's swaying relax me.

I would return the next day, for I dared not stay the night on the open sea.

Fifteen

"You were craven, Wendy, afraid of the water, the sand and the forest, the tide and the currents, the gorge and the highest peak of the island. What didn't frighten you, Wendy? Yes, you died a craven man, not a man to compare with my father Zach."

With so many questions floating in his head, Cassidy doubted he would sleep another night in whatever remained of his life. He looked at his watch. He turned in his seat and peered through the window. He had so many more pages to read, a mountain to climb and the day was coming to an end. Night would soon darken the sky. His is only light would come from the moon and his mind he went to Aayla lying on the cool sand of the beach, naked for his eyes alone and so beautiful.

He would give himself one hour more. Then he would leave.

*

Return I did, though my evening hours were less than idle. I scarcely slept, so intrigued was I.

My breakfast comprised strips of bacon between slices of fried bread and coffee that would create turmoil within the strongest of constitution.

I was eager, and skimmed the calm seas at maximum revolutions. The previous day's scar of desolate weather had abated and the day before me could not be more magnificent. I grabbed the helm and screeched. I yelled and jumped up and down for no one to see or hear, for a moment not lending credence to my more pragmatic arguments of the previous evening.

Despite my exhilaration, I spoke not one audible word to myself.

I arrived within an hour or two, oblivious to the passage to time, elated beyond description. I anchored precisely where I had laid out my scope the day before, my stomach knotted with anxiety. I did not pray. I could not. Rather, I wished for my most ardent desire to come true.

The ebbing tidal current had widened the rocky beach, though not to any great advantage. What had previously lain beneath the waters was now bare, sparkling under the sun and threatening. This was indeed a precarious shore.

I anchored Fortune twofold from the bow, well beyond the limits of her draft, yet not so deep that I could not achieve a steady foothold to protect my sidearm and rifle. I eased into the water, naked, each day more brazen in my comportment, each day more comfortable with my person, though my progress was slow, leaping high with each new wave, my weapons held at arm's-length over my head.

Closer to the shore, buried to my chest in swirling water, I resisted being swept this way and that, the focal point of my entire being the dark abyss and what lay in wait for me on the other side. In my heart of hearts I knew. This was the place…not far from my Eden where one day I would surely die.

Peering down I viewed my nine toes and the entirety of my person, yet I felt a strange sense of inhibition engulf me. Or possibly a feeling of disparity, as though my nakedness would somehow put me at a disadvantage with what I was about to encounter. To strengthen my resolve I left my weapons against the rocks and swam to Fortune for my swimming suit.

I spent the morning and much of the afternoon swinging

my machete, disavowing my hunger, hacking at vines that would not yield and dragging away those that did. With each cut I grew measurably more confident, disregarding the persistent ache in my shoulders and neck until I could no longer reach the higher branches and forced myself to desist, marvelling at the most haunting of passages I'd carved.

On either side stood walls of solid rock worn smooth by time and the sea, much of its natural dome now open to the sky: a veritable cavern equal in length to my vessel and twice the width.

To my dismay the water at my chest began to deepen, the tidal current reversing. I was at once disappointed and excited. My travail was not complete though I'd discerned a natural curve that would taunt me throughout what remained of my day and through another sleepless night.

The following morning the sun rose later than I, the journey to my destination done in half the time. Leaping from the bow I barely contained myself, this time properly attired. My efforts from the previous day were most impressive and not in vain, though much remained to accomplish and I set to work without delay.

I laboured for hours, the water never receding past my chest, the rock walls remaining wet several feet above my head.

Only once did I think to glance over my shoulder, shocked when I did not see the ocean or Fortune, unable to gauge my progress, determine how far I was from completion or imagine what might greet me or give me cause to retreat for my weapons. Then I worried for the safety of my weapons, unaware of time, uncertain when the waters would rise and I kicked my way to the sea with one hand clenching my machete, the other slapping at the surface.

I felt as though I was making no progress at all. On

Fortune's transom I lathered myself and plunged into the sea, not wanting to think. Thinking would lead me to the illogic of my situation and, perforce, to the logic of what I must do. I would return to the boatyard.

Sixteen

Cassidy reclined. He remembered when his father first showed him the way along the rocky windward shore, when they swam together into the channel and stepped onto the floating dock to see Tombolina. He remembered when they sat in the crystal pool and talked, when they strolled to the helicopter and wondered how such a thing might fly, when his father told him that one day he would know the answer and that one day he would fly across the sky high above the earth.

When his father was taken from him, five years in the past, his curiosity did not abate.

*

Dining with the harbour master I realized to what great extent I'd missed conversation, though he never enquired as to my destination and I felt no obligation to inform him. On the second evening we shook hands and bid each other farewell. I would never see him again, though at the time I had no reason to believe so.

Upon my return I steered a course directly to the channel, not wanting to waste a single moment, increasingly anxious to conceal myself and Fortune. On the horizon plumes of black smoke wafted into the air from a chain of naval ships.

I believed they might have seen me and been curious about my travels, though my concern was not one of conscription for they had no dominion over me. I was not one of them and cared as little about their war as they would about an errant foreigner. My worry was for the Isle of Tombola, their discovery of my paradise and the confiscation of my enviable yacht.

I anchored closer to shore, being better acquainted with the depth and the tides. At the entrance I tied a rope to a branch and walked 120 paces to where I had interrupted my clearing. Not three hours later, the chilling dampness surrendered to humid heat and the quiet dimness to sunlight reflected mere inches from my face.

I sheared away several branches blocking my view, sweeping away damp leaves until I saw what I believed was the most beautiful garden and I began to weep. I had yet to remove much of the ceiling to allow for Fortune's cabin. More importantly I had found her a wonderful berth with sufficient space to turn her about and sufficient depth to protect her hull.

I strode as quickly as I could against the water to where I'd coiled the rope and left my weapons. With one hand I dragged the rope 150 paces feet, with the other I kept my pistol and rifle dry. The ascent at the far end of channel was stony and unsound, causing me to proceed with caution, restraining my eagerness.

Standing with lush grass beneath my feet, I had no reason to cover my eyes against the sun or strain to see what was around me. I simply stared in disbelief. To my south, not far in the distance, was the towering stone precipice and within a mere few hundred paces ahead of me lay my private crystal pool and my tent. To the west, and of equal distance, lay my private beach and magnificent garden.

I thought of the mother superior's misspent prayer. I was already blessed with little need to see the kingdom of heaven, for neither was I poor in spirit or in pocket. Nor did I have need of another's comfort, as I had no reason to mourn. Though, perforce, I would admit to a Parkens' meekness, for I had, indeed, inherited the earth.

I have never sought to be righteous, though neither have I ever done wrong. Therefore in what manner might I decry dissatisfaction with my life? And what need have I of mercy, despite my kind nature? For have I not cared for so many in so many ways. And what was I to think of my pure heart as I stood amidst the most miraculous of places?

I confess that I broke my pledge, for a brief moment in time, despite being heard by no one.

"Father, or are you Aristotle Parkens to me now that you are dead? Have you made your peace? Are you a son of God? Verily," I shouted, "I believe that you are not. And is this the kingdom in which I shall dwell, for did you not persecute me, thinking yourself high above me?"

I fell to my knees and wept, so exhausted and elated was I, an orphan alone in the world. And who was the worst, my father for having struck me so viciously in my youth, or my unfaithful wife for having defiled our marriage, for had I not respected and loved her by the manner in which I treated the others not of my seed? I put them from my mind.

Within the hour Fortune was anchored close to the leeward shore and by nightfall the teakwood and tanks lay at the gorge ready for the morning crossing. By early afternoon the next day the wood was in place by the channel and well before evening Fortune's bow passed under the lowest of the overhanging branches in the channel which I soon hacked away along with many hundreds more.

By the first ripple of the incoming current Fortune was securely anchored to the channel floor, the surface and surrounding trees strewn with tangled flotsam.

For the first time I would sleep in my new home.

Seventeen

Cassidy moved the window to capture more light, insisting to himself that he would leave at the first hint of darkness.

He wondered who on the island might possess the knowledge he'd gained in less than a day. He doubted the eldest son's first-mate would be privy to the secrets of The Grand Guardian. But did he know? Did Dakota know? The journal hadn't been read. He wondered how much he knew that they did not.

He shook his head. He was certain. He was alone in what he knew. And as much as he loved Aayla, her body and her mischievous ways, he began wondering whether he could trust her mind to believe him and her tongue not to betray him in her sleep or in her current female state.

What would he say to her, and when? He took a deep breath and read.

*

By the end of September my dock was in place. I was proficient in piloting Fortune from her berth to the sea and entirely at ease when returning her through the maze of foliage which remained entwined to conceal the entrance.

My body was lean and toughened from my labours, sculpted from rigorous exercise and tanned from the sun. Each day I would swim from the dock to the sea and back. I would run along the leeward shore and often I would climb to the peak of the precipice to sit and gaze upon my new life.

I ate little and spoke not at all. My provisions were lasting longer than anticipated, for each day I discovered new fruits and dared to consume them. Consequently, not before the end of October did I leave Tombola to replace my depleted stock.

My one lament was my privation of things carnal, the feel of a naked woman's soft warmth beneath me, the adventure of someone new, her sounds and her smells, her adoration of me. The lack of her was a constant void within me and I planned an excursion that would last several days.

What was in her mind mattered nothing to me. I would, of necessity, leave her each morning and replace her each night. I could well afford the loveliest and most willing nubile bodies, many of them lonely, trading promises of fidelity for a fine meal and sweet words, many of them young widows wanting to relive his final, lingering touch.

I stayed one week, north of the boatyard, in a marina virtually deserted: a skeletal reminder of better days that were not to return anytime soon.

I rented the finest accommodation in what I knew was the finest hotel. I luxuriated in what was my first hot bath in two months; I went to a barber to be cleanly shaven and groomed, the steaming towel and his fine blade upon my face were luxuries and deservedly so. I purchased a new wardrobe in consideration of my new body and invited the clerk to dinner. I bought her a new dress and silk stockings and sent her home when breakfast was done.

The rest of the week was no different. The faces changed, of course, not the corporeal. In the dark they were indistinguishable beyond the tactile; their muted groans and muffled whimpers sounding alike. At week's end they were as one to me and I, to them, was an anomaly, a memory they would not soon forget.

I returned to the Isle of Tombola with sufficient supplies to sustain me through to the end of the year and adequate wood to build a storage hut. I bought seeds to plant and garden tools, fuel from several different locations, many more boxes of ammunition and a comfortable cot to lay upon by the side of my crystal pool. My one lingering doubt was whether to bring a woman with me to share my labours and complete my Eden, a woman I would return to the mainland at year's end to replace with another.

Though as I pondered in the silence of my mind what woman of sound thinking would not want to escape to Shangri-La during such difficult times, I also questioned what woman would want to leave. Therein lay my dilemma. What would I do, were she to refuse to leave? The persistent question in my mind was rhetorical, of course. I knew very well.

By the end of December my garden was flourishing, I was adept with a net for fishing and dissecting my catch no longer made me ill. At first I used my machete, until finally I could remove the thorny spines with a surgeon's delicate skill. I no longer stumbled while ascending the steep slope to the peak of the precipice where I taught myself to throw a knife and many days I fell asleep under a warm sun and atop the world.

I had not tasted beef or fowl in several weeks and began formulating plans once again to leave Tombola. What better time than New Year's Eve? I believed the war was not yet over, anticipating that so many broken hearts would be seeking repair.

I remained three days, wanting to forego the niceties, understanding I could not lest I debase myself and become a lesser man. I was, to them, an aura of brightness in a darkening world. I gave them respite in difficult times and I understood my responsibility to them. And, though I left each one without regret, I could not resist musing that one day I would not. Nor had I lost my appetite for finer cuisine.

I returned home temporarily satiated, burdened with a

cargo of several chickens and adequate lumber to construct a proper pen, thinking I would not leave Tombola again before spring, when I would celebrate my thirty-fourth year.

In the meantime my time would be well spent, not oblivious to the fact that I had much more to accomplish than ensuring my creature comforts on Tombolina. To that end, my cabin was strewn with dozens of newly acquired books on every subject of importance to a learned man, and others suited to a man who must learn self-sufficiency. Well-read since my youth I became voracious, dare I say insatiable in my quest for knowledge.

How could I not know whether a war involving the world was over? For that reason I purchased a short-wave radio and, to house the monstrous casing, a tent of greater proportions which would allow me to stand and spend more time away from the confines of my boat. I acquired equipment to catch the rain, never again would I lack drinkable water and Fortune was well provisioned with the finer elixirs required by men of impeccable good taste.

Some weeks following my return, I sat upon the precipice facing west throughout an entire day. To my right was Tombolina, Fortune and my newly erected camp. To my left was the gorge I no longer feared, Tombola and the wreckage which Aristotle Parkens once witnessed or caused. He was the last before me to set foot upon these shores.

Who once dwelled in those crumpled huts, now destroyed and wasted? Of what purpose was the larger structure? I feared I would never know.

I was decided. I could do no more to ensure a comfortable existence on Tombolina, to the neglect of the larger island, which was my quandary. What was I to do with Tombola? What did Aristotle Parkens intend? Was I to patrol the shores each day aboard my yacht to defend my lands? Was I to live as a hermit and one day lose my mind?

Was that what he wanted? And what of the squalor that lay amidst Tombola's lushness, a blight within a perfect jewel?

What masonry and carpentry skills I did possess were recently learned, insufficient to accomplish any task exceeding the most rudimentary. How would I as a single man repair such damage and rebuild even the smallest village, and to what end?

I believed then that I was midway through my life. How was I to imagine my centenary? I wondered with whom I would spend my final days. Or would I die alone? And what of my fortune, which thus far served no purpose beyond the purchase of a fine vessel and the beguilement of eager women?

I descended the slope and went to bed that night to lay awake, my many questions as yet unanswered, an undeniable probability gnawing through my resistance to reason. The Isle of Tombola was of no practical use to me and very likely one day would bring about my ruin.

At sunrise I ate a breakfast of fried eggs and toast before passing through the arch to the gorge where I stripped away my clothes and placed them in a rubber box with my weapon. On the other side I let the sun dry me. I dressed in long slacks, a shirt with long sleeves, sturdy boots and strapped my pistol to my waist.

I crossed through the foliage as one would a botanical garden, without apprehension. I soon came upon the abandoned settlement where I laid my satchel on the ground and stood quietly imagining men and women, children and yapping dogs. Or were they prisoners, slaves to the one once residing in what might have been a stately manor?

I walked on. I stood in front of each one. None was more than a glorified shanty when new, the current condition too disintegrated to suggest otherwise. The thatched roofs which I remembered had fallen were gone, dispelled by the wind. The crooked walls had collapsed, scattered splinters connecting one hut with another.

I turned my attention to the main dwelling. My body had strengthened considerably since my arrival; I was not the same man. I was limber, resilient and seldom gave much consideration to the possibility of personal injury.

If any part of the front door remained, I could not identify any particular piece of it. Inside the walls once badly cracked and chipped were a series of wide gaps held together by rotting beams. The windows were blank holes and the ceiling had collapsed, removing the second floor. Even the dust had blown away, leaving a sinister sculpture. Not even the decomposed birds remained.

However what I had not seen during my first visit so many years in the past, now in plain view amidst the rubble, was the strongbox. Perhaps once hidden behind a secret panel, or not seen by me by reason of my previous preoccupation for my well-being. I went closer and dragged the thing to the outer side of the walls. I stood well back and took precise aim, exploding the lock with the third burst from my pistol.

Inside was a package wrapped in layers of linen and bound with black ribbon. I reached in and seized it, surprised by the weight. I sat on the strongbox and began to undo the wrapping. Inside was a tome, leather-bound, its many pages coated with gold filigree and in a state of near perfect preservation. The leather was worn, though not by time, and I opened the soft cover.

The hand-written date was December; the author of the diary was Charles Weatherbone of Charleston, South Carolina. I read the first and second pages, wrapped the document again in the linen and returned to Tombolina. I spent that day and the next reading through what I suppose he felt should be remembered of his life, scarcely taking time to refresh myself with sleep.

Eighteen

Whoever Charles Weatherbone might be, he would have to wait. Cassidy's mind was about to explode.

He thought of the bedroom, the soft clothing he'd seen and he thought of Aayla, her body draped in soft fabric. He thought of The Seven Feasts in one year that would take her away.

He thought of Wendell Parkens who'd coupled with so many women before and after his wife and, when he was The Grand Guardian, how he'd bathed with so many young girls each year to make them ready for their first coupling. The man was a monster.

When was the monster born, he wondered, and how? He searched the walls. Somewhere amongst all those books was the answer. Somewhere on those walls he would find the Ancestral Tomes and the Twelve Scriptures. Cassidy knew they were the key to his escape from the Isle of Tombola with his mother. His mother, she'd be worried and angry.

He carefully closed the journal, gripping it tightly. He climbed to the far corner of the library; wedging the book into the narrow space Wendell Parkens had thought the most secret. He pushed in the chair, taking a moment to absorb what else was in the room, machines he didn't know and cabinets under each wall of books. What he did know were the pads of paper and pens filled with ink. He took one of each.

He closed the door behind him and went to the kitchen. He reached for the empty bottle and the brown apple core, wiping away the mark left behind with his elbow. The water on the floor was gone and he stepped into the garden where he lay down what he'd taken.

He ran to the south, away from the house, the pool and the lush gardens. He had to see the gorge from inside the arch. The water was high; the walls of the arch moist with dampness he believed must never dry.

He retraced his steps and stood, craning his neck. If he were to die, he'd do so knowing that one day Aayla would forgive him. With Aayla in his mind and in his heart, he climbed. At the summit he read his watch. Fifteen minutes had passed. He was at the top of the world.

He looked to the south, the east, the west and the north. He saw the house where he'd spent the day, the pool, the private lagoon and gold-coated sea. He saw Tombola, the village and the green forests. He sat, feeling content. He was at the top of the world and he spoke to his father.

Never had he seen anything as wondrous or as beautiful, were his eyes or his mind not on Aayla or his mother.

From where he sat he saw her father's hearth and Dakota's, larger than all the others and more elaborate. He stood, cupped his hands at the side of his mouth and cried out her name. Never had he yelled as loud. When he was done, his throat raw and dry, he sank to his knees and told her he loved her. He told her that one day soon she would know the word, and so many others. She would know the truth, and together they would do what they must.

They would leave the Isle of Tombola.

Nineteen

He crossed the mouth of the gorge with his hands held high to preserve the precious paper. He hurried to his tree where he buried the bottle and hurled what remained of the apple into the forest. He opened his strongbox to hide his watch along with what he'd taken.

At his villa he ate an evening meal quietly. Neither he nor Shakkra wanted the noise of the feast at the beach. She knew what was on his mind. She knew he didn't like the man asleep in her bed.

He sat with his mother and talked about his father and their times together. Her second-mate was a man older by half her age. Often he would lay in the sand near the trees or in the fields for a midday nap rather than consuming his midday meal with them, content to spend his night without her. They hadn't coupled once in their two years together and during The Seven Feasts the more alluring women wanted the most attractive and youngest men, not him.

Shakkra was thirty-five, looking many years younger to those who knew nothing of the passage of time. To them she was simply Shakkra, desired by men and envied by women. She was alluring and always pursued by those young men during The Seven Feasts which, for her, was the loneliest time of the year. She felt no emotion for the second-mate sent to share her hearth and her bed.

For the first three years since Zach's death she slept alone, her tears eventually subsiding by dawn's early light.

Then the man came. At first she would wait until he slept, then she went to her bed in her tunic and night-shield to dissuade him, preferring the thick humidity invading her hearth to his touch. Now she slept on her son's bed, squeezed into a corner.

She was content to spend her time alone, to remember Zach, not unaware of the attention the village men gave her at the beach. None of them was a match for the man she'd once loved and lost forever. Some of the men had fond and indelible memories of her, others would never know her. She no longer selectively shared her affection with other young village men and their first-mates were no less disappointed to no longer share their affection with Zach.

She remained alone throughout the week in her hearth, her sculpted body unpainted. Her memories were alive. The week for her was a solitary time of simple meals when she would knit or weave elaborate and colourful shields for her son and his little heart whom she adored.

The man knew and left her alone. He spent his week at the beach to sleep on the sand, quenching his thirst with tincture to dull his mind and his memories. She would never come back to him. She'd been lost to him at the pole. His one solace was the older women of the village whose paint could not disguise their years or the drudgery of motherhood.

All that he saw in their eyes was her. He understood Shakkra, yet she would never know. He'd known Zach. He knew he'd been sent to Zach's hearth not to console his first-mate. He knew the single motive was to punish her.

Before his death Shakkra and Zach would share affection with very few of the youngest and the most charming villagers who were their close friends, as was decreed, but she would always come to Zach late at night to tease him with exaggerated stories of the other men's prowess

They slept together each night, making noise and laughing until they went to the beach early in to refresh their bodies. Their minds and their eyes as clear as a perfect night time sky.

Not since his father went to the pole had she made noise the way Cassidy remembered. That first night Cassidy took Shakkra by the hand and led her from the sea. He filled her cup with tincture, much more than the few drops his father would have allowed and he sat with her until she slept. He'd promised his father to care for her.

She seldom laughed and seldom smiled. Cassidy was her single joy, her one way to remember.

He would take her with Aayla. He would find a way and he would take them away. He never spoke with her of Tombolina, neither did his father. Though she'd read his books with him each night in their bed by their lanterns until his death, and alone for three years since. She'd never known of the chest. Nor did Cassidy ever speak to her of the Jonathon's strongbox. Zach was afraid for her, as was her son.

She knew her son could read, that he could write. She knew what was in his mind. Her deception was Zach's final instruction to her. The boy wasn't to know. He was too young. Now he wasn't.

Jonathon Clayton wasn't the first man killed, and not at the pole. Many went before him. His body was found one morning at the edge of the sea. He'd drowned, though his son knew the truth and told his son who told Cassidy. The Grand Guardian wanted the strongbox and what he believed was in it.

When Cassidy woke the next morning, Aayla was first in his thoughts. He pushed himself from his bed and slid his legs into a fresh shield. Shakkra was in the kitchen. The man had gone from the villa to the blue water before she awoke.

The Seven Feasts was over.

Cassidy was famished. He sat, watching his mother. She stood watching her son. When he'd eaten his fill he watched her clear the bowls and the cups from the table, wash them and put them away. Then she went to the hook on the wall.

She reached for her tunic and draped the muslin around her neck. Her body was clear; her skin as smooth as Aayla's, her belly was flat, her legs and her arms firm from working in the fields and swimming in the sea. He read what was in her mind and knew she would rather go to the beach. She was so much like Aayla. The early morning was as hot as the previous day at noon and her brown skin glistened as much as the gleam of her chocolate-coloured eyes.

If she went to the fields wearing her maiden-shield and nothing else he doubted anyone would care. The other women were accustomed to their first-mates' undisguised adoration of her and he believed the men would work harder to finish early and get to the beach.

"You will tell me when you are ready, Cassidy, what you have done during The Seven Feasts."

"I have been with Aayla."

She shook her head. "Until you arrived at the last high moon, your little heart was with me."

"Before that, I meant. I wanted aloneness."

"You will tell me when you are ready." She raised an eyebrow, stepping in close to him. "She is unhappy with you."

"She is unhappy because of what I did not do, not for what I did do. She is a girl. Her mind is filled with affection. She is anxious for the next Seven Feasts."

"I am also a girl. Swim carefully in water you do not understand."

She smacked his faced, and kissed him.

He smiled. He lived in the hearts of the two most

beautiful women on the island. She returned his smile and shrugged. He watched her tug the thin tunic over her head and down her damp body. He imagined her in the fine clothes he'd seen.

When she'd knotted her belt he went to her and kissed her cheek. They left together and strolled to the fields. He always went with her to where she toiled. Then he left her and went to the sea to cast his net.

After his midday meal he went to the field where men laboured during hottest hours and the women worked at the shore to gut and clean the morning catch.

When her work was done his mother bathed in the ocean to wash away the smell and the blood. She went to her hearth to prepare the evening meal. No one spoke beyond simple words relating to their work.

Well-fed the man went out to sit on the porch. Shakkra and Cassidy were first at the beach, tossing their evening tunics onto the sand, turning to see Aayla behind them. His mother liked Aayla. Aayla liked Shakkra. Her own mother was much older and Aayla thought of Shakkra as a sister. She took the woman's hand, ready to lead her away, telling Cassidy with a familiar glare that he wasn't to follow. She wanted Shakkra to herself for a while. He could go to his tree and make raindrops in the forest.

He flushed the bright red colour of his shield. His mother's eyes sparkled. Her mouth beamed a warm, coquettish smile. Aayla simply shooed him away, wrapped an arm around Shakkra's waist and the two women left him without saying a word.

He stood his ground awhile longer, convinced. When they didn't turn around he hurried towards the north.

At the gorge he pranced into the high water until he could lunge forward and swim. He ran to the tree line and stayed as close as he could to the shadows. At the channel leading to the lagoon he stopped to breathe, wading into the water and letting the slight current take him further in. At the edge of the Sacred Pond he lay in the shallow water staring at the grand house and the precipice towering over it.

He walked to the front door. When he was dry he wiped the sand from his feet and went inside. He went to the stairs and climbed with a purpose to the library. He scampered up the ladder and reached for the journal. At the desk he sat as though the library was his and opened the book to where he'd left Wendell Parkens the night before.

*

At first I gave serious deliberation to rewriting the yellowed and flimsy pages that were the journal of Charles Weatherbone. In my view his words were his confession, which he first wrote near the end of his days some seventy-five years earlier. I did not. The tedious endeavour would have consumed too much of my time. Truth be told, I had no clear vision of what I would do with the island or whether anyone but I would ever read his words or, for that matter, the words of his son William, or of William's son Horatio.

These three journals, separated in a single tome by two black ribbons, are the Ancestral Tomes of this isle. With mine, these I write at the conclusion of my own existence, they are the history of Tombola for all that is good, and all that is not. For fear they might one day be discovered by prying eyes and curious minds not sufficiently versed to comprehend their meaning, or the Twelve Scriptures concealed within, they are shelved amongst the countless works of brilliant minds that line these walls. Their single distinction the leather binding that so closely resembles the newness of my own.

As days became weeks my sanity continued to preoccupy my mind as a matter of utmost importance. Increasingly I found myself willing to respond to one thought with another, addressing myself by name. On one notable occasion, I spoke aloud shocking myself with the quality of my voice. I suggested to Mr. Parkens that at some point I should take the responsibility upon myself to commission the construction of a bridge as a practical means of avoiding any future possibility of being swept out to sea when traversing from one shore to the other. To my surprise and my joy Wendell agreed, sharing my concern.

I remained on the island until New Year's Eve 1945, when perforce, driven by desperation and the fear of imminent insanity, I returned to civilization to replace what was lacking in my mind, the thoughts of another person beyond my own intelligence and, for the convenience of my person, the moist warmth of a woman. I spoke not a single word until I was well secured to the dock.

My primary concern was that of my outward condition and paid dearly for the immediate attention of a preferred tailor and personal groomer. My second and third were of companionship and dinner, both equally delightful. I had no need to wander the streets in search of homeless waifs. I was a man of considerable means with a natural disposition towards philanthropy and sought to enjoy the finest that my affluence could afford me. I was not for a moment disheartened by my selection. She was indeed the finest.

She was twenty and barely of age. At first my senses, overpowered by months of carnal neglect and morbid thoughts of a winter and spring of lonesome and long duration, filled me with the temptation to keep her as my companion, though I did not. In her place I departed Miami with sufficient quantities of food and intoxicants to last through the spring to the summer and allow me time to consider the words of Charles Weatherbone and of his son William.

The girl in my bed that first week of the year planted a seed in me of far greater worth than my own in her. And the world seemed to share the considered opinion that the war would soon reach its conclusion.

She was once an orphan, her parents dead, who married out of wide-eyed innocence or fear of further neglect. Then she was a widow and not yet a mother, the husband killed as much by some misbegotten semblance of valour and freedom as the bullet that deprived him of life. She was without him, without having known him, happily comforting me with her heated body as recompense for my kind words and my promise to see her again. I daresay, hoping to capture my heart with all that was hers to give.

I left her with sufficient funds to choose between one more night of luxury or a new dress and shoes. I confess, with certain regret. She was warm to my touch and moulded easily and without timidity to my contours and penchants. I would surely miss her, though my time, I decided, would be well spent.

In full agreement with myself regarding my eventual disenchantment with crossing the gorge at the discretion of the tides, my person in a state of perpetual wetness in good weather and bad, and the frightful prospect of being swept out to sea, I did in fact commission the construction of a foot bridge that would give me safe and dry passage from Tombola to the archway of Tombolina.

The barge arrived on the day following my return, carrying steel, wood and skilled craftsmen who had not plied their trade in years and were hungry for work. They erected their tents in the clearing where once a small village had thrived and then failed. Two months later I stood at high tide three feet above the water and with the steel that was left they crafted a magnificent gate that would make the gorge and its arch my own, for I had conceived a plan of considerable merit.

When they took their leave of me in early March I sent them away with plans authored by me and approved by their foreman for a magnificent home, one that was spacious and bright. I went several days later to pay for all they had bought and to select, according to my tastes, what they could not for they were men unacquainted with the subtleties of elegance and refinement.

Throughout my week in Miami she stayed with me once again, the girl who was warm to my touch and eager to please. I left her well-fed with more fine baubles to wear and convinced of my devotion. I would see her again and she promised to wait.

The war ended May 08th, and I thought of her alone in her bed without a husband or I to caress her and make her feel loved. The men of my crew were ecstatic, drunk with good cheer, news of the war and wine. Soon they would finish what little was left to construct of my home and leave my Isle of Tombola. Not so the foreman who begged my permission to stay.

How could I refuse a man in the winter of his years, when all he sought was a modest home far to the south on a beach of his own to live out his life? I could not. He was a man of tolerable intelligence and my evenings with him since our first acquaintance were my salvation. He had built me a fine home where at last I could sleep in a bed that did not sway, eat food not cooked over a campfire, take my relief protected from weather and store my collection of books not yet damaged by salt or the sun in a library of envious luxury and comfort.

Their labours were completed in June, anxious to return home. I went to their tents to bid them farewell, to pay them in full when, to my greatest and most wonderful surprise, I saw what had fed their night time fires over the past several weeks. The high walls and roof of the house once so alarming to me were gone; the floor covered over with fresh earth and large sods of coarse grass cut from the forest.

I paid each one a generous supplement and left one day

later in search of her, leaving the old man in his humble two rooms and a kitchen built at the clearing close to the leeward shore of the western shore, not the south for he was part of my plan.

I returned in a week with Irene, my unwed bride. In advance of the ceremony I'd met privately and in confidence with the preacher who agreed for sum otherwise beyond his reach to forego any official documentation of our union. If my memory serves as obediently as in past years I recall that my duplicate found its way atop brightly glowing embers.

That she believed in her mind that we were wed was sufficient to me. I harboured no desire to repeat a previous blunder.

I remember her name as though she had not died so many years in my past, never usurped by the memories of so many others whose names I do not and cannot remember. She was also a part of my stratagem, though I never intended her harm. And never once throughout her short life did I mention to her the name of Charles Weatherbone who was born into Southern aristocracy in the year 1815.

Charles was an educated man, the owner of a plantation. He was, according to his own assessment, a benevolent man and provider to forty slaves who would certainly not survive their freedom should the Union defeat the Confederacy in a war between neighbours.

War was imminent and Weatherbone feared the worst. Were the Union to succeed in its oppression upon the South he would lose all that he possessed. He vowed to his wife that such a horror would not come to pass. He hired two steamships, one captained by a despicable man whose sympathies lay with his purse, the other, a much smaller vessel, piloted by his son William who was not unfamiliar with a ship's helm. Together they fled in December of

1860.

By day, and at a safe distance further to the south, they loaded the ships with gold, foodstuffs, grain and bolts of fine cloth, pigs, goats, chickens, slaves and tools. Onboard one ship was William with his sister, younger brother and mother. Onboard the other was Weatherbone with his Negros aged from twelve to sixty years.

They arrived days later to a far-off paradise he had not previously thought to name and with the ships anchored not far from the shore, men, women and children, slave and master alike, worked hard to discharge the cargo. All but Weatherbone were taken aback by what they soon beheld, for he had not delivered them to a desolate island, rather to a new and wonderful home.

That evening the family slept in their smaller, yet no less pretentious manor, while the slaves shared ten modest huts of recent construction and comfortable proportions furnished with beds, sinks and pots, solid wood floors, doors and windows.

Set to return to the States, the captain enjoyed a parting repast and fine drink with his client. The next morning, having breakfasted with his family, the father walked the beach with his son. Surprised to see the two ships tied side by side in calm waters, William enquired as to the reason the stalwart captain had not departed. His father responded that, indeed, he had departed, and that the family was now safe from conspiracy and ill-intent.

For nine years Weatherbone and his wife tilled the land, cultivating crops with two of their three children and planting trees, toiling with equal fervour alongside their slaves. Only one of whom had died of natural causes and was buried atop the grassy and treed ridge not far from the village whence the man might look upon his family, the sea and his freedom. And more were born, increasing their numbers.

Two of the children were paler in complexion than the rest, though no one thought to accuse William. His ways were well known, as were those of his father, since more than one of the prettier Negresses had shared Weatherbone's bed in the past and, an equal number, his blood. His wife turned a blind eye to what was the nature of men. Of greater concern was her daughter who had blossomed into womanhood and dreamt of marriage and a hearth of her own.

For several weeks she pled with her mother and father that she might go with William on one of his many voyages until, at last, Weatherbone, much to his discontentment, conceded.

He took William aside, charging him with conducting his sister and her twin brother to Miami and what he prayed was the safety of trusted friends who would find her a suitor of sound upbringing and admirable qualities. Fearing reprisal, the family would never return to Charleston.

The younger brother went with them, craving his independence and employment unrelated to backbreaking hardship. He envied his brother's freedom and frequent excursions to the West Indies. Neither twin ever returned to the island, though William did several months later to learn of his parents' deaths, the final few pages of his father's diary stained by droplets of water, explaining his wife's demise and charging his son with the transport and well-being of his Negros for whom he had made provisions.

Charles Weatherbone took his own life, sitting alone atop the precipice of his small and private islet, looking down upon his wife where she lay buried by the side of her favourite crystal pool.

By the firmness of his script his hand was steady when he dated what was then the last page, June 30, in the year of our Lord, 1869, beseeching his Lord to forgive him.

Twenty

Cassidy stared at the date. Then he glanced at the clock on the wall. Charles Weatherbone was buried alongside his wife 141 years earlier, almost to the day, at the edge of the crystal pool.

He shivered. This wasn't what he expected.

He put a finger lightly under the page to see what was next. He saw William's name and July 15, 1869. He slammed the book shut and pushed himself to his feet. He hadn't much time. The Grand Guardian didn't possess dozens of books, or hundreds. Thousands lined the walls, so high that each wall required its own ladder with wheels attached to rails on the floor and the ceiling. He would need the rest of his life to find the Ancestral Tomes.

He thought for a moment of his father, his promise and what he must do. Weatherbone's journal lay buried in a strongbox for seventy-five years in a house that had fallen apart. Wendell Parkens had begun reading his collection of books sometime later to save his mind. Weatherbone's must be the oldest book of all, and in the worst condition.

He examined the journal closely, the size, the colour and the texture. He scanned the upper shelves of the wall where he'd found it. He looked at the clock and thanked his father.

He stepped into the centre of the room to see all the books more clearly. Not all were bound in leather. Many were shiny, like glass, others as though freshly painted in bright colours. He thought to search for the oldest, on the upper shelves, one that looked the worst, as though the pages hadn't been read more than once in over a hundred years.

He began at the third row from the top, removing and replacing each tome. Disappointed, he pushed himself with his hands against the ceiling to begin the second row. His feet began to ache from the weight of his body on the rungs of the ladder. He looked at the clock. One hour had passed. He was a third done. He knew the meaning of the Ancestral Tomes to the village, the spoken history taught to each new generation by The Grand Guardian. He'd been taught the lessons. He knew the meaning. What he wanted to know was Wendell Parkens.

None had ever seen the tomes.

Halfway along, he came to a book of similar description. He put his hand to what he thought couldn't possibly contain the most important history of the Isle of Tombola. The colour of the leather was the same. The pages were filigreed and coated with dust. The leather tome was small, not at all what he'd imagined and deceptively heavy.

Braced on the rung he opened the cover and read the faded words: To my son, William Weatherbone, for whatever purpose he might one day deem my words useful.

Cassidy hurried to the floor. He laid the tome on the desk and scurried to the ceiling to conceal the journal, holding himself securely, sweeping a hand across the dozens of spines thick and thin to conceal the void he'd created on the second highest shelf. Satisfied, he dropped to the floor, replaced the ladder and ran from the house, terrified. He'd stolen the Ancestral Tomes.

The sun hadn't yet set, a soft glow hovering in the sky. He would wait for total darkness. Until then he would sit in the sand to consider what he'd done, and what he would do. With no way to conceal the book he was afraid he might be noticed. None of the villagers had ever seen a book, let alone read one, though Dakota, he was certain, knew more than he pretended. Why else would he have spent so much of his youth away from the island when other boys stayed to cast their nets?

He wouldn't read a word until the seventh high sun, Sunday afternoon, decreed as the time of pleasure, when he would climb into his tree and make full use of his time to worsen his crime. He fanned through the pages, to search, not intending to read, ignoring the two ribbons, expecting a sheet of paper or parchment to dislodge. Nothing did. He fanned again, to the last page and to the inside of the leather cover, not recognizing the writing, wondering why his heart hadn't stopped beating.

The Twelve Scriptures, he imagined would be written in gold, preserved on parchment and in sacred scrolls. They weren't. To the village they were the Spoken Word, passed down from ancient times to modern times, intended for The Grand Guardian's eyes alone, he who would comprehend their meaning. And here they were, written in black ink by the nib of a pen and at the back of a worn and well-used book. At the bottom was the signature of William Weatherbone.

Cassidy closed the book, the strain on his eyes too severe. Yet he couldn't believe his eyes. How would he sleep, and what would he say to Shakkra in the morning, or to Aayla? What had he done? He would think of a way not to fish in the sea. He'd climb into his tree and read the words as his father once wished to see.

With the book safely concealed, he went to his villa. Shakkra was waiting for him, sitting on a stool by the door and dressed in her evening tunic, finer than the one she wore to toil in the field. When she saw him her face shone as though lit by a thousand fireflies. They kissed and went inside. She served him and sat with him as he ate his evening meal, but when she went to speak he put a finger to her lips and looked toward her private door.

Her smile disappeared into a frown when he stood. He didn't bid her goodnight as she'd expected, with the tight embrace of a son who loved his mother; instead he took her hand and led her through the darkness she knew to the quiet and abandoned beach.

"Shakkra, you are my mother."

"Cassidy, I remember your arrival. If not painted on my skin, you are surely painted forever in my mind. You were not easy to convince from your warm hiding place."

"I ruined you. I have heard what they say."

"No, you saved me." She smiled, "though you were too young to know."

"You went with Aayla between the late sun and early moon. What did she say of me?"

"She has very deep emotion for you; she wonders why you are not responding to her."

Shakkra giggled. To Cassidy's ears the sound was wonderful.

"She must know I cannot, and why I cannot."

"She is young, my son."

"And how did you respond to her?"

She squeezed his hand.

"Come, let us bathe and enjoy the din of the night. The blue water, Cassidy, is magical. The water knows what to take from the sand, and what to return. Let the water take our words, and bring us together with your father who waits to hear you what, at last, you will say."

"I do not understand."

"Yes, Cassidy, my husband's son, you do. Or we wouldn't be here together. You have something to tell me beyond the curious ears of the village. Now is the time."

She pulled her evening tunic over her head and flung the weightless fabric behind her; he hadn't yet dressed and stood in his shield. She took his hand and they walked to the sea.

"Shakkra…what she said…"

"What did she say?"

He went deeper.

"She told an untruth."

"Then so did your father, when I saw him in his favourite tree before we first coupled and joined. He promised to swim to the sky and drown, if he could not have me. And what do you do in your tree, Cassidy, when you're thinking of her, your Aayla, your little heart…and mine? I too feel deep emotion for her. In my heart, she's is my daughter. I love that little girl."

"I do not understand."

"Cassidy, don't you mean that you don't understand? What were your father's last words to you, Cassidy, before he sat at the pole without the foul opium and rum to weaken him and blur his mind to the pain of the stones? Tell me, because I know. I remember each word he told me. Didn't he tell you that he loves you, that you were to care for me, that he was jealous of the next man who would touch me and envious of you for what you'd bring to the world, that you should read each of his books many times. I've waited five years and five nights for this moment, Cassidy. So has your father who taught me to write in the sand and to read by the glow of our lantern when you were asleep in your bed. I know of the chest, Cassidy. That's all I know. I haven't touched one book since the other came to our villa, yet many are hidden beneath my mattress. You don't have fifty. You have ten more. You must know how I long to read by my lantern. I know that you do. You must now tell me the rest. And don't speak to me as you do in the field or at the ocean." She looked out, "this blue water. We're in the sea and you'll talk to me the way your father once did."

"I did not know, Shakkra. He swore me to silence."

"He swore you to discretion while in our hearth,

179

because he knew, Cassidy. He didn't tell you that he taught me because he was afraid for us, afraid we would one day make a mistake in our speech. This is a different time. The time is right." She put a hand to his cheek. "Not once have I allowed him to taint your father's memory, nor will I ever. He's old and he's vile. He snorts in his sleep and farts. Even if he were as brave and as strong as your father, you'd forever be my only child. During The Seven Feasts he leaves me to share affection with the old ones who are no longer pretty to the young men. When you're asleep, Cassidy, and he's somewhere in his own world of dreams, I sleep on your bed to remember your father. When you're joined I will tell the Chief Counsellor to send him away. I do like him and who else on the island can match your father."

"I know what you do. I hear your whispers and feel your warmth at my back each night. I would rather see you in my bed, than in yours with him. I know how you remember and honour my father." He put his nose to hers. "That's why, Shakkra, my mother, I can never tell you what I know. I'd rather go to the pole and follow my father. The offence I've committed is beyond the Twelve Scriptures. That's what I've done."

"And how would you know? None has seen the Twelve Scriptures spoken to us from the day of our birth."

He didn't reply. He didn't have to; the moon lit his face for a mother to see.

"Cassidy, how would you know? Tell me."

"I have them, Shakkra. I possess the Twelve Scripture, though I haven't yet read them. Today, when you walked with Aayla, and yesterday, I went to Tombolina. Mother, I possess the Ancestral Tomes and the Twelve Scriptures. Not long ago I hid them at my tree. I possess them. I've been to his home. I've been inside. He has a library filled with books. I've spent two nights reading The Grand

Guardian's secret diary. That's how I knew where to look. Now they're hidden at my tree."

She embraced him.

"What you're doing is dangerous."

"No one will know. Not even Aayla's father is allowed on Tombolina."

Shakkra snorted. "He's not a young woman learning to couple, or a lonely one who desires a strong man to comfort her. That's why I understand Aayla. Your father, the night before we were joined, brought me to the forest at the edge of the beach where we stayed until morning. We wanted to know that you would be his. That night wasn't our first. That's what Aayla wants, sweetheart. She wants her son to be yours." She kissed cheek. "I haven't called you that since you were a baby in my arms. I couldn't. You were too young to know what not to say."

"Now I do."

She beamed. "Yes, sweetheart, you do."

"I can't let her distract me. What I've read, mother, I'll tell you one day soon. The Grand Guardian wasn't a good man. But he left here many times, and now so will his eldest son who's replacing him. And each time he's gone with his first-mate I'll learn more."

"Is your tree the same tree treasured by your father?"

"Yes."

"Will you show me where the chest is buried, under the tree?"

"No, I won't. My father left me to care for you, to protect you. That's what I'll do. I'm no longer too young. I'm old enough to join with someone I don't love and give her a child." He paused. "I'm old enough to protect my mother. I won't fail my father, Shakkra. I won't."

"And I won't lose my son, Cassidy. I'd rather leap from the highest peak. And I will."

"I've been to the highest peak, mother." He kissed her

lips lightly and hugged her. "None of this earth created the world, Shakkra; I've seen the entire sea and all of Tombola."

She clasped his cheeks in her hands. "I will leap from that cliff, if anything happens to you."

"And I'll be one step behind you, without regret."

He swept her up with a roguish laughter in his voice and carried her into deeper water.

"You are your father. Put me down."

"Believe in me, mother. Keep Aayla from my sight until I finish what I must do. I love her. But I feel inside that I can't trust her tongue not to betray what we know." He pushed Shakkra playfully backward into the water. "And, mother, one day soon I will give my consent when you approach me for approval of your prospective and strong husband... when we're gone from this place, you, Aayla and me. The four of us will be married together. We'll be a family. And now you must go and wait for me at the shore."

"Why, Cassidy? We have so much to discuss."

"Go, mother. I must make myself ill for tomorrow. I can't possibly read all that I must in the four nights that remain before they return to this island. The writing is by hand and is sometimes difficult to understand. I'll spend tomorrow in my tree and you won't worry for me. I'll be fine. My heart is strong, for you and for Aayla. Before tonight, I didn't know what you knew as Zach's wife. Now that I do we must be cautious."

He took her hand and led her to shallow water. He kissed her and put his forehead to hers.

"We should never again speak together unless we are alone, Shakkra. No one here speaks the way we're speaking now and I don't want to see my beautiful mother stoned," he smirked, "while I sit tied to her side. As much as I loved and do love my father, I love you more, and we must live for that man we call Zach."

182

Shakkra walked to the shore. She waited, proud of her son and afraid for him. She slipped from her wet shield and into her evening tunic. She wouldn't abandon him. When he walked from the sea his stomach was bloated, His smile was weak. They went to their hearth where she fed him warm broth. She covered him in his bed with thin covers and lay by his side throughout the night.

Zach wasn't dead, she mused. He was alive in her son, reborn that night and no harm would come to him or she'd be the first to die.

Twenty-One

Cassidy awoke several times throughout the night in horrible pain, and each time Shakkra went outside to empty the pail and cover the vomit with earth. In the morning the pail was empty and clean. His body was cold with sweat, his every movement a torture. His hair was thick with the texture of kelp, his eyes red from a sleepless night.

They waited for the man to finish his breakfast and leave to cast his net before she fed Cassidy a bowl of warm fruit. While he ate she went to the Chief Counsellor to explain that her son wasn't well, believing he would go with her to her villa to see for himself. Instead he gave his consent, excusing her from a day of work in the fields to care for her son.

Aayla, however, wouldn't be left to wonder. When Shakkra left the fine house the young girl went with her, urging Shakkra to let her spend her day with Cassidy. Shakkra's response was firm. Cassidy was proud, she insisted. He wouldn't want the girl for whom he felt such deep emotion to see him unwell. He would be fine the next day, and soon they would have all the seventh high sun to play at the beach.

Aayla went to the fields disappointed, her heart somewhat lightened by Shakkra's promise to sit and talk with her at the blue water after the evening meal. Shakkra, for her part, was no less perturbed when she arrived at her home. When Cassidy heard the Chief Counsellor wouldn't be coming to see him, he eased from the bed dressed in a clean shield and went about stripping his bed of its soiled sheets for his mother to wash.

He promised to return for his midday meal, and again for his evening meal. He grinned. Then he would be well enough because of her fine cooking to swim across the mouth of the gorge while she sat with Aayla at the beach.

She wasn't amused. And she didn't pretend otherwise.

Twenty-Two

Cassidy took the book and his pocket watch from the chest. He climbed his tree anxious to discover, anxious for the night and to talk with Shakkra behind the low curtain and din of gently lapping waves. He fought the temptation to read what Charles Weatherbone penned when faced with his death so high above his wife's simple grave.

He inhaled a deep breath and opened the back cover. The script was unchanged by the passage of time.

*

1. The word of The Grand Guardian shall be decisive in all matters;
2. None shall dispute my word, nor that of any Grand Guardian who shall be my successor, nor speak ill of The Name lest they alone be banished from the Isle of Tombola;
3. All shall relinquish their physical past, possessions and want of all things material;
4. None shall practice any pagan worship or idolatry of past and intangible deities known to be false;
5. All shall embrace the traditions of the Isle of Tombola and seek guidance and comfort from me, The Grand Guardian, in all matters pertaining to life;
6. All shall embrace and partake of The Seven Feasts which shall commence at the last early sun of mid-season and last for seven suns, when;
7. All shall openly share affection with friends and

neighbours alike without jealousy, envy, hatred or ill-temperament, and;

8. One father shall be the father of all children without bias, and all fathers the father of each child, and;

9. Mothers shall not bring onto the Isle of Tombola any child imperfect in mind or in body for they shall be imperfect first-mates and bring eventual ruin to the island; nor shall the feeble or the frail suffer their misery, for I shall take them away and care for them;

10. None shall dispute the wisdom of my choice of first-mate for any of my flock to couple and be joined on the Eve of The Seven Feasts, nor decry my teaching of first-coupling at the sacred waters to those most timid and in need of me on that Eve in the year of her eighteenth birthday;

11. None shall dispute with any neighbour in the field or in the hearth, neither shall any be unkind towards any neighbour, first-mate or child, or do harm or cause injury to any person, or cause malice amongst my flock, neither shall any of my flock speak untruths or seek to bring about deception;

12. All shall toil equally in the field and in the blue water from the early sun to the late sun and for six of those suns, and on the seventh they shall take pleasure in the fruits of the land and of the hearth.

These Scriptures I have written and decree for you, those of the Isle of Tombola, so that you might prosper as one in harmony and peace.
*

William Weatherbone assigned July 15th, 1869 as the date to his first entry, though his father Charles had come to the island in 1860 and Wendell Parkens eighty-three years later. Cassidy knew each of the Twelve Scriptures by heart. He knew they mustn't be disobeyed. He also knew, as did

Zach, that they were written by a man and not some ancient guardian whose descendants were exalted beyond mere mortals. Now he knew that man was William Weatherbone.

When Jonathon Clayton set foot on the island, a small and empty village stood on Tombola. Away from the village was a hermit's shack. There was no guardian. He'd told his son Jacob of the old man who'd once implored Wendell Parkens to remain behind, and Jacob told Zach.

Cassidy glanced at the watch tied to his thong. He was excited, not at all preoccupied by his crime. He closed the book and looked past the tops of the trees surrounding and concealing him. He thought of his father. When he felt himself sufficiently composed, he began the first page.
*

Charles Weatherbone, née 1815.

I write these words not solely for my son William. I write them equally for his son and his son after him, boys I will never see grow into stout young men of enviable character.

We are here, all of us on this island, because of a desperate and generous man whom I knew for a very short while and by the hand of fate which brought us together. His name was Jameson Beachwood. The poor man's wife and daughter incurred irreversible smallpox in the year 1845 while travelling the many cities of Europe.

The mother was not yet forty. The daughter, her disconsolate father once confided in, early in our relationship, pined daily to return to her betrothed. To Beachwood's eventual dismay he and the girl's mother disregarded her pleas, not thinking their love for her selfish. Not long after, he left them buried in European soil and returned alone to Virginia to manage his affairs.

He lasted not one year before he abandoned his farm to the care of a good and thoughtful neighbour and came to this place which he intended would be his retirement with his adoring wife and the most favourite of their Negros. In fact, he became a recluse and remained on the island with a single Negro couple and a light-skinned Negress in the prime of her adolescence for whom he had long harboured particularly warm sentiments.

Still, he could not endure the loneliness of sleepless nights or the hardship of long days with naught to pass his time but the memory of his dear wife and daughter and the guilt that had taken dominion over him. He yearned to hear his daughter's sweet voice and to feel his wife's gentle touch once more.

He remained for nine years, visiting Virginia scarcely once each year so that he might attend to the well-being of his Negros and his young daughter. The woman required threads and buttons, wool and a new dress; the man, a thick pair of britches and new tools each year to replace the ones broken or dulled.

He returned with all that was needed by them, and more. For the man he brought a year's worth of ale and new boots, for himself an equal supply of patently fine scotch. For the woman he brought ribbons that she might wear in the evening and seeds to plant in her garden. For the girl he brought books and new dresses. His one diversion was teaching her, though, in truth, he taught all three.

In 1855, he could no longer bear to witness their loneliness surpassing his own. His Negros had become friends and his daughter a young woman of unquestionable appeal. I saw her on three occasions and, I do confess that, when first introduced she fully occupied my thoughts. I do not, however, confess any shame, for what man, who does not seek to deceive, does not imagine himself in amorous pursuit of a young and delightful woman? I daresay that even my now departed wife would condone my temporary distraction from her and forgive me.

Beachwood left his island and went with them to

Virginia. Once arrived, he bought them new clothes and went with the man and the woman to a church with his daughter, where he stood for the man to make their situation legal and binding in the eyes of God. He gave them their freedom in writing. He put them on a train and sent them north to much trusted friends with letters of introduction and sufficient monies with which to purchase a farm of their own.

To each one he gave a leather satchel, a gift he intended would surpass all others. In each were a Bible, a book of plain paper, a pen and a bottle of the finest India ink, for not only were they now free they could read and they could write as well as any other.

Those nine years were not wasted with their hands in the dirt.

When they were gone Beachwood divested himself of his farm and his land to the neighbour he deemed the most worthy and took his daughter away. She was, despite her formidable good looks, a Negress whose home could not remain in Virginia.

He went with her to Boston where together they spent a year and six months. He bought a fine home and gave her full title; he gave her his name, a certificate of birth and engaged the finest tutors to further her instruction so that she might be prepared for more formal education. He enrolled her in school and went to a physician to learn of his death.

He begged her forgiveness for leaving her alone in the world, though she had passed her majority and was a woman of strong character and enviable motives. She forbade him to die without her and for that reason I met her one night.

He engaged a courier to travel by sea to my farm in Charleston. The messenger spent the night as my guest. While he slept I read the letter once, twice and many more

190

times, thinking his employer quite mad. I had previously made his acquaintance on a single occasion and scarcely knew the man. In the morning we departed together, my dear wife believing a sick and dying friend from the days of my youth required of me to hear his confession.

Our meeting in Boston was informal. As we dined we spoke of abolition and secession and what we believed was to befall our beloved South, until the moment he deemed appropriate to explain his condition and his reasoning for the tombola: for him a matter of efficacy and fairness, for me a matter of complete disbelief.

When we were concluded he saw no purpose in detaining me further, denying me the honour of their company at dinner and the theatre the next day. Instead, we met with his lawyer and I took my leave of them by midday.

One month later he died. I went with him to Europe where I fulfilled my promise to him and attended personally to his interment. I laid him to rest in peace with his wife and their daughter, and felt certain he knew I had not disregarded his one request of me.

His daughter in Boston did not attend me and upon my return I forwarded to Miss Beachwood an invitation to join me for dinner, which she graciously accepted. She was a most fascinating and lovely young woman.

She thanked me for my kind consideration, disappointing me graciously. I invited her to become part of my family, to join us in Charleston. I felt I could do no less. Alas she had made Boston her home and I believed she would fare exceedingly well.

I returned to my home where I remained for one year to love my wife and manage my farm. I chose not to tell her the truth. She always believed my reason for crossing the ocean was to develop new interest in our crops, and not to bury a stranger. It is of course the true nature of men not to lament necessary untruths.

Two years later, early in the month of September of 1858, I took my leave of her once again, a similar voyage of commercial interest, I told her. Instead I came to this place, this wondrous isle with its majestic peak split in two where I now sit with my pen and my ink.

I had not more than the slightest assurance that I would not be abandoned here to die. I bade the captain a safe voyage to his home port, asking that he return in one week's time for his pay, were he able to extend his life by that many days. Amongst all the sailors I encountered and interviewed, he was the oldest by many years which served my suspicious nature well.

Seven days later I felt elated to once again see him and, of greater importance, I was decided in what I must do. I sailed with him to Georgia where I engaged a builder of wide reputation. I spent an entire week with the man, after which we came here with his son and a crew of five able bodies.

We spent the winter well-provisioned. By spring the village was built and Beachwood's great house was restructured to suit my particular needs and those of my family.

I returned home to my bed and my wife where I remained for a year and nine months, this lush paradise embedded in my mind. In December 1860, as was expected by all men of envious rank, South Carolina seceded, for many a boon, for many others their ruin. I went with good friends and good neighbours to a tavern not far where I bid them a furtive farewell, for in such times no man knows what truly dwells in the minds of his neighbour and friends.

Early the next morning I gathered my family and my Negros, each one willing, each one freely refusing my offer of freedom. The women we saw safely positioned in wagons, the men came with me.

Throughout the night, following my return, the stench of ale lingering on my breath, we filled our home and the huts of our Negros with hay from the barn. In the morning we dampened the hay with kerosene. We struck our matches to the top floor first, then to the main floor, the huts, the barn and finally my fields. I never once glanced back to see what destruction the first Union soldier would see. No vision could surpass what I saw in my mind.

The war began four months later and, to the greatest extent of my thinking, has never concluded. I sit here not faulting my wife, for I could never deny her. Yet I fear for the life of my sons and my daughter.

We journeyed to Jacksonville for ten days and nights at the mercy of uneven roads, meagre inns and pitiful food, our Negros left to sleep in the wagons or tucked into blankets on the hard ground.

Once arrived I commissioned a ship captained by a man whose name was Shaw. He was a man of contemptible character at first sight and not trustworthy to the smallest degree. His one saving grace was the proportions of his vessel, adequate for the conveyance of the many who were with me. For my family and my possessions I acquired another for my son to pilot, a capable young man whose reputation as a yachtsman was quite remarkable, as much the envy of his Charleston peers as the allure of many a young female eye.

The voyage through high and agitated winter seas lasted three long days and two dreadful nights, a memorable crossing by any measure and one I was content never to relive. When we arrived I leapt into the water without the cover of my shirt and swam to the shore in my britches and my boots, my Negros behind me.

My wife and daughter did not, as much as I attempted to taunt them. They thought me completely insane.

Twenty-Three

Cassidy reached for his watch. He tugged at a black ribbon and marked his place. He had much more to learn and so little time. He needed to clear his mind. He needed to think. The Ancestral Tomes were filling his mind and he couldn't do both.

He climbed to the ground. With his watch and the book safely concealed he hurried to his villa to see Shakkra lying on his bed, dressed in the tunic intended for work. She pulled back the covers and patted the mattress. He lay beside her and she covered him, her expression telling all.

"I promised, Shakkra, that I would return before him."

"You did not promise to make my heart stop beating."

"I am sorry."

She eased over him and brought him a bowl of soup. "What have you learned?"

"I would need 100 midday meals to tell you what I know. I have so much that is new in my head."

"Have you read the Twelve Scriptures?"

"Yes, I did this morning."

"Are they what we know?"

"Yes, Shakkra, but not one word is written of the Tombola Pole. And mother…"

He stopped at the sound of Shakkra's second-mate stepping onto the porch, grimacing. He finished his soup in silence, gave her the bowl and slid under the covers to feign sleeping away his illness and count the seconds.

"He is gone. Now tell me what he interrupted."

"The Twelve Scriptures, Shakkra, they were not written by an ancient guardian. They were written by a man whose name was William Weatherbone, the first son of a man who came to live on the island 150 years ago. He wrote them by hand on the back cover of the Ancestral Tomes which is a diary from what I have read so far, not ancient writings."

Shakkra listened to all that he'd learned.

"And now I must return to my place in the forest," he kissed her, "to learn more before my evening meal. Then I will go once again to the other place before we walk in the blue water where no one can hear."

"You frighten me."

"I am not afraid. I remember what Jon said to his son and Jacob to my father: Those who fear knowledge fear what they do not know and cannot see. I am seeing what they did not and I am learning what they never knew." He gave her a sly wink. "I will need a fine meal by the late sun if I am to feel well enough to swim with you under the high moon."

She let him go, as Zach would have wanted.

Again balanced on the tallest limb of his tree, the watch tied at his waist, Cassidy opened the book at the first black ribbon.

*

I daresay I was quite insane, albeit with joy. The Union would not destroy my lands already destroyed by my hand, nor would they benefit from its harvest or plunder my home previously ravaged by me and mine. My wife and my daughter were safely by my side, in a manner of speaking, and with us the full extent of my moveable resources.

I let the men and the children bathe and romp in the water. The females at first were more timid, uncertain of me, I would perforce suppose, though very soon after the dinghies were lowered to where we could grasp at the ropes

195

and guide them to shore.

I gave the men my fullest approval. Indeed I encouraged them, the lure of blue water too great to resist and soon all I could see were forty coloured heads afloat in the sea. Ebony heads and brown, their wide and excited eyes like cue balls travelling across a billiard table painted blue.

My wife, not always in agreement with my particular humour, arched an eyebrow and bade me go cool myself. She and my daughter, however, remained with their ankles and their shins cloaked in the familiar layers of Southern propriety. Captain Shaw remained onboard.

When I believed them sufficiently refreshed I clapped my hands, anxious to unload my cargo. We were equipped with food sufficient in quantity to last several weeks and medicaments for any emergency, the best of our wardrobes and gold sufficient in weight to buy 1000 such islands.

The guns, the whisky and cigars were last to leave my ship, taken by me and my sons alone.

At the beach I spread my arms and welcomed them home. They looked this way and that, my wife no exception while I sat in the sand, each one thinking himself marooned in an endless sea, my daughter on the verge of delirium, my wife's condition no less apparent. I leapt to my feet; sand glued to my britches and begged them to follow.

In the clearing was my home, less grand than the one burnt to the ground, yet superior in style and arrangement to the dreams of many I have known. In the distance stood ten huts of adequate proportion to accommodate my Negros in comfort, each with a shed equipped with tools for their gardens, tubs for their hygiene and large wooden barrels to capture clear water from the inverted roofs of those huts through spouts moulded from clay.

Much consideration was given to their construction. Nor did I neglect their private matters, each closet hidden from view between the rear of their huts and the edge of the forest.

That night I left them to become acquainted with their island and their new, superior lodgings while I dined with my family and the captain. When we were sufficiently satiated with food and fine wine the women, weary from travel and excitement, retired to their beds. My sons I sent to their rooms. One was too young, the other too curious. Truth be told, I saw in William certain characteristics which I deemed not entirely enviable or desirable in a man of his age and rank.

I walked with the captain to the gorge where his dinghy was anchored to the sand. He would sleep aboard and leave with the morning tide. I thanked him without unnecessary excess for his expedient service and gave him a bag of gold coins which he hefted in his hands without concern for my opinion of him.

I waited until the small craft was afloat and the captain was seated. He faced me and bid me farewell. I acknowledged his salute with a curt nod and a single bullet precisely delivered into the centre of his head, the sound of the explosion swallowed between the high walls of the gorge.

I retrieved my purse and hefted the weight. I tossed the pouch onto the sand. He had, in fact, done much of the work for me. What remained for me to accomplish would be much less difficult, or so I prayed. He was a stout man, thickly built and disagreeably unpleasant to the nose. I had not the slightest intention to haul the difficult weight upon my shoulders. I would let the steamship assist me in reclaiming its master.

Once hoisted to the deck I laid him to rest in the bilge. I could not imagine a more suitable berth. With him gone from my mind, I toured the ship and when I was done I went home to my wife.

The next morning, my stomach full, I strolled alone to

the shore with a shotgun and a box containing two dozen cartridges. The two ships were seemingly tied starboard to port. In fact, they were not. I waited with certain impatience for my son whose appetite was greater than mine. When he arrived he questioned the captain's delayed departure. I replied to William that, indeed, the captain had departed... to a place better suited to his disposition than this earth or mine.

Together we rowed to the smaller of the two vessels. William took command of mine while I made my way to the larger ship, using the ladder to climb onboard, leaving the dinghy to trail behind. My time spent from Jacksonville to the island was put to good use. I observed his every move and occasionally was permitted to take control of the wheel. That instruction, together with what I had learned while sailing with William in Charleston, served me well. If not a capable captain, I was certainly a sailor of some measure.

Some ten miles into the sea, I heard William's loud hail. I ceased all power and hurried to the bow to unleash the anchor. Nothing onboard was required by me to improve my quality of life, quite convinced that what I was leaving behind would ensure said quality.

I stuffed my ears with cotton and went to the lower deck to walk from the stem to the stern and into the bilge. Along my path I blasted into each side below the waterline twelve holes, each the diametre of a small plate. When I was done the ship's freeboard was much reduced and my descent into the dinghy was quickly done and well achieved.

Within the hour the ship was gone from sight, the captain with it. Not for one moment since has he occupied the slightest space in my mind.

The first year passed from one day to the next with a fresh appreciation for life. I often thought of Beachwood, who I once accompanied to Europe to bury his soul, and of his young Negress daughter residing in Boston. Because of her, I choose to believe, one night I summoned all my Negros together for reasons quite different from what any expected of me.

I had before me forty sheets of parchment on which I had previously and meticulously written the same inscription. To all the coloured men and their boys my youngest son gave cold ale, for all the coloured women and girls my daughter poured goblets of chilled wine. They were, I confess, quite taken aback by my actions. I made them all free with forty strokes of my pen and offered them, one by one, to convey them to the nearest Union port onboard my ship with sufficient money in their pockets to make their way.

The night was the most joyous of life. I shook each man's hand and embraced each woman and girl, handing each one in turn a simple scroll made of strong ribbon by my daughter. And when they were free, they refused me. The free choice was the first in their lives to make. From then we were equal in each other's eyes, though, truth be told, my eyes were the first to adjust clearly to our new situation.

In addition, from that night forward, a ledger was kept as an accurate account of their labours and the wages owed to them should they ever have a change of heart.

William was another matter. He was twenty and he felt the island was dulling his mind. He desired adventure, yet he was not well equipped, neither in mind nor in body to fight a war between neighbours who were each true to their beliefs. A concept, I daresay, quite foreign to William.

At the end of the first year he left, his course set for Cuba. He was gone for twelve months, ordered by me not to approach the American shores. He did not, to the best of my knowledge and returned laden with fine fabrics and lace for the women, whisky and cigars for the men who were now able to pay fairly for what they themselves desired. He brought a guitar, ukulele and mouth organ and books meant for leisurely reading and for learning.

In the year that followed my wife taught the coloured folk to read and to write. She was pleased to discover they possessed an inclination towards learning. As for William, he stayed with us for a year, content to remain on his yacht most nights in the seclusion of a deep channel not many paces from the gorge and along the windward shore in the direction of the northern tip of the island.

He left us behind in the spring of '63 and sailed once again to the island of Cuba where he remained a full year. He returned in the summer of '64 with the provisions we all required to live a decent life and news of a bloody war far from either side's decisive victory.

I had earlier expected that many of the older men would one day sooner than later meet their maker. Much to my surprise, we buried one. I believe without the slightest reservation that freedom and the occasional taste of ale made them stronger and more fit, for our fields grew more bountiful each year as did our population. We were now at sixty, each newly arrived duly documented and free.

William remained a restless few months, and how could I fault him. His brother and sister were children to him; his father was married to a woman endowed with ample good looks and the coloured folk were happy to sing and to dance at the end of each day or to sit with their mates by the ocean.

We knew he would soon leave us. And, soon, he did.

In point of fact, his voyage each year was important to our survival, though we could not and did not anticipate such an early departure. He set sail in the fall, much to his mother's dismay. To her delight he returned to her in June to tell her the North had brought an end to the war and to the life we had known in the South.

I assembled the coloured folk at the beach to tell them

the news, to give them a reason to leave. One man stood proud to remind me that he was no longer a slave. He was a free man, and he would stay where he was unless I would turn him away. I did not. Humbled by his forceful and simple words I was the one who turned and strode away.

William returned in the spring of '67 to a young woman who missed him and a daughter the colour of honey. That was her name and together we built them a home no better or worse than the others. At the end of the winter their second to arrive was the colour of caramel. That was her name and she was no less sweet. My wife was content; my daughter somewhat envious for my grip on her reigns was tighter than the ones tied to her other brother who was not far from his majority.

Since hearing of William's intended departure I endured their laments. Night after night we lay awake in our bed creating plausible explanations for why they could not and must not leave. Alas none was available to us either by logic or by our own creation. We were on the eve of our family's demise.

William fancied himself a worldly captain, when he was not, and I took him aside. He had not yet made his way in the world. He was a wanderer, a man of means not of his own labour and I harboured no doubt that he was more anxious to plant more seeds in the pretty Cuban fields he had come to admire than return to us with what we required.

He left with his sister and brother in the early winter of '68. The girl he would convey to a family known to us in Florida; she was never to return to Charleston where I have no doubt my name remained in question.

I sent with her a letter of introduction which she was to present in the company of her older brother, and a purse of gold which was her business alone. Our dream was to see her educated, to become a fine woman and return to us each year aboard my ship which my son had come to consider his own.

My youngest son left with a purse of equal weight. We believed, his mother and I that he might altogether miss the date on which he was to meet once again with his brother for their expected return. Not until several months later did we fully understand his eagerness to leave. I will never know her outcome, or his.

To see them standing onboard at the channel their mother wept openly. William's children knew no better and his young woman seemed to understand this was her lot in life.

Fifteen months later, missing her sons and with no news of her daughter, my wife closed her eyes one night and never awoke, neither her newest daughters nor I sufficient to sustain her. Her grave by the crystal pool is fresh, the flowers that adorn her not yet wilted from the hot island sun. And here I sit on the last day of June anxious to lay by her side.

I have left separate instructions for you, William, to ensure that our coloured friends will now have their complete freedom. In this you will not disappoint me, lest you atone most grievously when next we meet.

I was born, as were you, into the wealth of cotton and the disgrace of slavery. Each was equally natural to me, though never taken for granted. You, however, are quite different in that regard. You take your wealth for granted and grant your slaves nothing.

You shall therefore do this: You shall free them. You shall sail with them according to my wishes to a shore best suited to each one's future. They are, each one of them, compensated in full according to my estimated date of your earliest arrival. Further delay on your part will necessitate your goodwill for each day lost and according to our ledgers from your own pockets now filled with my gold.

Do not betray your mother's faith in you.

Do what you will with this island, once I am buried and lay by your mother's side without ceremony and without any marking to denote our final locality. Those arrangements are made. I shall be carried from here by a man of great courage, a man I respect, a man I came to know by virtue of another who taught me as though I was an ignorant child. I trust I shall meet Jameson Beachwood again soon, for I have much more to learn.

The wetness you see on these pages is the sorrow I feel for the loss of your mother and my joy in knowing she is now moments away from me. Do not infer anything more or anything less.

Written this day, June 30th, 1869 and signed by me, Charles Weatherbone, formerly of Charleston, South Carolina.

Twenty-Four

Cassidy closed the book and sat awhile longer, a dark thought persisting.

He believed Charles Weatherbone and Jameson Beachwood were good men, certain he would discover that William was not. Two chapters remained. Pages he could read at his leisure, not so what was left to discover in the home of The Grand Guardian.

One thing he knew: Jonathon Clayton arrived sixty-five years earlier and in that time he, his son and his grandson were all sat at the pole. And he, Cassidy, had learned nothing more recent than what he'd been bequeathed by means of the chest.

He could read and he could write, but to what advantage if he could eventually do neither. He glanced at his watch. Shakkra's second-mate would soon arrive from the fields and he promised her. His mind was so filled with swirling thoughts that he practically fell from the tree.

When he returned to the villa she had a bath ready for him to cleanse his body of his supposed day-long discomfort. On the edge was a clean shield which she'd once crafted from wool and stained a deep a deep crimson with field berries she'd gathered.

While other women wore the same shields for two workdays or more, and possessed not much more selection for the evening or the beach, Shakkra had many she'd crafted and dyed in the brightest colours and styles. They were the smallest and most intricate for daytime and evening, sleeping and swimming. Cassidy had as many, which set him apart, and Aayla, since Shakkra began to see the gleam in her eyes that was her son, was equally well fitted.

He stepped into the tub at the back of their home. Except for the coldest of days the village bathed outside. On the wettest they bathed in the rain or at the beach. Shakkra held out her hand, not willing to move.

He refused. She sat on the edge.

"You will ruin my good work. Your shield is not for swimming, and who wears a shield for bathing?"

"I have many more."

"I will call Aayla."

"No, you will not."

"She will come faster than a leaf in the wind, that mischievous little heart of yours."

"Mother, please, I do not feel well."

He clamped his stomach. Shakkra bolted upright, her smile gone. She reached for him, grabbed by her waist, her feet in the air, her evening tunic a layer of wet skin. She thrashed to no avail.

"I am your mother. Let me go now."

"No."

"I do not like this."

"But mother, I do."

"You have ruined my dress."

"Then take the thing off," he paused, not letting her go, "and we will call your fine mate."

She struggled. Then she gurgled. "Thank you. I will stay where I am."

He squeezed her gently. "Mother, meet me tonight, when the shadows are gone from the sand. Tonight we will not see the moon."

He kissed the back of her head. Then she was free to

clamber without help to the ground. She had nothing to say. She turned and pulled off her tunic. Wrapped in his towel she reached for his shield, smiled and left him to bathe. He would eat soaking wet, for what he'd done. She was a woman, as was Aayla. He'd learn one day, the poor boy.

Inside, Shakkra was dry and dressed in a shield the colour of a mango's bright flesh. When dinner was done she left right away. Aayla was waiting for her. Walking out she turned in the doorway for him to see her sad face and understand her worry.

He left soon after and made his way quickly. The sky was dark. He smelled rain in the air.

He ran and he swam. He ran again to the lagoon where he plunged into the channel almost losing his shield. He thrashed at the water with long, even strokes and bolted from the lagoon once his knees touched the sand.

At the house he slapped the sand from his feet and walked through the door. Again he was cold, traces of the hot humid air on his skin making him shiver.

In the library he wasted no time. He climbed to reach for Wendell Parkens' journal and sat in the chair to read.
*

What was written July 15th, 1869 was in the hand of William Weatherbone, sole master of his paradise the day he returned. He was twenty-nine and wrote of his destiny. His first words adequate proof to what great extent he was unequal to his father.

His sister's future was assured. She was enrolled in a school for young ladies, already an object of serious scrutiny amongst several young men of good breeding, men from scholarly roots and future captains of industry. His brother he left in Cuba with assurances to return one year hence to retrieve him or join with him in the pursuit of good and frivolous living, for their father had not been unkind in his final allowance to them. William never did see his brother again, though he did return frequently to Cuba.

What became of either twin is a matter of futile conjecture.

William would remain on the island, he decided. He felt no desire to commence a new life under the thumb of Northern oppression, servile to Union masters who had stolen his father's land. And theoretical abolition apart, his favourite was more black than white. She was a Negress, to him softly-coloured; to all others she was unequivocally black, or much worse. As were his daughters Honey and Caramel, and what would become of them?

White men of enviable rank would never think to contemplate wedlock with a woman of colour or mixed blood. Such women were distractions, the pretty ones at least, their offspring unfortunate occurrences. Where would they live? Where would they go? Even the purest abolitionist north of the Mason-Dixon was not that pure of heart, unless such God-fearing men of good conscience, William once wrote, left their hearts at home for a night of gentlemanly diversion.

At best his daughters, he believed, would begin and end their adulthood as favoured whores in the sophisticated brothels of Virginia, Charleston or Miami. In Cuba they would enjoy not the slightest difference or prestige in the quality of their natural make-up.

Before Charles concluded his life, he spent time with those who had become his friends. He gave each one, from the oldest to the youngest, a copy signed by him of their account and a handsome purse of gold so they would not fear the future. He remembered his short-lived friendship with Jameson Beachwood, content to have known the man and to have learned from him. He bade the village farewell and asked them not to worry. His son William would soon return to take them away.

He went to the man who once stood to declare his free

choice and took him aside. He beseeched the man who was his friend and equal. He was the man, the biggest and the most fit who would carry Charles from the precipice and place him into the ground without a single word of prayer, for none, Charles believed, could undo his wrongs.

In the months that followed William respected his father's wishes. He paid what was due the villagers from his own purse and conveyed the colony according to the lots they drew to the closest shore, though not everyone left the lush and plentiful isles.

His favourite remained behind with his daughters and, with them, a girl and a boy fathered by his brother and three women of passable good looks who, with no trust in their futures, let their men and children leave the island without them.

In the spring of 1870, his favourite gave him another mouth to feed; three others came to him by virtue of his wandering heart and his devotion to all the women. At the age of thirty William had fathered six children, all girls borne of different mothers not yet past their prime, and a niece and a nephew

In the autumn of that year, William took his leave of the island. He sailed his ship, once his father's, to Miami where he was largely unknown to search out four able men of colour or accepting of it. In addition he wanted a woman of his own kind and for his own purpose, a virgin not yet marked by the ravages of birth.

If he were to stay on the island, he could not do so by himself with no one to work the fields. Nor could he remain with four women and their children for soon, he knew, jealously would fester and his crops would fail.

The four men, not past their twentieth year, swore by all that was holy to take a woman unseen. In return he promised the men one thousand dollars apiece and paradise, an idyllic life, cultivated lands to harvest and a woman not unattractive. To further entice them he provided that, were they to experience a change of heart, he would return them to Miami with their pockets full. None of the four refused and he set them up comfortably at an inn whose primary colour of interest was green.

In the weeks that followed they provisioned the ship and were servile to his every wish. They came to know him, in accordance with his plan, as he came to know them. They shared four commonalties important to his need: two of the men were coloured, which the two others seemed not to mind, the four were handsome, down on their luck and their intelligence was well below what William considered a requisite quotient for any coherent thought.

On his own behalf, the woman he decided upon was of pale complexion with light-coloured hair, petite and delicate and recently arrived at the age of her majority. He was of the firm opinion that she met his need perfectly.

Her family had not recovered from the war. Their situation was quite destitute and for that reason the courtship was brief, by his account. The preamble was simple and unmistakeable. He paid her handsomely to spend a night in his bed, not unlike a common whore, so that he might see her naked, test her virginity, examine her beauty as well as her flaws and her apertures and experience his amiability or dislike towards her.

The former won out; though I daresay the girl had her parents' best interests deep in her heart as he invaded her as yet untested moisture, and not her selfish desire.

They wed that very week. To his wife he promised fidelity, a private island for her personal use, annual voyages across the West Indies and, in addition, he paid her family the weight of ten thousand dollars in gold: a king's ransom most certainly. Undoubtedly the young man was taken with her to the extent that logic and reasonable thought was beyond his then unsound mind.

The Feast of Tombola

William arrived home in June to his first son and three daughters recently born, undeniably of his seed, bringing with him a bride of legal age and four anxious men.

He summoned the four mothers of his children, assigning each one to a particular man according to her disposition. The men were anxious to see the women and to couple with them and he left them to their curiosities and devices. And with the women he sent his children, choosing to keep his first and second daughters, his niece and his son. The girls were the prettiest with pleasant characters which made them less burdensome.

Leaving his wife to attend the three girls and the boy, and to prepare his evening meal, he went out to meet with the men so that he might be certain of their contentment. They were very content and within a year four more newborns brought their numbers to twenty-two. One year later they were at twenty-six. Not twenty-seven or eight for they discovered William's wife had come to him in a barren state and would remain so. A year after they reached thirty.

The four men brought to the island unwed came for reasons William cared nothing about. More interested was he in the colour of their skin, for he wanted to achieve a balanced palette. One was a thief, one a failed carpetbagger who'd travelled south after the war in search of opportunity, finding hatred instead. Two others were wayfarers seeking adventure, men he believed would soon find themselves in a state of restlessness.

For that reason they went with him to Miami in the early summer of '74 so that they might take pleasure in whatever women's good looks and charms were worth what they were willing to allot to their purses. William's purpose was to recruit. For a good while his turbulent thoughts had been of the future. He wisely saw danger in men whose dull minds sought to wander, preoccupying his own mind with ways to dispel their restiveness.

210

As well, he went with another purpose in mind.

He returned his wife to her family. She was unwell and he feared her condition would worsen without the care of a doctor or the skill of a surgeon. That's what he explained and he paid them a generous sum so that she would not constitute a burden to them. Then he went in search of another female who would fill the void created by her absence.

She was eighteen, a waif he found begging for food on the street. Her person was dirty, her clothing soiled. However her eyes were clear, her teeth bright and her breath smelled clean. He took her to his room where he instructed her to bathe. He watched her disrobe and sink into the steaming water. Then he took his leave, returning not long after with boxes filled with undergarments, shoes, dresses, hats and bottles of perfume.

By that time she had not yet completed her bath. Neither had he been wrong by his account, unable to resist taking pleasure in her. He dried her; he combed her hair and directed her to the bed where he would verify his approval of her. He was educated in matters of the flesh and would easily discern a false yelp. She was, in fact, real. And upon hearing of the island, she gave herself over to him entirely in her body and in her mind.

They departed Miami one week later, William not seeing the need to pay a preacher for what he already possessed. With them went the two men, two others who were white, three who were not, their five wives and ten children.

Two of the men suffered from damage to their bodies caused by the war and could scarcely care for their families. They worked when they could. One wife was a laundry maid, the other toiled in a kitchen. A third man had stolen his brother's wife and worked in the stench of a livery stable to wash and clean up after horses he was unable to afford to ride or to rent. The woman, quite pleasant to the eye, served ale in a tavern for meagre gratuities, forbearing foul proposals from drunken men who sought to have her for an hour or less.

The fourth and fifth men had lost their piteous farms to the sadism of Union soldiers who'd burned their barns, their fields and their crops. That the Confederacy won out was of little solace to them, I daresay. They were land owners become slaves in their own right, destitute and defeated at seeing their women working the same fields as they.

The men were aged between mid-twenties and forty, the women some five years younger on average, the children between six and twelve and the prospect of an island life was impossible for them to deny or refuse. They came here willingly.

Now they were sixty and William Weatherbone was their leader. He was benevolent and caring. They lacked nothing and they trusted him. They went to him for counsel concerning all matters beyond their capabilities, for he had again chosen men of lesser intelligence and esteem than himself.

His paradise was not a place for thick britches and high boots, nor petticoats, long dresses and laced boots for the women. The island was lush, encircled by sand, the sea and drenched in hot sun. He and his false-wife, now a mother of two, left the others and voyaged to Cuba to see what they might do to alter the character of Tombola in keeping with a paradisiacal isle.

He had a dream, a vision long established in his mind. When they returned she stepped ashore dressed in a thin muslin dress daringly loose for the time, cinched at the waist with silver braid, and hemmed well above her knees: one dress for evening, one for the field. Her feet were bare. He wore muslin pantaloons belted with a gold-coloured cord.

The men complied quickly, the women not long after. The children wore flaps tied at the waist to cover their fronts and their backsides. Within a short while the oldest of them was oblivious to their casual state of undress.

Soon no one thought to feel shame.

He was becoming their guardian and to the children a mentor, though in 1876 they had reached eighty and he began to consider the wisdom of a code of law. The state of their contentedness also weighed heavily on his mind. In particular he worried about the men he once took with him to Florida. He saw how they leered at the women in the fields and at the beach, and knew the content of their distracted minds.

He saw in them mean spirits, causing William to suspect they might one day act upon their malice and disrupt village life. They envied his boat and his frequent voyages away from the island with his false-wife and often he would observe them standing at the gorge, facing toward his private stone passage.

One evening, not very long before dusk, he went to them, asking whether they might consider being his counsellors, which would require them to go with him in future travels away from the island. He saw by the guilt and the questioning in their eyes that they'd expected much worse of him.

Together all three traversed the gorge in his rowboat, passed through the arch and into his garden. He wanted to show them their magnificent island in its entirety as he did most every day and they ascended the steep slope, more eager with each step.

Once at the summit they gasped at seeing the setting sun, the spiny ridge of dark greens. What more heavenly place for men to die, one with his eyes fixed upon the leeward shore with its white sand and whiter foam lining the coast, the other spellbound by the silent, hectic collisions of endless rolling waves against the windward shore.

The next morning a distraught guardian discovered their bodies not far from the gorge. He'd seen them hurled from the high peak, and he struggled with how best to convey the terrible news to the men's families as he went to them with his false-wife so that she might help to console them. That evening he summoned every man, woman and child to admonish them, for none could read or write.

They must never cross the gorge or think to pass beyond the stone arch. Danger abounded on the small island after dark as the poor souls sadly discovered. Those men, he warned, went to a place they did not belong, a place of peril with no hope of escape. Any who followed would surely forfeit their lives, carried to the very top of the precipice by what lurked in the dark shadows and be flung into the sea, lest he be with him.

That evening he sent his false-wife to bed and went with the two women to his lagoon to bathe with them and comfort them with kind words, whisky and gentle touches, dissolving their fears. They were the first touched by The Grand Guardian and in the days that ensued he authored the Twelve Scriptures.

More children would be born and soon the oldest then fourteen would learn on their own what to do. In those scriptures he decreed that, upon reaching the age of eighteen, and midway through that year, the 30th day of June, on the first day of The Seven Feasts each child would couple and be joined with another not one year older and not younger by two.

Until such time none was allowed carnal knowledge. And none thought to disobey him.

The first Seven Feasts was five months away.

William's mind was increasingly troubled. He foresaw how the next generation might increase beyond his ability to care for them and, eighteen years after that he foresaw 500 souls or more. He would be well past eighty, if such was his destiny. His son, then five, was secretly learning to write, read and do numbers and would be past his midlife when chosen to take over the flock. Until such time they were all his children, schooled by him in matters of husbandry and left to romp by the sea and play when not in the gardens, learning to cook or to mend their homes.

They had no diversion beyond the beach, cleaning their work tunics and pantaloons as they bathed in the sea, the women less timid of what was impossible to disguise or conceal, learning to be unashamed of their visible breasts. They needed distraction, if he was to succeed.

During his next voyage he went not to Miami, rather to Virginia where he met a Chinese man of disputable character. While there he freely imbibed with his false-wife a tincture he first discovered in the genteel brothels of the West Indies years earlier. Her reaction to the drink that he told her was rum pleased him more each night. Unabashed was she, increasingly lewd at his slightest implication. He was certain that what would henceforth be called The Seven Feasts would be a success and make the village his devoted flock from the first day forward and for all time.

William returned home bringing with him cases of liquor, dates and figs. He brought another which he'd sealed with a lock which his false-wife knew nothing about. He went with her to his home where he prepared her a drink and gave her instructions to bathe and dress, adorn herself with fragrance and prepare the gifts she would share with the flock.

He went to his Twelve Scriptures. From that day forward she would be his first-mate.

When he was done they went together to summon the village from the fields. At the beach he beseeched them to hold out their cups and he filled them generously. His first-mate fed them with dates and with figs while he went to each one and filled their cups once again.

His decree was joyously received. He declared the big island would from that day forth be known as Tombola, the smaller island Tombolina, adding that they would all partake in a festive holiday lasting throughout seven days and seven nights.

On the first night, the young would couple and be joined as first-mates with plenty to eat from their gardens and plenty to drink. Neighbours would share affection openly with neighbours so that so that desire and covetousness might be dispelled and on the middle night one chosen from his flock would give of himself at the Tombola Pole and be revered by all, for Tombola was their island and all were equal in the eyes of The Grand Guardian.

No jealousy or envy would exist between neighbours in paradise, he proclaimed, for everything was shared and nothing was owned. Nor should they connote love beyond playfulness. He filled their cups once more, his first-mate following behind to offer each one a gift. When they were done they walked to the shore

William opened her tunic and let the muslin fall onto the sand where he stood to appraise her. She was naked, her single adornment a strip of soft leather which was the width of her hand and twice as long at her front and her back. He wore the same and together they walked into the sea beseeching the village to don their fine gifts and join them.

They did, slowly, hesitant despite being drunk from the tincture he hoped they would soon come to crave once each year. Drunkenness he would allow. He would give them full reign. He would never control them; never rebuke their lewd behaviour which he knew would take hold of them and bring them together as would the joining of their children.

In the morning the village awoke on the beach. Their

minds were unclear, their emotions uncertain. Men who were strangely agitated at seeing their wives' bared breasts in the open air gawked at the breasts and the bare buttocks of their neighbours. The women, flustered at seeing the state of the men, stayed as they were and searched for their muslin tunics to cover their nakedness.

William was gone with his first-mate, feeling content by what he'd witnessed. Soon, he knew, they would no longer wear their tunics to the beach. They would wear their leather strips instead.

For days after he spent his time walking the leeward shore of Tombolina, not searching for resolve, rather pondering his future and theirs because of what he would do. When he felt at peace with himself he erected the pole with the help of the men. He'd already killed two men and when the last day of June arrived he was ready, though none would be joined by virtue of their young age.

By midnight of the fourth night the young children were sleeping, their parents at the shore openly sharing affection with neighbours and friends as their older and soon-to-be joined children looked on with awe. He summoned them together for what they must do.

Once at the gorge he urged them to gather up a stones. He stood the young girls first by the pole, the boys he stood behind them. He placed the mothers and the fathers. The volley was poor; most missing their mark, prompting William to reach for another and hurl the last stone.

He'd chosen not the oldest, nor the youngest. He chose the most feeble, the man most drunk and not by the justice of any tombola.

When they were done he filled their cups and bade them go to the beach to sleep or share more affection with women who cared not at all that their breasts were bare or that their leather strips would eagerly be torn away by men who first sought the youngest and prettiest of them.

William waited until they were gone. He put the dead man onto his shoulder and carried him to the boat. At dawn he sailed to the north and dropped the corpse into the sea.

On the fifth and sixth nights he consoled the man's mate, on the seventh he gave her to another whose mate was not well and would soon be taken away so that she might be healed and brought back to him. She never returned, once claimed by the sea. Neither did the child with a crooked leg who went with her.

Soon the village forgot her, as they forgot the lame child and the others that followed: one year a man, one year a woman.

Twenty-Five

Cassidy sat stunned. The hour was growing late, darkness was encroaching and he knew his mother would soon be at the shore, feeling nervous, yet he couldn't bring himself to leave. He stood and went to lean over the lamp. He put his hand under the shade and pinched the small knob. He knew of them from Jonathon's encyclopaedia, though never before in his intrusions had he touched one or thought to experiment with light.

The glow was instantly as bright as the sun. Beyond the windows all was instantly black. He felt the heat on his face, the unfamiliar pain burning his fingertips. He sucked in his breath, willing himself to conquer his fear. He knew no one would see and he had so much more to read.

Shakkra would understand. Besides, he justified, she'd rather be with Aayla at the beach than with her second-mate at their hearth.

*

Each year William's niece grew lovelier, as he watched his son grow into a young man. In 1887 she was of age. He was sixteen, an accomplished yachtsman and compulsive reader.

On the thirtieth of June William's first-mate, now thirty-one, lay in her bed unwell. He lay on the warm sand of his lagoon with his niece and three others who would be joined that evening, teaching them what they should expect when he would send them to couple with their chosen first-mates at the beach before their festive joining.

When his teaching was done, the three girls then ready, he sent them away dressed in gaily coloured tunics and stayed with his niece to make her his own.

On the fourth night, he brought his first-mate to the pole and made her comfortable in the sand. Her eyes were cast down, her skin trembling from the damp air. He held the cup to her lips and helped her to drink. He tucked potent figs into her cheeks and left her to summon his flock from the beach. When they were assembled, their spirits high, a hail of stones sailed through the air, not all of them finding their mark. He hurled the last, the killing stone, ending his dolour and in the morning when the waters receded he freed her and carried her to his yacht in a wagon especially crafted for that purpose. The distance between the gorge and his dockage was becoming increasingly difficult to manage on his own.

He sailed north and gave her once again to the sea.

In the two years that followed his second-mate, who'd once been his niece, gave him two sons whom he adored. He left her immediately following The Seven Feasts of 1890 and took nineteen-year-old Horatio with him, so that he might begin to prepare the boy for leadership away from the influences of his daily life.

He did not intend that his son would remain with a woman beneath his station. The first-mate of The Grand Guardian would forever been seen by all as exalted. For that reason alone he had nurtured his niece throughout all the years of her life.

Horatio, fully endowed with good manners, gentlemanly comportment and language taught by his father, sat by William's side in Virginia as an equal for the first time.

Knowing his son was accustomed to unclothed females, William watched Horatio approach his nightly diversion with measured enthusiasm, seeing that his son did not like the whores as much as the island women for their scents were oppressive, their skin excessively pallid and their clothing too awkward to manoeuvre. Yet he was as white, despite his skin made ruddy by the sun, for his mother was of mixed blood and his high collar, vest and jacket were no less uncomfortable to him.

He was, however, unfamiliar with the fumes and taste of Cuban cigars and made no attempt to conceal his disgust. His familiarity with the tincture was of recent origin. His first taste was the day of his joining with Ophelia one year earlier and throughout week that ensued, his second the week recently concluded.

He knew to beware, for liquor was a source of vile self-loathing and incurable malaise, not so the calming effect of fine cognac which made the whore of his choosing no less tolerable. He made use of the same one each night, paying her well to sit fully clothed and without saying a word, lest his father also make use of her and discover his trickery.

Yet William Weatherbone was determined to know, his judgement confirmed by week's end. Horatio would not return home. Instead he accompanied his father who established him in a small and comfortable room whose landlady was anxious for a young and genteel guest. William returned to the island without his son, leaving Horatio to embrace an era of new enlightenment, cautioning the young man that nowhere on earth did such a place as Tombola exist.

He arrived home aboard a new and finely crafted steam yacht, constructed of the finest wood and fitted with the most modern conveniences. He would not see his son for twelve months. Nor would Horatio ever again see his first-mate, though he was unaware of her destiny and sought gentlemanly pleasures frequently throughout his first term of private tutelage that would prepare him for a higher education to come.

On June 30th the following year five boys stood at the

leeward shore. Five girls stood before The Grand Guardian who was cloaked in a white robe of fine cotton trimmed with gold braid. His hair was bleached white and, against his darkly tanned skin, he appeared not unlike a mythical god.

He gave them each their first cup and drank with them. He took away their simple tunics and walked with them to his lagoon where he watched them bathe as he told them what they should expect. None of the five was afraid. They remembered what they'd seen in years past and had played with the boys since their youth, gaily and carefree in the sea and on the sand. Still, they were untried and each went to him willingly to learn.

When they were cleansed by him he watched them dress in new tunics of different colours and sent them to the five boys, each one wearing a robe whose colour would tell the girls who The Grand Guardian had chosen for them.

By morning what remained of the first taste of tincture was unpleasant, their minds fogged, their eyes reluctant to open. They were of age, their union and first lesson forgotten. They lay naked at the shore, their parents, neighbours and friends dancing and singing around them and soon the celebration was in the fourth day.

The Grand Guardian took aside the young mother of Horatio's first child late in the day and lay with her in the shallow waters of his lagoon, warmed by the sun. He offered her refreshment and they drank together. He spoke of his son, the next Grand Guardian and she was so proud.

They spoke of The Seven Feasts, his strong drink unspoiled by the tincture in hers, the very opium the others had drunk for four days and three nights. She, more than they, would be soothed by the welcomed euphoria for she was the one chosen. He gave her more drink and walked with her into deeper water where he undressed her and gave her comfort.

She gave her affection with pleasure, for she did not know jealously or envy and he was The Grand Guardian who loved her no less than he did his own son. He fed her with figs and dates, recently prepared. He gave her more drink and soon deemed her ready.

He left her undressed. He carried her to the arch and through to the gorge. He traversed the low water, keeping her warm flesh dry and laid her in the damp sand on a blanket at the pole where then 101 torches stood flickering and 101 stones no smaller than his fist lay in a heap. He placed a potent date in each of her cheeks and left her to the invading darkness.

At the shore the evening air was humid and hot. Some were dancing and singing, others splashed in the sea and others lay in the sand to watch or be seen. He loved them and yearned for their happiness. He went to them and refilled their cups, giving them more dates and figs. He called them his children and told them to gather round him.

They were drunk from good times, insensate with happiness and affection for each other. He spoke over their singing, and looked past their dancing. Yet they were in danger of losing that happiness, the love they now felt, and Ophelia wanted all to know that she felt such affection for them as the sisters and brothers they were. She was waiting for them; she knew she would always be with them in their hearts. She was ready to leave them, to give of herself so that they might be saved.

The Grand Guardian held his cup high and drank deeply. They all did the same and went with him to the gorge. He was chanting, and they chanted. He leapt to the right and to the left, and they leapt. He led them to the very edge of what they knew, the gateway to what they all feared, yet they followed to see Ophelia tied to the pole, her legs covered by water, her eyes glazed, her hair hanging in thick strands across her naked shoulders and breasts.

He went to her and kissed her. She saw nothing, he presumed as he stepped back to signal with his arm. The first stone struck her chest, ninety-nine followed, the revellers gleefully prancing into the air, praising her, thanking her amidst gruesome shadows dancing on the stone walls. William's stone was the last and the truest. He would see none of his flock suffer.

In the morning he waited alone for the sea to uncover Ophelia as the others danced, swam or shared one another with abandon on the beach. He took her upon his shoulder to the cart and brought her to his yacht. From Tombolina he cruised past the northern tip where he would not be seen. Of greater importance: she was gone from him and his son.

Three days later the effects of poisoned blood began fading and no one remembered what they had done. No one but William who thought the girl irksome, mischievous and ill-suited to stand by Horatio whose destiny was to rule. Within a few days William sailed to the coast of Virginia. From the harbour he travelled inland by coach to meet with his son, believing they would return together to Tombola for what remained of the summer.

Horatio was grief-stricken at hearing the news of Ophelia. He listened to what his father calmly recounted of Ophelia's eagerness to share her affections so freely to the men of the village during the first nights of The Seven Feasts, knowing full-well how deeply his son adored her. And that she gave of herself no less freely when chosen to sit at the pole so that the island might continue to flourish and be strong. He did not hear how his father had taken her to the lagoon to fornicate with his young wife before he carried her to her death naked and drunk.

Images of her broken body and torn flesh sitting in the shallow water with her hands bound ransacked Horatio's mind. He asked whether Ophelia was dead before the flood waters covered her over, and William said yes. The

Tombola Pole was not a symbol of violence or cruelty, her life was given for the greater good and Ophelia understood the importance of her sacrifice.

Horatio at once and vehemently refused his father's choice of replacement, despite the intended temporary nature of the union. He had in mind two others of much greater promise, not yet of age. And, again, Horatio refused.

William had no election but to acquiesce, despondently assuring his son that whatever girl he might choose to betroth during his time away, or bring to the island as his first-mate, and hopefully of a tender age, would be accepted by him and by all. He, William, would attend personally to the girl's well-being should she arrive before his education was complete.

He asked simply that Horatio make his selection wisely, that the girl of his choosing be schooled and that she not demean their station by either her manner or her speech.

Horatio had spent many recent nights anxiously awaiting his father's arrival and news of his treasured isles. He longed to see Ophelia, dispelling images of her sharing affection with other men for she was attractive and would spend The Seven Feasts without him. Now hearing of her killing, he could not possibly return to the village without regarding them as maniacal murderers and deviant hedonists much worse than the ones of ancient Greece he'd studied.

William was dumbstruck, reminding Horatio of his obligation to return once each year during his summer recess, lest he forget his past and come to ignore his future. He feared that Horatio might never return to Tombola to one day rule and he urgently sought affirmation.

His son held fast to his decision. He would indeed return home, upon completion of his education which would last four more years. By then his crushed heart would be healed and, he hoped, he would be able to forgive his father.

He enquired of William as to whether he planned to continue with the stoning, William answered yes. He asked what the criterion truly was and William lied, contravening an all-important article of the Twelve Scriptures he once penned onto the rear cover of his father's journal.

He explained the selection was a matter of a random selection made by him in keeping with the name of the island which he chose to signify the manner in which Charles Weatherbone had come to inherit the islands years earlier from Jameson Beachwood: a simple tombola, the luck of the draw.

At that point Horatio made very clear to his father that further conversation would be difficult. He could not condone murder. Above all, what sane and sober man would receive news of his first-mate's death with any sentiment other than deep sorrow and loathing of the assailants? And that his father might believe otherwise was beyond words.

Horatio was decided. He stood to face William and bade him farewell. The men shook hands. He would return in four years' time, on the Eve of The Seven Feasts and not a day earlier, to once again partake of island life and with a woman of his choosing if that's what fate intended.

Horatio had no doubt he would return, whereas, in his heart, William did not believe his son. He returned to Tombola provisioned with personal comforts for himself and his niece and in the four years that followed he made regular voyages to different ports, avoiding Virginia and his son as the village continued to prosper and grow.

He was fifty-five when Horatio was twenty-four, who, good to his word, stood at the docks on June 20th, 1895 to solemnly greet his father as a man of good character and firm beliefs. No longer was he a child to be taught or guided.

Respected by his peers and educators alike, he had not

misspent his time courting potential brides, rather he strived to achieve the highest honours in his class, fulfilling the occasional gentlemanly need with the charms of a young widow whose own need was his money more than his devotion.

Throughout the four years she had never strayed to another, to the extent that he believed her and, when he took his leave of her, he treated her well.

Stored with his luggage were letters of presentation to the most prosperous banks in the States. With those letters, concealed more cautiously amongst the folds of his clothing, was a pistol.

He was an educated man; he had adapted to the fashion of the day and was accustomed to conversation with men of equal standing. How could he then submit to any man of mortal birth who placed himself above all others, whose name was The Grand Guardian and not father or William?

Were they to have crossed paths elsewhere, William would likely not have recognized his son. He was at first pleased, and then furious. His son stood alone and not with a woman on his arm, which he could abide for he had made his own provision for that circumstance. However, hearing from Horatio that he would not return to Tombola as a son by his father's side, rather as an equal aboard his own yacht, or that he would not return at all, was excessive.

Still, Horatio did not retreat.

Much had changed in his absence of five years. The world had changed. He would no longer be content to grow crops, pluck coconuts from treetops or spend leisurely hours frolicking in the sea. He would have his own ship, one previously chosen and awaiting him. Or he would remain in the States and regret that he would never again see his mother who William had given to another man many years earlier.

They departed the following week, each vessel well

provisioned. Each man stood at his respective helm miles apart. William was happy for the distance. He was pleased with his choice of mates for Horatio, the youngest and the prettiest of the island girls, secretly anxious to teach them and make them ready for his son.

Upon seeing the isle he once treasured, Horatio remembered his youth. He remembered his hours of learning while other boys worked in the fields or played. He remembered that he was different, that he knew what others did not. He remembered Ophelia, her body and her curious mind.

He arrived midday on the Eve of The Seven Feasts, docking alongside his father's vessel with ease. When they left Tombolina through the arch to row across the gorge and stroll to the beach, the village assembled to greet him. His mother wept, not expecting she would see such a great change, feeling humble beside him.

After their midday meal together, he went again to the beach where girls and boys played.

When he was younger, after his physical changes and before his departure, he thought nothing of seeing the girls and women, other boys and men unclothed by the sea, their nether parts covered by narrow strips of leather, the women and girls with their breasts uncovered. Now he felt embarrassed by seeing them, and for himself as he walked past them covered with a strip of leather not much wider than his cravat.

He knew by their descriptions which were the two women available to him. They were indeed beautiful, their tanned bodies toned from their daily travail and he asked them to walk with him.

They were Tora and Oona.

He asked each one to turn, and they did. He ran his hands over their breasts and closed his eyes. He clutched their buttocks and examined their bellies, neither one stained by the birth of a child. He looked into their thin strips of leather, ignoring their eyes; each was clean, well-groomed and untouched. He took them into the water and bathed with them, talking in a way that made them feel safe.

He asked each one whether she was fearful of not being chosen. They each were. He asked whether they were excited by the thought of coupling the next night. They each were. Then he asked what might happen on the fourth night, as though he might not know, when he did. The girl not chosen would sit at the pole. No further provision had been made for her.

He saw no need for further delay and coupled with each one as they lay on the beach, his embarrassment dissolved. To a sightless man they would be twins; he felt no difference in touching them or being touched by them.

That night he took Tora and Oona to his bed and on the second evening he declared them his own without ceremony. Upon seeing the rapid commencement of drunkenness and lewdness, the prelude to week-long incest and depravity he'd forgotten, he forbade them both to partake of the tincture and took them from the melee.

Early in the evening the women went to the leeward beach and waited until he came with his yacht to take them several miles out to sea. Neither had ever beheld such a breathtaking sight. Never had they seen the Isle of Tombola from afar and in the morning they saw the early sun rise over the precipices as never before.

They remained onboard seven nights and seven days. On the seventh day he swam with them to the shore, their tunics wrapped tightly in waxed paper, and sent them to their daily routine. Then he returned to his dock and went to his father who chose not to contain his displeasure.

The Seven Feasts gave meaning to their way of life, William insisted. He demanded to know why his son had taken the women away and Horatio responded that he intended no insult. The women were very much to his liking. He had lived a monastic life since learning of Ophelia's murder and merely sought to indulge himself. In addition to which he was not inclined towards sedation beyond the effect of his favoured cognac and did not intend to involve himself with those who did.

Nor would his first-mates give themselves as convenient vessels to be filled and possibly fertilized by drunken and crazed men in search of variation. Virginia had indeed changed him and the fault did not lie with him. He did not consider himself responsible for the predictable results of his father's initiative.

The once playful nights between neighbours and friends were now corrupt, borne of the need to disavow what they could not alter. Nor could he alter or forbid what was decreed by his father. And for that very reason neither would he partake or forgive. Nor would he openly dissent, and with that remark he left The Grand Guardian with much to ponder. They never spoke as father and son again. They met as the heir apparent and master at the behest of The Grand Guardian.

Over the next nine months Horatio tutored his first-mates in matters of the sea. He spoke to them of tides, which they had seen since their birth, never understanding the rise and fall. He spoke to them of piloting and taught them all facets of seamanship. He taught them numbers and taught them to read and to write. He spoke to them of Virginia and Charles Weatherbone. He showed them maps and charts, pointing to a speck in the ocean that was their home. He spoke to them of courage and beseeched them to trust him, for he would never do harm to them.

To Horatio they were one, without discernable distinction. He supposed that he loved them, not giving much thought to the matter, the larger part of his heart infused with Ophelia, despite his proclivity towards fornication with many and the one chosen in Virginia to routinely act as a good friend.

These girls were different. Where they went, they went together. When they slept, they slept together and when he instructed them in worldly matters, together they learned. He was with them always, for he knew that one day he would leave them and that, without his tutelage, their innocence would succumb to the malice of others.

They were beautiful and flawless and thus far his seed had not taken root in either, for which he was grateful for his carnal demands upon them were frequent and ardent. As they were weeks earlier, at the shore, past the beginning of autumn, the workday done, after he watched them slipping from their tunics and wondered what he must do with them.

Then without warning, he knew.

But winter was nigh without much change in climate. And Christmas, the purpose of which he had not known prior to his time spent in Virginia. Though the seas were more forbidding at year's end and he knew to wait for spring when the voyage would be less frightful to the women. Until then he savoured them and protected them.

In the early spring of 1896 William took his leave of the island once more on a voyage to the States with his niece who was just twenty-nine. Three days later Horatio also departed the island, taking the girls with him. He would never see his mother again, nor his father for many years.

From 1896 to 1906 more children coupled and joined, and with those couplings came another generation, more mouths to feed and more fields to till.

William, since his return ten years earlier, learning of his son's departure and soon realizing the theft of his gold, wrote not one word more about him, nor did he keep a journal of much else, forbidding the people of Tombola to speak his son's name. Until, in 1906, at the age of thirty-five, Horatio returned to the island alone on the third day of

July. The Seven Feasts was in its fourth day.

William was sixty-six and nothing had changed.

Horatio arrived at the island by night, approaching the craggy entrance of his father's docking channel shortly after dawn. Securing his finely outfitted yacht he waited inside the arch leading to the gorge, knowing his father would soon arrive for his morning bath in the crystal pool.

He suppressed his pleasure at surprising William to within a breath of his demise, as he had intended. Tombolina was forbidden to all but William's first-mate, who was his own brother's daughter, and those most beautiful whom he sought to comfort and came with him to the lagoon and not through the arch, and never without him by their side.

There was no elation, merely the silence of disbelief confronting disdain. Horatio asked his father without preamble how many had died in the ten years gone by. William responded by asking what fate had befallen the women kidnapped from his flock. Father and son walked together into the light and went to the pool where William, accustomed to obeisance, sat at Horatio's behest. He had no other election, for he felt consumed by danger. He knew in his heart why Horatio had come to stand over him.

Slavery, Horatio argued, was a blight long dead, a disgrace for future generations to read about and ask themselves why. Those who toiled the land across the gorge were slaves, each one persuaded from birth and by another more zealous and despotic to believe they were free. Yet they received no payment and enjoyed no freedom of movement, each woman raped once in her life and at her most tender moment.

William demanded that his son not concern himself with business he had no familiarity with. His people were content and well-fed, the women soothed by his comfort of them, the young girls honoured by his teaching of them.

Horatio asked in reply: What person, man or woman or child would be content to live one year in fear of not living another?

At that moment Horatio held the pistol in plain view. He had come for the sole purpose of giving reprieve to whichever poor soul was chosen to sit lashed to the pole and be stoned. That night, he, William Weatherbone, The Grand Guardian, would sit at the base of the Tombola Pole, his blood not infected in the slightest with opium, and give of himself with the fullest awareness of his cruelty. Not one other would give up their life so that he might rule supreme over piteous women and men whose spirits were broken.

William guffawed. His people would never permit his death. Horatio allowed the laugher,   for he knew better and without further preamble he shot his father once in each of his legs and made him a cripple. Then he bandaged the wounds so that the old man would not die before his time.

With William bound and muffled so that he would not cry out, and dragged beyond his sight, Horatio went to the dock and boarded his father's yacht. His search was extensive. He found guns and discovered the tincture that would satisfy the cravings and prolong the stupors of his father's minions throughout the night and into the next day. He found two wardrobes of fine clothes and with them he found the documents important to his present and future quests.

Onboard his own yacht he filled a large goblet with cognac and clad himself in the leather strip he once chose never to discard. He went to the pool, sinking in to soothe his body and mind, ignoring the whimpers nearby. When his body relaxed, warmed by the liquor and the sun, he poured another and strolled to the lagoon he remembered from his childhood where he once listened, read and learned, thankful that he did.

He swam through the channel to the ocean where he

remained until late in the day.

As the sun began to set he returned to his yacht and dressed. From William's yacht he carried the many cases by himself through the arch, placing them into the rowboat and crossing the gorge. He went to his mother's hearth, where he learned of her death, returning to his father's home to search his den for whatever might serve his purpose.

What he discovered was the voluminous tome first begun by his grandfather Charles and neglected by William throughout the ten years past. Horatio would very soon after take upon himself the task of writing the final passages into his father's journal.

In the bedroom he saw his father's first-mate asleep or unconscious in her bed between silken sheets. He left her undisturbed and continued to the beach where he shed his clothes not wanting to appear very different from the others; pleased the passage of time had not greatly altered his youthful physique.

At the shore he saw many splashing in the water, others lay amidst entangled limbs upon the sand while others slept, their soiled tunics flung in reckless patterns as far as the eye could see. Boys and girls a year from their time to couple and join watched from afar, giggling, prevented by decree of the Twelve Scriptures to do as their mothers and fathers were doing, lest they be punished by The Grand Guardian.

The girls were proud of their newly nubile bodies, the boys anxious for the year to pass quickly, as he was once anxious to couple with Ophelia. He knew what they must know, that once each year, and cloaked by the dark sea, they could pretend.

He wondered how they would endure beyond their pending expulsion from the island, content in his belief that Tombola was not their home, rather their prison under the sun surrounded by a sea they would never escape without his intervention.

He paid no further attention to the children, dispelling from his mind the sweet memories of times spent touching Ophelia under the water. He called upon those men not fornicating or dancing to assist him with the cases. Then he mingled with them to play and frolic as he filled their cups and gave the women instructions.

When the cups were drained he filled them again and he left.

When he returned the beach was strewn with tables in careless rows, covered with food. They were gorging themselves. He ate with them and gave each one more tincture to drink. When they were sufficiently drunk, he gave them another and left them once more. His intention was not to fornicate with naked young girls in front of their newly joined mates or, for that matter, their mothers. Such deviant thoughts were far from his single preoccupation.

He went to his father with calm assurance and sat with the man. He laid out the documents which William readily recognized, and his pen, instructing William to sign the transfer of deed. When William refused, Horatio nodded. With grim determination he put the barrel of his pistol against a trembling foot. He cocked the hammer and tilted his head as though posing a question and William knew all hope was lost.

Horatio Weatherbone was at that moment the most recent freeholder of the Isle of Tombola according to a document first signed by a dying man whose last wish was to lay with his wife and his daughter as witnessed by Charles Weatherbone.

He heaved the man who was no longer his father onto his shoulders in the low light, turning a full circle and telling him to gaze upon his precious Tombolina one last time. He carried William through the arch and across the gorge, ignoring the sea, kicking his way through the receding waters to the Tombola Pole where he dropped the man into the shallow depth and stripped him of his robe while ignoring the pleas.

When William was tied, his body naked, Horatio left him and went to gather The Grand Guardian's flock.

He gathered them together and thought to make them dress, though he did not for he wanted them not to think, or be distracted. Instead he incited them. The Grand Guardian himself awaited his children at the pole, he declared, wanting to give of himself so that they might endure. He loved them to such a great extent. And he, Horatio Weatherbone, who once came of age amongst them, and who was called upon by his father to return at this time of sacrifice and devotion, was their new guardian appointed by him who waited to behold them one last time.

Together they marched to the gorge, elated and drunk.

Horatio placed the youngest girls in front, dressed in their thin strips, and the boys he saw swimming with them in the sea, for their arms were not yet the strongest. He gave each one a stone. Behind them he placed the youngest and most intoxicated of their mothers and gave them each a stone until one hundred were counted and one was left for himself. He bade the children not to come closer, but to stand where they were.

They knew what they must do. Waiting for his arm to drop, fifty stones assailed the water, not one reaching the mark. Then the women, all of whom The Grand Guardian had swum with in the lagoon to comfort or teach, stood where they were to await Horatio's command.

Few stones found their mark. Then Horatio stood before his father, clutching his stone loosely and without malice.

He was uncertain whether William could see him through eyes glued together with thick tears. Or hear him over the cacophony of the drunken cheers of those who once were in awe of him, who once praised and adored him, who now abandoned him to frolic naked in the sea.

Horatio watched them leave, believing William's punishment insufficient. He bid his father farewell with a smirk and dropped the killing stone into the water.

He stood throughout the night in the arch as the tide water rose high in the gorge and subsided with appropriate indifference as the sun lazily illuminated the horizon.

Then he knew Ophelia was avenged and he left William where he lay, twisted and washed by the sea, if not cleansed.

Twenty-Six

Cassidy closed the book and placed it in the middle of the desk, rubbing his eyes strained by the script as much as the glare from the lamp. He stood, replaced the chair and went to a ladder, climbing to the midway point. The names of the authors meant nothing to him; he was looking for what he did know.

He wanted to learn about what else he'd seen in the house. He wanted to know what all those things were. He wondered whether Dakota knew. He must. He wanted an encyclopaedia of a recent date and novels more recent than those left by Jonathon Clayton. He wanted magazines so that his mother could see beautiful women in beautiful clothes. Then how would he fill those empty spaces. One book might be lost amongst so many, not the armful he wanted. He'd find a way.

Three nights remained. He would need two full nights just to finish what Wendell Parkens had written, another to read what was left of the Ancestral Tomes. Aayla would give him no peace on the afternoon of the Sunday afternoon. She'd give him no choice. He'd have to stay with her at the sea.

He hadn't thought of her much since they last slept on the beach. At that moment he did and he smiled. The Grand Guardian left the island with his wife several times each year and Aayla's father always knew the times in advance.

He replaced the journal. He put out the light and left once his eyes adjusted to the dark.

There was no moon. The sea appeared black. Shakkra was barely visibly where she sat in the colourless sand by the trees, her knees tucked into her chest. He held out his hand and helped her to her feet. He kissed her and when she went to remove her tunic he stopped her.

"The water's too dark for us to stand or swim tonight, mother." He took her hand. "Come with me. And don't be afraid."

"And where are you thinking to take me, my brave son?"

"To paradise, Shakkra," he answered matter-of-factly, "to Tombolina."

She recoiled, held in his grip.

"Let me take you to where my father has taken me. The water's low and I can tell you all that I know." He urged her with a wide smile. "Come. We'll swim in The Grand Guardian's Sacred Pond."

"I was in that water once before, Cassidy. I saw nothing sacred in the water. What I saw were girls dizzy with tincture, an old man and a lewd woman who has memories the girls can't share. I do, Zach and I knew to limit the tincture. The memory is buried deep in my mind where I wish it to stay." She snorted. "By your calculation he was then eighty-three, which doesn't make me want to remember more than I do."

"I'm sorry. I wasn't thinking. I'll take you to his crystal pool. The water's clear and warm. It's like standing in a bath as deep as your shoulders. Come, Shakkra. I have so much to tell you."

She glanced behind her for no reason. She took a deep breath and squeezed his hand. At the mouth of the gorge he swept her into his arms and carried her across the waist-deep water, not that he had to. He wanted to allay her apprehension. They walked along the ridge where the sea met the sand, to cover their footfalls and soon he guided her to the right where he swept away the branches overhanging the inlet.

They waded along the channel and across the lagoon; they walked across the lush garden to the pool. He went in first and waited quietly for her to join him. Shakkra pulled away her tunic and eased into warm water, her feet barely touching the bottom as the gentle ripples tickled her lips.

She whispered. "I don't like this."

"I won't let you drown. Who would feed me?"

"How can we talk when I'm standing on my toes?"

"You look like a siren of the sea fanning your arms."

"I hope you mean a gorgeous siren of the sea."

"I do, Shakkra, and one day very soon you'll swim freely and lure a man of your choosing with your soft voice."

"I'm doing that now, sweetheart, on my toes."

"I said a man, not a son who dreams of a wife as stunning as his mother."

"Your father is alive in you. I was never angry with him for very long."

"Anger isn't allowed."

"Neither is lovemaking one week before an old man pushes himself into you. And why are you higher in the water than me?"

"I'm sitting on the ledge."

"Is the ledge big enough for two?"

"No."

She splashed hectic water into his face, pushed herself forward and clung to his neck, pulling him towards her. When he surfaced she was sitting with the water at her shoulders.

"Now tell me how you will take me from here."

"I don't know. What I do know is that each time they

leave together; I'll come here and learn more. The first Grand Guardian, mother, wasn't a good man and I've learned more of the Tombola Pole. The first Grand Guardian killed his son's first-mate at the pole because she was too curious and not worthy enough. Then the son, many years later, killed his father because he knew his father was insane. He knew what was happening here. And, mother," he smirked, Charles Weatherbone and his wife are buried right here by the pool. Their ghosts are swimming with us."

She leapt to her feet, taking a fountain of water with her. "That's not funny."

He took her hand and made her sit.

"I think they're the only ones, mother. All others are taken out to sea when we sleep and given to the fish. Think, Shakkra. Have you once seen a tombstone or even a wooden cross? Did you see my father buried?"

"No, I didn't."

"Because he wasn't, there is no grave. And the sick children or feeble old women and men, they're not taken to be cared for. They're taken to a deeper part of the sea where the tidewater won't return them. I won't let that happen to you, Shakkra, if I must kill him first. And the drinks at The Seven Feasts aren't wine or liquor. In fact they're both, but in them he puts opium."

She squeezed to the side to make room for him.

"Cassidy, do nothing to bring harm to yourself. Anyone who can do such a thing is not well."

"It's too late. I can't make myself forget what I know."

Cassidy took almost two hours to recount all that he knew in detail.

"I'm afraid. If any of the others discover what we're doing they'll betray you. Our strength comes from having known your father. The others come from the seeds of simple men and none on the island are truly aware of what man is their father."

"I am."

"I went with your father each night for a week before the old man brought me here with the others." Her smile was dreamy. "In the sea and in the forest," she giggled, "because he didn't like the sand. Yes, Cassidy, you're my son as Zach was Jacob's. It's what Jonathon wrote in his letters. He didn't want his lineage soiled."

"Don't be afraid for me, or of them. They won't know. I'm very careful. You'll know everything I learn and we'll be ready together."

"And what of Aayla, will your heart beat without her?"

"Will yours beat without either of us? She'll come with us. Together she and I will find you a man you'll love as much as my father."

His mind wandered.

"What are you thinking?"

He grinned, pointing to the house.

"In there, on my first night, I saw a magazine for women. I saw pictures of women in fine clothes and what they wore under their clothes. I was thinking of you dressed in those clothes and how happily a man would undress you, of how jealous I will be of him."

"No one will undress me except your father in my dreams until I'm ready. So please put those pictures from your mind." Shakkra paused. "And now what fills your young head?"

"It will happen, I swear. For now, mother, I've told you enough." He smirked. "You're not as young as you once were and you won't remember all that I have to tell you. I won't confuse you, old one. Give me your hand. Let me help my aging parent onto the grass."

Shakkra nodded dolefully in agreement. Then she shoved him from the ledge, leaping onto his back and his shoulders, forcing his head under the water. When she was satisfied that he was sufficiently rebuked, she hugged him, swam to the edge and pulled herself onto the grassy edge to let the warm air dry her skin.

He climbed from the pool, ignoring the defeat and took her hand. He guided her to the lagoon and through the shallow water to the beach where they walked once more in the gentle surf, until at the gorge when he once again ignored her and carried her across the ebbing waters. At the beach by the village she left her tunic over her shoulders and they turned towards their villa.

Inside he went straight to his bed and counted. She went into her room and changed into her night-shield, not the least uncertain. No man would tell another that his mate would rather sleep by her son's side than with him. In her mind, until she was free to choose for herself, she had only one man in her life and by the time Cassidy had counted to fifty he felt her weight behind him and felt the warm breath of her sigh at his ear.

"Take us away soon, your little heart and me...and find me another good man. I cannot sleep with my son forever."

She turned into the wall and fell asleep.

When he awoke his morning meal was on the table, the man had gone to the sea and Shakkra was dressed in her work tunic. The day had just begun and was stifling. The work would be hard and she promised to keep Aayla from him as long as she could after the evening meal. Mother and son would meet later that night, though she wouldn't see him before and he asked if she might bring him a sandwich and a clean shield for the beach.

He had a surprise for her. He would come to her by the early moon, when Aayla by then would be in her hearth pouting.

At noon, his stomach rebelling against its emptiness, his shield soaked from working in the sea he climbed the tree.
*

I was not aware, father, that you harboured such a low

estimation of me. And now you are gone, to my great regret, and with you my dear mother, my brother and my sister whom I shall never see again. Had I known, I would have shot you myself. Or, at the very least, I might have seen you hanged for the murder of our long-forgotten Captain Shaw. Farewell to the both of you, my loving father and mother and thank you for sparing me the discomfort of seeing your disgust of me.

I doubt whether we shall meet one another again, as I am already in heaven and you most assuredly are not. Nor shall you be greatly missed. No one survives to know you are dead, other than a handful of mournful souls whose burden and expense you bequeathed me?

William Weatherbone, July 15, 1869

*

I offer no plausible or valid explanation as to why I sit here today atop this precipice well above your grave to pen this addendum to a notation written by me so many years in my past.

To remember where I last placed this tome, forgotten by me lo these many years, was a matter of some deliberation and I debated at length with myself the rational extent of the need when what is done is done.

Therefore I must determine that I write what I do not for me, that in fact I write these few words for you my dead father.

The sun is not bright, the sky is ominous and the winds from all quarters are aggressive at my back. Perhaps the dark mood which is conducive to my current thinking serves as my catalyst.

I know now, father, these twenty-seven years after your death, how a man suffers to have his heart pierced by the treachery of cruel disappointment inflicted by a son, if not the bullet from his own pistol. And for his treachery toward me, I will never think to bequeath to him my Isle of

Tombola or the bars of gold which he has not already made his own.

He, Horatio Weatherbone, is no longer my son and what I now choose to write I do so for my own assuagement of his thankless heart.

Farewell once more from me, William Weatherbone, The Grand Guardian of the Isle of Tombola, April 1896
*

William Weatherbone, née 1840.

My sister I left with family friends in good social standing who, by coincidence, had a son and nephew both of marriageable age, each man unmistakably taken with her charms. Each one, in fact, and before my departure with her twin, declared himself an ardent suitor.

Her twin, my brother, I left in Cuba to discover of his own accord his particular devices and notable vices which, he disclosed to me during our voyage, he had begun to perfect several months prior to his departure with me from this island.

I was of the considered opinion that he would fair quite well, were he to discover, sooner rather than later, the distinction between the sweet smell of a clean woman's sluice and the stench of a whore's gutter. And sincerely I wished them both well, as much as I felt little or no need to see either of them again.

Over the first several months I did my father's bidding and conveyed his Negros whom he believed were his friends to the United States of America, his homeland where a wrongful war overnight made free white men into slaves of the North and black slaves into free men of the South.

I decided that I must remain on this island. I had my father's gold and, as I discovered while delivering my sister into the care of others, the South would never again be free lest I change the colour of my skin to that of a Negro. Then what of my favourite whose colour, until her death, reminded me of fine brandy?

Better that my skin be black as molasses had I once considered a life together with her in my native South, or in the North. What magnanimous Yankee gentleman would ever think to tolerate a black woman dining by either one of his elbows, lest she be serving him from the kitchen or from under a finely set table? None, I daresay. And what of my girls, who would never be white and never be black, destined to remain Negresses in the minds of one colour and half-bred in the minds of the other? They would degrade to women of questionable calibre and be much sought after until the desire which is so fierce in the eyes of young men would become disgust in the eyes of all men.

The three remained with me, as did my niece whom I adored and my nephew. And three others who saw me as preferential to their futures with men of little or no ambition whose free money would soon be ill-spent. I was scarcely returned a week when each of the four women gave me a daughter. I was a man barely thirty years of age in possession of my own and twelve other mouths to feed.

If not for the work in the fields by my father's amiable Negros, until I took the last one away, I fear we would have confronted starvation and lost. The future was of great concern to me and gave me cause for the deepest reflection. Nor were my deliberations and worries founded on sustenance alone, for the women began slowly to contribute to the cultivation of my fields, albeit not entirely to my satisfaction. Despite my expectation of much more, I quelled my discontent with understanding.

My greatest concern was one of contentment, mine as well as theirs. I was unprepared in my mind and my body to till the land for no other purpose than the nourishment of four women whose then current allure would certainly fail them one day and disappoint me. And of my nephew and the seven girls, what was I to do with them one day? These were preoccupations I was not reared to entertain, let alone seek to determine a satisfactory resolve.

I much preferred the sea and very much desired not to endanger my love, neither of the sea nor the pleasant diversions available to me at various welcoming ports as a gentleman of discerning taste and obvious means. Yet how could I in good conscience leave my children and their mothers without my protection? I could not, and I deliberated into this late autumn in search of an adequate resolution to my quandary.

I sailed my ship to Miami, where after several weeks and due consideration of the many candidates, I elected the four most appropriate men. Two were the colour of charcoal, the others white-skinned, no less impoverished and in equal need of deliverance. Each was well-suited to my need.

None had yet reached his twenty-first year and each had sworn with their hands on the Bible to take a woman with their children unseen. To the whites I intended to give the palest of the four, most notably my favourite, firmly of the belief the two others would be no less pleased as not one of the women was intolerable to the eye.

I spoke to them of a paradise each was incapable of envisioning, the lush land and gardens laden with fruit, warm ocean waters and white sands so bright as to blind their eyes. Furthermore I promised each one a thousand dollars in gold, once we were sailed, and my assurance to return them should they renege once we were landed and upon gauging the women externally for themselves.

In the meantime I saw to their comfort at an inn while they followed my instructions each day to provision my ship and affect minor repairs without the slightest disagreement amongst them. The women left behind would be pleased by my selection and, for my part, I would no longer fear the jealousy that I believed would soon fester in their minds had I not acted with such alacrity to care for them.

The men I brought to them were young and handsome and strong, with minds not more developed than their own. I came to know the men well, content in my choice. My favourite, of course, would no longer be mine to enjoy. Though, in truth, she was more the mother of my then current children and was never intended by me as the sole object of my affection beyond a gentleman's need.

With that void in mind I devoted much of my time to enlisting a suitable woman of my own. Many were adequate; none were suitable until near the end of my sojourn when I came across a particular young woman.

Her family was in desperate straits and I considered her quite charming, if not somewhat timid. She was pale, not pallid, her skin perfectly clear unlike the many whom each day avoided the curative nature of the sun with wide-brimmed chapeaus and delicately laced umbrellas. Her hair was not quite red and not quite blonde. Her blue eyes appeared to occupy more space than necessary amidst a face as fragile and translucent as fine porcelain. She was petite and delicate, not frail.

She was recently arrived at her majority and, until I believed the moment propitious, I met with her formally.

Her family had not yet recovered from the war. The father and mother were desperate and I doubted whether any future prosperity was possible. However, nearing the date of my departure, I invited her to dinner and spoke with her not unkindly, rather pragmatically, my intentions explained simply yet frankly with little opportunity for misunderstanding. She would live well. She would travel across the West Indies, dress in the finest clothes and fabrics and drink the finest wines.

Our courtship, of necessity, would be brief, more a

matter of what she believed in her mind. Beyond which our marriage would take place without the slightest pretension in the few weeks that remained to us. As for her dowry, I suggested the excessively adequate sum of 10,000 dollars in gold for her father.

To her I gave 500 dollars, which she accepted upon her father's approval, and she came with me to my room. I undressed her and bed her with all the lamps lit to test her virginity and to see with my own eyes her beauty and flaws thus far hidden from casual regard. Her beauty spoke demurely for itself, her flaws, if any, were invisible to my eye. She was uneasy, despite my gentleness, never before stretched out before a man and prodded for the sake of determining her newness and our mutual contentedness.

In the morning, and each of the several that followed, I woke her with ardent attention. She remained with me, forgoing what I believed was unnecessary contrivance and we were wed the morning of our departure. She remained on the aft deck with sadness in her heart until she could no longer see the harbour. I left with a much lighter purse; much to her father's delight who I imagined would dine that evening in the company of his wife as a result of monies once mine.

I arrived home after two days and one night at sea. Gwyneth was paler than when I first undressed her, each of the four men eager as much as curious about the look, the smell and the feel of his woman, for none wanted to return to the dusty streets of Miami to rely on the unsure and meagre sympathies of strangers.

I instructed Gwyneth to remain onboard the boat and I took each man to his assigned woman and hut. None were displeased, despite infants wailing in the corners, though I was not wrong to anticipate a certain annoyance and hostility on the part of my favourite who by that time had become too accustomed to the finer amenities of my home.

I sent her away without my first two daughters, my niece and my first-born son. Still, she had her arms full.

I gave each man his time and strolled with my new bride along the beach, leaving my girls and son for a short while in the care of my precocious young niece. My wife was enchanted, splashing and kicking at the water, the hem of her dress soon soaked and stained with salt.

The dilemma was one I had never considered as my father's Negros were content with their short britches or skirts the women would often fashion into something not dissimilar by drawing the back of their hems into the front of their waists. I made a mental note and when we returned to the house I left her to take charge of her children and to cook me a substantial meal for I was famished after a day at the helm.

I met with the men to assess their mood. Each one was pleased and the sounds that travelled through the night air to my bedroom bore them out. I must believe the women were equally satisfied, my favourite in particular for how quickly she adapted to another.

In a year's time the gardens flourished all the more, as did the women. The subsequent year was no less fertile. We had food in abundance, and children. Sadly, we were two fewer in our number.

Each night throughout the two years, despite my best efforts, my wife refused to bring forth a child of her own. Most disturbing to my mind was that she gave not the slightest consideration to her predicament. I believe her unnatural lack of interest was intended to spite me. This in response to a malaise brought on by her lament of not having constant companionship of a female of equal standing, despite our several trips to Cuba and other West Indian isles when she delighted in being amongst others of similar rank.

One year later we were at thirty and her condition was

not improved. Alas, Gwyneth was not my primary concern.

The four men who came with me to the island had once told me their stories. At the time I was content to have a full pitcher of wine which helped me to disguise my lack of interest in their hard times. I was more interested in the colour of their skin. One Negro was a thief, which did not concern me for I had nothing for him to steal and he would have nowhere to escape. The other came from the North, foolishly seeking a better life. What he found was more of what he had left behind and in ample quantity for a dozen or more of his kind. The two others, white men of the South and maimed by the war, I found together looking for adventure, riches and women. Though I believed at the time they were seeking to escape whatever situation they chose not to confide in me.

They were restless in their manners and, I knew, in their minds. I saw malcontent and danger forming in their hearts and their thoughts. Their women began showing signs of wear, becoming less attentive to their needs, which made me all the more diligent in my regard of them. They were, in fact, the catalyst for my decision.

I brought them with me to Miami and left them for a week to reduce the value of their thousand dollars by whatever amount they believed a woman's mercantile attentions were worth. I, on the other hand, went with my wife to return her to her mother and father. I saw no point in continuing my ruse of endearment as she became increasingly abject in her treatment of me.

Her arrival, naturally, was unexpected and the man was ill-prepared to disguise his displeasure at having a married daughter returned to him, particularly one previously given away and discovered to be incomplete as regards a woman's primary function. We agreed on a sum equal to the original cost of my acquisition of her, plus one thousand more for my legal divestment of her. I daresay our memories of each other are equally poor.

Try as I might, my search for a suitable replacement was proving impossible and I had little choice each night other than to seek comfort in the welcoming arms of a whore. She was the youngest and the prettiest in the house and certainly no less timid with her body than in her valuation. Sadly she was a whore and I was in search of newness, which I discovered quite by accident as I was leaving the bordello late one evening.

Her name was Elise. I was at once taken by her name and her voice as I was by what I imagined of her person, though she could not have been more dishevelled. Her clothes were ragged, her face and hands soiled to where any true indication of her colour was a matter of supposition. Yet she had an undeniable quality that drew me to her. Her eyes were filled with hope, her teeth unspoiled, her breath intoxicating to me. She was begging me for money with which to buy a bowl of soup, though she did not appear the least bit malnourished and I found myself all the more fascinated.

My proposition was open and frank. She would accompany me to my hotel. She would bathe and we would find a suitable eatery. In the event she would enjoy my companionship I would pay her one thousand dollars for a night's worth of her. If not, I would pay her 100 and send her away well-fed.

In my room I instructed her to bathe and left her. I returned sometime after, my arms and my hands laden with undergarments, dresses and petticoats, shoes and hats and bottles of perfume. I found her reclined in the tub, delighted not to have ignored her pleas on the street corner. I sat on the bed and told her of my island, my ship and my predicament of loneliness.

I dropped ten gold coins into the water and told her to stand. She was mine in body and soul. I dried her and within the hour I had verified my approval of her. I was, and remain, a man of the flesh, well-versed in the behaviour of women. Her cries sounded real to me, her physical statement irrefutable. I watched her dress and when she was fed she came back to my room and was my constant companion as I continued to ensure the future of my island.

When I returned home Elise accompanied me, not yet a full month into her eighteenth year, albeit not as my wife for I possessed her already.

With us came the two men, then greatly refreshed. Five others I found on the street, two of whom were white, three of them Negros, all of them married and each of them fathers of two children. Two were casualties of war, still capable of work in the fields. The wife of one washed the soiled clothing of strangers; the other worked to prepare the daily nourishment for a family of means.

Another man had run to a new and better life with his brother's young wife, and paid for his treachery with the stench of horse dung in his nose and on his fingers each day, caring for horses he would never afford. His wife, a true beauty indeed, worked in a tavern and each day heard how men befouled with ale would pay her well for an hour's worth of devotion.

The other two were driven from their burnt out homes and fields, earning what little money they could by working another's fields with their wives by their sides. They agreed to life on my island as greedily as the others, some of them ten years younger than me, others ten years older.

I was generous towards them. They lacked nothing and came to me as children to a father when matters exceeded their capabilities as none was gifted with recognizable astuteness. They trusted my word and my leadership and took comfort in my protection of them.

Elise, by then a mother of two, was no less loving of me and, I discovered, was as enamoured of fine dresses and shoes when we travelled as she was disinclined to wear them at home. Often I would see her at the ocean, my private lagoon or my pool enjoying the warmth of the sun to its fullest and most pleasurable extent. The island she often complained was no place for petticoats, long dresses and laced boots. And how could the men bear to labour in their thick britches and high boots?

Her point was well taken. By 1876 our numbers had grown to eighty and the state of their contentedness was of deep concern to me. We travelled to Cuba with a particular purpose in mind and when we returned Elise stepped from my ship wearing not more than the thinnest of veils, a muslin dress unabashedly loose and cut to a length not longer than the midway point of her thighs. Cinched at the waist, the edges were braided with gold and her feet were bare. I was dressed in pantaloons of the same fabric, belted with hemp laced with gold thread.

The men of the island adopted the fashion without hesitation, the women not long after and soon they wore one tunic for work in the fields and another when all work was done. The children adapted well to flaps made from fine leather that gave modesty to their privates and their backs and again I was praised, though not by all, and I began to recognize the need for a code of law. The two men I had taken with me so that they might release their anxiety had soon relapsed into their previous state of restiveness.

I saw daily how they regarded the women in the fields and at the ocean where their tunics did little else beyond shading their bodies in some small part from the sun. I saw lasciviousness in the men's eyes and their minds. They were ill-intentioned and I worried that when I left the island their maliciousness might undo all the good I had done.

I went to them one night as the village prepared for sleep. I wanted to make them my advisors, a position which would give them cause to travel with me on several occasions. And, of course, I would pay them well. They were the first men to set foot on Tombolina, and the last. I saw in their eyes that they had suspected much worse of me and they quickly accepted. They rowed me across the gorge and walked with me through the arch, not believing their good fortune.

We climbed the precipice, each one far above me, for none had ever seen Tombola from the sky. Nor had many seen my isle from the sea, at once mesmerized by what they beheld and gleeful when hearing of my next voyage to Cuba where young women were known to give their charms freely and unabashedly.

They stood side by side, slapping each other's back. As one looked to the north, the other to the south, I shot each one in the back. They fell quietly forward and down.

At the gorge I waited for the tide to begin its retreat. I secured them to the small boat and rowed to what I believed was a mile out to sea. They never came back and the next morning I went to their huts with my Elise to tell their families how I had witnessed their fall from the precipice and how the tide had swept them into the sea whilst I stood unable to help them.

That night, after the evening meal, I summoned the village to caution them with gentleness in a way they would understand; warning them of the dangers that lay beyond the arch. I sent Elise to her bed and went with the two widows, one of them once my favourite, each one a mother to my children, to my pond where I comforted them with assurances and whisky they had never before tasted.

In my mind, they were the first to know The Grand Guardian and over the weeks that followed I wrote twelve scriptures that would bring evolution to Tombola and with that evolution a festive week each year to ensure that never again would I fear disruption enough to kill.

Their simple minds had no distraction from their daily

travail other than to swim and to bathe in the ocean.

I saw how the women dressed in their muslin tunics now went into the water to wash away the dust from the fields where before, dressed in cumbersome clothes, they did not. I saw how at first they were shy of their visible breasts and how they had eased into familiarity with their neighbours. I thought to a time long since past when I would travel to the brothels dotting the West Indies, however this time I went with Elise to Virginia where I met a Chinaman of despicable character who was able to supply me with ample quantities the finest opium.

Elise, of course, was unaware, which enhanced my delight immeasurably. She drank her first rum not knowing, her second not caring and her third in a state of complete abandonment of her senses and decorum.

She was lewd beyond my highest expectation, acting readily at my slightest suggestion and was not easily satiated. We stayed a week longer, each day visiting a seamstress who believed us demented for what we commissioned. Despite her critical opinion of us she put aside all others and worked for us alone until she was done and handsomely rewarded.

At the island I instructed Elise to bathe and anoint her skin with oils and perfumes and to dress in her finest evening tunic, which she preferred to any of the garments in her wardrobe, and to prepare the gifts for my flock. She was truly excited and while she was gone I unloaded cases of wine and liquor, dried fruits and more.

One case was locked for I had not yet confided in her as to the contents.

Together we went to the beach to gather the village around us, my Twelve Scriptures committed to my memory and my heart. We filled their cups and fed them all dried figs and dates as I revealed to them of the island's name. We filled their cups again and I told them of The Seven

Feasts that would last seven days and seven nights without labour and without sleep. I told them of the Twelve Scriptures. Both were joyously received.

The young would couple on the first day and be joined to a first-mate on the first night. Neighbours would show their affection openly to neighbours without shame or jealousy and without envy for they possessed nothing, save what came from the ground or from me and was to be shared. Nor should the essence of love exceed playfulness which would lighten their hearts rather than burden their minds with guilt.

On the fourth night one of my flock would be chosen to sit at the Tombola Pole and give of themselves for the betterment of all the island, for they were all equal in my eyes. I bade them follow me to the water and we gave them each a gift. When we were done I went to Elise. I took away her dress, leaving her naked but for a small patch of fine leather no greater in width than the palm of her hand and twice that in length to cover the least of her that she could.

Her skin glistened with oil. I stood with her for a long while allowing the men to enjoy the tightness and smooth curves of her person. And for the women to see that she was not shy or made by me to go naked before them. Indeed, she stood before them of her own accord, delighting in what was her nature.

I loosened the hemp at the waist of my pantaloons and let them fall to the ground for them to see that I wore the same, and together we walked into the sea. And soon they followed as none of the young was yet of an age to be joined. I knew they would from then on and I would forever be a guardian to them in their eyes. I would encourage them always and never scold them.

In the morning we stood by gorge, in the distance, watching them through my nautical spyglass as they awoke naked and uncertain on the beach.

At first men's faces grimaced at seeing other men regarding the naked condition of their wives, their expressions becoming pleasant as each man took in all that they could of every woman. The women became anxious at seeing so many men not their own in a state of first light readiness, though very soon after they would not think to wear their tunics at the beach or in the water.

That day and the next I spent deep in thought as Elise saw to my flock's pleasure. I was firm in my resolve. The village would, of necessity, be pure and without illness or imperfection to diminish us.

I chose the man for that reason and saw no purpose in deterring. I raised the pole on the afternoon of the fourth day and at midnight, when the water was at its lowest, the others came from the beach, drunk with tincture and eager, the women with the breasts bare and their privacy shields askew.

I hurled the stone that killed him, after all others. Were it not for the sureness of my sight and the strength of my arm, the man would have died a miserable death.

His neighbours left him and quickly forgot, such is the nature of man, returning to the beach to have their shields torn away and their breasts fondled, to prod and be prodded, to fall asleep and awaken unrefreshed to begin anew, unaware I had taken the man to northern most sea to dispose of his person.

On the fifth and sixth nights I took the man's mate with Elise to my pool where together we comforted her. On the seventh I gave her to another whose mate was not well and who I decided I would soon take from the island so that she might be restored to good health.

And with her I would take the lame child who would never work well in the fields and cause resentment that would diminish us.

I do confess to a persistent and derogatory belief in most

men. By week's end none questioned or gave thought to the Tombola Pole. Nor, eventually, did they question the absence of a broken child and sickly woman.

Of greater importance was their continued inclination towards unashamedly frolicking in the sea and basking in the sun at the beach in their shields.

It is undeniable that mankind is amongst the easiest of species to train.

Twenty-Seven

Cassidy sat in his tree, pensive, his groin itching from the dampness of his shield, wondering how he would survive in the fields on the verge of starvation.

He thought of his mother the night before and how she'd looked with her hair fanned out across the water. At times he was hard-pressed to think of her as a mother. She was Shakkra, young, attractive and desirable, and feeling her warmth through his bed sheet each night was increasingly difficult when he was already racked with so many amorous thoughts of Aayla.

One day soon he would take them away. He would marry one and give the other away. If the black men and women owned by Weatherbone were slaves, and the villagers who came with his son were not allowed to leave, then what were they if not slaves? And what was he?

His father had taught him to read, telling him often that to read would one day be his salvation. Now he had thousands of books to read, to learn of the modern world, of sixty-five years lost to him since Jonathon Clayton first came to the island. And he would. He would replace those books with his own.

The Ancestral Tomes, he decided, he would return that night.

He buried the book and his watch and ran to the fields, smiling and waving to Aayla who shunned him. Late in the day, when his work in the field was done, he left and returned to learn more of William Weatherbone, anxious to read what his son Horatio once wrote.

*

As much as I was devoted to Elise, my niece was becoming lovelier each day and was of age. She was eighteen. Elise was thirty-one. My son, Horatio, was sixteen, a splendid yachtsman. He possessed a natural familiarity with the sea and an irrepressible inclination towards the West Indies. He was to my credit, a voracious reader and masterful at his numbers.

On the thirtieth of June of that year, Elise lay unwell in her bed. She was not in a festive mood. In spite of her I went with my niece and three others to the lagoon to prepare them for joining that evening. The day was humid and oppressive as I taught them what they should know of a man and his appetite. I was patient and took pleasure in each one, as they sought their first pleasure from me, their parents oblivious at the beach, sharing pent-up affections with their friends and their neighbours in the water, on the sand and in their huts.

The girls were in awe of me, for I was their Grand Guardian and they were eager to give themselves to me so that they might be taught and prepared, not fear the excited probing of young men anxious to prod into depths beyond what exists. When I sent them away my niece stayed with me and I made her my own.

That night she would couple with me once more and live with me as my second-mate.

On the fourth night I alone bore the weight of taking Elise to the Tombola Pole. I made her comfortable on the ground and gave her more tincture to calm her mind. Her eyes no longer shone brightly, nor would she look upon me. She had forsaken her love of me, her damp skin trembling in the warm night air. Yet despite her rejection of me I kissed her and put figs soaked with tincture into her cheeks.

Soon I summoned the village so that we all might praise her and when they were done I hurled the last stone. I could not bear to witness the slowness of the water that would bury her until the morning's ebbing tide. Instead I returned to her at first light to release her, to carry her in my arms to the ship and sail northward to where I returned her to the sea. I remember her to this day and quietly reminisce about our first years together when she took pleasure in the bordellos of Cuba and the West Indies as much as I.

Such was her private diversion for none of the island was permitted to share affection with the first or any mate of The Grand Guardian.

In two years my niece gave me two sons. She was twenty and I adored her, delighted that, not unlike my previous mate, she was not in the least tentative in sharing my proclivity for the practised ministrations of young and pretty whores. In fact, she proved a willing student and I daresay many a gentleman was dismayed to discover she was not available to them. In addition to which she had, the previous year, convinced me to let her attend my duties at the lagoon with those I would bring there to prepare for their first coupling. She embraced the experience with remarkable enthusiasm.

However in the summer of 1890, at the conclusion of The Seven Feasts I left her and took my son at nineteen years of age with me so that I might extend his education beyond my limitations and begin to properly mould him, shape him for the demands of leadership. Nor did I intend for him to remain joined with any island female who was not in most ways superior to the common characteristics of the village. And she most assuredly was not.

She was in my view a potential danger to the peaceful co-existence I had achieved on the island.

Throughout their first and second Seven Feasts they shared affection with not a single neighbour or friend, nor

262

did they partake of the tincture after the first morning of the first year when they awoke feeling wretched and repugnant by reason of their indulgence, refusing to hear the wisdom of others, refusing to consume more so that they might dispel the initial affects and feel better.

What then would he do once I was gone, no longer able to conceal his disregard from all others? And what of his first-mate, should she one day contemplate sedition, this Ophelia of his, the one girl to weep in my lagoon as I prepared her body and her mind to couple with my son.

He was, at this juncture of his life, a handsome specimen, well-mannered and comported himself with marked gentility. His language during our travels was always gracious and he was regarded by all who met him as mild-mannered and unobtrusive.

Seated in Virginia's finest bordello I sensed his discomfort. He was as acquainted with unclothed women as I, subsequent to his active participation in two Seven Feasts and seeing my island women virtually unclothed at the beach.

These women however were laced with fragrances; their skin was untouched by the sun and their apparel he found difficult to manage. Despite having seen women fully dressed in his travels, he had never seen one attired in her stockings, bloomers and corset. Nor had he ever been presented with the opportunity to unwrap one from her bindings.

Yet he was as white in spite of his parentage, albeit evenly burned by the sun and his starched collar and fitted waistcoat were no less binding to him.

In addition he particularly disliked the taste and the fumes of Cuban cigars wafting through the common rooms, failing miserably in his concealment of that unpopular opinion. He did, however, take well to the finest and most expensive of cognacs which did little to alter his opinion of the women and their time-honoured profession.

Not surprisingly, he selected the prettiest and youngest of the whores, who, I learned at the end of our week, had passed her time with him in a settee, paid by me not for her charms but to sit quietly and fully clothed lest I discover his deception. The fact that I did made my decision final.

I needed no further time with him to prove or disprove my motives. I went with him to a boarding house and rented a room of adequate size and appointment so that he would spend the coming year in comfort. When he was settled I went with him to a tutor of considerable reputation and left them to become acquainted after cautioning him that the Isle of Tombola was a figment of his imagination, that nowhere on this earth did such a wondrous paradise exist. And that he was not to defy me. In that regard I was not his father, I was The Grand Guardian.

I left without him and went to the harbour to take delivery of my newly constructed yacht. I arrived home two days later to my niece and would not see Horatio until a full year had passed.

On the last day of June of the following year I coloured my hair white by design, made whiter against my dark skin, and had by that time adopted that colour for all my regal robes which were long and crafted in cotton, not muslin. The braiding was gold-coloured and I adopted the practice of wearing sandals, which prompted my niece to comment on my god-like manifestation.

That Seven Feasts would be my first, presenting myself in such a glorious manner and I was anxious to witness my flock's acceptance of my glory.

That year I joined five boys and five girls. The boys I sent to the beach to wait. The girls I took with me to my lagoon where I took away their tunics and my niece gave them their first taste of tincture. They came to me willingly and I made them ready. When they were clean we watched them dress in robes of different colours and we sent them away, knowing that in the morning they would awaken feeling unpleasant and not remember the ceremony of their joining, the feast or their first-mates first knowledge of them. Though, unlike my son, they would know to enjoy The Seven Feasts as was intended.

On the fourth day I brought Horatio's first-mate to my pool. Many had come to my lagoon, though very few had seen the lush garden surrounding the crystal waters of the pool. This time my niece did not attend me.

Together we drank our tinctures, for she dared not refuse me, and we spoke of my son. She told me of her love for him, and of her pride in knowing that one day he would be The Grand Guardian. She missed him and longed to see him in the coming days.

I was, of course, adamant that she would be insensate beyond misery. To that end I poured her a second cup and a third, for she was the one chosen and I would be no less kind to her despite my resentment of her.

I undressed her and eased her into the deep water to comfort her in my arms until she felt the time right to share affection with me and did so readily and wantonly, her eyes wet with tears, her murmurs I believe were words of adoration whispered to me, though I cannot be certain.

When she was depleted I pulled her from the pool to give her more tincture and filled her cheeks with potent dates. I left her undressed, laid her upon the soft grass and went to partake of the evening feast.

When I returned to her I carried her through the arch and across the receding waters of the gorge. I laid her onto a blanket to give her warmth against the damp sand and filled her cheeks once more with fresh dates. When she was tied I went to gather all those who were now my children, leaving her alone to dream of my son and to see the stars from between the massive walls of the gorge.

They were intoxicated from their reverie, dancing and sharing affection while others bathed in the sea or lay in the sand. One by one I gathered them, calling their names over the cacophony of their merriment. And one by one they came to me hand in hand with their neighbours so that I might remind them of my devotion to them, and their devotion to each other.

Ophelia was waiting for them, I implored. She was anxious to bid them farewell and to tell them of the deep emotion she felt for them. I saluted them. I raised my cup to them and they followed me to the gorge, dancing and singing with me to where she lay half-covered with the rising tide and looking like an unfortunate urchin. I went to her and kissed her. I bade her farewell.

The first stone was flung by my niece and struck her chest with determined accuracy, which surprised me. Ninety-nine more travelled the short distance amidst gleeful shouts. Mine was the last and the truest. I would not lie to my son when telling him she went quickly to her lasting peace.

In the morning I rose from my bed and left my niece. I waited at the pole for the water to recede to a depth that would allow me to unlash Ophelia and carry her gently upon my shoulders to my yacht. Not one hour later I gave her back to the sea and returned to Tombola to make ready for my voyage to Virginia believing in my heart that my son would return with me.

I was sadly mistaken.

He was disconsolate to hear of her passing, despite my assurances that she did not suffer and was not left to drown in the flood waters. And for the first time I discerned disbelief in him. He questioned the Tombola Pole and my right to determine a person's demise by lottery. Then he shunned my choice of replacements and, in the end, refused to return.

I had determined that he would join at once with another chosen by me, a matter convenience, since I intended that he would one day succeed me with one of two others of notably higher intelligence than what was the village norm. He knew of them and thought unkindly of them. Nor did he share my regard for the first.

Each was then fourteen, each one a creature of remarkable juvenile beauty, each one thus far protected by me during his time away to the extent I saw fit. They swam in my pond and soaked in my pool each day when their labours in the field were complete.

They were content, neither one afraid of what they imagined. The first-mate of The Grand Guardian would forever be exalted, they knew, and I can but imagine that in their dreams each night they fancied themselves in the finery of the station.

Neither was I oblivious to their natural attraction towards one another.

Horatio, however, saw no value in my thinking. He refused all three, yet saw fit to question their destinies. He demeaned my flock in the vilest of terms and dissented with no consideration for my station or sentiments.

I left him with a promise that I would accept whatever woman he might in time bring to the island, unable to imagine I would not see him for four years, during which time I continued my kind treatment of the girls. To see them mature was not unpleasant.

When Horatio did return I was elated at first to greet him alone at the harbour, unprepared to confront a man whose bearing was equal to mine, equally ill-equipped to sail home alongside a yacht more magnificent than my own.

Once arrived at the island he at once displeased me and proved me correct in my view of his future. He took for himself both the women first selected by me as his first-mate, when what I clearly intended choice and not self-indulgence. He denied me my privilege of rank.

He belittled The Seven Feasts with complete disregard for what his future flock held in such high esteem. He denied the girls their right to partake and kept them to himself throughout the week, to this very day claiming them as first-mates of the future Grand Guardian and, as such, forbidding them to share affection with the village.

He distracted them from their work in the field and took them in their spare hours to the sea from which place a mere few had ever beheld Tombola.

Had I been aware of the thoughts festering in his mind I would have granted his unspoken wish. I would have sent him away with instructions never to return. And with him gone I would have lashed the two to the pole without benefit of tincture or the last stone for defying me and defiling my Scriptures.

I did not and I lament my leniency to this day when I have learned of his betrayal.

Horatio Weatherbone is this day dead to me.

William Weatherbone, April 30, 1896.

Twenty-Eight

Cassidy snapped the book closed and rubbed his eyes. The sun was low in the sky. He'd waited too long. He wouldn't have time to retrace his steps to The Grand Guardian's home and return for his mother. Yet the sky was still too bright for him to walk the beach with books in his hands. Most of all he feared Aayla's curiosity.

He went to the tree line and waited, watching his mother swim with Aayla. With their backs to him, and if not for the colour of their hair and their bright shields, he was hard-pressed to tell them apart and he wondered what other secrets they shared at his expense.

Most of the village remained in their villas, weary from the past week. Those at the beach were the youngest and soon they began to dry and dress themselves. Shakkra and Aayla were the last, strolling from the water like girlfriends or sisters, their arms wrapped around each other's waist.

Cassidy walked to the water and waited for Shakkra who came to him a short while later with a sandwich and a flask of juice in her hands.

"That little girl loves you, Cassidy. You're treating her badly."

"No, Shakkra, I'm treating her well. I mean what I say. I'm taking you away. To succeed I must avoid her until I can no longer go to the house. Until then you must keep her away. My head has to be clear for what I'm doing."

"Right now she prefers me to you. Her company is easy

to enjoy, and you should be enjoying her instead of me."

"That's what I want, after I succeed. If I don't I'll never have her until an old man takes her first…and then Dakota."

"She says she won't join with him, or couple. She wants you and has no interest in sharing affection with others. I understand her."

"That's because of you and the trick Zach taught us about the tincture."

"Your father saw no harm in sharing affection," she smiled, "selectively. "He always told me that he required the practice with others so that he might be perfect for me, but each morning we woke together."

"I know. You kept me awake. Green was his favourite colour…on you."

"And he was handsome in red. Those younger women miss him, as I do. The truth is your father equated sharing affection with survival, yours and mine. The Tombola Pole didn't come as a surprise to him. He died for us."

"He was never jealous?"

"Yes… and no. It's a natural thing…selectively, and with good friends. We always went to our bed at night and woke with clear minds. We shared our affections with the same few couples each year, the ones Zach and I chose together. They welcome me each year to their villas, but not as before. They know what's in my heart." She smiled. "Unfortunately for the women there's one less handsome and strong man to enjoy."

"And one less painted young woman for the men who miss you," he smirked, "so near to their hearts, yet so far from their…"

She smacked him, and giggled.

At the gorge she tugged her evening tunic to above her waist. He raised his arms.

"What books are they?"

He stopped at the edge of Tombolina. "These are my

own. I'll leave them at the house when I leave with two or three others. This one, Shakkra, is the Ancestral Tomes. I can't chance that he'll discover it missing. And mother," he opened the book to the last page, "these are the Twelve Scriptures. Look at the signature. He was a man like any other, and very cruel."

She took the book and fanned through the pages, unimpressed.

"I expected more."

"There is more Shakkra, much more."

Walking to the channel leading to the lagoon he told her of what he'd read. At the receding water they pulled away their tunics and held them high, Shakkra believing she'd sit with him in the pool to hear more. When they passed through the lush garden and went closer to the house he told her to dress, explaining the cold air she would feel once inside.

The house was dark and Shakkra at once felt the chill. He put on a light and she was amazed by the instant brightness, shielding her eyes. He knew she was afraid and took her by the hand. He guided her through to the kitchen and explained the few amenities he could. He showed her the dining room, the parlour and the many magazines displaying women and their elegant clothes and many others filled with pages of couples and women sharing affection.

They climbed the stairs and he led her to the bedroom where he put on the light and watched her amazement. He took her to the closet and showed clothes as elegant as those in the magazines, more than she'd seen in her entire life. He opened a drawer to show her what she thought must be a hundred shields meant for the evening or sleeping in all manner of colours and styles. He opened each one until she fell back against the ball.

He took her into the bathroom and to the room he had

no idea about. He showed her Dakota's room and took her to the library.

"Your father wouldn't believe that you've done this."

"I'm beginning to believe that I know a way to leave."

"Tell me."

"I can't. Thinking isn't the same as believing. You'll know when the time's right, Shakkra, when I'm certain. And I want to show you this."

He reached into the cabinet he knew shelved the album and thumbed through the pages to the photo of a beautiful brown-haired girl lying in the shallow water of the lagoon with two others.

"That's you, Shakkra. That's what he did, and what his eldest son will continue to do with Aayla and others. He took pictures of the all the girls he brought here to make ready."

"I want to be sick. He must have done this from far away."

"He's got many more albums."

"And you found this one by coincidence, I suppose. Why are you looking at a picture of me without my shield?"

He smirked. "Any real man would look. You're the most attractive female on the island. And you weren't my mother then."

"You were already inside me."

He shrugged. "My father was always proud of you."

"Female?" She smacked him and closed the album. "You need Aayla more each day."

"I need you both. What is this place, Shakkra?"

"We're learning more with each page you read."

"I brought you here to show you. Not even your shields are as fine as those in her drawers. And what materiel can be so smooth to the touch? You saw for yourself her dresses and her shoes. He's got just as many. These are the clothes they wear when they leave or when they're here alone. Yet we wear tunics and loose-fitting pants. And when we sweat in our beds from the heat of the night, they sleep here in a bed covered with thick blankets to protect them from the cold air."

She pulled up her tunic and looked at her shield.

"You're right."

"Shakkra, mine are the finest in the fields and at the sea when I cast my net. I'm as proud of my mother as Zach was of his wife," he smirked, wickedly "whether she's in her shield or not. You would be painter's perfect model."
She smacked him, shaking her head. She kissed him and smiled, seeing the clock.

"I haven't seen one since your father's watch with its gold chain. It's just after ten. What will you do?"
"The watch is fine, Shakkra. I wind the crown each day. Tonight I'll sit here at his desk and read. You'll walk through the house and be curious. Be sure to replace everything you touch in the same manner. I'll find you when I'm finished here and tell you what I've learned."
She left him and went downstairs, curious to see what women did wear under their clothes. He climbed to reach for Wendell Parkens' journal, replacing The Ancestral Tomes. At the desk he thought of Shakkra, took a deep breath and smiled. She was perfect, and one day he'd lose her to another, if not easily, he promised.
*

William Weatherbone died in 1906. He left behind a village whose populace exceeded 400, his last entry the vindictive response to an insane father's lament before the penmanship changed and Horatio's hand became apparent.

I read late into my second evening, scarcely believing a fraction of what I'd learned, drunk from knowledge and not daring to consume the most infinitesimal drop of liquor, fearing I would miss or misconstrue the slightest meaning of what remained to discover. I was weary, my vision blurred.

I was at the second ribbon and knew what lay ahead was the memoir of Horatio Weatherbone and the fate he enforced upon more than 400 souls, yet I thought I might sleep awhile rather than exert myself unnecessarily. Until upon turning the page I came across what I believed was a single sheet of precisely folded onion skin, the edges pressed to razor sharpness. There were, in fact, three.

With a surgeon's skill I straightened the delicate pages that were in pristine condition and sat entirely dumbfounded and perplexed until a cold so paralyzing shot through me and I convulsed involuntarily with a violence that jerked me from my seat.

I forewent that much needed respite and read the letter with trepidation, my mouth dry, my eyes scarcely able to convey what I was seeing to my brain. I could not read the words. Instead I turned to the next page to see what I believed was a card inserted as another bookmark. What I discovered instead was a photograph of a man I grew to loathe and once thought I knew so well.

Below the yellowed image was written: To The Grand Guardian of the Isle of Tombola, Wendell Parkens, left this day by his father, Aristotle Horatio Parkens, first born son of William Weatherbone and his first and most preferred concubine.

The date was two weeks prior to my father's death, my mind an explosion of angry memories, confusion and disbelief. I read each word so intently that I was able to disavow my weariness.
*

Cassidy put aside the journal and scurried to where he'd squeezed The Ancestral Tomes into its place on the shelf. He skipped to the floor and ran to the desk, opening to the page bookmarked by the second ribbon. He turned to the next page. The letter was there, as was the photograph.

274

The paper was frail, the creased edges split apart and yellowed with age. He was truly afraid; his heart beating faster, thankful he'd decided to return the book. How would he dare to touch the ancient paper, how would he not? Would he understand the words of Horatio Weatherbone without first reading the letter to his son?

He could scarcely breathe. His fingers trembled, wondering what might have happened had the letter come away from the book and taken flight into the forest or onto the beach. He sucked in air deeply, noisily and unevenly, thankful Shakkra had gone, opening the first fold, hesitating to unfold the second and then the third.

The script was written in black ink, the letters of each word close together and slightly smudged. That was half his ordeal completed. The pages were so tightly pressed together they could easily have been mistaken for a single page. How would he separate them? And what if they didn't separate, or what if they tore?

He read the first page.

*

Greetings to you, Wendell Parkens, albeit that I send them to you posthumously from the grave.

I am certain that you have by this time seen the entrance to Tombolina from the windward shore, where my father once docked his much prized yacht.

If you have not, then you must, for your own safeguard and that of Tombola. The inlet will serve to protect you against ill winds and conceal you against ill intent. The destruction and removal of its infrastructure you have witnessed, except for the remaining ten huts, was my last commission before leaving the island for good twenty-six years ago, three years preceding your birth and two years prior to my legal marriage to your mother. An event, which you understand by now, was pragmatic and of mutual advantage to both parties.

I return now for one specific purpose, which is to place this letter into the shared journal of my father and grandfather whose final pages are written by me. The duration of my stay will not exceed by one second the time required by me locate the strongbox in which I first buried this book and depart.

Charles Weatherbone, my grandfather, was a man of goodwill, if not at first misled by the values and teachings of his epoch. My father William Weatherbone was not. He was, in fact, quite insane and decidedly cruel.

I returned to Tombola at the conclusion of my education so that I might save a life. I had formed the opinion over my time away that, were I not to choose either girl or both, the one or both not chosen by me would surely be stoned at the pole as they were in their eighteenth year.

For that reason I took both girls as my own and, in the spring of the '96, I conveyed them to the most extreme and southerly point of Florida. I travelled with them to where I would be certain of their personal security during my frequent absences and the least unencumbered by restrictive social mores and attitudes.

The most difficult part of our absconding, without the slightest uncertainty, was my need to have them cover their nakedness or conceal themselves upon our arrival in numerous ports, as their participation in our voyage of several days was mostly accomplished in a natural state.

Soon after, I brokered my yacht for a handsome profit. I no longer had need of it. I arranged for their tutelage, their melding with the current times and remained with them for one year to ensure their futures. I left them substantially endowed with a portion of William's estate, his gold, derived in large part from what Charles had bequeathed him.

To my greatest pleasure and delight, they have done well for themselves.

They developed with commendable enthusiasm into educated women, well-received in the world of art for their many paintings, many of which now hang in our home and in my bank. Though who can say for how much longer?

Both are alive to this day, mothers of your half-brothers who have greatly exceeded my demanding expectations of them. They have no knowledge of you, nor do they know of Tombola which I never believed would suit their life's purpose.

Now you know the motivation behind my twice yearly absence throughout your own development. This was my final visit to them, my farewell to beauty and a love that did not diminish with time.

I daresay, had Ophelia not been killed, I might well have exempted the two from my disgust of The Seven Feasts and made them recipients of my carnal avarice, during a week which you must understand by now was seven nights of drunkenness and deviant adultery.
*

Cassidy took the bottom corners gently between his fingers and meticulously peeled the first page away from him, letting the translucent paper float to the desktop. He rubbed his face hard and shook his head to clear his mind.
*

Had William not stoned Ophelia, certain he would one day lose dominion over so many, he might not have died and Tombola might have become a paradise of free tenants, not slaves, free to come and go and be recompensed for their work.

He did so because I was where he had put me, unable to prevent him, and his reason for disclosing his cruelty to me in Virginia was one of cowardice. He knew what would forever dwell in my heart and did not want me to return with him.

I cannot conceive that he believed otherwise. I would

have killed him where he stood. His sole protection from me was the rule of law in a land he considered as foreign. For that reason I did not. I chose patience over imprudence, anticipation over fleeting gratification. However, I harboured no doubt whatsoever that I would return to Tombola once my education was concluded.

I fully intended to avenge Ophelia prior to his summer trip of '96, until he departed three months earlier and without warning. Perhaps he suspected, suspicious of my actions which I chose not to disguise. In any event the timing and the condition of the sea were propitious for me to escape with the two women and I chose not to endanger them by staying one day longer.

I remained in the States those nine years, visiting Tora, Oona and my boys twice each year. My career advanced steadily, as did my wealth accumulated from wise investments and hard work, though not everyone was enamoured or in agreement with certain of my practices and I thought it wise to enjoy a vacation of extended duration.

At that juncture I left Horatio Weatherbone in Virginia and went with the fruits of his good fortune to Tombola where I remained for one year aboard my newest yacht, one whose decks you were not unfamiliar with throughout your youth.

The year I refer to was 1906. I killed my father happily and without much delay, devoid of the slightest regret. And this is what you do not know, Wendell Parkens.

William was soon sucked away by the sea. When the minds of the enslaved were clear, and their bodies clean, I went to them as The Grand Guardian. They would believe no one else. They were men and women equipped with simple minds. They knew no better. I separated them not by virtue of their masculinity, femininity or age, rather by what they did or did not know. Those who were not yet joined remained with their families; the young girls spared his

278

single-minded intrusion into their nubile bodies.

I chose the smartest first, the strongest second, and thirdly I chose those I discerned were of less than average wit. Finally went the meek, those less least likely to survive. They required the longest time with me.

Those in the first category I delivered to various ports within a short distance of one another and over the course of ten weeks, with sufficient monies and newly purchased clothing to see them on their way to opportunities in the west. To aid me in my ultimate intent, I decreed as their provisional guardian that during each of my voyages, the homes of those conveyed by me must be burnt to the ground during the hours of darkness so that the ensuing smoke would go unnoticed by curious eyes.

Between each voyage my tutelage of those who remained continued, the second lot completed by autumn's end. They went in the same direction from ports not as far to the south and, upon my return, the last of those meagre huts were fragmented and charred sticks.

I returned with clothing for those eager to depart, yet fearful, as were all those who preceded them. Their accord regarding their new attires was not easily achieved, accustomed as they were to bare skin, loose fitting tunics and pantaloons. I spent the winter continuing their lessons, despite my realization they were lost, despite being found. I worried for them, concealing my uncertainty at times with great difficulty.

In the spring, the ocean much calmer after a winter of raging seas, I took the most dimwitted to the gulf coast where they might work in the fields and the marshes. By June I had deposited the meek onto numerous island shores within two days of Tombola.

*

Cassidy held the two sheets lightly under his fingertips and blew soft, continuous breaths to separate them. He persisted over several minutes, frustrated, resisting the urge to call out to his mother whose hands were more delicate than his. At last the two sheets came apart, fluttering, stopping his heart. He laid the second as evenly as he could over the first.

*

My sense of obligation to the village was at an end. I returned to Tombola where I remained a two weeks longer, surrounded by the charred and skeletal remnants of the past and a lingering smell much less offensive to my olfactory senses than the oppression of men. Ten huts remained, and my father's home where I sat abhorring the man for his life's work.

I chose to destroy neither the huts nor the manor house, believing myself better served by nature. To that end I nailed the doors and the slatted windows in a manner that would prevent their closure against the onslaught of predictable foul weather. In my mind I saw the eventual devastation and was content with the outcome.

The Tombola Pole was long since gone, burned like a hideous candle with the first homes. What was not undone, what was left for me to destroy on my own, was William's private dock. I laboured relentlessly until I was done, each board and floating tank secured to his vessel which I stripped of every possession and amenity as my grandfather once did to his advantage.

On the last night, the vessel fully burdened to within inches of the gunwale, I towed her several miles out to sea where I removed the bolts from her bilge that would allow her to sink. With her went any memory of William Weatherbone. I have not thought of him one day since.

My course over the next several days was north by west, to another country where I was unknown and reborn in name, if not in philosophy. What mattered most were my resources and my ability to convey sincerity to those around me.

And what must I say of your dear mother? And what would she say of me to know I am the bastard son of a beautiful black slave? Your mother was a woman, when I met her, in search of opportunities. She had no family, though she was not orphaned as her parents went to their reward, deservedly or not, after her age of majority. She was some ten years my junior and not unaccustomed to the company of men who would treat her well.

Who was I to disparage her, I who kept two women and two children in the South, women I went to on four occasions immediately prior to the day your mother and I expressed our devotion till death do we part, and twice each year thereafter.

What you should know of your mother was that she was not borne of particularly good stock. She was, in fact, quite average as regards her parents and her education, if not her original ability to beguile and entertain men of substantial worth. You should know now, that I did not love her, not on one occasion I can remember. We were not that way. She was easy on the eye and finely crafted; a distraction, and soon she could not help her dissatisfaction with each new thing she acquired by virtue of my success. With you, Wendell Parkens, she was particularly dissatisfied.

Her contempt of you brought on by the accelerated damage you caused to her person and her vanity. Men no longer observed her from the peripheries of decency, women no longer envied her attractions and I began to call her Mother, as though by her Christian name.

In my defence, despite being harsh on you for your errant and promiscuous ways, I was never dissatisfied with you, save when came home with a trollop as your wife, your actions no less deplorable to me as I write this addendum to what I have penned in my forefathers' journal.

The two women of whom I write are angels to me. The

woman in Virginia was my salvation during a time of difficult loss, a poor widow who traded her warm charms for my money to the exclusion of others throughout the duration of our time together.

Neither was your mother given to nurturing. You constituted her one experience, sufficient for her to refuse me from then on. We were Mr. and Mrs. Aristotle Parkens when the need arose. When we were not, I never questioned what was in her thoughts since I was forever preoccupied with joyous times past and future in the warm South.

On that I have written sufficiently to satisfy you.

I imagine at this juncture that you remember questioning your childhood nurse as to my cowardice. Indeed, I trust I have redeemed myself in your heretofore low opinion of me. I do not now, nor have I ever seen myself in that light, despite what you certainly will believe in a few weeks from now which, for you, might possibly be weeks or years in your past.

I fathered not only you, and two others by women of greater character than your mother and yet another by Ophelia. I saved 400 lives and more, placing my own person in danger to dispatch another in search of redemption he will not find and, I hope, his failed quest for eternal peace.

The Weatherbones are at an end, as you possess no validation beyond this journal that you are not a Parkens, a name of convenient fabrication. The writings of three generations long-buried in a strongbox constitute our single legacy. What is done is done.

You are left with an island paradise blessed with a pool as clear and as brilliant as to appear filled with crystals. In that clear water I leave you my silver and ruby ring, of which I am certain you treasure significant memories. The infliction of those memories was intended by me to strengthen your character and your determination, perhaps in vain.

Perhaps for the better, though one of us will know the outcome of my thinking past and present as I believe the quantity of gold beneath the floor of that pool is sufficient to support you or ruin you. The other will not.

Tora and Oona never again set foot on the island, nor will the gold do me much good in my next planned endeavour.

And now I forewarn you, Wendell Parkens, Grand Guardian, against your certain insanity. Nothing good will come of the prolonged existence I believe you will one day come to desire on this isle. You are, after all, a Weatherbone and we seem somewhat predestined to abrupt and violent ends.

Aristotle Horatio Parkens, June 1933

Twenty-Nine

Cassidy aligned the third sheet with the second and first, leaning over them in the light to make them perfect before pinching the corners and turning them over. He made the first fold holding his breath, and the second. The third fold fell into place on its own.

He thought back to what he'd read of Aristotle Parkens the banker, his wife and the wife of Wendell Parkens in the furnace. He put the letter to one side and opened the Ancestral Tomes at the second black ribbon.
*

Horatio Weatherbone, née 1871.

This year is 1907, and nothing matters but the ruin which I see around me. My name is Horatio Weatherbone and once I have written what I feel I must for reasons unrelated to personal absolution I shall quit this island and never return.

I have shared the years since my escape from Tombola and my father between the industry of Virginia and the white shores of southern Florida. In one I have lived a hectic and commercial life, most hours of the day consumed by matters of finance. That particular existence is over. In the other I continue to share two women whom I love deeply, regarded by their neighbours as affluent young widows who choose not to remarry because of their young sons.

I believe Tora and Oona were created, not born, to walk

this earth as eternal examples of all that is beautiful and all that is perfect. After these many years, I cannot choose one over the other, or be with one without the other. Nor will I desert them when I leave this place.

When I first left the island they were young girls, devoid of breasts, their maiden-shields a matter of acquiring the habit of proper comportment and not one of necessity. They were children and I, of course, was blind to all but Ophelia.

My youth was spent in luxury and excess. From my twelfth year I travelled often each year to several ports in the West Indies, Cuba and Miami with my father and until her death Elise came with us, after which my father's niece found pleasure in voyages across the seas and I went with them until my final departure and the commencement of my formal education.

I wore fashionable clothes which were uncomfortable to me and I dined in the most elaborate eating establishments, at first finding the fact that I could not at once see a woman's or girl's nakedness to determine the full extent of her person. Until my eventual habituation of the dress code, the concealment of one's nature was a matter of their personal shame and my fertile imagination.

At home I wore silk pyjamas to bed and drank wine each night with my meal. I was competent in reading and writing and soon arithmetic was uninteresting to me. I required more to satisfy my hunger for learning. The most difficult part of my early and informal education was not betraying what I knew to others.

Ophelia was different. I loved her with all my heart and told her the word that she must keep secret. I showed her my books and taught her to read. I told her about my travels and what I saw. I told her that one day she would sail with me as the wife of The Grand Guardian and not my first-mate, a ludicrous appellation that existed nowhere else on earth.

The Feast of Tombola

When the time came for us to join my father was not the first. The preceding week was amorously spent by us so that the result of our intercourse would be ours and not some aberration of another's deviant nature. When she was returned to me from the grim water of the lagoon her eyes were red with tears. When she gave me a son we knew without question was the boy was ours. At barely three months old I was taken from him, and from Ophelia.

The journey to Virginia was arduous, if not tedious. I discovered my father's proclivity for whores, though not until one year ago, after I killed him, did I realize that his first and second mates were also taught by him to take pleasure in the amour of women.

They smelled acrid, these women of convenience. No worse or better than the taste of bile rising to my throat. Their skin was rough, the texture no different from my shield left to dry in the sun. Their breaths were artificially sweetened and the pungent scent of their portholes and underclothes belied any recent cleaning.

They were no less repugnant to me than the dense blue smoke of cigars stuck between the fingers of men twice my age and more, their waistcoats and collars undone. As I sat amongst them I wondered at what point they would seek the privacy with which to culminate their evenings. They seemed in no apparent hurry, quite content to reduce the state of their sobriety and to unabashedly fondle the woman of their choosing from all quarters.

I could not remain to witness the debauchery. I had upon my lap the most beautiful and the youngest of the whores. I excused myself to my father and with a bottle of fine cognac in hand I went with her to her room where I drank quietly, deep in thought. I poured her a dram or two and she sat quietly, no doubt thankful to earn her remuneration that evening and subsequent evenings for the pleasure of her own fanciful dreams.

I could not bring myself to commiserate on her behalf. She was a whore and I was in a miserable state of my own, knowing that for at least one year I would be confined in North Carolina without Ophelia and without my son. Father had not conveyed me all the way to Richmond to sleep with a young whore. I would not see Ophelia for a long time and felt her absence and that of my son grievously.

At week's end he departed without me and I spent that year succeeding beyond the rest of my class, not more than occasionally succumbing to my elemental urges with the sisters of my classmates and occasionally the younger wives of my tutors. My skin was well-darkened by the sun, my body hardened by work in the fields and toned by my time in the ocean. I was the very antithesis of what they knew.

And then he returned. I barely recognized him; he had altered his appearance to such an extent.

Hearing the words I sat enshrouded in disbelief. She was dead, my son given to another. And he sat as though talking of the weather or the condition of the sea. I despised him and I know he saw in my eyes that were we not amidst a genteel and law-based society, I would have murdered him where he sat. He knew I would choose not to return with him, for he would have died soon after whether at sea or on this treasured isle.

I bid him farewell, the grip of my hand firm. His, I remember, was moist. I put Tombola from my mind throughout four more years of education, unaware until one year ago of his abhorrent and deviant behaviour towards her.

In those four years I sought solace in the arms of a young widow I had come across by chance. I did not love her and did not live with her, nor did she love me. She required my particular generosity as much as I required hers and our relationship was amicable. I could no longer rely on the dreamy moods of the sisters of my classmates or the urges of my tutors' wives. My familiarity with either was too fraught with potential disaster. The widow was less hazardous to me and stayed faithful to my need and my purse throughout the four years.

When I left her I did so with nothing to explain to any future pursuer of her affections. She had one child, not of my doing, and was respected by the bank as a result of her weekly and substantial deposits. She would do well for herself. She was, in fact, left unspoiled by our need of one another.

I travelled to the coast and met my father with gentlemanly civility.

I must concede that I took great pleasure in seeing the immediate transfiguration of his mood. In the final six months of my studies I travelled to the shore on several occasions with one purpose in mind, that I would never again be subjected to the whims of others, that I would no longer be enslaved to a man who thought of himself as my guardian and not my father. The cost of the yacht and its most modern of amenities would cause not the slightest deficit in the pockets of The Grand Guardian of the Isle of Tombola. And we sailed here on a date of my choosing.

My mother welcomed me with open arms and her warm heart. I had not worn a man-shield for five years and my body had paled somewhat by virtue of strict social mores. The sensation of being naked in public, my nether region scarcely concealed, was unfamiliar to me as I walked to the beach.

I scarcely recognized them in spite of detailed descriptions recently implanted in my mind. I knew the girls six years younger than me more by their smiles and their waves, if not by their bodies which had blossomed under the sun into magnificence.

I walked with them and spoke with them. They were easy and comfortable with me in both regards. I brought each one in close to fondle their breasts which were equally firm and equally soft. I held each one against me and filled both my hands with the flesh of their bare buttocks and could not tell one from the other. I kissed them and their breaths were sweet. I felt their skin which had the texture of silk and their hair which was lustrous and fell like straight curtains across their backs to the thin bands of their leather strips which I pulled away to confirm they were clean and well groomed.

I asked Tora what she felt in her heart. She desired me as her first-mate. Oona replied in the same way and no less hopefully. I asked Oona whether she was afraid that I might not choose her. She was, as was Tora. We spoke of the fourth night. They shrugged, so engrained was the event in their lives. Yet I could see the fear in their eyes. I took them immediately into my heart and onto the warm sand where once again I could not tell them apart.

That night they slept in my bed, as Tombolina was forbidden to them and I would not spend a single night in my father's home.

The girls were inseparable. They worked, they played and they slept together. When I was with one I could be no less affectionate towards the other. The next night, the first evening of The Seven Feasts, I joined with them away from the others to make them officially mine. I required no murderous Grand Guardian to sanctify what I felt in my heart.

He was furious at being denied their nubile bodies by me, and by my disruption of his feast.

Upon seeing what I had not for five years, I forbade them their first and subsequent tastes of the tincture. They, of all women, did not require artificial accelerants to stimulate their bodies. Nor did they need, or would I allow, a man three times their age to putrefy what was pure. I did allow them what had become my preferred relaxant and I took them to sea where we remained far from sight to acquaint ourselves more intimately under the sun and under the stars.

They were amazed, and at first somewhat apprehensive of the engines' ceaseless rumblings, until they discovered the thrill of diving into the sea from such a great height and to this day I remember their playfulness and eagerness to study and learn.

They were excellent students and did not disappoint me in my need for secrecy. I remember as well my father's harsh rebuke and my undisguised delight at detailing my week afloat that began with his privation of Tora's and Oona's youthful apertures.

I knew of the opium from previous years and would seek all my pleasures of the flesh with whom I pleased and with a clear head. He had already stoned one woman of mine, he would kill no more. And what I did onboard my yacht, I reminded him, was not a matter that required his slightest concern.

All that he might expect of me was my silent disdain, though I would not oppose him. I could not amend what was so entrenched in the minds of weak men and servile women, neither would I partake, from which deciding moment we met and spoke as The Grand Guardian and his eventual heir. The date and cause of that future event indelibly noted in my mind.

Tora and Oona spent each night in our newly constructed cabin, their faces buried in my books. They discovered the capitals of the world, modern machinery and current fashion which the two decided with equal conviction was unnecessary.

I believed they would never stop questioning me as to the reason any woman would cover their breasts and bind their bodies so tightly or how they might possibly purge themselves from under such a restriction. The idea of hiding their faces from the sun under umbrellas, they decided, was ludicrous, though despite their incontrovertible opinions by year's end they required very little assistance from me and their handwriting was passably good.

Each Sunday we ate our noonday meal onboard my yacht. We sailed from a point where we could not be observed from the shore and in just as much time they were comfortable at the helm with considerable knowledge of the sea. Unfortunately, to their dismay and mine, the winter seas were higher and less inviting than other seasons and our excursions were fewer in number.

They learned of Christmas, though that particular feast meant nothing to them. Nor did they mind the prospect of foregoing any future Seven Feasts. For my part I was most glad that their bellies were as flat as when I first acquired carnal knowledge of them and my fervent desire was that they remain so until such time as an infant or two would be more convenient.

I would wait until summer, at the time of his seasonal voyage to wherever he went for his narcotic supplies and cases of rum. By then the girls would become graduates of my class and ready for teaching beyond my capacity. In truth, they gave me no respite, reading by their lamps as I failed each night to evade their curious minds with slumber. Not each day, rather each hour they learned more than they had the hour before. Each girl was Alice and was living in Wonderland where they witnessed my anger but once.

The Grand Guardian left once in August and again in November, when I judged the girls not quite ready. I did not anticipate his next departure until the late spring and again in early summer when my intention was to go with him and at some point not too far out to sea, dispose of him, and return for the girls.

Not unfortunately and much to their credit, each was increasingly difficult to contain, impossible when together and I began to consider late springtime as more appropriate timing, if not requisite to our flight and my continued protection of them.

The two had achieved a state of learnedness beyond all others on the island save The Grand Guardian, his depraved niece and me.

By February I decided they would be sufficiently tutored by April, not expecting he would cheat me of my one chance to avenge Ophelia. He sailed in March without the slightest indication to me. To say that I was furious says nothing of my mood.

I sailed with Tora and Oona three days later, fully provisioned with food and drink and much of my grandfather's gold stored in my hold. I waited until the last moment to embrace my mother for the last time. I would not see her again. She was unprepared and untutored; to take her with me would have been to set a newly born child adrift in a furious sea. My girls, at least, were commendably prepared.

We went first to Cuba where I bought them colourful dresses and sandals. We proceeded to various island ports where the manner of dress was simple and easier for the girls to accept. Still, more than once ,while approaching harbours or passing nearby ships I was required to send them below deck as they refused to wear clothes onboard and had tossed their shields to the wind.

During our first year I made a handsome profit from the sale of my yacht, which was the original motivation for its purchase, not knowing the full extent of my father's wealth. I bought them an enviable and spacious private home by the sea and in that year they each produced a son, neither girl marked in the slightest by the event. Nor did the arrival or the anticipation thereof interfere with their continued education. I hired tutors and retained a woman to help them care for the children while they studied and each discovered an undeniable ability to draw.

In the second year I travelled north to Virginia where I purchased my own fine home and each year established myself all the more as astute and knowledgeable in matters of finance and investment. Those who were not acquainted with the elegance of fine living were not acquainted with me and twice each year in the spring and the autumn I travelled to see my never-to-be wives and my children. I daresay I loved them, though Ophelia had long ago depleted me of that emotion. She took all that I possessed and I never ceased to lament my short supply.

My career endured nine years, the sale of my home undertaken surreptitiously, my accounts closed and withdrawn in the same efficient fashion. I had made many wealthy men wealthier at what we agreed was an equitable fee to profit ratio.

However I arrived more rapidly than my most liberal estimation at a juncture where those captains of industry might possibly deduce that their wealth might have been substantially more had I not invested in myself by virtue of their resources. In my view an explainable fee for such high returns brought to them through diligent management of their interests, though I did not disregard their likely and discordant point view.

At the harbour, now more than a year ago, I paid for a remarkably fine craft with gold, documented to and owned by Aristotle Horatio Parkens. I voyaged first to Florida a very wealthy man to spend time with Tora and Oona who are now thirty, their remarkable beauty and charm of sufficient quantity to grace their patio overlooking the sea however they please and to the delight of all my natural senses.

My children know me as father and one day soon I will tell them of their half-brother taken from me seventeen years ago. Of course, I no longer regard him as my son, his mind inevitably reduced to the lowest common denominator of the island, which I was displeased to confirm one year ago. At that age he would be impossible to incorporate into my plans and too old for any adaptation that might be undertaken by Tora or Oona. I would not impose such an impossible task upon them. The boy will make his own future as a free man to the best of his abilities.

We left the boys in the care of their lady servant and we three went on a long vacation to the islands through to the third week in June. They have lost all trace of Tombola in their voices, also having taken to wearing loose-fitting silk garments, recognizable in the islands and quite acceptable to the American perspective of the South.

Under those garments, or when gracing their patio, never having adapted to corsets or girdles, they unabashedly wear shields made of silk.

Upon our return I took my immediate leave of them and sailed here to Tombola, denying them for the first time. I saw no advantage in tainting their new-found freedom by allowing them to relive a time when once they were slaves who believed themselves free. My simple response to them was that no one this coming third day of July would sit at the Tombola Pole if not The Grand Guardian himself.

I arrived here in the early hours when the sky was the colour of pitch and waited at the most southerly point of the leeward shore protected from the wind. When the sun was a slim golden glow emerging from the sea I travelled north along the opposite shore to the channel where I docked my yacht by his and concealed myself in the arch to wait for him.

I saw him appear and watched as he rowed across the gorge. As he came closer I cloaked myself in the dampness of a dark corner. He looked like Moses in his white robes and long hair, and comical to an erudite man, his mouth opened sufficiently wide for me to reach in and deprive him of his merciless heart. Yet I could not laugh as this was the man I had come here to kill.

He chose not to answer. No response was necessary. I knew how many more had sat at the pole. I can only surmise how many others gurgled in the sea before succumbing to its depth by virtue of some malady imagined or created by him. And to spite him I told him of Tora and Oona, the two women to escape his fornication in the waters of his private lagoon.

They were well-established with my children and successful in careers unknown to most women, independent with enviable finances and living in a grand home which I was able to afford by reason of his gold. And, as for me, I was at my young age, a millionaire and would by the end of that day be considerably more affluent.

Though not before we arrived at the pool, once I commanded him to sit, did I achieve my greatest gratification. He knew why I had come. Neither his arguments nor mine served any purpose other than to prolong what was inevitable. Whether his people were well-fed or not, they slaved in his fields not theirs, while he travelled the seas, wore fine clothes and slept with decadent whores, while they wore thin strips of leather to conceal their parts and thin tunics and pants to protect their skin from the sun. And which of them did he believe in his twisted mind wanted to toil in those fields with no certainty of living another year.

Then I disclosed to him how he would die. He choked; his laughter was so coarse, insisting that his loving minions would protect him. Those words were his final argument, one which I debated with the discharge of a bullet to each of his knees.

He would die that night and without the aid of narcotics to dull his mind. He would endure the ritual to its fullest and cruellest extent. His guardianship was terminated forthwith. I would free his slaves and leave Tombola to its fauna, the hot summer sun, the harsh rain and winter tempests.

In the meantime and until dark, I bound his hands and his feet. I ran the same cord across his mouth to a knot at the back of his head. I bandaged his knees for fear of seeing him dead from my own negligence. Then I dragged him to where I would not see him.

I went to his yacht to initiate a thorough search. I found opium in plentiful supply and rum. In his main cabin I found what would make Tombola mine for whatever purpose I one day might choose.

Onboard my yacht I poured several measures of cognac into a goblet. I dressed in my loin-shield that I now wear exclusively in the company of Tora and Oona on their patio or with them onboard my yacht. I went to the pond to relax in the warm sun, shutting out the nearby wailing, letting the liquor relax my mind.

On the verge of slumber I went to the yacht and poured another of equal measure. From the dock I strolled to the private lagoon, a place where I once studied and learned as a child, never thinking I would evolve into my tutor's assassin, ever thankful that learning came easily to me. Once at the channel I swam against the incoming current and spent my day at the beach.

At sunset I dressed and carried the many cases of rum from his yacht to the arch, rowing them across the gorge, thinking my shield inappropriate attire for the work at hand and for the first encounter with my mother in ten years. Alas, what I found at her hut was a woman whom I did not know living with a man I cared little about. My mother was dead and I chose not to enquire as to the cause.

Regarding my sisters, Honey and Caramel, they would be amongst the first to depart. I felt no particular devotion or obligation towards them, nor do I particularly miss them.

They are of above average good-looks, sisters with first-mates and children. I can but imagine the basis for my father's early attraction towards them. Nevertheless on their eighteenth year, and irrespective of what else he might have done, he sent them to join with men of no great distinction from the others.

I went into his house. His niece was in her bed and unaware of my intrusion. She was fully naked, covered to her waist and not the least desirable to me, though I drew back her covers to examine both sides of her, curious to see what might possibly lure an uncle to his niece.

There was no part of her to critique, beyond her stupor. And what I later discovered of her proclivity towards her own kind was not in the least distasteful to me, lest I be hypocritical in my thinking. Her commendable attributes were all that I found of any particular value in the house and I left her to go to the shore where I disrobed so that I would not stand out from the others.

For as far as my eyes could see bodies were twisted around other bodies, moving in every conceivable way. Along the trees those believing themselves a year or two from their first coupling were watching and giggling. I gave their silliness no further attention, remembering my times with Ophelia and our explorations of one another beneath the water's surface. This occasion would be their last to see such a natural act displayed so wantonly.

I enlisted some of the men unencumbered by their neighbours' legs or frolicking to assist me with the cases. I filled their cups four if not five times and joined them in their evening meal, refusing young women and old. I was not on Tombola to fornicate, though I was not entirely displeased by their attention or the preserved condition of my person.

Instead I went to my father. I put a lantern by his side. I asked him to sign the documents that would release the Isle of Tombola to me, his son. When he refused I cocked my head as well as my pistol that I put his foot. Clearly he understood my sincerity and my intent. From that memorable moment I was the owner of Tombola passed down from Jameson Beachwood to my grandfather, neither of whom would ever have envisaged what they had made possible.

I hauled his weight onto my shoulders, securing him with one hand and holding the lantern with the other. I turned a full circle, swinging him with me and telling him to fill his eyes with his last glimpse of his secret and much befouled Tombolina.

I carried him through the arch and into the gorge. I disregarded the rowboat and kicked my way through the ebbing waters with little consideration for the location of his head in relationship to that water.

At the Tombola Pole I dropped him where I stood and stripped him of his regal robe leaving him looking ridiculous and shrivelled as much by fright as by the water. I lashed him tightly and indulged myself with a modicum of sadistic pleasure at seeing the discoloration of his hands. I knelt to within inches of his face and let him read my mind.

His pleas fell on deaf ears. Pathetic cries from a desperate man not wanting to suffer the reality his own decree.

At the shore I incited the village without delay, giving them no reason to dress. The Grand Guardian was ready to give of himself so that the island might endure. His time was nigh to sit at the pole and he awaited their joyous mood as much he desired to behold them one last time, to see them all and to bid them farewell.

Together they marched to the gorge, hand in hand, naked and drunk, young and old.

I stood the girls closest to their joining year and dressed in their maiden-shields in front. Behind them stood the boys of a similar age who had been with the girls in the sea and along the trees. They were not the strongest and I gave them each a stone. The youngest mothers, naked and excited, stood behind them and I gave each one a stone until one hundred were counted.

The men stood at the back, most of them naked, all of them with empty hands. I held the last and most precious stone. When I dropped my arm very few of the one hundred hit their mark.

The village was dancing and cheering loudly. I beseeched each man to take with him a woman to the beach to delight in their pleasure, to honour my father with whom I must share a son's last words before hurling the stone that would sanctify him.

The children needed no further prompt from me. They ran quickly into the night to emulate their parents who followed behind them as though hurrying to their final night when, in fact, three remained.

The damage to my father was evident, though not to the extent that I could witness in his eyes that he desired.

I asked him a question which I did not previously. I was certain he would refuse to answer; falsely believing that he might survive the night. I would, I assured him, send him to hell quickly in exchange for the gold that I knew remained but did not discover throughout my close investigation of his home.

He told me, and I left him to ascertain his truth or his lie, returning within a very short while, my body wet with the crystal water from the pool where he had, once discovering my original theft, buried his bricks of gold under the stony floor.

I squatted so that our eyes were level, so that he understood my eyes. He did, at once.

He saw me drop the killing stone into the water by his side. He saw me walk to the stone wall that was the abutment of Tombola. He saw the ghastly and flickering flames around us, lighting my face, lighting the dark water creeping to his final and most precious gasp of air, his nose and to his eyes until his last attempt at life delivered him from me.

At that moment I prayed to Ophelia and begged her to forgive my neglect of her so many years in my past. In the morning he lay twisted and blanched, his eyes wide open and his mouth twisted into a ghoulish configuration. I unlashed him and soon he was gone from my sight and my mind.

The next morning his niece, upon hearing of his passing, was beside herself. Strangely, when at the conclusion of The Seven Feasts, some of the village became slowly aware of her absence, we were unable to account for her. My suggestion to them was that she had likely gone into the forest to remember him and to honour him.

In truth, she was violent with outrage when I woke her. I was surprised not to see foam at her mouth. My blow to her temple was unequivocal; she remained unconscious until well out to sea where I was certain Ophelia was regarding the completion of Tombola's cleansing with certain pleasure.

That was one year ago.

At the end of each freedom crossing with his slaves I went to Tora and Oona. How could I not with so few miles between us and my devotion to them so boundless? Now, at the end of my year-long work, I will remain with them until the autumn, when I will leave them with fifty more bars of gold, an endowment made possible by father's posthumous charity and properly invested.

For my part, I leave Tombola with few hundred more; my newest destiny is a blueprint in my mind. I will sail north to a new homeland and a new existence. I came here one year past as a wealthy man. I leave with my resources handsomely increased, exclusive of the 200 bars of gold left at the bottom of a crystal pool certain that Tora and Oona will never be in such desperate straits as to consider for one moment my offer to them.

I am left with nothing more to write and to wonder who one day will read these words, perhaps a trespasser, a thief or pirate. Not my sons, nor the women I can never marry for fear of denoting a preference between them which has never existed. Nor I, for I wish never to see this hell once more in my life.

Thirty

Cassidy blew air through his pursed lips and slouched into the chair, disappointed he'd finished the book. He'd read the last page and reread the Twelve Scriptures. All four Weatherbones had died violent deaths, Charles and Horatio by their own hands, William at the hands of Horatio, who was Aristotle, the father of Wendell Parkens killed by his eldest son.

He had too much to digest and felt as though he wouldn't sleep for a year. He also felt increasingly chilled in a room whose air he had no idea how to warm. He replaced the letter and photo as he'd found them. Satisfied, he climbed to the shelf from where he'd taken the Ancestral Tomes and replaced the book.

On that wall he spent several minutes and saw nothing of immediate interest. On the centre wall he found a recently published encyclopaedia and filled the void with a book of his own. From another wall he chose a dictionary, one of many he hoped wouldn't be missed, filling that void with another book of his own.

He positioned the chair and ladders as he'd found them and went to find his mother who was in the living room.

She looked up at him and smiled.

"I'm learning new words, Cassidy. Look, these aren't shields. They're thongs and that material we didn't know is silk." She turned the page. "These are stockings and garters, but not like the ones in your old books and magazines.

These are called bras. They're worn under their dresses." She shrugged. "I don't understand why. If they're so delicate and beautiful why do the women hide them under their clothes?" She turned another. "These are what they put on their faces to make themselves beautiful." She closed the magazine, looking at the others strewn across the table. "She has so many."

"She has more upstairs."

Shakkra sighed. "Her silk thongs felt so nice to my touch. When did you say we would leave this place?"

"I didn't, Shakkra. But I know whatever I do, I must do quickly. My father, his father and his father have all been killed. It's not how I wish to end my life. You and Aayla are too pleasant to my eyes for me not to see both of you for many more years." He hesitated. "Stay here."

"Where are you going?"

He left without answering, coming back before she could call out his name.

"She has many. You're right. I counted dozens. I'm sure she won't miss this one."

"Cassidy I can't."

"She won't know." He turned. "I'm counting to ten, unless you want me to see my beautiful mother without her…thong."

He turned at ten, smiling to see Shakkra was holding her tunic at her waist.

"Yellow suits you. And soon you'll have more, and Aayla You must believe me."

"I'll come here again tomorrow with you and the day after. If you're discovered, they'll find me with you."

"No one will discover us. Come, let's go to the pond and sit for a while in the warm," she grinned, "and golden water."

"No. I'll sit in the grass. I don't want to ruin my thong."

"And when we arrive home you'll hide it under my

mattress. He won't find it there if he looks. I don't trust him. At night you can wear it under your evening tunic," he pointed to the magazines, "like them." He grinned, stepping back to study her. "It will be our secret."

She smacked him. She was smacking him a lot recently, not unhappy that her son was proud of her body, as Zach had once been proud of her at the beach and in the ocean.

They turned out the lights and went to pond where Shakkra did sit in the grass without her tunic, with her feet in the water, admiring the gift from her son. Cassidy sat on the submerged ledge and told her what he'd learned about William, his mates, Horatio and Wendell Parkens. He told her about the gold.

When they could no longer see the moon he carried her along the channel to keep her dry, and across the gorge. She carried the books and for the first time Shakkra saw his tree. She saw the strongbox Zach had kept hidden from her. She touched his books, the watch and Cassidy let her weep in his arms.

When they arrived at their villa they went in quietly. Cassidy changed into a sleeping shield and crawled into bed; Shakkra came out wearing hers and slid her tiny silk triangle under his mattress before easing herself onto the bed between her son and the wall.

He didn't turn to kiss her. She was a stunning young woman. She deserved a man to hold and make love with, not the back of a son who lay awake each night silently promising his father that one day soon she'd be free and marry a man who would love her and be kind towards her.

The next morning was stifling and work in the field progressed slowly. At midday all the women went to the beach to refresh themselves with their mates who were already enjoying the sea and their catch. Aayla was no exception, walking directly towards him, this time without Shakkra attached to her hand or her waist.

"I cannot see you if I do not come to the blue water to clean my work tunic."

He attempted a weak chuckle.

"I thought you preferred my mother to me. You are always stuck to her like a wet tunic."

"Shakkra is my friend and she is beautiful. I hope I am beautiful like her when I am twice my age."

"You are right, Aayla. Sometimes thinking of Shakkra as my mother is hard for me. Her skin is the same as yours with not one mark like many of the other women."

"The men like to look at her."

"So do I, when I am not looking at you."

"Now two less women will share your affection next year: Shakkra because she is your mother and me because I feel no more emotion for you."

"You spend too much time together. And why does my mother know what I do in the forest?"

"She told me all the boys find a place to do that, until they are men."

"I am a man."

She shrugged.

"Aayla, on the last night of The Seven Feasts, did you hear your name."

"Yes, the whole village heard you. The next day they laughed at me."

He paused, pointing "I called your name from the tallest peak."

"No, you did not."

I did." He took her hand. "Come, I will take you…and then you will believe me."

"Do not tell me untruths, Cassidy. No one goes to Tombolina who are not The Grand Guardian and the young girls who go to his lagoon before their joining."

"You are right, Aayla. I am sorry. Come. Let us swim before I go to the fields."

"And where do you go after your evening meal, Cassidy? Tell me. Shakkra does not tell me. She says she does not know."

"She does not know. I go into the forest to think of you and the many new suns and moons ahead of us. Aayla, when Shakkra was near her time to couple my father filled her with me before the old man took her to his lagoon to teach her what she must know."

He grinned.

"Why are you smiling?"

"One day soon I will tell you before an old man takes you for teaching and before Dakota sees you without your maiden-shield."

"When I join with him he will have the most beautiful girl on the island, and you will be with the fat one who looks filled with children already."

"I will congratulate him on his beautiful girl and express my sorrow that he must listen to your constant talking until he jumps from the highest peak."

She jabbed his stomach with her fist, reached down and jerked his feet out from under him.

She waited with her arms akimbo.

"You will jump from the highest peak, when I am under him and you hear my loud sounds of affection. Your heart will cry. All the girls want to take my place. He is very handsome."

"We will all hear him first, Aayla; when he passes through you and into the sand while you scratch him with your skinny legs and bony arms. My heart will be fine."

She gasped for air. Her eyes glared and her lips curled into an instant snarl.

"I hope they stone you."

"They will, Aayla, like Zack, Jacob and Jonathon. And all you will remember of me is standing here in the blue water talking like children."

306

"I am a woman."

"And I am a man who will couple with you when the time is right, and not after two others. First, Aayla, you must help me."

"I do not understand."

"You must swim in the ocean and talk with Shakkra. In her heart she loves you like a sister."

"What is the word you said?"

"I said she loves you. I also have deep emotion for you. Now come. You have fish to prepare for your meal and I must till the fields."

At the sand she squirmed into her dry tunic and looked down, not knowing what to think of him.

"You made the same markings in the sand before, Cassidy, the last time we slept against each other on the sand. When my eyes opened to see you, I thought you were dead in the blue water."

"You felt sorrow in your heart, believing you would never see me again because you feel deep emotion for me."

She shook her head and looked into his eyes, uncertain. "No, Cassidy, I felt sorrow because I love you." She knelt and touched the sand. "And this is my name."

He nodded. "Yes, and soon you will write in the sand with me, and on paper. Now we must go and when your evening meal is finished you will come here to swim with my mother and share secrets about me."

Thirty-One

On the second to last evening and after his meal Cassidy kissed his mother and went to his tree. He turned each page of the illustrated encyclopaedia more carefully than he wanted, resisting the urge to hurry and possibly miss important information. He was looking for what he'd seen at The Grand Guardian's home, angry with himself. He saw everything in those pages he'd hoped for, with no way to mark the pages.

He saw art and computers, facsimile machines, maps and automobiles more modern than the ones he knew from the books in his strongbox, printers and scanners, airplanes and jets, cell phones and words he had no idea about. He saw New York, Paris and London. He saw where Tora and Oona once lived near the sea and where Horatio Weatherbone fled to become Aristotle Parkens. He saw stovetops and ovens, microwaves, televisions and remotes, busy streets and airport terminals. He saw all of these things in an hour and wondered what he should do.

He had twice that time left to him before he would see Shakkra sitting in the sand, waiting for him. He turned to the first page to retrace his curiosity one difficult facet of what was missing from his mind at a time.

When he was done he understood that he didn't understand. What he did know was that he would never return the two books. Wendell Parkens never found Jon Clayton's strongbox, nor would his eldest son find what

Cassidy had inherited or taken in exchange.

In the dim twilight he walked to the tree line. He was alone. He laid the two books onto the sand strolled into the sea to take his bath. When he was done Shakkra was at the shore.

"What have you done to your little heart? She couldn't stop talking about you."

"What did she say?"

"Nothing I'll tell you," she put an arm around his shoulders, "without betraying my little sister."

"Now I can't even trust my mother. And when I marry her away from this place, will you be my mother or my sister-in-law? Should I be worried?"

Shakkra took a moment. "We're at an age now when you and I are friends. Cassidy, you know more than me, as did your father. And soon you will know much more."

"We'll learn together, Shakkra, my aging mother."

She shoved him into the sea.

"Knowing more than me doesn't mean that you're smarter or stronger. Don't make me trade my son for a daughter. Often, and increasingly, Aayla is much better company than you. I think I'll adopt her. At least her legs and arms aren't as bony as yours."

"That's not funny."

"No. What you said to her wasn't funny at all."

"You're both against me."

"Of course we are. We're girls. And we both love you. At least you said something nice. I cautioned her against using the word."

"Does she know you can read?"

"No. It's enough that she knows you can."

"I want to tell her about the strongbox, to teach her, but I can't"

"And you shouldn't. What will you gain by giving her a delicious meal she can't eat? She'll know when the time's right. When and if the time comes."

"It will. I promise."

"I believe you. Now carry me across the gorge and once again into the channel. I don't want to spoil my silk thong. Imagine what your father would have thought to see me dressed so wonderfully."

"Shakkra...he did, and he does."

He eased her to the ground at the shore of the lagoon and together they walked to the house. He reached for the light switch as though by second nature. He held her hand and they went to the far end of the parlour to sit on the sofa that he knew wasn't a chesterfield. He reached for the remote which was entirely new to him and pressed his thumb onto the green button.

Shakkra shrieked, seeing the people, hearing the cacophony of sounds, the cars and the bursts of gunfire she'd never heard suddenly screaming from the black picture frame. Cassidy thumbed from channel to channel, not knowing, stopping when they saw a man and a woman openly sharing affection and seemingly unaware of them.

He didn't care that they were naked. He knew they were real, somehow. They were at the helm of a large boat and that's what he wanted to see. Shakkra was more shaken. She went unsure of each step to the screen. She touched them, recoiling, not understanding the sensation, leaping backward at the sudden explosion of thunder and the thick plume of smoke shooting into the sky. Then she saw nothing but blackness and herself, as though in a black mirror, and turned to him.

Cassidy replaced the remote where he found it. He told her he'd wait until they were at the pool to explain as best he could. As he stood to leave she went to a low leather seat surrounded by magazines. He climbed the stairs to the library, he climbed the ladder and at the desk he sat to read from Wendell Parkens' journal.

*

I absorbed each word without the slightest pause, either in my father's story or my disbelief. When I was done I read each word again. In all my years until his suicide not once did he betray himself: my father, the straight-laced and judicious banker, the keeper of two mistresses and the father of three bastards. Yet he believed my juvenile predisposition towards amorous women intolerable. What a truly undeniable hypocrite he was. What was his thinking to bury 200 bars of gold, knowing or believing he would not return? And when he did return, to toss away a ring and not make slightest effort to confirm its continued existence in such times of human strife.

I would not on my life touch his gold. I had no need of his posthumous charity. I would prove him wrong. Nor did I need his forewarning. I was not the one to choose death over life or a woman such as my uncaring mother over women of undeniable appetite and whose bodies, I must imagine, were far superior in many ways.

He would take mother to the seasonal shores of the Northeast, often without me, while maintaining a grand home at the southern tip of Florida where he would sail twice each year aboard his yacht in these warm blue waters with those naked consorts.

I believed him born and educated in Montreal. Now I discover he was born not far from where I sit to a black slave who William Weatherbone saw fit to give to another man so that he might marry another. Perhaps his single truth in life was that my paternal grandparents had died a few years before my birth. I can vividly imagine my mother's expression were they to have extricated me from her as a child of colour. Or, for that matter, the facial distortions of my dearest Charlotte had providence chosen to transfer that particular gene from me into her.

My father, the righteous Aristotle Parkens, was many

men. He was the son of a slave and her master's son, his father's assassin and the murderer of his father's own niece. He was a breeder of bastard children and fornicator, despising others who sought the same pleasures of the flesh. He maintained a widowed whore and bedded the women of friends and associates. He was truly a man who lived duplicate lives and died because he misused or exceeded his time in one of them.

I wondered at the time of my ancestral discovery whether the consorts remained alive. And what was I to suppose of my three brothers, despite possessing no knowledge of their names or their whereabouts. I could not imagine that he would curse them with Parkens as a lifelong penance as he did with me. Or Weatherbone for that matter, all of them killed by the cowardice of self-loathing or hatred.

His bastards exceeded his expectations of them, yet not a word of praise did he speak in his lifetime with regard to my own achievements, which makes me ponder all the more why he chose not to bestow upon the three others this island which is now my home and his pot of gold at the end of the rainbow which everyday hovers over us.

What was in his mind? Or did he possess one near his end? What did he know or believe of me, and with his father's gold what was his need to cheat and deceive to the point of his requisite demise?

In the years that I knew him he played a heartless gentleman of commerce in the North, a father with no interest in that aspect of his existence and a husband whose wife was a social convenience as much as a domestic necessity. While in the South his role was conversely that of generous benefactor and devoted lover. Why did he not after all those years return to the South as Aristotle Parkens to live out his remaining years? In truth, I never knew him. Nor do I to this day comprehend his dire need to return here, to his hell, as a postscript to his illicit life, his final farewell to his consorts and bastards. On my life would never touch his gold.

He killed his father to assuage his memories of a woman long since dead and fled north to evade those who realized too late his true nature. His true nature not fully recognized and his life two-thirds over at the time of our first meeting when I came to him as his fourth child and one he would abandon no less than his first, the son of his beloved Ophelia who was left amongst others to make his way unskilled and untutored save for the most rudimentary curriculum to assist him.

As for the cruelty I endured as a result of his cowardice during the latter years of the First Great War, the fact that I employed the Second Great War to my own advantage did not then, nor does it now, acquit him of his indifference towards me. He was never redeemed by me. Nor shall he ever be.

I was wrong to previously believe that I loathed him to the greatest extent possible. I recanted that misconception at once upon reading his journal. My loathing of him at that moment was immeasurable and remains so. I believed, and will until the end of this my own final day, that this island was intended by him as his final and posthumous punishment of me, that he intended my insanity so that he might, in his troubled mind, negate his participation in my existence. Clearly I forestalled my intended insanity with the strength and determination of my mind and my character.

He failed. Do you hear me, father? Your words did not deter me. Each day I grew more determined to make the Isle of Tombola my home.

Though give the devil his due, Dakota, as you complete your private reading of this journal and theirs, my Ancestral Tomes. Without Aristotle Horatio Parkens the Isle of

Tombola would not exist, nor would I The Grand Guardian who cares for all others on this magnificent isle. He, Horatio Weatherbone, planted not only his seed into the womb that bore me, but into me directly. If not for him we would not exist. And, for that, we must in perpetuity be grateful to him.

Thirty-Two

Cassidy went in search of Shakkra. He found her sitting on the sofa, her face buried into another magazine. She saw the concern etched into his face.

"I'm being careful, my son," she smiled, "the son I'm going to trade one day soon for a precious young girl."

"You'll make each other deaf with your female chattering, and rub off your skin with all your hugging and kissing. I see you from behind the trees. If you were a man I'm sure you'd have her child."

She twisted her mouth and arched an eyebrow in a way particular to women.

"She needs someone to hug and kiss her."

Cassidy shook his head, defeated. "She's stolen you from me. She's a witch, Shakkra."

"Yes, she's a pretty little witch who's trying her best to work her magic on you." She paused. "Cassidy, listen to me. I want that girl as my daughter-in-law when we leave here. We have to succeed. I won't see her with Dakota as much I like the boy. He's a good young man, and I see in his eyes how he loves Xandra. What's decreed isn't right. It can't happen. It won't happen."

He scanned the magazines.

"I've returned each one to its proper place. I told you. I'm being careful."

"I know, Shakkra. And you're right. It won't happen, not on my father's grave."

315

"Are we leaving?"

"No. I have more to read. I think about two hours. Then we'll sit in the pool and I'll tell you all that I've learned. Shakkra, I believe the gold is still there."

"I'll sit in the grass, and before you leave me make that black frame come to life again. While you're reading I'll learn here."

"It's called television, Shakkra. I'm not certain how we see what we do, but I know it will teach us what we don't know."

He explained the On\Off, the Volume and cursors. She fought the confusion in her mind and when he left her she spent several minutes mesmerized and listening to each channel before thumbing the cursor to another.

One floor above Cassidy went directly to the desk and Wendell Parkens' journal, proud of his mother.

Charles was a good man in Cassidy's mind, William wasn't. Horatio was in the first part of his life; Wendell wasn't at any time in his life. He believed Horatio would have remained a good man in the second part of his life, had he remained with Oona and Tora. Did he really despise the island that much that he never returned for the gold, taking his life instead?

He married a woman for her good looks, when he already had two and was wealthy. Did he need to escape the island so badly that he married the wrong woman for the wrong reason when no one would have known him by his new name? Cassidy wouldn't. He loved two women and one was downstairs working as diligently as he was to escape the island and respect his father's, her first-mate's dying wish.

He snorted loudly at the thought. Shakkra was never Zach's first-mate. She was always his wife.

Cassidy put his hand on the leather-bound journal. He knew he would discover no more about the Weatherbones.

They were a family long dead and forgotten, save the eldest son and Dakota. He had more than a hundred pages to read and one more night. Then what would he do?

The evasive answer was a matter of considerable concern each sleepless night as his mother's quiet whimpers engulfed him.

What he needed now was to learn more of Wendell Parkens and his sons.
*

My bride was as much infatuated with the island and her new home as she was with me. She loved the sea and was endlessly exhilarated by the hedonism of swimming naked in the middle of it.

She was carnal by nature and by summer's end she was as pleasantly coloured and toned as entirely as I, proving a worthwhile companion each night and most days at the shore, though not all my hours or hers were spent in wasteful indulgence of one another. When I was not keeping pace with her my days and evening were spent in consultation with the old man.

By late March we were ready with plans for a village of ten villas and a garden sufficiently large and varied to sustain ten men and ten women, until a year later when I would bring ten plus ten more.

We set out with the old man on a voyage to Miami. She to await the arrival of my first son, he to purchase all that was needed to achieve the secondary half my dream while I undertook to fulfill the primary.

We remained two months during which time the old man returned weekly onboard a hired barge with cargo required to construct and properly feed the village. I leased for my wife and me a pleasant accommodation and engaged a young woman to act as her servant and as her companion during my frequent absences of which she was, in her mind, fully apprised.

My quest was threefold. The first was my application of citizenship; the second was the acquisition of people and the acquirement. The third, and of equal importance to me, was a supply of a tincture that was well beyond my then current knowledge. To that end I followed the path of my grandfather. I made myself well-known to a brothel of formidable repute and their recognized rival. I was disappointed in neither establishment and spent my afternoons alternating between the two.

The women were of a quality equal to or exceeding my girls in a Montreal that would never again be my home. They were varied in nationality, colour and mother tongue, their accents as colourful and as charming as the whores themselves who were not my objectives, rather my facilitators and pleasant diversions.

By the conclusion of my time with them I had acquired the name of a man who without much debate acquired me as his newest and most desired client. He was my junior by a decade and our relationship endured until his untimely death at which time his son succeeded him.

The mornings and evenings of those weeks were no less critical to my vision. During those hours I sought girls and young men I considered most suited to the peaceful and idyllic existence I would offer them. Unlike my grandfather, I decided on single men and women, childless and of equal in age within a year or two and discovered them in no particular order.

The men I wanted were not yet past their mid-twenties, and for good reason. I cared not at all about their past, concerned that they could and would till a field and cast a net, take another man's waif and the women I would assign them. Each was able-bodied and of passable good looks, deprived of the fullest use of their minds and eager.

To each one I explained the Twelve Scriptures and required them to sign their mark as contractual proof of their acceptance. In return I would give them a life free of disease and poverty in a Shangri-La endowed with white sands, blue water and lush green gardens.

In addition to which I would cloth them and feed them.

I found half the number on the street searching for employment, indifferent to their colour, some white, some black. A few were itinerant and one I found with a woman of his own. He carried a strongbox which seemed impossibly heavy strapped to his shoulders and back. He was twenty-two and fit, she was eighteen with an appearance that would serve her well at the brothel and make her a favourite which he certainly could not in any dream of his afford.

I deliberated the better part of the last week whether or not to except them, and at last I did.

I gave each man two-hundred dollars so that he might find lodging and equip himself with certain essentials which I enumerated to each one. None but the last man and woman had possessions of their own to bring.

The women I found were not younger than eighteen and not older than twenty, each one single, a virgin, attractive beyond the norm and varied in their extraction. I gave each one a gift of silk stockings, underpants and a chemise.

I took each one to dinner in a new dress and shoes and let them taste the sweetness of wine and the heat of fine cognac. I brought each one to my bed to test their honesty and their bodies; however the first test was their acquiescence. I rejected very few who sought to deceive me, determined that the men be content with my choices.

I found the nine girls in turn a comfortable room and paid them sufficient funds to maintain themselves through to the end of my explorations, though I did not neglect them. I continued to assess each one's appropriateness for each man and to reassure them. When we left port each man was indeed content, each woman excited by her unforeseen salvation delivered by me. The children sat quietly in wonder, uncertain of their new parents.

They were ten boys and ten girls aged between ten and twelve, all of them orphaned and of mixed breeding. The holy sisters charged with their care equally delighted to be rid of twenty children and to enrich their coffers by one thousand times that number.

In a ledger specific to its current and future purpose I noted the name of each man, his woman and the children assigned to him. I noted their dates of arrival and their ages, leaving blank those columns required for their future joining, their children's names and their dates. The farthest column would note the date of their expiration, the first of which I did not anticipate would occur within such a brief number of years.

None of the children and none of the women had previously experienced the sea, a certain number of them succumbing to debilitating mal de mer. To my starboard side was the barge burdened with supplies I could not transport in excess of my human cargo, save a single strongbox the man with his own woman declined to relinquish.

The barge anchored at a point where at low tide she would sit on the bottom, the captain anxious to rid his vessel of the pigs, goats, sheep and various fowl. I anchored not far off her portside, the women regarding my dinghy with some reservation, not completely convinced of their uneventful arrival to shore.

The boys scrambled over the gunwale from where they stood and plunged into the saltwater. The men leapt in behind them, their pants and shirts already soaked with sweat. The girls went with the women, I suppose lamenting their dresses.

Jonathon Clayton, I remember, remained onboard for the dinghy to return for him, his woman and his strongbox.

I joined him with my wife and first son.

Each couple was anxious to see their new home, a villa of solid construction built with wood and covered with slate atop foundations of concrete some four feet above the ground. The windows were wooden slats crafted from teakwood, as were the front and back doors, each home possessing a kitchen and sitting room, two rooms for sleeping and one to accommodate matters of a personal nature. Outside at the rear were an enclosure for their personal bathing and a shed for their tools which were all new and of the most modern design.

The plumbing as well was ingeniously designed by the old man, each villa's need supplied by rainwater captured on their rooftops. The containment of clean water was sufficient for a week, fed by dual conduits into the villa for cooking and hygiene, the grey water disposed of by gravity into individual deep pits carved into the ground far into the forest.

In their rooms they found closets filled with cotton knee breeches, loose-fitting shirts, berets and sandals for the men and boys. Each had a change for their travail in the fields and one for the evening. For the women and girls I commissioned tunics to conceal the lesser parts of their legs and none of their arms, sandals and gob hats to protect their heads from the harsh sun. For their time in the sea I provided cotton shorts for the men, bloomers for the women and girls with middies to maximize their comfort and freedom to frolic.

The males would have appeared ludicrous to continue wearing thick, woollen long johns under their new garb, as would the women were their underpants to extend below the hems of their tunics. To the males I gave newly fashionable briefs, for the females I commissioned smaller underpants to complement their tunics.

The fashion was beyond the pale for them and I left

them to tire of their existing wardrobe in their own time, which they did. Within a few days the men saw the obvious benefit. The women continued a weakening disinclination awhile longer, forming a better opinion of their new wardrobe upon seeing my wife in her tunic and at the beach in flared bloomers and middy, relaxed and entirely comfortable.

By June 30th all were habituated to their homes, to my fields and Tombola. Each morning boys learned to fish by the side of their new fathers as daughters worked in the gardens with new mothers. They sought shelter from the hot sun to consume their midday meal and when they were nourished the women prepared the morning's catch for the evening meal or preserved what was caught to store in their sheds.

At night neighbours sat on their porches and conversed with neighbours and became friends. They strolled in the forest and swam at the beach.

Often in the low light before dusk I would stand atop the precipice to observe them through my telescope and witness their contentment with me and with each other. I chose well, each of them living what most of the entire world could merely fabricate in fantastic dreams of limited duration. And that day, above all others, would be the telling of my certain success or my pending defeat.

I planned a great feast of roasted meats with legumes, vegetables and fruits from my gardens. I gave them no tincture that night. To quench them I brought wine and liquor and beer and joined them in a simple ceremony.

In the morning a few awoke on the beach, unaware as I watched them timidly clothe their naked bodies. Others awoke in the privacy of their beds, each one bathing in the sea before the morning meal. They were happy and I determined that each year, until year six years hence when I would join the first of the girls with the first of the boys, I would extend each feast by one day.

In the spring the village was in the throes of maternity, eleven women delivering a child not many days apart, leaving the men in the latter days to toil alone in the sea, at the gutting table and in the fields. I suspect many were the product of my initial investigation of the women.

The one man, in fact, who could claim full responsibility for his eventual fertilization, was Jon Clayton, a responsibility he delayed for reasons of his own.

Before my departure in April for reasons of further recruitment, my census counted fifty-five, upon my return we were at ninety-five.

The old man went with me, returning without me onboard a barge laden with lumber and slate, beds and dishes, baths and clothes. Aboard my yacht were wine, liquor and beer for the two nights of feasting and condoms for the men. Some had confided in me worries of their hearths growing too small and, truthfully, in my mind I had begun to consider that very dilemma, that my island would grow beyond my ability to guide them.

My criteria had not changed and my absence was of much shorter duration. The ten men were of a lower class, the women attractive and childless. And again I went to the nuns to relieve them of their best children which were available to me in abundance.

The third year was no different. Tombola was a village of thirty villas, Tombolina home to me and my wife alone where she continued her hedonism and enjoyment of her life with me. We drank wine with each evening meal in our home, we wore fine silk to our bed and twice or three times yearly she voyaged with me to various ports where we mixed with people of an enviable station, Irene adapting well to the their society after many years of my osmotic influence over her.

Those of the longest duration on the island had not tired

of their idyllic existence and in the spring of the fourth year I brought the population to 135 souls and forty homes. Three years remained until my truest test, when the first children would join together and each year thereafter when I would cease to import strangers and begin to fully cultivate the true people of Tombola.

My stores of unused opium had quadrupled and that year I deemed them ready to fully partake of our festive viand over four days and four nights. On the first night the newest were joined during a magnificent ceremony and all took well to their first taste of mild tincture. Each day and night the men grew more daring, the women more brazen. Some swam naked in the dark night time water; others prostrated themselves across the warm sand to bathe their bodies with sun, the women daringly so without benefit of their middies to cover their breasts whilst they on their fronts to tan their backs.

By the fifth morning I was pleased by what I had witnessed and they went willingly to cast their nets and tend to their gardens. I went to my crystal pool to begin teaching my son who was three and of an age appropriate for his initial instruction. I went also to read in the quiet of my garden and reflect upon a matter of mounting anxiety to me, uncertain how to approach the man.

By my records Jon Clayton was then twenty-five, his woman twenty-one. She was the loveliest of my flock and each year more men admired her. I confess that when I saw Irene as often as I did in her natural state I saw them both.

I was and remain unaccustomed to being denied. Yet to this day I harbour no doubt that he would have killed me had I once thought to share my affection with her or replace my false-wife with her. He was unlike the others in his manner and his speech and not once since his arrival had I seen his strongbox. He sat upon the lid throughout the entire voyage and once at the shore conveyed the cumbersome thing to his villa without moment's delay. Not long after, when I went to them in the company of the old man, as with all the others, to verify the condition of his home, the box was gone.

There was no visible indication of the thing which was too large and excessively heavy to conceal under a bed or place upon a shelf.

I went to him and sat with him on the fifth morning. I proposed that he accept to act as my Chief Counsellor in matters of daily importance, that he assume the role of guardian of the village when I was gone on business requisite to the maintenance of the island. I wanted him close to me so that I might glean from him what he knew, that I might discover evidence beyond my well-founded suspicions that he felt himself above reproach, that he thought himself an island unto himself.

To my absolute astonishment he shook my hand in agreement. In return I gave him status.

I built him a wonderful home twice the others in dimension and comfort so that he might be respected by the village, in a place easily viewed from my perch high atop Tombolina and sought his counsel in many of the island's quotidian matters.

He was a man whose eyes could not disguise his curiosity or natural intelligence. Mine to this day are the only books on Tombola, save his. This I know. Literacy for many is a burden which provokes thoughts and dreams and breeds dissatisfaction. My flock has no need of such disappointment, for what would they accomplish beyond my shores. They are content, as they were then and during the time of William, their lives are simple and complete for they lack nothing. Remember this throughout all your days.

Yet I know that Jonathon Clayton was a man well-read, not unlike Jacob his son, his son Zach, and the one who is left, this Cassidy, who conceals somewhere on this island the fodder of his dissatisfaction and, I suspect, his mother's.

Beware of him, Dakota. Beware of her in the time she has left. My single consolation is the increasing obsolescence of what they possess. Yet books alone did not create such a burden upon Clayton's back and I wonder to this final crossroad in my life what young Cassidy has truly inherited beyond his father's tools. Be cautious of him. He, as were his forefathers, is deceitful.

One year later I became an American citizen. The island grew to 185 souls and fifty homes. Ten men were joined with ten women of formidable good looks, all of them virgins save the necessity of my assessment of them. Each was given an orphan boy and girl, in their twelfth year. The feast lasted five days and nights, the strength of the tincture somewhat increased and in the sixth year my flock had grown to 235 and sixty villas.

The seventh year at last arrived, the truest test of their devotion to me and all were joyous at the expectation of a true Seven Feasts, except the old man, the builder of my village and my manor. He was sickly ill. A soiled rag his constant companion, a wicked and vile cough his final penance in life. I sat with him to bring him comfort, despite his putrid breath suffocating me.

He drank one full cup, then another and a third. Several months earlier he'd gone with me to the States where I commissioned a pole crafted from oak with an altitude of some sixty feet, a diametre equal in breadth to the shoulders of a large man and treated to resist the sea.

The hewing lasted an entire week, the transport to the harbour and the voyage across the water one week more. The crew of the barge remained four weeks longer constructing a dam against the flood waters of the gorge and when they were done the Pole of Tombola stood forty feet high above the lowest water and would never be displaced by the sea or set aflame as a pyrotechnic by someone searching to assuage his past or confirm his redemption.

This Pole of Tombola stood erect in a depression 200 feet from my bridge and towards the leeward shore. At the lowest tide one could splash in water as deep as his ankles, at the highest even the tallest man would drown were his feet not to leave the floor.

I thought I might miss the old man for without him the village might likely have been no better than William's crude cluster of shacks. I did not miss him, and do not. He faded from my memory quickly, which I discovered was requisite to my exalted position. I could not favour the weak, for weakness would ruin Tombola. He'd be the first, I decided.

The village grew to 285. The final ten men and ten women, then comfortable with their new children in their new villas amongst their new neighbours, were curious about The Seven Feasts. They would be the last of any unfamiliar persons to set foot upon my shores and the first joined by me on that thirtieth of June, behind them stood the original orphans then in their seventeenth and eighteenth years.

At the shore after the morning meal, they filled their cups measured by me, and soon began to sing, dance and frolic in the sea.

The ten girls did not know. How could they? The ten boys knew from the time of their first change and were anxious to couple and be joined. I left them to talk amongst themselves and went with the girls to my pond at high water where my false-wife greeted us with plates of fruit and cups of tincture.

Irene was as excited as I, and forbidden to partake in the festive sharing of affections as was I by my own decree so that my rank might be upheld. For one woman or a few to gain my favour would be unfair and possibly lead to jealousy and envy. She and I sought pleasure in our travels beyond the scrutiny of my flock. The ten girls were at once taken aback by her as she stood before them in her shield and bolero that was left untied.

I was sufficiently pleased to observe them, to witness them increasingly sharing affection each year with neighbours and friends so freely, without refrain or jealousy. They understood that open affection towards one another was the one true exorciser of covetousness. Tombola was truly my Eden and they were indeed my flock.

With our first cups emptied, our appetites sated, we went into the water with another. Irene came with us. She had no designation beyond her name. She was my first-mate to all of Tombola and no other girl child henceforth would be given her name. She was Irene and was then twenty-seven with the countenance and body of a woman much younger.

The girls took easily to her. They drank and swam together. They emptied their cups to splash and giggle and when she threw her shield and bolero to the sand the girls did likewise with their shorts and boleros which had earlier replaced the bloomers and middies which had served their purpose of diluting their parents' inhibitions.

Over the years I had commissioned smaller and more comfortable clothing for their time at the sea. The females now wore shorter and more flared shorts constructed of a lighter fabric, their tops were boleros adopted from European fashion that tied at their breasts and were infinitely more desirable to the male contingent of the island. The men's fashion was equally modern. Irene had worn her own trend of late beyond their inquisitiveness and would be tested that evening as much as I.

I spoke with the girls of what they should expect and answered their concerns with gentle strokes and warming endearments. I spoke of The Seven Feasts, the joining and

328

sharing of affection. Since the first taste of tincture one year before the village had become closer and I recited the Twelve Scriptures to reinforce what they should know as faithful adherents.

We waded with the first into deeper water where I was gentle so that she would not cry or cry out. She did not and when all ten were taught we left the water to dry ourselves in the low sun.

They dressed in tunics of different colours. I sent them to search out the boys who wore the same colours, who knew to go with the girls to their new villas and couple without apprehension for they would soon be joined as first-mates and free to share affection from that day forward. They would no longer share their parents' hearth. Ten of the then ninety villas were theirs with which to begin separate and contented lives.

I remained at the pond with Irene who had not mislaid her carnality in some dark corner of motherhood. She understood what I must do and was not jealous in any way. Nor did I deny her nature throughout our travels abroad.

We went to the festive tent by the shore when the time was right and joined the twenty children who would soon bring forth the purest generation to my isle. We feasted with them and when we had eaten our fill we went to the sand with our cups. The air was thick with merriment and sensuality. I raised my cup and praised them; Irene went amongst them and gave them all gifts.

When her coffer was empty she returned to stand by my side self-assured. She let her robe drop to the sand, attired in a tightly woven shield sufficient to cover her pubes. The back of her was entirely bare. Her breasts, not different in colour from the rest of her, were covered by the smallest of boleros constructed without ties. She told them to open their gifts and walked into the ocean without waiting to see what their reaction might be.

I joined her, my own robe not far from the water's edge, my shield not more than a cod of soft leather, my backside uncovered across half its width to preserve the sanctity of my position.

We waded and swam towards the gorge, watching, our hopes mounting at seeing the confusion.

The men were first to run to their villas. Installing their shields required the removal of whatever garment they wore; though I suspect the uncertainty as to how they should wear the new article was more worrisome. While they were gone the women chattered excitedly, transforming into a kaleidoscope of arms and legs.

They were first into the water. We left when the men filtered through the trees onto the sand, wearing shields in no way as modest in construction as my own.

The shield from then on was important to island fashion, worn by the men in the sea when they fished, or on hot day afternoons in the sun, which they came to know as high and late sun. By the women when they stood at the gutting tables cleaning the day's catch or swimming in the blue water. The small piece at the shore was a common sight.

William was not wrong in his evaluation. Minions were easily trained.

By the fourth day as many boleros covered the sand and the grass by the trees as they did breasts. I was alone with Clayton. I recall that he not once called me by my title, nor by my name. We simply spoke. During his epoch they all knew my name, until eventually they forgot.

Nonetheless for all but him and his woman I was The Grand Guardian. Better he called me nothing than to diminish my stature with familiar address.

I believe several conditions existed and conjoined at a propitious moment to inspire Jonathon Clayton towards an island life. The reason he never attempted to leave is a matter of conjecture. Possibly that I possessed several weapons which he did not. I possessed seamanship and a vessel, which he did not. And possibly those combined elements were sufficient to discourage him, lest he feared the hangman or jailer in relationship to what lay secreted in his strongbox, which I strongly believe to this day is a viable suspicion.

I went to his hearth as a courtesy for discussion. He did not want the old man to die, not that way. He disagreed with the Pole of Tombola and, I knew then, with many more aspects of my island. His wife did not share affection with anyone, nor did he. When others bathed in the sea or under the sun, their bodies stretched upon the sand, he was invisible to my eyes. He was gone with her. While others celebrated joyously and drank of the tincture, their eyes glazed, their bodies and minds relaxed, his eyes, I remarked, were clear, his body and mind equally alert. Hers close to his. Try as I might, I never discovered his path.

The pole would remain. I had no election. The pole was humane, and remains so to this the eve of my death: 101 stones cast into the air by those whose vision is no less weak than their limbs. Were I to have put a hole in the old man's head or tie his wrists and give him to the sea, what then?

The old man died at midnight by my hand. He'd survived beyond his own expectation and wanted my mercy. I could do no less. Many of the 100 missed. Mine did not. I freed him from the pole and the receding waters at first light. I carried him to my ship and sailed north where I buried him in the sea.

Jon Clayton viewed me differently from then on. I was, in my view of what festered in his mind, a real threat to him. As I harboured no doubt that he was to me.

Three days later The Seven Feasts was at an end. Men fished once again in the sea and women worked their gardens and fields. On the Sunday, the seventh sun, they amused themselves at the shore, where I saw not the slightest indication of him from my high peak, yet I had no resource with which to ascertain his movements or hers. What was certain in my mind was his dislike of me.

For five years the island prospered. We were then 350 and content. Of course, I sailed on several excursions to East coast and to the West Indies, each time bringing with me supplies for the men and women under my care.

Alas, with so many came burdens and difficulties. I could not return with necessities for so many, their tunics and pants, their shields and their boleros, their blankets and sheets and quantities of rum and tincture sufficient to sustain them through The Seven Feasts. The weight alone would most certainly sink my vessel.

On one such voyage I returned with a tailor of advanced age and his wife, a capable seamstress. I brought with them many dozen bolts of fabric, a sewing table, balls of yarn and needles.

We came by a circuitous route. They were my guests for the better part of one month and not once did I mention Tombola by name.

Throughout the duration of their sojourn they met each day with a handful of my female flock whose capacity for learning was deemed adequate. They were given instruction in the knitting and weaving of shields. By month's end they were passably good at stitching and sizing, adding small details I never gave thought to and did not disallow.

When the task was done I returned them by the longest route possible and paid them well for the work they would no longer enjoy for I commissioned them to make me self-sufficient in that aspect of the isle. I suppose he might have come to his end not long after as he was not well and his wife, throughout her brief visit was constantly sullen when she might have rejoiced at her good fortune. Now they are both forgotten.

The island was self-sufficient and continued to grow in equal parts to my love for them and my suspicions of one.

Thirteen more had gone others had gone to the pole, Jon Clayton refusing on the first few occasions my instruction that he cast the last stone until I asked no more.

His son was twelve. One Clayton was worrisome, double that number would threaten me.

Hence, subsequent to the evening meal of the fourth day of The Seven Feasts at the beginning of his twenty-first year, I walked with him along the leeward shore of Tombolina to discuss the woman sitting lashed to the pole.

I wanted him to view the pond and my pool, to fully understand me, and we walked through the shallow channel to the lagoon. We went to my dock where we boarded Two Fortunes, my newest yacht, and he saw for the first time my private passage. We returned to the pool where I poured two cups of the finest French cognac from a bottle I opened before his very eyes so that I might circumvent his suspicion of me. I offered him a Cuban of the purest quality and he refused. I drank the cognac, he did not and I saw in his eyes that he knew.

I reached for a cigar and lit the tip with a gold-filled lighter and inhaled the aroma. I reclined. I offered him, as would befit his station as my Chief Counsellor, and his woman with him, the privilege of bathing in my pond and my curative crystal pool. He declined. He was content with his then status quo. I beseeched him to reconsider my impression of his duty to cast the last stone. He declined.

He wanted the woman that night set free, not punished for her condition. He wanted the woman conveyed to the States for care, as though Two Fortunes was an ambulance vessel.

He confronted me in the most daring fashion, defying me. He wanted to see with his own eyes the tombola which decided at random who would live another year and who would not, which of course has never existed. I told him so.

What fairness would exist in a random draw which would certainly place happy and healthy people in jeopardy without any sane justification, I questioned? Cleansing the Isle of Tombola of those who would contaminate us by virtue of their discontent, infirmity or frailty was and remains the single and most efficacious means of ensuring our continuance. The eve of my own submission to the pole and to my flock that is now upon me can be no greater testament of that most sacred doctrine.

I confessed my curiosity as to the contents of his strongbox, the remnants of his past life. Had he replied books, private papers or gold he might have survived the evening. He didn't, and my subterfuge was exhausted. What I wanted was his devotion to me, which I recognized would forever be denied me.

I reached into a box by the side of the Cubans and shot him once with the pistol concealed within. I saw no purpose in prolonging his demise with threats or idle banter. His wound exploded three inches below his groin from the inner thigh into the bone, catapulting him from his seat onto the soft grass.

I cocked the hammer of my pistol once more and waited, drinking my cognac, filling the air between us with blue smoke. A drowned man will not wear the same expression as a man whose end comes from a bullet. I waited two hours by my count and my memory, my body infused with the warmth of strong cognac, my person cloaked in the delicate aroma of aged tobacco.

He spoke not one word, nor did he groan a single murmur. He lay on the ground bleeding, dying in defiant silence, not one word spoken of his woman or their son or their daughters.

When at last his time was near I stood and went to him. He was balanced between life and death, clinging to life at the threshold of his demise. I went to his feet and turned my back to him. I knelt, grabbing his ankles, raising them to a manageable height and dragging him with considerable effort across the garden and into the pond. Not once did he cry out, neither in pain nor in desperation and, in water sufficiently deep for my purpose, I inverted his body facedown and left him to drown or to bleed. Whichever he chose, I had no reason or desire to bear witness.

I went to the woman at the gorge and plucked the figs from her cheeks. I tilted her head to its limit and poured tincture into her mouth to soothe her and went to the shore to summon the village.

Within the hour she was forgotten, memories of her expelled by urgent desires to share affection. When the tide reached her shoulders I too left her. My task at hand would last until the ebbing waters of early dawn.

I stood over Jon Clayton. He was dead. His subsequent conveyance to my yacht would be a Herculean effort of needlessly long duration. First I went to the yacht alone to ready myself, my instruments previously laid out. I fortified my mind and my body with a generous measure of cognac and was not for a moment indecisive as I strode to the pond. He rolled in the water without objection and I was able to beach him without great effort on the sand, the weight of his torso anchoring him in place. I jolted him from his pants and knelt close by the cleansed wound.

I raised his leg onto my shoulder and with the sharpest serrated blade I possessed I tore at the entire circumference of his upper thigh, separating the flesh. I was covered with blood, yet I persisted until I sensed a significant resistance requiring a more appropriate tool. With my razor I sliced through his sinewy matter of ligaments and muscle and finally was able to drop the leg and disrobe. I plunged into the high water and bathed meticulously.

When I was clean, and with my hatchet, I knelt once

again by my work. Adrenalin was my tincture. Never before had I dissected a man. The first blow was insufficient to separate the limb, the second no better. The third attempt caused the amputated part to split away without much noise and lay inert by the stump. What little blood exited from either extremity drained into the sand and discoloured the water.

Once again I left him to compose myself in my crystal pool, this time with Irene who was in no way complicit in my surgery or my dispatch of him. Her purpose was to comfort me until I would free the woman from the pole and secure her to the transom of my launch which I was by then adept at piloting inside the gorge.

The sky was dark when I freed her in waist-deep water. Urgency did not allow her to remain past high tide. I weighted her, as I did all of them, and hauled her onto the low platform. Once clear of the gorge I motored north beyond the shores of Tombolina where I discharged her.

When the launch was once again floating at dock I proceeded to Clayton.

Guiding him from my pond to the sea he was not in the least cumbersome, though I admit to certain nausea at having to convey his tattered limb with him. Together we waded south towards the gorge at a depth equal to my shoulders. Invisible to all, I could smell the smouldering fires wafting from the village to the sea and hear the ardent cries of neighbours and friends strewn upon the cool sand.

There I released body and limb to a flooding tide.

That very morning Jonathon Clayton was discovered, his leg torn away by a creature of the deep sea. I heard the hysterical cries from my home and went quickly to console his woman and son. Later the same day, his remains clad in cotton ribbons out of respect for his woman, and without her to hinder me, I sailed with him onboard my launch to afford him a decent burial far to the south in a sacred place then known to me alone. Such was my final respect towards my flock; such was my final devotion to each of them in turn and in their minds.

They must never know of the non-existence of such a place. Indeed, far from the shore I gave him to the sea. What became of the man's leg remains a mystery of little interest to me.

Thirty-Three

Cassidy wanted his mother. He was sitting at the desk of a conscienceless man and somehow he felt powerless. He didn't know what he felt, yet he did. He felt consumed by evil. His mind was black. He felt nauseous, his limbs catatonic. He was cold, his head was spinning. In his space and time the library didn't exist, nothing existed. He was somewhere he didn't know in a time he'd never lived, but he knew that was wrong. He had been there, often, always the same place and time, but when and where? What cloaked his mind in darkness to haunt him, and why?

When the sickening numbness subsided he went to Shakkra in a daze and sat beside her. She was transfixed.

"Cassidy, many of them speak no differently than we do, you and I. Others I don't understand at all. The ones I don't understand are the prettiest. They must be the foreign tongues Zach spoke of. I've learned more than I could have imagined. I'm really beginning to hate this place."

"Shakkra…"

She faced him. "Cassidy, you're white as a ghost. Why? What have you learned?"

She put a hand on her son's and waited. She knew.

"You've seen the evil darkness again?"

"I don't understand why it takes me over without warning. I'm always in a place I know but where I've never been. I'm in another time, never sure whether I'm in the past or in the future. And how can that be when I've never

338

left this place?"

"We're here now, Cassidy. One day you'll discover the answer, when we do leave this place."

"Shakkra, I'm not finished upstairs. I still have much to read in his journal. We have time left and most of the day tomorrow. I have more to show you."

"I also have much to tell you."

"They won't return until the day after. When we're done here we'll sit in the pool and exchange what we've learned."

"You have one hour, Cassidy, and one after that to talk before we walk home." She beamed. "And, yes, you can carry me through the channel to the sand and across the gorge. I've never felt so good in my clothes. You've spoiled me, Cassidy. I'm seeing so many wonders on this television. I also saw the value of the gold in your chest. Much has changed since Jonathon's time. Cassidy, your gold is worth over three million dollars."

He shrugged.

"This house, and ones much nicer, is bought for one fifth of what you have. And cars, much nicer than the ones in Jonathon's pictures..." Tears formed in her eyes. "That's what he wanted, Cassidy. He wanted Jacob or Zach or you to live well. I think you really are wealthy. You can live like The Grand Guardian when we leave this place. That is why he killed your father and Jacob. He wants your gold."

"The gold is yours as well as mine. When we leave, we leave together. And, mother..."

"What is it, your little heart? Does she still trouble you?"

"She's a girl. She'll always trouble me, the same way you troubled my father. That's why I must find you a man; I can't manage the two of you by myself."

She pinched him, but his smile was weak.

"I've put her from my mind until I feel safe to think of

her, Shakkra."

"Then, what is it, sweetheart? What did you learn that caused your dark dream?"

"Jonathon, he didn't drown in the sea. No sea monster took his leg from him. He did it, Wendell Parkens…and soon his eldest son will think to come for me."

He kissed her cheek.

"He'll come for me before you. I'm Zach's woman. The new Grand Guardian won't wait long."

"He won't come for you, not for you, not for me. I promise. Before the next Seven Feasts we'll be gone from here." He looked at screen and forced a grin. "Then you and Aayla will wear the finest silk thongs under your beautiful dresses like they're wearing."

She slapped his cheek with an open palm, gently.

"Club dresses, Cassidy. And don't presume to know what I'll be wearing under my dresses." She chortled. "I really have so much to tell you. Thank you for bringing me. Now, go upstairs and leave me to my black frame. We must have one of these when we leave here, Cassidy. It's like the moving pictures Jonathon once described to Jacob, and he to your father."

Cassidy made her a promise, kissed her and left. His mind was clearer, his body stronger. Shakkra did that to him, and Zach. He was his father's son, and he could be no less for Shakkra who was as much his sister and close friend as his loving mother. No, he mused climbing the stairs, he wouldn't be stoned. Neither would Shakkra sit at the pole as did the wife of Jonathon and the first-mate of Jacob.
*

The subsequent six years passed me by uneventfully, my registry of births and deaths a veritable ledger of pluses and minuses. The population was at 500 and stable. The advent of ingestible contraception was a twofold blessing in that regard. Fewer births occurred as an aftermath of The Seven Feasts and the celebration was truly one of gratification and abandon, though none were permitted the convenience before their first joining.

The few girls who chose to disobey me were forthwith taken by me so that mother and child might be cared for.

Jacob reached his majority and was joined. I recall with fondness my first-teaching of his first-mate, my enjoyment of her in great measure a derivative of my punishment of a man who had disheartened me and acted subversively toward me. She was a girl of uncommon good looks amongst a population borne by a parentage first selected by me and soon after I recognized an evolution within her that did not diminish throughout her lifespan.

One cannot contain or disguise intelligence and what I saw unmistakably in Jacob's eyes I began to distinguish in hers.

On that fourth night I sat Jonathon's woman at the pole despite my inclination to stone her earlier on. Her longevity was a matter of pragmatism and throughout those years she steadfastly refused to join with a second-mate. Jon Clayton had left his mark on this island, my quandary since his demise a question of timely eradication. Clearly the women and offspring mixed with Clayton's blood were and remain no less a threat to Tombola.

One year later Zach was born to Jacob Their second child, a girl, followed a year later. She died not long after. As for Jacob, he lived thirty-one years. His first-mate followed six years later. Happy no doubt to have seen her son joined with Shakkra.

I have maintained a separate record of that family from Jon and his woman to the current Cassidy and his mother. Their blood has not thinned to any degree and I worry the time is nigh to staunch the flow.

Not once did I invite their women to my pond so that I

might give them comfort. They thought differently of me and I saw the wisdom of disregarding that aspect of them. In fact, with age, my desire to comfort any of the bereaved females decreased markedly. I discovered that with age what I desired most was youth, content to sail the West Indies and the Southeast with Irene in search of diversity and nubility.

Irene was forty-eight. To a keen eye and intimate touch one could not discount that her years and proclivity for good living had begun a usurpation of her once undeniable allure. Her carnal appetite was no less ravenous than her taste for fine cuisine and, at her age, no less costly when not in the company of our closest acquaintances or when she desired something much younger and prettier, or handsome and virile.

At her mid-centenary we celebrated gaily in Miami with champagne. We dined with good friends onboard my yacht who thought us delightful and different. We danced and laughed and went our separate ways for the diversity that was habitual to us and shared with our friends.

I was then sixty-five, though graced with a youthful physique and visage uncommon amongst men of my age.

The final morning we bade them farewell and set a course for Tombola. Irene laid bathing under the hot sun, her body naked and splayed across the forward deck. When she sat to reach for her glass she turned and smiled at me for the last time.

I remember her as though she was here with me now, guiding my pen. She sipped once, then again. She put aside her glass and stood, stretching with her feet wide apart, letting the fine mist cool her. She died quickly, the better part of her head surprisingly intact, her body flung by momentum into the sea.

I would miss her deeply. We were so close throughout those many years. How could I see her sat at the pole? I could not. Nor could I see her grow old. I believe she would have agreed with my immediate dispatch of her, irrespective of the grievous pain I brought upon myself.

Yet I could not reside on my own in such a large home, nor could I manage the island, the village or The Seven Feasts on my own, and what of companionship to fill the lonely voids between my travels.

My station required Irene. She was as important as I in the eyes of my flock. Nor could I take for my own any of the girls at their majority. To act upon such a foolhardy notion would imperil me. Not one of them would ever comprehend a transition from the fields to Tombolina, nor could I possibly educate the brightest amongst them in worldly matters so that I might avoid certain humiliation during my many sojourns abroad.

In any event, how would I explain such a young companion or wife despite existing in a decade of free thinking and indiscriminate emotion?

Of equal import was and is the mystique of Tombolina and me, The Grand Guardian. Any who would be Irene would have knowledge of me. She would see me in my entirety; she would know my weaknesses and strengths, my pleasures, my fantasies and my secrets which are the fixative that binds us together.

One month prior to The Seven Feasts in '76 I found her in Miami. She was a newly hired serving girl in my preferred establishment, engaged no doubt by reason of her endowments, equally delightful to one's eye as to one's imagination. She was a sculpture of perfection and I had not long to wait to see for myself what lay beneath what little she wore.

I wanted her for the week, to test our compatibility. I was not tentative in my request. I was decided. Nor was she falsely demure. She was, by her own admission, practised, her appetite capricious. She would have lied, and for that reason I chose not to enquire. Had she said one or two, she would have meant four or five; ten would have meant twice that number and I would have left her in search of a less accommodating female. She wanted ten thousand for the seven nights and I considered the fee agreeable.

Her name was, at first Taliah. Once upon the island however she was Irene. She was ideal. She was twenty and insatiable upon hearing of my island, my yacht and my wealth. She was sufficiently educated to act as my constant companion abroad, though not to any extent that would cause me to worry here on the island. She would adapt well to Tombolina and to me.

She slept onboard Two Fortunes each night and by week's end she was mine. Her body bartered willingly for an island.

She could not believe her eyes and, at first sight, did not believe me. At her behest I circled the island twice and when I motored though the channel to my dock she gasped at seeing the overhanging ceiling of interlocking vines and dense foliage. I docked alongside the launch and took her to the crystal pool where she could gaze upon the lush gardens and the tall precipice of bare rock. We strolled to the lagoon and through that channel to the ocean where we bathed and later she marvelled at my home.

The Seven Feasts was one week distant. She did not know of the tincture, nor would she until acquainted with the taste and its enrichment of her. Then she would know of the Tombola Pole, my first teaching and the festive ceremony of the first night.

My eldest son, your brother who was then thirty, disliked her at once. Taliah was eight years younger than his own first-mate and considerably more pleasing to the eye, though I believe in my heart his loathing was directed at me. He was not allowed on Tombolina save by invitation on those occasions requisite to his advanced education upon the sea or the desire of a mother now dead to see her son.

He was also the son of The Grand Guardian, his single distinction on the island, and subject to my decrees without privilege. I would at all cost forestall any misconception that Tombola was ruled by a family and not by one who was omnipotent.

He did however love his mother and, I suspect, never truly believed how one night she slipped into the sea as I slept.

Garrett was taught privately as a youth in Virginia. He pursued his mid-years and collegiate studies in Miami, spending his summers at home onboard my yacht and in my private lagoon. He was joined in '64 with his mate whose name was Blaque. And once joined he was sent from my home to begin a more humble hearth of his own.

In the early autumn I sent him away, to fill his mind with advanced knowledge. Arriving home the next summer he found a daughter, and one year hence a son.

During those first seven days in my home, and within the shores of my Tombolina, Taliah romped freely. She practiced the manner of our speech and understood her place as Irene, anxious to meet her village. Yet she requested of me that I call her by name at home. I acquiesced, firm in the belief that she would be my finest woman, disinclined to recommence my search and preparation of yet another.

June 30th was a brilliant day, our morning meal magnificent and later we sat in the curative waters of my pool. Thus far she had worn clothes to prepare and consume her meals, her body as golden as my own. I told her of the five girls who would join and how they must be made ready as decreed in the Twelve Scriptures of my forefathers.

When the five arrived clad in shields and boleros, they were the first of the village to see Irene. I daresay shocked to see someone not much older than themselves completely naked, her skin coloured bright orange, serving their first taste of tincture with breads, figs and fruits. Irene played her part well. She swam with them, splashing and laughing while together we comforted them and made them not afraid.

When they left us, a rainbow of colours romping through the channel, she laid in the sun to dry. She was anxious for the girls to be seen, for the feast and the joining of others. As Irene she was exempt. Her station was understood and she was well accepted by all, regrettably to the exclusion of my son and his mate which did not bode well.

On the fourth night I paid particular attention to Taliah's inebriation. She was young and new to the island, not yet familiar with tradition. She did not cast a stone, none was left, and neither did I. I no longer flung the killing stone. The Chief Counsellor held that stone in his sling.

She was not disinclined towards children, simply not enamoured of stretching her body beyond the point of repair. For my part I had three already, my daughters gone ten and eleven years earlier to their own hearths and I saw no purpose in providing further evidence of my prowess. If I am no longer The Grand Guardian beyond this week, I am and shall ever be the one true father of this magnificent isle.

I tolerated Garrett's malaise three years longer, instructing him on several occasions not to permit his thoughts to fester into jealousy or envy. Tombolina was mine alone until such time as I saw fit to relinquish my time on this earth.

He was unhappy with life, which I understood. He was educated, the first-mate of a woman not his equal. He wanted more and I sent him away to learn aviation. He was gone three years, returning once each quarter and summer for The Seven Feasts. My words of caution to him were succinct. He was not in any way to betray Tombola. And he did not.

It sufficed that he learned to betray her.

In the first year his homecomings were times of happiness for Blaque I daresay she coupled with him and was content to hear the fiction of his fabrications. Predictably, throughout the second year her enthusiasm diminished with each visit. She was his first-mate, no longer first in his heart. Such aspects of a man are inherent when separated by distance and reason. He was a man of means living in a land of excess at a time of indulgence.

To Garrett she was the mother of his children; to me she was the first-mate of The Grand Guardian's son with responsibilities and in the spring of 1982 I forbade him to return that summer. He knew, or at least he surmised. What other reason had I to deny him his homeland?

Four girls and four boys were joined, the feast the most extravagant thus far. I observed his first-mate from afar, partaking to the fullest in the ecstasy and abandon, her carnality seemingly unquenchable. On the fourth day I drank with her as we strolled across the low water of the gorge. Irene joined us at the pond where we swam and filled our stomachs with fine food that was unfamiliar to her. She drank more and we comforted her until the water was once again at its lowest.

I sent Irene to Tombola. I went through the arch and across my bridge to the pole where I set the woman Blaque onto the sand and denuded her. I filled her mouth with a full measure of tincture and stroked her hair. I filled her cheeks with the saturated flesh of figs and lashed her to the pole. I put fire to the torches so that she would see light and left to gather my flock.

Most were excited, I daresay exhilarated at the thunderous and then familiar reverberation throughout the village and along the shore. Only one man and one woman did not keep pace with the others and my thoughts leapt to the not too distant future when I must surely address them.

Blaque went quickly, her lower extremities buried under a blanket of stones, her forehead cracked beneath her broken skin where she lay until early morning when I could safely pilot my launch into the gorge to retrieve her.

When Garrett did return he was an accomplished pilot in fixed-wing aircraft and helicopters. He said not one word about his first-mate. Possibly he had tired of her; perhaps he realized in his travels the magnetic attraction of young flesh to affluence and breeding.

He would take another the following year, he insisted, and he wanted the pick of the young litter. I refused him bluntly, giving him leave to journey as he pleased away from the island so that he might gratify his natural urges, my thinking not in the least benevolent towards him. I wanted his leering eyes away from the most nubile of the island or the youngest and most beautiful of those previously joined.

To him, they were his by right of his birth. Of equal import, I required time alone with Irene to consider what I must do. I reasoned that I had two courses of action available to me, debating throughout the year as to which one he would travel.

One year later I was certain. I chose the lesser, not to this day certain of my prudence. He was not yet The Grand Guardian and for the betterment of the island I banished him for his insolence and self-righteousness. He was thirty-six and unprepared, as was I at thirty-six when I first held his small weight with such wondrous dreams for him swirling in my mind. He had not the slightest notion of equanimity or compassion, temperance or the virtues of quiet supremacy, each one fundamental to the nature of any who desire to succeed me.

He would learn forbearance and restraint, or he would not. His banishment to last not a day less than ten years, his punitive absence intended to prove his worthiness to me or diminish him all the more in my opinion of him.

He would leave forthwith without his family. Nor would he witness the joining of his son or daughter. He would return to Tombola on the prescribed day with a woman of recent acquisition, not better educated than he and not yet with child, devoid of a troublesome mind and nature.

He left me in Miami, his allowance ten-thousand for each year of his exile. Neither of us thought to shake the other's hand.

In the year that followed his daughter was joined, and one year later his son was sat at the pole. He was dim-witted, idle and troublesome, thinking himself superior to the village by virtue of his birth. He was not and his sacrifice served me well as a timely demonstration of my sense of impartiality.

The village flourished to beyond six hundred and Taliah was indeed Irene to them, regal in her every action and word. Her only restriction her shield, when most others now wore only their colours throughout the seven nights.

We voyaged frequently to States and throughout islands, as I once promised, and she continued to adore me. She did not lament her exemption from the eroticism of The Seven Feasts for she had Tombolina to herself and full reign to seek release when not wearing the guise of Irene. She was always the premier attraction at pools, on beaches or cruise ships. I denied her nothing.

We celebrated our tenth year together with champagne in the company of new and desirable friends and gave neither my son nor Jacob the slightest consideration until I stepped onto my dock with mere days to spare, refreshed and determined; my yacht filled to capacity with all that was needed to complete the celebration.

I avoided him, not wanting the faintest glimmer of satisfaction to betray my eyes. On the afternoon of the first day I allowed Irene time alone with the girls. I joined them much later, envious of her. Never once did I think to disappoint them, to shun my duties and deny them my knowledge and my comfort.

When I sent them away I lay upon the sand with Taliah who understood me. I was fearful. He was not like the others. He and his woman did not partake as did the others. Their scanty sips of the tincture did not deceive me and whatever affection they shared was pretence for my benefit or hers and not in the least wholehearted.

His mind and body would not be weakened by the calming elixir, yet I could not dismember him or shoot him or push him from the precipice. He was stronger than I and would know my purpose. In truth, Taliah was my guiding light.

On the morning of the third day I summoned him to Tombolina, to my pond, where once I sat with his father.

Few are the men whose words endure even the shortest time in my mind; this man was one, as was his father before him. I greeted him at the arch. His eyes were clear, his body relaxed, yet alert. He was unafraid. I extended my hand. None on the island dared to lay their hands upon my person. I was, in their eyes and in their minds, untouchable. That I might choose to place my hand upon them was a matter of elation and pride to them, my first-teachings of their daughters all- glorious. To his credit, he refused my greeting.

My memories of him are vivid.

"Sit, Jacob, please. May I offer you food or drink? The night air is stifling."

"I prefer to stand. Thank you."

"And I prefer that you sit. Please, we are alone here, your invitation a matter of some importance to you."

He did, as did I. He was silent, his eyes fixed upon me,

not once glancing across my gardens.

"The tombola, Jacob…the name is drawn."

"And I suppose the name drawn is mine. Shouldn't you have summoned me on the 30th? Isn't that the way the tombola works? You choose a name and give him or her three days to fornicate and drink themselves into eternity."

"Indeed, Jacob. However you are not like them, are you? Three days or one, what would you have done differently? Nor did I announce you publicly to the village. I summoned you privately so that you might return to your hearth and share time with your family away from the jubilation of your neighbours who will see your departure as your everlasting gift to them. However I will expect you here tomorrow when the tide water begins to ebb and the moon is high. I beseech you, do not dampen their spirits."

He smirked. "By my estimation, Wendell, that would be late evening, about eleven o'clock. Or should I say PM?"

The affront was outrageous. I leaned forward.

"Choose whichever one pleases you, Jacob, as long as you come to me alone before the hour."

"And if I don't, Wendell, what then? What if I do choose to dampen their spirits?"

"You have known the day might come since your youth and at your majority you swore with the others to honour the Twelve Scriptures. You have no place to hide. You cannot conceal yourself beneath the ground or in your father's chest and to quit this island would require that you grow fins or master a vessel. You are a tiller of fields and a fisherman without such appendages or knowledge. No, Jacob, you will sit at the pole. Be thankful not to have known earlier than today. I delayed this pronouncement out of consideration of your father, my first Chief Counsellor. His death was a grievous loss to me. Know that the fear of one's death lies in the anticipation of the event. Those who drink the tincture, who go to the pole with their cheeks filled with potent figs, are insensate to the event. You would be wise to allow yourself a lapse of restraint and pride. No one will think you a coward."

"Ah, yes, you are a kind and generous guardian. And did my father drink much of your opium-sprinkled rum before you ripped away his leg?"

"I would never commit such an atrocity against one of my own. He drowned…sadly."

"Of course he drowned. He had one leg and was never a swimmer. When he did go into the sea, he did so no deeper than to fish or to piss. His feet were as flat as cobblestones. A man like that doesn't drown and I can't believe he hacked off his own leg to prove himself…Wendell. And what do you suppose the shark did with his fucking pants? Or don't you know the word fuck. It seems to me that you do."

"You test me."

"My father taught me well. It's a family trait."

"With books from your chest."

"There's no chest, Wendell, and you have no reason to talk like the so-called grand guardian now that we're alone."

"I suppose not. I've seen the chest with my own eyes. He let no one near the precious thing and damn near broke his back under its weight."

"I never knew Jon Clayton to complain of a sore back, or broken a spirit for what it matters."

"I wouldn't refuse your son his inheritance, Jacob, or the knowledge within. I simply desire to know what he once brought to the island and for what purpose. We came as equals, all of us, one no better than the other."

"If he'd wanted you to know the contents of the chest you believe he's hidden somewhere he would have told you himself. And now that I know we're equals, you and I, why don't we take a cruise onboard your yacht?"

"What he hefted onto and from my boat was no

illusion."

"Those first people came here for a better life, Wendell, or for whatever their reasons were. The rest of them remain because they know nothing else."

"Those not derived from Jonathon Clayton's blood."

"Believe what you want, Wendell. I believe Jonathon might have said those who can't swim a hundred miles or more. Did your previous Irene try? Tell me. Your secret's good with me. Did she succeed or fail? For my money, if I had money, I'd say she succeeded and then fell...overboard. Come on, Wendell, we Claytons are good at keeping secrets."

He was a difficult man, unyielding and not in awe of me.

"We're done here, Jacob. Further banter between us will serve no purpose. Go to your woman. Tell her what lies ahead for you and, if you prefer, I'll take you this very night onto the sea and return alone so that I might convey her to you tomorrow...and your son a year from now. I won't deny you, should you wish to match your arms against the ocean and the dark night."

He stood.

"She'll follow me one day, as will he. Anyone with a brain would know that, Wendell, which is your saving grace. Ignorance is bliss, isn't it? And you've managed to master the concept. She just won't leave this earth or island tomorrow unless you have a gun under your robe as I suspect you do now. You'll see me at the gorge tomorrow, before the hour, and don't think to lash me to the pole or strip me of my clothes, Wendell. I'd spoil your day despite your weapon and show them you're a man like any other. Stay a safe distance from me."

And with that threat he left without the slightest courtesy.

Thirty-Four

Cassidy pushed himself from the desk. He slouched, inhaled a deep breath and blew the air from his lungs in a gust. He knew that, once arrived, Cecilia was never told where Jonathon chose to bury the strongbox. Nor did Jacob's first-mate know, nor did Shakkra. Now he believed she must know. He must tell her.

None of the women save Cecilia had ever seen the box. They'd never been told of the letters passed from father to son or the gold until Cassidy thought that night to give his mother hope. He would take her to the tree not the next evening, but the one after. Sunday she would see the launch concealed in the channel, she would swim to the western shore where she'd never set foot and she would touch the helicopter.

Yes, he thought, she would swim with him to the windward shore and she would wear a fine new thong made from silk and tied with pretty ribbons.

He stood, his mind made up. He strode to the bedroom, switched on the light and went into the closet. He opened the drawer where he knew he would find them and rummaged through the jumble of coloured triangles and strings. He took a while longer to choose. Most everything was new, he decided by touch and by smell, chuckling at the thought of having his nose so close to Irene's forbidden parts.

He chose the blue-white of pure snow she'd never seen.

He grinned, remembering Zach, for a fleeting moment forgetting why they had come, and not much bigger than a single flake, he thought.

"Thank you, Zach," he whispered, "for who I am. This gift to Shakkra is from you."

He left the silky clutter as though untouched and strolled to the library, eager to read what remained for him to discover in the final pages.

*

Jacob came to me the next night at the gorge. I remained with him and bade Taliah summon my flock in my stead. I stood at the foot of my bridge observing him warily. He stood erect by the pole, his expression sombre, not fearful. He wore the look of a man whose time was nigh, his eyes black and dry amongst the bright red and orange of flickering flames.

As they gathered he sat freely and willingly at the pole, his arms by his side, his first-mate and Zach in the first row, disrespecting tradition, each one with a stone. I could not deny them, he knew, and I harbour no doubt or suspicion that he suffered no sensation whatsoever from the third or subsequent stones.

Mother and son walked away last. In the morning I came across him lying in peace upon dry sand, compounding their insolence.

She and I understood each other. I would let them be. I would not insist that she join with a second-mate, nor did I deem any such union wise. Her current son occupied sufficient space in my mind. Nor did she, from that time forward, share even the coolest of affection during The Seven Feasts with those around her, her only colour her natural tan.

Indeed, her six remaining years must have seemed unbearably long.

I was then eighty-two and guiltlessly anxious for

Garrett's return for the most selfish of reasons. Travel by yacht seemed much less compelling, much less pretentious than in previous years, though, despite my recent perspective, I did the previous year purchase a fine sixty-foot craft. Her lines were sleek, though her dockage on Tombolina was a matter of precision. She was a veritable floating home.

Taliah was thirty-six, her body unchanged, her adoration of me more likely a figment of my imagination.

When first we met society was decadent, a world in search of novelty and gratification of oneself. She was young and I was then formidable in my physical presence. In '92 society was equally decadent, yet beyond the shores of Tombola I was simply Wendell Parkens, a man in the winter of his years. I chose to remain onboard and let her wander freely in search of a man or woman whose pockets or purse were sufficiently deep and well-stuffed to accommodate her natural inclinations, or those whose bodies were chiselled into muscular sculptures or warm and yielding to her delicate probing. I was content to hear her vivid descriptions.

At the end of each sojourn I was fatigued, despite my weariness longing each time for yet another voyage and for that reason I wished for my son to return so that he might captain my yacht on extended excursions and pilot my helicopter recently delivered to Miami and awaiting his trials. I would have access to anywhere along the East Coast and West Indies within an hour or two, my yacht in reserve for pleasurable daytime sailing alone with Taliah.

That summer is indelibly etched in my mind. The fourth of the four girls was my most pleasurable in all my years of first-teaching. Her slender curves painted green by Taliah, her soft skin, her whimpers and the tears squeezed from her eyes. I took pleasure in her for she knew who I was, yet I could not admonish her for my suspicions.

She was not with The Grand Guardian whose purpose was to gently break a path for the one I would later join with her. She was with Wendell Parkens, in her mind a fornicator, a man who once sent Jacob to the pole for no reason other than the workings of his mind. And soon I would give Shakkra to Zach, her fertile body my garden no less so than the fields of Tombola planted with my seeds and bringing forth each year a bountiful crop.

When I was done we watched her wade undressed to the beach, exempt from a robe as were the others. When she was gone from sight I forgot her and swam with Taliah.

Four days later Jacob was reunited with his first-mate. She was given no choice by me when summoned on the day of her departure from the island. She drank each drop of tincture measured for her and she did so in my pond. She did not appeal to me as regards matters of the flesh. I would derive no pleasure in humiliating a father and son long since dead. My purpose was to silence her wailing tongue and dim her bright eyes.

I stood behind her at the foot of my bridge to witness her son hurl the first stone. Shakkra's aim was no less accurate, no less swift, the Chief Counsellor's blow meaningless. Now Zach was alone to pollute Shakkra's mind against me, and soon his progeny.

Her whimpers in my pond were not caused by the pain of my intrusion into her, rather my intrusion into the grandson of Jonathon Clayton. He was the true source of my satisfaction, not my intimate knowledge of her.

Garrett arrived at the marina in Miami at noon on the prescribed day, one week following The Seven Feasts. On his arm was a woman half his age. Like Garrett she was tall and blonde, her body lithe and athletic. He went with me to the heliport, she went with Taliah who knew what was right and what was wrong for the Isle of Tombola.

There was no subterfuge of emotion between my son

and me. To this very day, not long before my final walk across my bridge, I feel he never forgave me my preventative action against him. Indeed education does breed malevolence in men, and Jacob was not wrong in his belief that ignorance is bliss. Yet as Grand Guardian how would Garrett preserve one without the other.

They were not married. She was his recent acquisition, more beautiful than mindful, more avaricious than kind. For all I know she might have been a street whore wanting to escape her procurer, or quite possibly another man's delinquent wife. She was able to read and write. I would say best described as minimally literate. She knew of the world, not worldly matters and clearly she dressed to please my son's acquired taste in feminine fashion.

Nor do I harbour any doubt that she applied her cosmetics in such a manner as to offend or provoke me, which was unmistakably the case. Not a soul on Tombola knew of the female penchant for face-painting, or any adornment beyond their coloured trinkets fashioned from vines and shells, their tinted shields and their painted skin once each year as much to disguise their complete nakedness as to enhance and to entice.

Throughout my life I have slept with a plenitude of whores, the wives of good friends and wives of my own, a euphemism certainly, and no less true of those whom I have comforted in my pond or first-taught. And she would be taught, with her face and her twenty digits wiped clean.

She was comfortable in stilettos and short skirts; she would not comport herself well in evening gowns and elegant sandals until tutored by Taliah. Nor was my son, despite his finances and until his conversion, an elegant gentleman. They would conform to island dress. She would wear tunics and when at the shore she would wear what other women wore, not satin or silk tied with fancy ribbons.

Garrett flew the machine through the air with the ease of

a bird. I remained on the ground and when he was done he went with Taliah who was, to him, Irene. In that recognition I permitted not the slightest latitude. Perhaps he suspected, or was certain that, had Taliah indicated to me otherwise, I would have brought him to his homeland and laid him to rest with his woman. She did not.

I went with her, Forrest. She was twenty-three and I asked her to speak with me of my island so that I might understand what she knew and what she did not, what she might expect and what she did not. She would oversee the work in the fields and watch over the women at the gutting tables, she would swim in the sea and once each year she would celebrate with the village, yet she would not. She was the future Irene, when my time was nigh, not a day before, and she would be fully prepared for her station.

She was agitated and would learn serenity; she was giddy and would learn calmness. I approved her after long deliberation and subsequent consultation with Irene. Some days later she landed with my son upon my helipad not a moment after I docked my yacht, by which time Jacob's first-mate was forgotten by all but, I suppose, her son and his first-mate.

Garrett's eventual application to me, I confess, was appropriate. I expected no less and was not disappointed in him. Avarice was his nature, guardianship his destiny. How could he, they, as future Grand Guardian and Irene, dwell in a hearth less substantial than that of the Chief Counsellor? Still, I denied him, restrained him, reminding him of my meagre beginnings, the dilapidation of the island upon my first and second arrivals and my years of sufferance so that Tombola might once again flourish as in the time of William.

Forrest seemed not to mind. She took readily to her position and the current island garb of tunics in the field for the women, evening robes and shields for the beach. After not much time with us, she was one with us, embracing us. And why would she not? She went with Garrett once each month to wherever she wished by air and by sea. She wore imported clothes from the houses of France and Italy and dined increasingly with friends befitting their station. I issued one dictum: Tombola did not exist. No one was to know of my island paradise, nor was anyone to bless us with a casual visit. And one concession was made: Upon my invitation to Tombolina I permitted her to wear her silk and satin, as did Taliah.

One year later I joined them officially in keeping with the Twelve Scriptures. He did not allow her right in my Sacred Pond, yet she painted herself in silver to match her finest shield which she wore so that the village might not the full extent of their future Irene.

Her first child, Fontaine, Garrett's third, was three months into his life. Taliah, by design or by negligence, gave me a son, you who are now in your seventeenth year.

Garrett's adaptation was more complex, more a question of generational differences in my view, his current mind and reason consequences of his time away.

His mind was constantly troubled subsequent to his return, despite his increased responsibilities. Clearly he aspired to rule Tombola in a fashion more in keeping with the modern world, whereas I saw no need for advanced data systems, surveillance cameras and cell phones

Tombola has thrived thus far for sixty-five years under my guidance and forty-six under the Weatherbones without the implementation of devices created by men to ensure jealousy, envy and mistrust. The slightest misjudgement or slip of the tongue, a flickering light seen from my garden, a gold ring or bracelet forgotten upon his hand or hers, a lustrous cosmetic, would ruin my Isle of Tombola in a breath cut short.

My single ring is the symbol of what I am, my single

lock latches my gate at the arch; any other is in the minds of the village. Though I do not deny the killing stone will scarcely be hurled before all trace of me is swept from my home and my study by him. Beware of him. He does not consider you his brother. He will be false in any consideration of you.

Garrett has, in fact, managed the island for some time; Irene and I content in these latter years to act as figureheads, my primary purpose to audit my son's administration of my island and the disbursement of my wealth while Taliah devoted her time to doting over her one child.

Garrett did not hold me in contempt for sitting his first son at the pole. I could not imagine him more disinterested. Nor was he remotely interested in the life of his daughter. Forrest was and is the epicentre of his world and together they enjoy life to the fullest at my expense. My yacht and helicopter are their prestige, my island their private resort and sadly I have no one but a child too young to replace him.

Would that Taliah had brought me Dakota ten years earlier. He is strong and possesses the intelligence required of a Grand Guardian. He would now occupy this seat so that I might spend my days at my pond and end my life in peace, not assailed by a hundred and one stones and swallowed by the sea, were it not for his youth.

At five you went to school on the East Coast, Fontaine went with you, against my better judgement, to placate Garrett, each of you returning home for the summer. Neither one of you befriended the other as the years passed, as though by design or intuition, or possibly by virtue of my forbiddance of Fontaine on Tombolina once his brief education was begun. I saw no purpose in causing him to dream.

Taliah did in a single moment alter the future of

Tombola with her carnal desire of me.

One day soon he will serve you, when you are joined next year with the daughter of my Chief Counsellor. You will impregnate her, and leave her to complete your studies. Fontaine will not. The boy is not given to leadership, nor does he comprehend the complexities of human relations. He was born to follow and he will. This Garrett knows, as do you, Dakota who, once joined, will continue to live on Tombolina in a hearth as magnificent as my own with the girl Aayla and your mother, Taliah.

You shall wear the gold braid so that none shall entertain misgivings as to your destiny. My most ardent wish is for you to one day assume your rightful place as Grand Guardian and your first son after you. My greatest lament is that I will not witness the day. You will be the third and the most exalted Grand Guardian of Tombola. You shall wear the ruby ring.

Fontaine, for his part, will remain as he is, his education degrading over time to the mean intelligence of the women in the fields and the men who cast their nets over the sea, destined to follow his father one year later to the pole so that harmony might exist on the island.

Dakota, whom I soon expect so that I might spend what remains of two fleeting days with you, you know of Judas and of the evil borne of malice and envy. Be cautious in what you do, and do what one day you surely must. Wear the ring only when you are ready. With it you will find the keys to your salvation, my will and my most prized possession that will no longer carry me across the blue waters that surround us.

We will not speak of this, for I cannot ascertain nor believe that I am not spied upon by his gimmickry.

I did not then, nor do I now, intend for any of Garrett's seed to ever wear the gold braid of The Grand Guardian. His first son was born dim-witted to the extent that he was more than likely unaware of his own passing. His second son is no better. Any further education is a futile effort, any attempt to activate and thereby remedy his dull mind completely without merit.

Garrett himself is, for me, an interim measure to ensure the continuance of Tombola. He was for me an interim measure. He is no longer for now I sit here helpless, subject to his most dastardly whim. I am healthy in my body and in my mind, a man whose appearance belies his advanced age by many years. Yet how was I to defy him, to stand against him, when yesterday he delivered to me the news of my pending death? He must not possess the ring.

I could not. My victory over him is in what Dakota knows in his mind, in what Taliah knows in hers, and what they will each know before my death. They alone are not subject to the laws of this land and upon reaching his twenty-fifth year he will assume his rightful place without the wise counsel of his mother so that he alone might one day be kind and benevolent towards those beneath him.

I hear a knock at my door. My son has come with his mother. I see the glaze in his eyes and the torment in hers.

And now they are gone. I will see them tomorrow, when my mind shall be clouded with tincture, for truly I am not a brave man. I am a Parkens, after all, despite my genealogical bond with a man of such high calibre and determination as Charles Weatherbone. I drew from him his strength, and from his son my legacy that is Tombola, to do what my own father could or would not do.

What reason did he have to desert such lovely women so tied to his heart, so that he might give himself to avarice and a woman whose icy heart was housed in a body sufficiently chilled as to prevent the bloodless mechanism from melting? I forget her entirely, though not him, never Aristotle Horatio Weatherbone who came here seventy-seven years ago and before his deserved death to guide me or ruin me, to free me or entrap me with his last and compelling articulation to me which he knew I would not ignore. His intent was to ruin me and, in that, he failed.

Dakota was gone seven years; his fleeting summers spent onboard my yacht studying every aspect of seamanship while Garrett went with his son to wherever he and Forrest might show themselves in the best light.

That summer I was ninety-five. Dakota was twelve, unafraid of the sea, anxious to pilot a vessel of his own. Taliah was forty-nine. I understood her, as she understood me. She adored me, as I adored her, her charms compelling me to please her on rarer occasions yet no less ardently in the warm water of my crystal pool or upon Tombolina's heated sands. Her future is secure for I have decreed that the status of Irene shall never be revoked. She is, and will forever be, Irene.

On the eve of the fourth day of The Seven Feasts that seventh summer I sent my Chief Counsellor in search of Zach. I waited for him to cross the bridge to my arch. I stood alone without Garrett to assist or defend me. The first-mate of Shakkra, the father of Cassidy has not traversed my thoughts in these five years since.

My study is cold, or is my blood cool with trepidation? I wonder whether I shall cry out in pain or whimper with fright, for I am a Parkens. The accumulation of my years has not effaced that fact. My father, once a Weatherbone, a man with a brave heart, somehow metamorphosed into a Parkens, a banker, a coward. And I, The Grand Guardian of Tombola, now shiver at the prospect of my death for, in truth, what else have I to fear? And what does that speak of me?

I have not yet touched my tincture, nor have I ever. Nor has Irene. We are forbidden by custom as much as by decree. Yet despite my law tomorrow I shall drink to the fullest extent my body allows to free my spirit and fog my mind, to dispel my mounting uncertainty and dread. I am fortified with not the slightest consolation in the knowledge that Zach, that summer now forgotten, went to the pole of his own volition and with a clear mind.

Why do I remember only them and their women? Why did they forever distrust me, suspect me? That is why. That alone is the root of my discontent with them. I have always known. They sought to deceive me, undo me, bring jealousy and envy to my island. Not once did they confide in me, entreat me on their behalf. Not once did Jonathon Clayton think to seek my counsel when I, so often, sought to know his mind.

I beseeched Zach to sit by my side. He did not. He stood in casual defiance of me, as though I was a simple minded villager and not in the least exalted in his eyes.

He said: "Wendell, you're fast running out of Claytons."

"You leave two behind. Be cautious in what you say," I replied that day.

He said: "And tomorrow I'll sit at the pole, to once again see my father Jacob, his father and the Father of all mankind."

"If such is your belief. No other on this island knows His name or any other false or pagan deity."

I remember pausing, deciding my purpose in our conversation.

"I derive from your premonition that within your hidden chest lays a Bible. A very old Bible amongst other ancient works of so little value in today's world, a world of computers made of glass and plastic, where children kill children without remorse, where cameras are concealed in phones so small they can be hidden in a man's hand to record such violent acts for amusement, where television details those accounts for sensationalism and ratings, where spy satellites in the universe, and cameras on every street corner from which we cannot hide lest we be cloaked from head to foot, track our every move."

He guffawed, blatantly. He understood not a single word of what I said. And what does that speak to the value of his treasured chest?

"You're talking of the mysterious hidden chest. Yes, I've heard tell of your suspicions. No, Wendell, my grandfather was a man of the cloth. Didn't you know? He committed his scriptures to heart, as you did yours. Although his didn't include debauchery and fornication or a woman never being certain of her child's exact parentage…save a few of us."

"You were never timid, the times I observed you. Neither was she, your woman Shakkra."

He stood staring at my glorious manor, not once thinking to comment on its splendour.

"I've enjoyed a few of the prettier ladies before they lost their ability to speak clearly or to appreciate my expertise because they were filled to their brims, if you catch my meaning. In any event, I was already with the prettiest. You can appreciate my dilemma, I'm sure. As for Shakkra, she certainly has deserved more than me, not that such a perfect person exists on this island. Or don't you recall her precisely. In the States, or anywhere for that matter, I can't imagine the life she'd lead."

"You refer to my first-teaching of her."

"No, to your second so-called teaching and I thank you for making me appear all the more superior. She hasn't complained a single day since. You were second to me, as you were to Jacob. We Claytons don't need a Grand Guardian to dig our holes for us, holes left too shallow for the task. Didn't you sense the extra space I drilled for you, Wendell? No matter. I suppose and I pray that when Cassidy's time comes to join there won't be much of a seedless twig afloat in that lagoon of yours."

I pointed my gun at him, commanding him to stand

back. He was unequivocally unafraid. What manner of men were they? I, the most illustrious man to know him, with him on my private isle, and he was not demeaned in any way.

"You need not concern yourself. Be content that the father goes before the son."

"If you don't mind, I'll keep that insight to myself."

"I have sworn that no Clayton or his woman shall outlive me."

"That doesn't give either one much time. And who did you swear to, my father or Jonathon?"

"To the hearing walls of my manor that know all that I know. I have no secrets from them. Now go to your first-mate, and hold your tongue. Remember what you leave behind. Be at the pole tomorrow when you have said your farewells."

"I've said them silently each night for the nineteen years since you killed my father."

Killed his father, yes, for the betterment of the village, so that we all might prosper and live in peace.

"I will send full measures of tincture to your hearth this evening and tomorrow throughout the day."

"To denigrate me and shame me before my forefathers. Don't bother. I'd prefer you to shoot me where I stand, Wendell."

"And I would prefer that you leave, without the utterance of a single word. Leave me."

He did take his leave of me, his gay whistling the vilest sound permeating my quietude until his echo at last died with his passage through the arch.

That next evening he came to me no less steeled than his father for what he was about to endure, no less resolute in his determination not to falter as his first-mate Shakkra and the boy reached first for the stones. I could not see the man's eyes; I saw hers and understood her communication to him without the slightest misinterpretation. She was bidding him au revoir, not adieu or farewell. She would see him again one day soon. She knew well, as did I.

Her stone was hurled with violent passion, not once theretofore witnessed by me. He died that instant. The son's stone, from my vantage, struck not a second later with equal devotion. Then he waded into the shallow water and turned to face the throng, leaving them naught to do but drop their stones where they stood. Were I a younger man I might have waited a day or two and hauled him to the precipice to fling him into the sea for such intolerable contempt.

The next year the name of my Chief Counsellor was drawn from my tombola. His practice with the sling was less precise each day, his manner not in keeping with his position. He began to think highly of himself, confusing counsel with instruction. I replaced him with a man whose comportment was quiet, his performance in the fields and in the sea commendable, his character above reproach in my opinion. He and his family exchanged hearths forthwith with the widow of his predecessor.

Not long after I came to know his daughter more intimately. I studied her. I saw in her a future with Dakota until such time as he inherits the guardianship of Tombola. I instructed my son that he should come to know her better from that moment on, which he has managed with the uncertainty of youth or, I daresay, the uncertainty of his conviction. Now I will convey this, my final instruction to him, tomorrow.

The girl Aayla must never know the privileges of Irene. She is unlearned; best suited by her looks to give him pleasure and bear his children until such time as Dakota is the rightful Grand Guardian of Tombola. For her to journey from the island for the briefest duration would certainly incur jealously and envy. She is unrestrained, too advanced in years to comprehend the essence of a simple and carefree life juxtaposed with lavishness and its requisite discretion. He will, in due time, deal with her appropriately.

Dakota must do as I and Garrett have done before him. He must renew the island with the fresh blood of a woman whose age will maintain his interest in her, one whose schooling is beyond minimal standards, who is attuned to this island life and of enviable character when in gracious company.

With all such matters of considerable import preoccupying my conscience mind, condemning me to sleepless nights, still I had not forgotten Shakkra or her son, the boy who stood with arms by his side to defend his lifeless father from what was decreed. In the second year following Zach's departure a woman, barely past her fiftieth year and worthy of no particular mention, fell deathly ill as I began my deliberation as to which person that summer should pay obeisance to the village.

She was stricken with fever, her person and her bed drenched through with transpiration. I beseeched her to be strong, to endure the few days left to her. She would not recover, nor would she suffer unduly. To abet and assuage her I decreed that she be fed with tincture without delay, cleansed and clothed with fresh linen to comfort her. I saw no purpose in prolonging her affliction.

She died a beneficiary of my compassion, her final days and hours spent in euphoric bliss until the Chief Counsellor's steady hand performed his duty in perfect harmony with the acuity of his eye. She was buried in the sea by my eldest son at low tide.

One year later, two full years ago, his mourning expired, I sent her first-mate to Shakkra so that he might complete her hearth, once joined. She knew this time not to oppose me. He was the age of Jacob, had the latter not scorned me. Be aware and cautious of the last of his line. He is the son of Zach who learned from Jacob. The blood of Jonathon Clayton is undiluted in him.

I grow weary. My eyes are heavy. My hand cramped from the urgency of my words, yet I persist for tomorrow is unknown to me. I am uncertain as to what I might expect from my first taste.

Dakota, and Taliah who is Irene, I have told you where to find these words amongst my many tomes. Read them together. Keep them safe from harm together with the Ancestral Tomes. Conserve them. They are the addendum to the history of the Weatherbones from whom you are directly descended as much as they are my confession and confrontation of self as I steel my mind and my person against the dark thoughts that endeavour to invade me and pervade me.

My night was uneasy, my sleep a restless turmoil. My mind filled with the spectres of bad dreams. I am weak, a sensation unknown to me. I did not eat, not my evening repast nor my morning meal. No such pleasure will sustain me through this last day of my life. But, yes, the tincture is poured for me, awaits me. Have I not the right to end my life with the blissful ease of those less deserving?

My first taste is pleasant.

My second infuses me with warmth.

My daughters, are they dead too? Or do they survive me without any memory of me? Will I meet their long-departed mother, her body charred, my dearest and licentious Charlotte? Or my father, his head half gone? And when I am cast into the blue water, will she greet me one last time, the one I gave to the sea so that I might be one with Taliah?

Taliah, who stayed with me throughout the night, is free of me beyond her finest memories of me. And Dakota, who left me once more this morning, whose mind is in possession of all that he must know. I leave them both. They shall not attend me at the Pole of Tombola.

I deserve not to die, though I am content with my existence and with my paradise, my lush Isles of Tombola. I must, however, despite giving sufficiently and magnanimously of myself to all those who needed me and adored me.

I have not, in this considered account, encountered or written a single fallacy or artifice in respect to my life.

Wendell Horatio Parkens, the second and most exalted Grand Guardian of Tombola.

Thirty-Five

Cassidy possessed no other name. He was a Clayton, but to whom. A teary film glazed his eyes. He imagined his mother, her face glued to the television. How could they now return to a simple villa lit by the dim glow of lanterns? He could not. Nor could she, he knew.

He had no further reason to trespass the manor. He studied the walls and the journal. Nor did Dakota have reason, except for the journal which was no longer his to read and conserve. He no longer had the right. He was displaced with his mother from the manor. The entire island knew. He and Irene were sent by The Grand Guardian's successor to his former house on the hill on the afternoon of Wendell's stoning.

He wondered. Did he know more than Dakota who was aware of his father's journal? He must. How would Dakota know what was written? He couldn't. The timing was wrong. Dakota couldn't know more than what Wendell had told him, father to son their last evening and last lucid morning together.

Did he know of the gold? Did he know of the ring?

At top rung Cassidy dug behind the row shelves, his heart palpitating wildly. He grasped the cluster in his hands, keeping his eyes closed tight until his feet touched the floor. He held Horatio's ring in his hand and, with it, keys to the yacht. A second key looked not much different. A third had Box 318 stamped onto one side.

Cassidy's decision was beyond his years, and no less crucial than when he hurled the second stone against his father's temple. The conflicting rationale had crept into his mind with each page turned and was irrepressible: He mustn't, yet he must. Go or stay. Escape or remain. Either way the danger was clear for him and for Shakkra.

Whether he was discovered for what he was conceiving and taken to the sea, or not, the next year he would sit at the pole and, the year after, Shakkra would follow.

He forced a thin smile and glanced up to the Ancestral Tomes wedged into the second shelf. He looked at Jonathon's books, the works of Dickens and Dumas he'd read so many times. And again he searched the walls. He pushed away from the desk and climbed the closest ladder, replacing a voluminous world atlas with The Mystery of Edwin Drood and The Count of Monte-Cristo, the margins of each filled with the writings of Jonathon, Jacob and Zach, committing to memory where he placed them. Then he climbed another and reached for the Ancestral Tomes.

Cassidy sat at the desk depleted, all doubt eradicated from his mind. He would take with him the island's history. He believed Garrett hadn't read the Ancestral Tomes. He would have had no time, and possibly not the journal. What he would do with them Cassidy wasn't entirely certain. He wasn't certain at all. Nor did he know what he could not do without them.

He returned the library to its original state; he switched off the light and went to his mother.

What he did know was that he could never undo what he had done.

She saw through him.

"Cassidy, what have you done? What's in your hands?"

"Come, Shakkra, let's leave this place for tonight and spend time in the pool to talk."

She gave him the remote.

"Tell me. What have you taken?"

"I will, at the pool. I promise."

She knew her son, although at that moment she saw Zach in his eyes and relented.

"Cassidy, this television is teaching me so much. I can't believe what I've learned in so little time. Today is Saturday, July 10th. When was the last time I knew the date? Or did I ever? What I see isn't real, yet I know it is."

He shook his head and smiled. "It's past midnight. Sunday, July 11th and I know what you see is real. We just don't know how, but soon we will. Now we must leave to spend a short time in the pool before going home to sleep so that when we wake we're alert. There's more I want to show you, and I have a surprise." He pressed OFF and reached for a magazine. "Take this one. She won't miss one of so many."

"What have you learned? And what's in your other hand?"

"What I hope will one day help us, Shakkra. We're taking them to the tree, both of us. You'll see my tree and the box, our gold, and touch your books once more. It's time for you to know what I know in case I fail. From now on you'll come with me to the tree and read your magazine and this atlas until we're ready to leave here. We must learn as much as we can to prepare ourselves, something we can't do at home."

He led her to the entrance, turned out the lights and swung the brass door closed. At the pool he opened his hand to her.

"This is for you, Shakkra. I chose the nicest one."

She clamped a hand over her mouth. "She'll know."

"She has dozens. She won't know. So put it on and sit with me in the warm water." He turned his back to her and eased into the water, waiting.

Shakkra hesitated no longer than a breath or two,

tugging her tunic over her head, pushing one thong to her ankles, pulling the other to her hips.

"Are you finished?"

"I'm not sure." She giggled: a sound he didn't hear often enough. "Am I missing a piece, Cassidy? I've never worn anything as delicate or as tiny."

He looked up, visibly taken aback. His mother was backlit by a perfect moon, the edges of her near naked silhouette emitting a silver glow. "A real man should see you like this. You belong under the brightest sun where many can see you, not a clumsy son."

"Thank you, Cassidy. And you belong with your little heart, not me."

He held out his hands to her. "I belong with both of you. That's why we'll leave here before the next Seven Feasts, the three of us together."

"What did you learn in the library?"

He grinned. "If we remain, this time next year you'll be in this pool alone. But, Shakkra, as much as I miss my father, I'm not in a hurry to see him."

"Your time is decreed?"

He nodded. "As I've told you, there's no tombola. He decided who and when. Now the other one will do the same. We weren't meant to survive him. He died too soon, Shakkra. He didn't want to. He expected to live longer, to see us dead. His son killed him so that he could be The Grand Guardian. He made him drink the tincture and before his death the old man warned Dakota about me. That's why I've taken his journal...and the Ancestral Tomes...and his ring."

He opened his hand.

"Why, Cassidy? I'm afraid. What you've done is dangerous."

"I'm not afraid, Shakkra. I'm my father's son. He made me unafraid, for you."

"I don't want another brave dead man in my dreams. I want you and Aayla beside me always."

"That's why I've taken these books, mother. They're just books. The Ancestral Tomes are confessions of dead men. They're not divine. Neither are the Twelve Scriptures he stole from William Weatherbone who was insane. And Parkens' journal is worse. If at this moment I can't tell you why, neither can I tell you why not. That's why I took them, because I didn't know why I shouldn't. If these books were important enough to conceal from us, and I know why he did, they should be important to us when we escape. They might even help us escape. These keys will free us as much he intended for Dakota to be free. Without them he's not."

She exhaled a loud breath. "What else have you read?"

"What I've read is for you alone, mother. You must not betray us with your beautiful eyes when you play in the ocean with Aayla." He paused. "The old man has decreed that Aayla will give Dakota a family, also that she'll never be Irene. Nor will she ever share affection with others because until the time he takes his brother's place all must believe she will be Irene. Then he must find another woman not of the island and Aayla will be nothing to him... if he lives."

"Don't talk in riddles, Cassidy."

"I don't think he'll live. The old one has warned Dakota about me in his last words. Much of what he wrote is about Jonathon, Jason, Zach and me. He also warned Dakota about his brother who didn't wait to send him away. He was supposed to live here on Tombolina in a house like his. Now he lives with Irene on the hill overlooking Aayla's villa. That should tell us something. He's disobeyed The Grand Guardian's wishes."

"He is The Grand Guardian."

"He's a man, who pisses the way I do, and so does Dakota who may not warm the water close to his loin-shield much longer."

Shakkra eased from her stony seat into deeper water, clinging to the side of the pool.

"I worry more for your little heart than Dakota. He'll know what to do when the time comes for him to confront his brother. She won't, and I won't see her little head split in half, Cassidy. I won't. I would kill first."

"You won't. Nor will she feel the first stone or the last. She won't be here. She'll be with you, her big sister and confidante, making men blind on the beach with your tiny thongs and keeping secrets from me."

She kicked a wall of hectic water over him.

"Should we bring her here, Cassidy? We can trust her. She would do nothing to harm us. If not for her we wouldn't be here now. We wouldn't have seen the television and you wouldn't have stolen these books."

"I borrowed them, Shakkra, and left mine in exchange."

"She's a daughter to me and I don't like deceiving her."

Shakkra pulled herself from the water onto the grass, standing to dry herself in the warm night air.

"Her father's Chief Counsellor."

"Yes, who's unaware that he tells Aayla what you must know." She stooped for her thong that was dry and her tunic. "How will we leave her alone tomorrow at the ocean, Cassidy? When the entire island is swimming and playing she'll sit alone and cry."

"How will she cry when she hears the first stone bounce off my head, if we don't escape?" His voice took on a defiant tone. "I think, Shakkra, I'd rather see her cry than sit at the pole. You know I leave her alone so I can succeed." He clambered from the pool. "When I'm not thinking of your happiness and hers, all that fills my mind is escaping. I won't sleep another night until we leave here. I can't."

He knelt for the books.

"We have one day left to us, Cassidy. Then we'll read

and study until their next journey. Will we hide at your tree without her? Or will she one day come to find us together with our heads in these books? Or will you lose her because you don't trust her as Zach trusted me."

He didn't answer. And she didn't press, maintaining his stride through the gardens to the lagoon and through the channel to the ocean. When they'd crossed the gorge she stood aloof, her thoughts traversing a private world beyond a dark sea. She let herself dry and stepped behind him, slapping her thong over his one shoulder, her tunic over the other.

She tugged at the ribbons clinging to her legs, slapping the wet triangle over his shoulder, whipping away the one that was dry with icy silence. When she'd tied those ribbons precisely to her satisfaction she swept away her tunic and finished dressing. Then she studied him, waited, opened a small palm flat and wide, drew her arm into a wide arc and smacked his buttocks to make him wince.

She inhaled deeply. "That felt so good."

"No, it didn't."

"Then wear something that protects you more."

"You wait until I'm a man to spank me?"

"A man knows who he should trust. And, yes, you're a man. That's why you must trust your little heart as you do your own."

Shakkra massaged her hand. "You hurt me with your thick skin."

"My skin is half yours, half Zach's, and I don't think his was the thickest." He hugged her. "Thank you, for the lesson. I think. Maybe you're right. I hope you're right and that you'll support me in everything I do and say. You're my counsel, not her. She's the student. She has to learn what we know, and what we don't yet know. Then we all must learn together. We'll teach her to speak differently…and teach her when not to. Now, because of us, she'll have to think each time before she speaks a single word. This won't be easy for her, or for me. You must tell her that everything I say is true. She hasn't seen a book, or a magazine, or pictures of beautiful she's never imagined like the ones in that magazine in the sand. At first she won't believe that she too can cross to where the blue water touches the sky or that she can one day fly across the sky at the tip of thin white streaks that grow wide and disappear."

"She'll be a good student." Shakkra smiled. "Come, I'll prepare a warm salve of ground roots and leaves to soothe your injury."

"Thank you, Shakkra. You've touched me enough for one night. My injury is fine and our night isn't finished. We have a lot to do."

Thirty-Six

They went to the tree as Cassidy did each day by a different route so that his feet wouldn't leave depressions in the grass over time for others to follow.

Shakkra saw the books she'd read each night with Zach in their bed and she wept. She held gold in her hands and nestled her magazine safely between the atlas and Wendell Parkens' delirious work. She saw the scratch marks made by her son and ran her hands across the chest that Zach had once touched, as though the box was more precious than the gold inside. Cassidy simply dropped the once-sacred Weatherbone chronicles on top and closed the lid.

At their villa she kissed him goodnight and turned her back to him. She slid her thong from under her tunic and hid both under his mattress. When she was gone he changed into his night-shield and covered himself with a thin sheet to dispel the chill brought on by weariness despite the thick humidity.

Shakkra went to her room. She tiptoed through the dark to her drawers and rummaged blindly for a clean night-shield. Properly covered she stood listening, the shape of his body gradually more defined.

"I am awake."

"I heard your breathing."

"I am awake every night."

"I did not know. I do not stop to listen each night."

"You stay long enough to believe that I am sleeping

while you change your shield and go to your son's bed."

"I go to his bed as a mother who feels deep emotion for what is left of her life, nothing more. You are not prevented from looking into his room to see that I sleep against the wall."

"I do not believe that you do not couple with me because you couple or share affection with a son. I know why you do not come to me as a woman."

"Your arms are never open to me. All I see is your back."

"You speak an untruth. You slept by my side at first, with your shield tied to you as a second skin until you went into your son's room."

She wiped a hand across her brow. "Zach is alive in my heart and in his eyes."

"You believe me unequal to Zach; you care nothing about the position of my back."

Shakkra remained still. "All men are unequal to Zach. You were the one sent to me. Anyone else would sleep alone in your place. I feel no need to spoil what I remember, as though he is in my bed and not you."

"Where do you go until the early sun thinks to brighten the sky?"

"I go to the ocean, to the south and to the north, to remember Zach, to talk with my son of his dead father."

"That is good. He should not forget." The man rolled onto his other side, facing Shakkra and the door. "Will you couple with me now?"

"I cannot."

"You will not." He snorted, swallowing hard and breathing a loud intake of air through his nostrils. "I am glad. I put my back to you each night because I wish not to spoil memories of my first-mate. I understand you. I miss her as you miss Zach. She was sick with fever and gave of herself so that the village would not suffer; Zach gave of himself for the village to prosper. You are not different from me. You hide yourself in the dark. You believe I want what is hidden behind your shield. I do not. I lie here to remember."

"I do not hide in the dark. What is hidden by my shield was meant for Zach, none other."

"When he lived you shared affection with others."

"We shared affection with others, together."

"And you are content to continue with my back to you, you with your back to your son?"

"Yes."

"And one year from now, when he couples and joins with a first-mate?"

"I will feel happiness for him and make his bed my own."

He groaned. "I am content to know the truth, content with my memories."

Shakkra didn't move until his second snort, then his third.

She stepped into the living area, closing the door behind her. Slowly she opened Cassidy's door, stepped in and stood against the wall. What would she do in one year if they didn't succeed? Would she cast the first stone with a mother's love? Or find her way through the channel to the lagoon, from the lagoon to the precipice to fling herself into Zach's strong arms?

The heat was oppressive, her body and tunic damp with humidity. She went to the window for relief and found none. How would she feel in a year to sleep alone, to live without her son if they did not succeed? They must. They would.

She pulled her tunic over her head and crawled onto the bed, curling onto her side close to the wall. She was frightened and struggled not to cry, giving in to herself for Cassidy, Aayla, and for Zach.

When she woke she was in his arms. His strength and his warmth flowed through her. He was stroking her hair and humming. She was safe. Her world was perfect once more. She was with Zach in his arms and her son must be waiting for his morning meal.

Streaks of bright sun filtered through the wooden slats in the wall. She squeezed her eyes shut, clearing her mind, the dazzling light now a kaleidoscope of distorted images. She wanted Zach never to loosen his grip that held her tightly in place, never to stop stroking her hair.

She whispered his name.

"Zach loves you."

She sighed. "He does, but you are not Zach."

"No, I am not. I will never be Zach. My wish is to become half the man he was, that he is in my mind. Until then I am a son who loves his mother, who does not like to see her cry."

"This is another night you have not slept because of me."

"There is no better reason to lie awake."

Cassidy freed his arm. He eased their bodies apart, sitting with his back to her to give her privacy.

"How long did I cry?"

He chortled. "How much of the night was left to us? Not long, five hours."

She sat beside him. "I heard something last night that you should hear, on the television."

"What, Shakkra?"

"Get a life, kid." She put a hand to his face. "Thank you. I was dreaming, Cassidy, of Zach."

"You do each night. I hope Aayla does not talk as much in her sleep."

"But now is the time for you to hold her, not an old woman."

He stroked her arm. "Old women do not feel this way,

Shakkra. They do not have hair as soft as new grass or eyes as clear as rainwater." He put a fingertip to her lips. "Zach would not want these to go untouched by someone you will soon meet."

"I am afraid of what will finally come to pass, and when."

He squeezed her close. "And I am afraid I will die from hunger before I leave you to cast my net in the sea."

She whispered in his ear. "I love my brave son."

"And I love my mother who forces me to tell a little witch the truth. She will hate me, Shakkra."

"Of course she will. She is a woman."

"You will defend her, a woman who will hold a knife in her hands this morning to gut fish?"

"Yes, a young woman you have treated badly."

He nodded. "Perhaps when I am in my tree, when you are showing her pretty pictures and teaching her words, I will bash my head with a coconut or drop from the tree on my head."

She patted his knee, pouting. "We'll miss you, sweetheart."

Thirty-Seven

Cassidy stood at the shoreline, cooling his feet. Shakkra strolled lazily away from him, hand in hand with Aayla in shallow turquoise water. He watched them as long as he dared. When they turned he looked out to sea.

They were coming closer, closer still; their lips curled into secret smiles, each silent word a conspiracy against him. Aayla wrapped an arm tightly around Shakkra's waist; Shakkra cupped a hand at girl's shoulder, rubbing. Rubbing, he mused: a mother's comforting caress, a sister's cunning solace. He was doomed.

They were wading into deeper water, observing him, their heads bobbing, their bright teeth shining like beacons against their dark skin. They were laughing at him, revelling in his discomfort and he could do nothing. He was defenceless against them, waiting until mother and daughter, or were they sisters, he didn't know, hugged and kissed. He didn't know what to think anymore, his mind a whirlwind of joy and doubt, suspicion and anticipation at seeing them separate, Aayla carving a seamless path through the water, propelling her sleek and sculptured body to shore, directly at him, her target, her enemy.

She sauntered from sea to sand dripping, adjusting her shield. She went to him, stood by his side and gazed across the same blue water that coated her body in glistening beads. His fixed his eyes on Shakkra. She was nodding, not at him. Even at such a distance they spoke woman-talk.

"Will you stand beside me all day without talking?"

"Excuse me. What did you say?"

"Will you talk to me sometime today?"

"No. I feel no emotion for you. I am watching my friend, someone who does feel emotion for me."

"She is my mother."

"I feel sorrow for her. She is too kind and too beautiful to have such a stupid and skinny son."

"I am sorry, Aayla. My emotion for you is much greater than when I left you. Today I will stay with you until the late sun disappears below the water and you will eat your evening meal with me in our hearth."

"I will not."

"I know Shakkra has told you. I believe she is your sister more than my mother. Look how she watches over you like a mother hen. You are both against me."

"What do you wish to tell me? Shakkra said you have much to say, much to show me. She said I must believe what you tell me. She said I must do what you tell me to do, to trust you. She asked me to smile, when under the water she squeezed my hands and I saw in her eyes that she was not calm."

"Do you trust her, with all your emotion? Do you feel deep emotion for her, enough to believe me, to do as I say?"

"Yes, more than what I feel for my own mother. I will do what Shakkra asks of me."

"Aayla, go to the trees. Find your bolero and hers. Return to me. We will meet her at the shore. See how she swims away from us. She is waiting for us to join her. Do not hurry. Do not stop to talk with anyone."

Aayla left him. She walked to where she'd tossed her bolero beside Shakkra's onto the sand, hoping she'd walked slowly enough. She didn't know how slowly to walk, or how fast. She was Aayla and never gave thought to how she should look to others.

She looked across the sand to the shoreline. Cassidy was walking as though he was dreaming, towards Shakkra who'd swum into waist-deep water. She would, she decided, walk two steps to his one, anxious to hold Shakkra's hand. She knew her friend would protect her, keep her from being afraid.

The tidewater was low, Cassidy and his mother exchanging smiles, each holding out a hand for the other amidst the crashing waves.

"Thank you, Shakkra. Now can you tell her to listen to me always, to do what I say always?"

She shook her head. "I learned something else last night, my son."

"I'm afraid to ask what."

"Get real."

"What does that mean, get real?"

"I don't know. I believe it means that I won't." She shrugged. "I'm learning."

"More quickly than me, I think."

"Cassidy, my second-mate, I spoke with him when we arrived at our home. I've changed my mind about him. He feels nothing for me and wants nothing from me. He sleeps to remember his first-mate. He misses her. He understands why I don't share my..."

She felt an arm at her waist.

"Why have you stopped talking?"

"Walk between us, little one. Aayla, today you will see what your eyes will not believe, when in your heart must believe. You will hear what your ears will refuse to understand, but you must in your heart understand. From now on my son will not leave you. I will not leave you, and very soon you will know the reasons why."

"I do not understand. Where are we going, Shakkra?"

Cassidy took her hand. "We're walking into the gorge and beyond the pole to the windward shore." He pointed.

"The tidal current's at its lowest point so we'll be able to swim easily to the far blue water and walk along the shore to a place you've never seen. We're going to Tombolina."

A spasm cold gripped her. Shakkra's warmth across her shoulders did little to dispel the chill.

"What did he say, Shakkra? I did not understand his strange words. The fast water is forbidden to us when no one sits at the pole and the bad water beyond is filled with dark creatures. No one has ever gone to Tombolina."

"Don't worry, little one. He loves you with all his heart. He won't let anything bad happen to you. We're going to Tombolina because if we don't next year he'll die four days after you're joined with Dakota, four days after an old man fills you with his ancient prong in his pond for his own pleasure. What we do today will save my son. What we do today will save you as well."

"You are talking like him, Shakkra. I do not understand. Never have you talked like this with me."

"Because I couldn't, today I must so that you'll believe us. It's the only way to show you the truth. We haven't lied to you. We've deceived you to protect you, and to protect ourselves." She stopped to hug the girl. "Aayla, we live here in danger. We all do, everyone, above all the one who is my family, my son."

"The name is not yet known."

"The name is known. He'll be first; I will follow the year after. It's written in a book you can't yet read." She paused. "Aayla, we are certain of this. We know."

Aayla stared in disbelief.

"You see, Aayla, already you don't believe my mother. What chance do I have that you'll believe me?"

Her lips quivered, her eyes welling with tears.

"So, this is the Aayla who wants to marry me, who wants to have my children, a little girl who cries for no reason, who's afraid of the fast water and little fish in the bad water?"

Shakkra pushed him away, gently, guiding the girl closer to the trees. She was smiling, lightly brushing her thumbs across Aayla's wet eyes.

"We will teach you to read and to write so that you can see your name is the sand, understand all our strange words and speak them. We will show you many things that will scare you, many more that will make you happy and curious. Soon, Aayla, you will become unhappy with your life here, as we are. We alone do not speak this way. The Grand Guardian does when he leaves this place with Irene whose real name is Forrest, as does Dakota and his mother, whose name is Taliah, as does his cousin Fontaine."

"How do you know all these things? How do you know what others do not?"

Shakkra shook her head. "Little one, do you trust me?" She saw the doubt. "If you do not, tell me now before we pass through the fast water, through the gorge to the far side where the water is not bad."

Aayla wrapped her arms around her friend and squeezed, relaxing under the warm pressure of Shakkra's arms.

"How can I not have trust in you, Shakkra? You are his mother." She turned to Cassidy. "And we are better swimmers than him. Hold my hand. I am not afraid, if he is not."

Aayla had never seen the Pole of Tombola in daylight, nor the bridge or the dark cavity behind the wrought iron fence which led to Tombolina. Nor had she ever seen the blue sky from between towering precipices. Neither had Shakkra who suppressed her awe for the sake of her young friend.

Once past the bridge they stepped into the shallow water, wading to the depth of their chests, swimming easily with the current towards a sea that was forbidden to them.

The ocean was agitated, the swells higher than the calm leeward shore. The coastline was dotted with boulders and lined with wet sand that was coarse, not fine. Across twenty-one of the huge stones twelve rows of scrawled vertical lines were etched into their surfaces. He slowed by each, running his open hands over Jonathon's work, telling Shakkra the significance of the now barely visible lines.

They might have been in another world, the women walking tentatively, their bodies wrapped closely together, Cassidy walking inches ahead of them as much to listen and search the sea as to conceal the humour etched into his face.

"We're here, ladies."

Aayla wrinkled her brow. "Where are we? I see nothing and what is a ladies?"

He pointed. "That's his secret entrance to Tombolina, where he hides his boat, the huge machine that floats on water. You and my mother are ladies. At least she is."

Shakkra punched him.

"The water isn't deep, I don't think so. We may have to swim a short distance." He took their hands and led them several feet into the channel. "It's a little gloomy."

"What is gloomy?"

"The bottom is sandy and the water is clear. We have nothing to worry about. At the end, where we can see no more, the channel turns to the left and continues the same distance. That's where we'll see the small boat and climb onto Tombolina."

"You have come here before?"

"Yes, now that you believe me, with my father before he was killed. I have walked on Tombolina and I have been in his house, with my mother."

"This cannot be true."

Shakkra nodded. "This is my first time in the channel. We are both nervous, little one. And, yes, I've been in the house."

"I am ready."

They half swam, half waded three abreast with wide strokes, Aayla sucking water into her mouth at the sudden light of day and sight of the launch tied to the dock.

At the wharf she reached for a cleat, not certain of its purpose, letting her feet touch against flotation barrels coated with barnacles, kicking herself away. Cassidy hauled himself onto the dock. Shakkra didn't. She went to Aayla instead, not quite pleased with her son's lack of gallantry or his smirk.

He took Aayla's hand first, then Shakkra's. They stood in a row facing the portside of the fibreglass launch, Cassidy the first to break the timorous silence when he leapt over the gunwale.

"Come, ladies. Come, Shakkra. Come, Aayla, now you'll learn The Grand Guardian is a man, no more special than you or me. Tell her, mother."

"What he says is true, little one. Go. Stand on the boat. Nothing bad will happen to you."

Aayla followed more tentatively, her hands gripping the gunwale before thinking to lift one foot then the other from the dock. Shakkra followed.

"Thank you, Aayla. Now, come with me. Sit here, at the helm. This is what makes the boat travel and churn the blue water white. The boat does not move because The Grand Guardian sits where you sit. It would do the same for you or for me. Come, we have more to see. "

He scrambled onto the dock, taking his mother's hand, then Aayla's. He was excited. Once off the boat she released him and held Shakkra's. They walked into the clearing, Aayla as though each step was her last, her eyes adjusting to the bright light. Neither mother nor son surprised the by the girl's reaction.

Aayla shrieked.

"That's where he lives, Aayla. That's his home. The

walls shine because the sun is high, not because he's The Grand Guardian. It's paint, like the white paint on yours and ours. And the windows are mirrors, reflection plates. That's why they appear so brilliant. They aren't special. We'll go inside later when you'll see things that will scare you," he looked at Shakkra, "but you have your big sister with you."

"Don't bother with him, Aayla. He's rude and, as you once told me, sometimes he's stupid when you're near him. He acts this way because he loves you, he has deep emotion for you and sometimes he's silly," she raised an eyebrow, looking directly at him, "at the worst times. All men are. Sometimes it's best to ignore them. Come."

They left him. They went to the crystal pool where Shakkra removed her bolero, telling Aayla to do the same.

"Inside the house is cold, little one. Your top must dry before we go in." She eased into the water. "Come in. The water's as warm as it is clear, and deeper than you are tall so sit here with me. He won't be long. He's thinking of what he will say to make us like him again."

"I love him. I remember the word. He made my name in the sand for me."

Shakkra beamed. "As do I love him, even when he's a little silly. We must accept that we're superior to him and those like him."

"Men?"

"Yes, of course, all of them. And the one who lives in the golden house is no different. Very soon, little one, you'll write Cassidy's name in the sand and on paper. I will teach you. Shhh, let's be quiet. Here he comes."

"I'll sit on the grass, since the best seats are taken."

They said nothing, their hands laced together underwater.

"Shakkra, it's time for me to be serious. You don't know what I'm about to tell you. I'm sorry. It's what my father wished. It's what Jonathon wished and now I must betray them because I'm the last descendant to live on this island. Aayla, what you'll hear is worth my mother's life. If you tell anyone, if you speak as we do to anyone, you'll lose your friend to the sea. Not everyone on Tombola goes to the pole, and none go to the Sacred Gardens or are taken away for care. They are taken to the sea and given to the sea, to the blue water you call bad."

She looked at Shakkra.

"Believe what he tells you, little one. Every word he says is true."

"Mother, you didn't read the three letters in my chest because the lighting was poor. You didn't because I couldn't let you. Zach forbade me with his last words to me," he put up a hand, "which doesn't forbid me from speaking them to you. I've read each one a hundred times. I've studied each one a hundred times. Each word is in my mind and my heart. Each night I lay awake and recite them. I will never forget my father, or Jacob or Jonathon who first came to this island. To begin with, Shakkra, his name wasn't Jonathon Clayton and he wasn't really American. He was Johann Gerson. He was German."

"Cassidy, did Zach leave more than one letter?"

"He did. He wrote many for your eyes alone and, of the three, he wrote the most difficult to read. The ink is blotched with my tears. I swore to keep three promises, Shakkra. I promised I would never tell you of the letters until you were safe from harm. He knew your strength, your determination. He knew that if you read his letter you would place yourself in danger because of me. My second promise was to keep you by my side always. I haven't yet failed him, Shakkra. And I won't"

He stopped. Her face was wet with tears, Aayla's small wet hand wiping them away.

"What was the third promise, Cassidy?"

"The third was the easiest promise, mother. I promised

to take you away from here and, with you, this girl I love in the way Zach loved you."

"Shakkra, what is he saying?"

"We are leaving Tombola, little one. That is why we are here, to discover a way."

"Mother, I want to read those letters from my heart, and once we're safe from here you'll hold them in your hands and read them with your own eyes. Not before."

She nodded and held Aayla closer, kissing the girl's cheek for comfort.

*

Jacob, my boy, I write this letter without your mother's knowledge sometime before my death and I wish her to live out her life without the slightest awareness of this our final communication.

I have no firm date in mind as to the timing of my expiration, neither do I have long to wait. The event is not unexpected, though our destinies are seldom in our own hands.

You're a hard-working lad, your mother's pride and joy as much as you are mine.

I came to Tombola under false pretences, Jacob, though I won't waste valuable lead lamenting the fact. All who live here came for a particular reason or purpose, some honest, some not. Who's to say which was mine?

I don't regret coming here. I regret bringing your mother with me and loving her to the extent that your sisters preceded you. Their names might well have been Passion and Desire to celebrate my feelings for Cecilia. We waited for the first, I believe with good reason, which I'll soon allude to, not expecting that the girl would bring Cecilia such joy that your mother would want a second daughter to cuddle and nurse. But a man needs a son and I didn't waste much time once I saw the beauty of the second. I needed a son, Jacob, without which we Claytons would've stood a bugger's chance of escaping this paradisiacal hell.

You weren't any easy experience for her, lad, although, as pleased as I am to have known you, I'm no less pleased to have closed her gate. The fewer Claytons delivered to this place the better. Remember that, and spend yourself with some degree of restraint when the time comes. Girls are fine in the hearth, lad, for cooking and making us laugh, though they'll never do what needs to be done in the thick of things. For that reason, implore the lucky girl who wins your heart to give you a son as strong as my own, and quickly.

Now here's what you don't yet know, what you'll pass on to your son, and his son to his until we're expired or free. And when your time comes you'll add your words to mine and your son to yours. Not for the sake of familial history. Eventually all families dilute themselves into nonexistence. Leave your thoughts for the sake of a single purpose: Free yourself of this place.

The one reason I've not killed this deluded Wendell Parkens is the fact that I possess no knowledge of things nautical. I can't swim. I never saw the need to soak myself so extensively if not within the confines of a wash tub. So what was the point in learning seamanship when drowning was quite in the realm of possibility? At this time there's no escape from here, which will change one day, Jacob, if not in your time, in your son's.

But there's another reason I couldn't leave before the first of your sisters, or after, even if I could swim a hundred miles or more with a box on my back, or captain a boat. .

Jacob, I'd be hung for treason or shot as a spy. A matter of perspective, I grant you, although I wouldn't have been in a very favourable position to argue semantics. And I sincerely doubt whether their view of me would be much different on this beautiful summer's day of 1967, if the scratches on my windward rocks are the least bit reliable.

They're my sole tie with freedom, my sense of time and place, though I admit that living on a tropical island is preferable to swinging from a noose or having my chest perforated with a foreign bullet.

When I came here I wasn't twenty-two. I was thirty-two and I was Scottish to those closest to me, though not by birth, my citizenship more a matter of convenience of the times, much as I adopted the United States as a matter of expedience. I went to Scotland to complete a higher education, to learn their speech and their ways. Upon completion of my studies and the successful erasure of my natural accent, I was sent to the US to work. I was sent with very little choice in the matter, though I was very enthusiastic about my mission. I was an officer in the German army at the tender age of twenty-three, which isn't that outstanding. If caught, not one of my medals, awarded to me in absentia, would have covered the hole in my chest.

My employer, well-known for his work ethics, had deep pockets. I wasn't alone in my quest by any means and within a very short time I was a US citizen and the Terminal Manager at the prized dockyards of Savannah not long before war broke out in Europe.

My primary task was one of information gathering. I compiled information on local opinion, politics, convoys of allied troops and American readiness to join the fray. In American jargon I was a spy. However, to me, I was doing an important job for a simple reason. I was highly paid for work I did well: one pocket filled by my homeland, the other by virtue of my privileged position. I enjoyed a plethora of perquisites and very soon I wanted more money as much as I wanted more adventure and women.

I wanted the war never to end, however we seldom get what we wish for and not much time was left to me after the disheartening declaration heard round the world in May of '45. Apparently my superiors forgot me, more concerned with their own skins, a decisive action that served me well. I didn't want to be remembered, by them or the Americans. So I did what any good spy would do under similar and dire circumstances. I ran like hell, and not empty handed.

I wasn't working alone throughout my time in Savannah; I had a good bit of help from people who I'm certain continue to run the place, no doubt their pockets as heavily weighted as their minds. More to the point, when I left I did so alone with 150 lbs of gold and a charming brogue that never seemed ready to leave me, accumulating sufficient reading material along the way to see me through several months if not years. What I didn't take, to my great regret, was my revolver. Had I taken that I wouldn't be writing this letter to you now. I'd be learning how to drive a boat, or more likely sink it.

I suppose the war did end at a convenient time. Eventually prying eyes would have discovered the missing gold acquired over several years. Not stolen, Jacob, rather diverted from whatever purpose it would serve an enemy.

I fled first by bus to New York, to lose myself in the crowds, which I did quite successfully. Unfortunately, postwar was a suspicious time. The FBI was everywhere searching for retired or neglected spies. I couldn't look for work, let alone find any suitable employment to match my particular skills. I was an intelligence officer in a defunct army and any thought of travel to Europe seemed somewhat irrational at the time.

I left New York. I travelled west, then south, then east. I saw the country, mostly bent over with my face to the ground, dusty or wet, in dry heat or rain strong enough to blind a man, labouring in fields of corn and cotton amongst whites and blacks, all of them honest men living free and poor. I was the richest of them all, yet the poorest.

I travelled at last to Miami in search of work and good food as much as good wine and a good woman to drink with me. I didn't expect to find a waif of incredible beauty and charm living on the street, begging for food or pennies for a night's shelter to avoid the disputable luxury of St. Jude's.

The place was an orphanage, a stockpile of derelict children once abandoned, unwanted by others, all of them troubled or simple in their interpretation of the world. I loved her at once, and took her as my own, albeit not in the biblical sense. She wasn't yet eighteen, Jacob. Your mother was fifteen when I found her and she remained a virgin three years longer, which did nothing for my spirits. Yet I wouldn't see her harmed by my impatience. She's slender and delicate to this day. I wanted her not to die in labour, and now you'll take care of her in this island prison when I cannot.

Her tender age is the true reason you came late into the world, as did your sisters before you, not to discount the dimwits we took possession of upon our arrival. They were the brightest of the lot, manageable in their own way, and six years later they were gone from our home not a moment too soon and forgotten, replaced by those we love.

I can't imagine the future weakness of their family trees long since planted. More importantly, I can imagine the strength of yours.

Remember this, lad. You've got 150 lbs of gold buried beneath the ground. Not your mother, or any other woman derived from me is to know of its existence or location, not until you're certain of success. They can't be trusted by virtue of their weak and loving hearts. The same holds true for each generation to follow. If no longer a man's world, lad, it's our job to make it appear so.

Once free, whoever carries the gold won't know of the world. My sole advice at the end of my imprisonment is for you or yours to seek out a barrister, one who's trustworthy and not the first in line. He'll know what course to take on your behalf and fit you well into any future society.

Your mother knows not to expect me for dinner any one of these coming nights. We say our farewells each evening and each new day. She knows as well that she must continue your lessons in the sand and in the sea, by the lantern near your bed one book at a time while your sisters are asleep.

Goodbye, Jacob. I trust I won't be meeting you anytime soon. You're too kind of heart to follow my preordained path.

Jonathon Clayton, (née Johann Gerson)
August 18th, 1914 - July 02nd, 1967

Thirty-Eight

Cassidy hurled himself into the water, crouching, slowly breaking the surface. He needed to clear his eyes.

"Shakkra, he was writing of me. Now do you believe me...without the slightest doubt?"

"Yes, Cassidy, since I first came here. You're Jonathon's son as much as Zach's. Those markings on the stones, they're his?"

He nodded. "Aayla, it's alright to open and close your eyes, to blink...before the sun dries them like figs."

Shakkra kissed her head. "Don't be afraid, little one."

Aayla squeezed herself closer into Shakkra's arms.

"What am I hearing, Shakkra?"

"The telling of Cassidy's past fathers, the one who came first to Tombola. The rest you will one day understand very easily. Now Cassidy has more to tell us."

She looked to her son.

"Cassidy, each word, you've made no mistake? You're certain?"

"I spoke each word as he wrote it. I wouldn't say anything different a second time."

"I would have liked him, I think."

"I would have also, I think." He turned his attention to Aayla. "Don't cry. I've known since my birth and Shakkra since before her first-coupling with my father. Now that you've discovered the truth, soon you'll know what we know. When you stepped into this pool with my mother you

400

lost your girlhood, Aayla. Now you're a woman, and you must act like one. You must not tease me. Now you know why I haven't paid attention to you, because I do feel deep emotion for you, because we're leaving this place together the three of us and my head must be clear."

"My mother and my father will not permit me to go."

Aayla craned her neck to see Shakkra behind her, barely hearing Cassidy.

"Listen to him, Aayla."

"They won't know. If they want to follow later, I promise they will." He grinned. "Once I'm finished with what I must say to Shakkra, and after to you, so that you will understand, we'll take you inside the house and you will see how badly we live."

"Cassidy, this little girl's heart is beating loudly enough. She doesn't need…"

"I'm sorry, mother. She does. She must know that being on Tombolina isn't a childish prank. Aayla, forgive me, but do not for any reason tell your parents. Your father's the Chief Counsellor. He's too close to The Grand Guardian. Your father won't understand all that you're learning now. How would you explain this to him? Even he is forbidden from crossing the bridge or passing through the arch. We won't forget him or your mother when the time is right, that's what you want."

Aayla retorted in a tremulous voice. "I will tell them nothing, Cassidy, and I am not a child. I am a woman."

Shakkra squeezed the girl's shoulders.

"Cassidy, Jonathon was right in what he wrote. We're learning by what we see through the television. What he didn't write was how we're supposed to carry so much gold and who will we trust? We won't know anyone."

"I'll find a way. What good is gold under the ground," he smirked, "or under the water?" Now we are poor. Our hearth is a humble villa, yet we have great wealth. Won't our lives be better with our freedom, and alive, even if we must leave the gold hidden until we are certain? We'll know when the time comes who wishes to cheat us and who won't. The gold's less important than you and your little friend nestled in your arms."

He fell backward into the warm water, sweeping the water from his hair when he surfaced. His eyes and his skin glistened, his matted hair resembling a thick skullcap.

"I have more to tell you, Shakkra, but the water's soothing and inviting, at least to me. Why am I standing here by myself?" He smirked. "Are you also afraid of this bad water?"

He knew the weight of what he was passing from his shoulder onto theirs, a burden lightened by light-hearted splashing and shrieking until he hauled himself from the water in a single movement; Shakkra and Aayla did the same.

"Where are you taking us?" Shakkra asked.

"To the whirring machine, Shakkra, to the helicopter that carries The Grand Guardian through the air."

Shakkra took the girl's hand. "Come. Let's see the noise-making monster together for the first time. We've only ever seen it in the distance, like a big bird in the sky. Haven't we, Aayla?"

"You know the helicopter isn't a monster, Shakkra." He looked at Aayla. "It's a flying machine without a single feather. Come."

They walked along another of four paths leading from the manor. Three led to the dock, the pool and the pond, meandering through the gardens. This one led to the helicopter and Aayla recoiled at first sight. Shakkra's reaction was no less expressive.

The tinted glass enclosing the cockpit sparkled under the sun, imposing and sinister. The maroon and black metallic paint was smooth and hot to the touch as Cassidy ran his hands along what Aayla believed was indeed a monster, its four eighteen-foot blades drooping ominously towards the ground.

Shakkra's voice was firm. "Cassidy, don't touch it. It's dangerous."

"It's a machine, a dead machine until he's inside. I've touched it before." Cassidy fiddled with the door release and climbed in before his mother could catch her breath. "Here's what I didn't tell you, because I knew you wouldn't believe me."

"What do you think you're doing? Get down from there before you're trapped inside."

He didn't. Instead he rested his hand on the cyclic pitch stick and grinned, making a guttural whirring sound.

"Cassidy, do what I ask."

"Mother, I will, if you promise to sit here in my place...and Aayla." He clambered to the ground. "Didn't we agree to learn as much as we can, as quickly as we can? Didn't we agree to teach Aayla what we know?"

Shakkra shook her head, took a deep breath and pulled herself quickly into the cabin before she could change her mind.

"I don't feel good in here."

"I don't believe you. I don't see fear on your face, I see wonder. Now you know. The thing is made of metal and glass with no eyes, no wings and not a single feather," he chortled. "And with our new books we'll learn more about how it works."

Shakkra eased herself through the door to the ground. Aayla backed away; she knew what he was thinking. She was right. But rather than coaxing her he went to the co-pilot's side and climbed in to watch her through the portside door. He didn't wait long.

"Aayla the white lines in the blue sky come from flying machines not much different than this, only bigger. I wasn't telling you an untruth. One day we will fly together over the sea, the blue water."

"Do they fall from the sky into the sea?"

"I suppose they do sometimes. I don't know."

"Then I will never go with you." She looked behind her. "There are more chairs." She bounced a little in her seat. "Never have I felt anything so soft under me."

"Soon you will, every day, and you'll dress in beautiful clothes with my mother. But now we must go."

Cassidy swung himself onto the ground, closing and latching the door. On the pilot's side Aayla was standing with her friend, chattering. Cassidy closed the pilot's door and all three walked away without once glancing back, bypassing the pool, strolling to the pond where they splashed through the low water of the channel to the leeward shore. Aayla stood staring out to sea, then north, then south to Tombola, her hands clasped in front of her.

Cassidy sat in the sand to watch her, Shakkra stood by her side.

'Never did I think I would be here."

"Or you didn't want to think you'd be here, little one, for the same reason my son wants us to leave before the next Seven Feasts, for the same reason you must never tell your father of this."

"You are speaking of the first-teaching. I will couple with Cassidy, never Dakota."

"Yes, when we have gone from here, not before. You would have his child, not him. The Grand Guardian would take him to the sea and return without him."

"I will tell no one, Shakkra."

Cassidy interjected. "I believe you, Aayla. Thank you for not getting me killed." He stood, pointing to the horizon. "Now, come. We'll go to the pond where the ocean and the wind won't distract me from what is left to recite of the letters. The weather's beginning to change and we're not finished what we came here to do."

He followed behind. At the pond he sat in the direction of the dock; the women lay on their fronts in the heated sand, facing him, propped onto their elbows. Shakkra was fearful of what she would hear, Aayla certain she wouldn't understand.

He began without preamble or inflection, his face devoid of expression.

*

Zach, we'll speak later this morning for the last time regarding your future and your mother. You'll know then that by the time you read this I'll be dead and gone. I hope that tonight your arm was strong and your eyes were keen. Tonight I sat at the pole by invitation of our divine Wendell Parkens and trust I went well without bringing shame on you or your mother.

I met with Parkens yesterday. My feeling is that I might easily have bartered the contents of my father's strongbox for my life, or the briefest extension of it. He knows of the chest; the existence was never in question, merely the contents and it's eaten at the bugger for forty years. And remember this. What the bugger doesn't know will keep you alive now that I'm gone.

Jonathon was a good man. The gold, he told me often, wasn't stolen. He was a soldier sent onto foreign soil to wage a secret war I can't imagine for his country. What I do know is that whatever courage we possess is derived from him. He often joked that if the gold didn't exactly constitute the spoils of war, then certainly he must think of the 150lbs as the fortunate proceeds in his possession for the purpose of weakening the enemy.

Parkens, on the other hand, isn't a good man. He has his sights set on us, Zach. My father went on this date nineteen years ago and not by the jaws of a shark, my mother six years later, three days after my joining and four days or more after your conception. I was next in line and, given that Parkens rid himself of his beloved Irene, I can't imagine that he'll spare your mother when her time comes, or you unless he makes a mistake to your advantage.

He knows we're a different breed. We haven't forgotten our past, Jon or Cecilia, or our family name when others have. Your mother's unlike the other women, you're unlike other boys, and that won't change. Waiting for the privacy of our villa when the day is over to speak freely and to read by your bed is a small price to pay for what you'll achieve one day. In fact it's no price at all; it's the one freedom you'll know until your escape.

The people here, the other villagers, won't be any help to you. They won't believe you. Those who are left of the originals were never brilliant thinkers to begin with and their offspring are even less equipped to do what must be done. Imagine living in a world without the slightest notion of what lies beyond these narrow shores. That was his plan, which sets you apart.

You know of the world, of what existed until 1946, and we know the world hasn't stood still since then. Think of what lies in store for you, once free of this place, of what new world you'll encounter with your sweet mother by your side. She's as beautiful as she is smart, a rarity here, and she's passed her finest qualities to you to compensate for my very few natural shortcomings.

That time will come. Parkens is old. His son's gone, his grandson likely dropped into the sea to swim with fish smarter than him. Keep a keen eye for your first opportunity. You'll have one try, and your mother with you. Do nothing to put her in the ground before her time.

She knows to continue your lessons, your reading and your writing, though she must never know of the box's location or of the gold, as was your grandfather's wish. The danger is too great. Any amount of gold will drive any man to the farthest reaches of his dark side, and this fellow Parkens arrived there some time ago, very comfortable with, or very unaware of his insanity.

Do what you must to care for your mother.

Best regards,

Jacob (Clayton)

March 25th, 1955 – July 03rd, 1986

*

"Jacob's first-mate was killed at the pole six years later, Aayla. And nineteen years to the day after Jacob my father was stoned first by Shakkra and me. He didn't suffer, not for one second.

But what I will read in my father's letter is the most important to us."

She sat straight, crossing her legs, completely engulfed by confusion.

"You know I do not understand you, Cassidy."

"The first Grand Guardian, Wendell Parkens, killed my father and those before him because of a box I possess, because he wanted to know what is in that box."

"The box is at your tree?"

He looked to Shakkra.

She nodded.

"Yes. The tree is where I hide my books. Studying them is how I know to make your name in the sand, how we know of the world beyond this island. There is also gold."

"I do not know gold."

"Here we grow food in our gardens; we have sheep and pigs for our meat. Once each year The Grand Guardian gives us what we need for women like Shakkra to knit or sew our tunics, our pants and our shields. Across the sea, the blue water, gold is given in exchange for what they wear and what they eat. It's the colour of his house."

Shakkra spoke. "Aayla, if you tell anyone of the tree my son will be killed, and not at the pole. The Grand Guardian wants what we have, what he must never find if you want in your heart to couple and join with Cassidy.”

Aayla turned to him. “I love you. That is all that I know.” Then she looked to Shakkra. “Never will I speak against him. Never will I hurt you, Shakkra. I will say nothing,” she forced a weak smile, “because I do not yet understand and what he is speaking is difficult for me. Never have I heard you or him speak this way together.”

“Soon you’ll speak this way, Aayla, before you leave the island with us and go to where gold, helicopters and boats are known by everyone. Soon, after I’ve recited my next letter, we’ll go to the house and show you many things.” He glanced at his mother with a smirk. “And Shakkra will show you thongs made of silk.”

Aayla looked to Shakkra, desperate to understand, her eyes imploring her friend to hold her close. Shakkra patted the sand beside her, giggling when Aayla galloped on all fours to her side.

“Never will I let anyone hurt him, Shakkra, unless it is you or me.”

“I agree, little one. Now listen to me. Each night in the sea, not the blue water, we’ll talk this way far from the others. You must be ready when we leave. We’ll teach you to write your name, the way Cassidy did once in the sand, and we’ll teach you to read so that you’ll know your name, you’ll know Shakkra and Cassidy. And from now on he’ll be with us, not sitting in his tree alone, she winked, “but sitting with us on an old box full of books.”

“I will be ready, Shakkra, and I will say nothing. I want to see these books and the gold.”

“But for now you must be patient and listen to what else he has to say. His next words are important to me. Zach wrote them.”

Aayla nodded, squirming onto her knees to put an arm around her friend’s shoulders.

Shakkra squeezed her and kissed her cheek.

Cassidy took a deep breath. He hadn't moved so much as an inch.

Thirty-Nine

Cassidy, no surprise is contained in this letter, one of three now hidden in the box. We knew the day would come, and we had a good idea when. My first inkling was his invitation to cross the bridge and pass through his hallowed arch. My first thought when I saw him standing there, hunched over, was to snap his withered frame in two. I didn't for two reasons close to my heart: you and your mother.

It's difficult to fathom that after these fifty-nine years he still hasn't found the chest. Now he believes we're concealing a Bible of all things. I never met the man, sadly, though what I know of him never led me to believe that our Jonathon was a righteous man. I suppose, given a choice between a fifty-pound holy book of little use and the same weight in gold, I would have made the same choice, hopeful that one day I might spend it. Such isn't the case. That's your destiny.

If not certain of the gold, which he likely sees in a festered mind as a result of our secrecy, he's certainly aware of our books, despite his mockery of their usefulness. He'd have to be deaf and dumb not to see the difference in us.

There's no better time to prepare, Cassidy. The man's ancient and weak. He's no match for you, and Garrett spends much of his time away from the island with his woman who places herself high above us despite her frequent condescension, though don't be in a hurry to fail.

Pace yourself, but get your mother off this island well before the sixth anniversary of my death. By then you'll be close to eighteen and man. She'll be twice that age and much too young to follow after me, which she will. Make certain that I'm the last Clayton to die on this island.

He told me himself that none of us will outlive him. Let's prove him wrong. If he dies first, you'll soon follow your mother and you won't have to wait a full year.

Jonathon made his calendar along the windward shore because he could, Jacob each morning in his books and I scratched my days into the frame of the bed I shared with your mother so that I would have space left in those books to write letters for your mother to read once I'm gone, once she's free to place my words on a proper shelf and not before.

You must do the same. You must know when the time is right to leave here, though I have no idea what lies in wait for you. He was ranting, his words sometimes indiscernible between his laughter and his spittle.

He raved about what he called a writing pad made of plastic and glass, something no bigger than our largest book that contains the history of the world and of each living person. He carried on about a person's written word being transmitted through the air, travelling across the world in seconds, of cameras hidden in phones so small they can be concealed in a man's shirt pocket, radios that fit in a man's ear and a glass tome with not a single page that once opened contains thousands of books. I can't imagine the strange workings of his deluded mind.

He believes every street corner in the world is fitted with cameras that record each person and what they do, and of machines hundreds of miles in space that watch every person's every move making secrecy or hiding impossible. Apparently because, beyond Tombola, children are killing children, men are killing their wives and people are afraid to leave their homes because the world is running amuck. The man was delirious; his eyes were glazed over, his lips quivering. He was afraid, Cassidy. Now he's afraid of you and your mother.

I can't speak to how he sees the world, or even if he does at this point. The only certainty is that he's done his share of killing. And he doesn't care much about age or gender.

You've been to Tombolina with me, Cassidy. We've swum into his secret channel. We've seen his little pool and his pond. I hope that will help you a great deal once you decide to act.

I bade Shakkra farewell this morning, joking that she should put as much passion into the hurling of her stone tonight as she did upon me last night. She didn't laugh and I hope she's not angry enough with me to drop her stone. I suppose I'll know soon enough. I'll make the same request of you later, that you not fail me should your mother's heart weaken. A terrible burden, I know, though I see no reason to denigrate our history with tincture. I'll go the way Jon and Jacob would expect of me. Nor will you ever feel the effects of the tincture.

A drop or two of the rum when you're of age will suffice as subterfuge, nothing more. You'll be gone long before you'll have to worry about stealing into the bushes or onto the sand with your woman on a moonless night to make certain your first son is your own.

We'll meet again, many years from now, when the three of us are ageless and free.

Until then, make her laugh and smile.

Zach (Clayton)

March 19th, 1974 – July 03rd, 2005

*

Cassidy stood. He strode into the pond and dived into the waist-deep water. He returned to them slowly. Aayla somehow felt she should speak, Shakkra couldn't.

He said: "What you did is what he wished you to do. You couldn't have honoured him in any better way."

"I killed Zach."

"You saved Zach, and I made certain that you did. If I'd seen the slightest hesitation, Shakkra, the first stone would have been mine and yours the second. Then what? Would you have blamed me as you've blamed yourself for five years?" He was numb. "You heard his last words. He wants you to laugh and smile."

"All this, Cassidy, what we're doing, this isn't by chance."

"No, it isn't. This is the time, Shakkra, the sixth year. We must be gone from here before the next Seven Feasts ends the year. Being here is no accident. Those lines scratched onto the lid of my box serve a purpose. They are my calendar. Since his death I've made a line for each day, for each month a number. Today is July 11th, Shakkra. The coming months will pass quickly with many sleepless nights," he paused, "and many smiles for what lies ahead of us."

"He's written letters to me."

"He has…on the inside covers of books you once read. Each of the covers is full."

"You've known all this time."

He nodded.

"Can you speak them to me, now?"

"You know I can't. I've never read them. They're not mine to read." He filled his lungs with air. "The old man, Wendell Parkens," he turned to Aayla, "The Grand Guardian, in his journal he wrote of how the village and your father dropped their stones once seeing Zach was killed by us. He wanted then to throw me from the precipice. His son is no better. This is why, Aayla, I needed to know when they'd be gone, and why I couldn't tell you.

This is the year we leave." He stood. "But we won't do that by sitting here. Come."

They walked to where one path crossed another and led to the pool where Shakkra and Aayla found their boleros. The day was mercilessly hot, the humidity hanging in the air like thick rain. Aayla didn't want to wear her top, doing so to imitate Shakkra who hadn't said another word.

"Aayla, up there, past the house, at the top the precipice, I stood there alone the first night to call your name. I saw the entire island, Tombola and Tombolina together, and the entire ocean. I told you the truth."

She shrugged. She'd seen the stone walls from Tombola each day of her life without knowing the number, and one evening each year. During the day she paid no attention to them, those rare nights the damp walls and dark shadows frightened her. Shakkra was more important to her than stone walls. And right then she didn't know what to think about Cassidy.

She wanted to be brave for Shakkra, yet her heart was at the point of rupture as Cassidy put his hand to the huge brass handle and swung the door outward. He went in first, the women followed. Once inside, Shakkra stood Aayla in front of her. She wrapped her arms around the girl dispelling the sudden chill, explaining each of the rooms from afar. Then she guided her to the sofa and sat, patting her lap so that Aayla would sit on her and not the cool leather. Somehow Aayla knew to lock her arms tightly around her friend's neck and remain quiet.

"Make the television work, Cassidy. Put the volume to its lowest point. Do not scare my daughter." She paused while he went to the black screen. "Don't worry, little one. Nothing will happen to you. We don't know everything about this black glass, except that each time we learn from what is inside. The people aren't real, yet they are. They're like the people you will soon see, the reason you must learn with us."

She nodded to her son and held Aayla snugly in place.

Aayla jerked more than lurch forward, startling all three.

Thunder reverberated through the room, rain slashing at the man's face. His eyes were red, his mouth distorted, his lips trembling out of control. The blue-white glare of the vehicle's halogens camouflaged the backdrop, not the man on his knees or the black silhouette and gloved hand pushing the gun against his forehead.

What the fuck. I mean what the actual fuck are you telling me? You mean he's fucking dead, that asshole? Shit. You killed a fucking cop.

Boss.

Shut the fuck up. I don't want to do this. I don't.

Cassidy clicked the cursor.

The older woman was blonde, dressed in a décolleté black dress with a gaudy faux-diamond pinned in place between freckled breasts. Her hair wasn't real, her skin the texture of wet leather left in the sun to dry. Her veined hands were skeletal and spotted, decorated with clumps of gold and zircon. The woman beside her was younger, attired in red satin, her blonde hair sprayed to resist force nine winds, her sculpted face too perfect, her eyes too blue, her lips too full, too red and wet looking. Her hands were smooth; her nails painted bright red, a single zircon adorned a slender finger.

Aayla leaned closer, not letting go of Shakkra.

Ladies, for only 129.95 this three-way bra and matching panty set can be yours in large, extra-large and double extra-large for the perfect shape after that perfect baby.

Shakkra whispered, "They are to cover their breasts. They're ugly, for girls like the one intended for Cassidy. Not for you. Not like the pretty shields I'll show you in a few minutes."

Cassidy clicked again, ignoring his mother.

The man and woman sat behind a glass tabletop, appearing rigid. She was white, her lips painted to match her mahogany hair. He was black with no hair, dressed in a suit and white shirt making his head appear detached. She was smiling, he wasn't. Neither one looked at the other.

Gill, the governor denied all allegations of wrong-doing. His wife of twenty-five years has not commented as of airtime.

That's right, Simon. She's standing by his side, as she did last year. She must really want to live in Washington. What was he thinking?

Aayla said. "She is beautiful, Shakkra. Why does her face not move when she talks? And what are those on her feet?

Shakkra chuckled. "I don't know about her face. But, yes, she is beautiful and she wears elegant sandals on her feet, as you will one day soon."

"Is she in the wall with the others?"

"We don't know where they are. We're learning."

The news duo disappeared.

The woman wore her bleached hair cropped, a form-fitting white V-neck sweater and tight linen pants. On one hip she wore a gold badge, on the other a black gun appeared inordinately large, more comedic than threatening. Her unshaven partner wore high-waist white slacks and a loose-fitting white suit jacket over a white singlet, the grip of his black gun protruding just so as a perfect fashion statement.

No, ma'am. We're with the Special Victims Unit. It's your daughter. I'm sorry, ma'am. We need you to come downtown.

My daughter, is she alright?

No, ma'am. She's dead."

Aayla twisted in Shakkra's lap.

"Shakkra, the mother is so young like me and her

daughter is dead. Do you think the daughter was stoned?"

"I don't know. This is the first time I've seen that woman."

"It's television, Aayla. That's all we know." He grinned. "We can even watch people coupling. They want us to see them. We can tell by their faces. Can't we, Shakkra?"

"No, we cannot."

Shakkra's expression spoke volumes. Despite his rapid emergence into manhood, she was still his mother. The screen went black.

"My skin is cold, Shakkra. Why?"

"There's much we know, Aayla, and much more we do not. But, come. We'll see the house and show you many things you won't understand, but soon we will. For now, let's see all the rooms. Let's see where he sleeps with her and what she wears when she's not here with us. She has tunics and robes like the women behind the glass and so many shields as soft as your hair."

"While you're doing that, Aayla, with Shakkra, I'll find a book for you to read."

He hesitated.

His mother asked, "What's wrong, Cassidy?"

"Nothing' wrong, mother. I feel a great weight lifted from my shoulders. I'm sorry I didn't tell you what I know. I couldn't. And, Aayla, I'm sorry I couldn't tell you the truth. Without you we wouldn't be here. Thank you."

Shakkra eased her little friend from her lap and went into the kitchen. Aayla went to someone who looked very much like Cassidy. She wasn't sure anymore.

"Will I be different to you, the way you are to me?"

"Yes."

"After, will you feel deep emotion for me?"

"Yes."

"This is why you did not touch me at the beach?"

"I never said I didn't touch you, Aayla," he smirked,

"when you slept in the sand like an angel."

"What is angel?"

"Beautiful young mermaids who swim in the dark sky between the stars."

"We are leaving here."

"Yes, before I lose my mother to the pole, before you lose me to Dakota. And I will need your help. I must know…"

"Each time he leaves from Tombolina on his," she thought hard, "boat." She turned to see Shakkra gently tapping her hands together in praise. Then she put her nose into the air, snubbing him. "I will do this for Shakkra, not you. But I do begin to feel emotion again for…"

"You love me."

"I feel love for Shakkra more." She pranced to the kitchen. "You can leave from here with us if you want."

Forty

Aayla adapted to the chill of The Grand Guardian's manor. She marvelled at the kitchen and the bathroom and held crumpled silk to her youthful face for the first time. She lay on Irene's bed, closed her eyes and imagined herself floating, catapulted into the air with the flick of a switch, soon after burning the tip of her finger against the white heat of the light and shrieking.

In the library, touching her first book, seeing the words and hearing Shakkra read aloud, she didn't know what to say or feel. She'd never known what she'd missed. So how then could she feel sadness or loss?

He scanned the walls row by row and chose Little Women for her, commenting that the title seemed appropriate since she was a little woman, garnering no particular favour in their current view of him.

When they left the sun was midway through its descent, blinding halos outlining threatening clouds suspended over the island and the sea.

They went first to the tree where Aayla saw more books and felt the weight of gold in her unsuspecting hands. She was less afraid with each passing moment, more curious with each new word.

At their villa Shakkra prepared a special platter of legumes and red snapper. Aayla and Cassidy ate quietly, Shakkra and the man spoke of the next day's work in the field and the sea. When the evening meal was done the man went out onto the porch curtained by teeming rain.

For Aayla what remained of the evening was complicated. She didn't know what to say and wasn't certain what not to say. She thought she would never sleep again and decided she didn't like Shakkra's second-mate. Because of him she couldn't listen to Cassidy and Shakkra speaking to teach her and she wanted to become exactly like Shakkra who was prettier than the women on the shiny pages. She was the prettiest woman on the entire island.

She wanted a beautiful shield like those in Irene's closet, which she knew wasn't possible, delighted when Shakkra promised to design the prettiest and softest of any shield on the island. One she would wear on Sundays when she could make all the other girls crazy with envy, Shakkra whispered.

The man was in bed sleeping, or not, as the night grew increasingly wicked. Aayla didn't want to leave. She wanted to stay with Shakkra. Deafening wind wailed through rustling wet leaves, the evening sky prematurely black with raindrops the size of pellets. Shakkra wished Aayla could spend the night, disappointed she had nowhere for the girl to sleep.

Instead they kissed at the door and hugged like mother and daughter, sisters and best friends, Shakkra murmuring to Aayla that she wouldn't forget her promise.

From her window she watched the young girl disappear into the village with Cassidy, walking as though the summer's worst storm wasn't swirling around them.

At the stoop of her villa she kissed him.

"Cassidy, I will never sleep again in my life."

He smiled. "Yes, you will. You will sleep with me in our bed one day soon."

"Because of you I am a bad girl."

"Why, Aayla?"

"Because now I am envy and I was never envy before

today. I did not know to be envy before."

He cupped her face and touched her nose to his. "Aayla, do nothing to hurt my mother. From today you must think before you speak one word unless we are at the tree to read after our work in the field or in the blue water after the evening meal to speak of what you will soon learn."

"Never will I hurt my sister. I love her."

"No Aayla. You feel emotion for her, unless you are at the tree or in the blue water. To say you love her will hurt her."

"I will never, and never will I sleep."

"I must go. Your tunic is clear with rainwater and your skin looks like a chicken ready for the fire."

She pulled away and punched him.

"I meant to say a beautiful chicken."

She punched him again and leaned into his ear.

"Cassidy, the rain…"

He shrugged.

"My little women…"

He chortled. "They will stay dry all night."

She wrapped her arms around his neck, kissing him. "Goodnight," she kissed him again, "darling."

She sauntered inside, leaving him on the porch with his mouth agape.

He meandered through the downpour, humming and smiling, convinced he should never completely trust his women together. His future wouldn't be a good one with them constantly conspiring against him. He was anxious and excited. He was in the sixth year of his father's wish and he would succeed.

The year, for Cassidy, was the day he'd waited so long to see.

His villa was dark, the lanterns snuffed, the rooms quiet. He knew, and he knew one day soon that would change. Shakkra lay in his bed, dressed in her night-shield and curled into the wall. He changed in the dark and eased between his sheets close to the edge. He lay on his back, quiet, deep in thought, his arms crossed over his chest.

He knew she wasn't sleeping. She was thinking. Her mind was filled with images of all she'd seen and heard in the house and Tombolina, shivering from the warm dampness lingering in the air. He covered her with his sheet and rubbed warmth into her arms and her back, thinking she was shivering from the heaviness in the air, discovering she wasn't. She was weeping as quietly as she could.

He lay still, giving her time and space, giving her freedom to remember or regret. He wanted not to breathe, each breath resounding in his ears. He wondered what Aayla must be thinking, possibly about the man inside the television, cowering in a rain as violent as the storm howling across his slatted windows, or the young woman in her elegant shoes. Or was she thinking what she might do with all that she would soon learn?

Then he felt Shakkra's warmth infused in the sheet she flung over him.

"Thank you, Cassidy. I was not cold." She rolled onto her other side. "We cannot disappoint your little heart. We cannot be that cruel. We must succeed."

"I will."

"The letters, you did not mistake one word."

"I did not." He kissed her nose. "And, Shakkra, one day soon you will stop crying in the dark. Then you will have the letters to console you, and a man to share affection with you. You heard my father's words. He does not want you to live your life alone."

"I have you, and soon I will have Aayla and your baby."

"You speak like an old woman near the end of her years. You are young and, Aayla was right, the prettiest woman on the island. I will have a difficult time protecting you from the men who will soon chase after you. Did you not see yourself in The Grand Guardian's reflection plates? Beside you the women on this island and in your magazine are goats. If you were not my mother, and I did not feel so much emotion for Aayla, I would not look at another woman."

"You are your father."

"I will never be as brave or as strong."

She put a hand to his cheek. "You already are."

"You listened to him, to everything he said."

"Not everything. He was a man after all, and was right only some of the time. We are right all of the time. Soon you will know the difference. When Aayla is your first-mate she will teach you what you must about our ways."

"Then I will stay here with the goats and send you away together."

She snorted softly, her lips curling into a thin smile. "Cassidy, the letters that Zach wrote to me..."

"They are safe, as clear as the day he wrote each one."

"If we do not succeed..."

He put a fingertip to her lips. "Shakkra, my lovely mother, you should know better? Listen to me. We have succeeded. All we must do now is leave. The hard part is done. We have done what no one else would dare to do. We were in his house, and on his bed. I now possess his father's journal, the Ancestral Tomes and the Scriptures, not him. We have new books that will help us learn. We have touched his clothes, you wear her thongs and we have swum in his sacred water. You sat in the helicopter and at the helm of his boat. We were free in our minds, and that will soon free our bodies with Aayla's. On that day you will read the letters in our books, not before. It's what Zach wished. He also wished for you to smile and laugh."

"On that day I'll sleep in my own bed, not on yours to whisper like a child afraid of her father."

"I prefer you here, where I can watch over you. Zach

would not want to think of such a man touching you."

Shakkra inhaled deeply. She kissed his lips and patted his cheek, turning and nestling against him. "Goodnight," she waited, "darling."

She giggled and fell asleep.

Yes, he thought, he should stay with the goats and send them away together.

Part Two

Forty-One

That night was six months earlier and Shakkra hadn't waited long before sleeping alone in her bed. She hadn't slept with her son since the last day of summer by virtue of her good fortune and another's unshakeable grief.

Still, she missed his warmth and his comfort.

The Sunday afternoon was idyllic, bodies strewn lazily along the sand, heads bobbing in the ocean. Wading and playing in turquoise water to their shoulders, Shakkra and Aayla talked in low tones and laughed in high-pitched squeals until the man strode from the trees into the water.

Shakkra felt compassion for him; she understood what he felt, yet she was unable and unwilling to assuage his loneliness with words or tenderness. Aayla hadn't changed her opinion of him. She watched him come closer, wondering why he stopped fifty or more paces away. He tilted his head and smiled at Shakkra who saw him fill his lungs with air and stare with blank grimness towards the horizon. She was numb with intuition. She held Aayla's hand.

The man had wanted her to see him swim with measured strokes, gliding resolutely across the surface until she could no longer see his arms or kicking feet splashing the water. He'd wanted her to know he wasn't coming back.

Despite her certainty she shielded her eyes from the

425

glare of the sun, helplessly searching for him to no avail. He was lost, yet she felt no regret, she felt empathy. If not for Cassidy, she'd thought more than once.

Aayla went to her father so that he might advise The Grand Guardian of the island's loss and from that first evening Shakkra laid awake in her bed most nights struggling to dispel her loneliness and mounting apprehension until sleep consumed her.

Separated from his mother by a tiled wall and not a thin sheet, Cassidy missed her clandestine whispers, he missed seeing her, though in his dark room his mind was no less agitated. How would he tell her? What would he say to console her once she knew?

And what of Aayla who, since that afternoon, once each week talked herself to sleep with her nose not far from Shakkra's. On those nights they slept in night-shields woven from silk. Cassidy slept in leather with his head buried under his pillow to muffle the giggles and laugher from his mother's room.

Every afternoon since the man had gone they went to the tree to learn when the workday was done and the sky was still bright. She was invited each evening to dinner, working with Shakkra in the kitchen to prepare the meal. And each night she went with them to the sea to bathe and to talk until the water cooled and the shadows disappeared from the sand.

Aayla quickly came to know what they knew and together they learned about television, computers and cell phones with cameras, though they didn't fully understand.

She learned of days, weeks and months, hours and minutes, day and night, and she saw his watch. She learned of aircraft, not how they stayed in the air. She learned of cars and boats, theatres and restaurants, of motorcycles, not how she would ride one, or why. She learned of dresses and lingerie, shoes and silk stockings, not how they felt on her body, deciding she wouldn't like bikinis with triangles that covered her breasts.

That's what she wanted most, to wear the clothes that Irene wore when she went with Garrett across the sea. Until then she lived her dream once each week. Being with Cassidy in his home she was his woman in all ways except one, and Shakkra was her sister.

Garrett and Forrest were no longer The Grand Guardian and Irene in their eyes. They had visited the manor on many more occasions, each time Aayla overheard her mother and father discussing and confirming the absence. She believed her father enjoyed his frequent mandates to oversee the island in all matters, elevated in rank as Chief Counsellor beyond Taliah and Dakota.

Time was theirs, Tombolina now no more frightening or intimidating to them than their own humble villas. Little Women was back on the shelf and Aayla had gone through another with Shakkra's help, her fingertip tip highlighting each spoken word. The third book she read aloud by herself with Shakkra by her side.

When Garrett flew from the island he was never gone longer than a few days, precious time spent by Cassidy on Three Fortunes writing notes and discovering how to decipher charts. He discovered VHF, GPS and radar, engines and propellers, each time more brash in his search, exploring the ship from stem to stern, finally opening the marine radio to channel 16, all three forgetting why they'd come, intrigued by the voices.

He'd discovered the yacht's log book which Shakkra read from cover to cover while Aayla studied from magazines strewn about the main cabin and berths. He came to know the layout of the ship intimately. He knew each stateroom, each closet, the afterdeck and the crew's quarters below that led to the powerhouse. But they had no crew. They sailed alone, at least from the island. Visitors never came to Tombola.

On those occasions they never went to the pool or the pond. Those forays were the briefest, the most exciting and the most uneasy despite the accuracy of Aayla's information. They were concealed from the sky by a ceiling of thick foliage, as protected as they were vulnerable, ready at a moment's notice to slip into the channel and swim to the windward sea.

When Garrett travelled by sea their work was more relaxed. Cassidy searched for books that would help explain his many notes while Shakkra and Aayla watched television, sometimes finding their way into Forrest's wardrobe and into her clothes. Aayla wanted those days never to end.

She decided she didn't like stilettos; she did like short linen sarongs and silk panties. She liked barrettes in her hair and silk robes, not garters or bras. She asked Shakkra what they would wear on the day they would leave. Shakkra didn't know and they went to Cassidy.

They'd seen women inside the television who wore clothes like men; others wore elegant gowns or short dresses, shorts and tank tops, and others who wore no clothes at all when not alone. He didn't know, suggesting that if Forrest wore a thong at the beach and muslin robes during her times on Tombola, yet she possessed such fine-looking clothes in her closet, then she must certainly wear those clothes during her time away. So would they somehow, which made the wardrobe and its frequent additions a compulsory part of each subsequent visit.

On those extended incursions they would lounge by the lagoon before returning home to prepare dinner, luxuriating on chaises-longues upholstered in European fabrics, sipping wine Cassidy early on discovered in a room beneath the floor of the pantry off the kitchen.

Hundreds of bottles lined the walls, hundreds more

stacked in open boxes strewn across the floor. He knew nothing of Pinots, Bordeaux, Alsace, Margaux, Lafitte or champagne. He understood red and white. He'd studied the cellar a good while, deciding that the oldest wines would be the least likely to be missed, and not those coated in thick dust or those from boxes with one or two missing bottles.

In bed alone Shakkra often thought back to a recent day on Tombolina when she climbed with her son and Aayla to the very top of the precipice. Cassidy thought she'd be thrilled at seeing the extent of the lush island encircled by white sand and the entire ocean. Instead she was dismayed to finally see how small Tombola was in the midst of an inhospitable sea. She didn't remember the view; she remembered peering into the swirling violence of the gorge, the bridge and the pole that appeared so indestructible and accusing as though pointing at her.

She remembered Aayla feeling her sadness and taking her hand as the young girl tried to imagine a vaster place.

What she didn't see was Cassidy's inner conflict pitting rational against emotion, strength against fear, nor would she.

Shakkra never questioned Cassidy about the passage of time. Little more than five months remained until The Seven Feasts and he knew that in her mind nothing had changed beyond their acquired knowledge. Inwardly she was preparing herself.

Cassidy was aware that her dreams had gradually transmuted into hopelessness. What he knew, what he hadn't told her, what was so indelible in his mind, she would not like. The words she would soon hear would make her afraid. He'd known for a month or more, since the day he'd decided there was one way to leave the island. Yet he'd let her suffer through diminishing hope and uncertainty, and Aayla with unquenched curiosity each day learning more for possibly no reason.

He felt the anguish of cruelty for what he'd done. Yet what choice did he have?

He heard footsteps in her room. He imagined her dressing in her field tunic when she knew the touch of fine clothes made of satin and silk, he thought of the coconut milk he would drink with his breakfast and the smooth taste of the wine from Garrett's cellar.

Her door opened and closed, and other where she went to pass her water and wash her face in a small damp room with small wooden windows, not a large tiled bathroom with hot and cold water, soft towels and fleecy robes.

He heard her padding into the kitchen to prepare his morning meal. He wanted to spend the day in bed, or in his tree, not to see a single soul.

She tapped on his door. He wasn't ready.

"Good morning, Cassidy."

"Good morning, Shakkra."

"Come, sweetheart, breakfast is ready for you."

He swept the sheet to the foot of the bed, squirmed from his night-shield into one suited to casting his net in the sea and went into the kitchen. He kissed her, and left her to make himself ready for the day. When he returned, he draped his arms around her neck and pulled her close.

"You're sad, mother. You should be delighted. Today's Saturday. Tonight you'll giggle and chatter with your little friend."

"She makes me happy."

"And I don't."

"You make me proud. You make your father proud."

"We miss him." He eyed her tunic. "It's difficult now for me not to see you and Aayla in anything that isn't silk. When you surprised me in those fine clothes I didn't see you as my mother. I saw you as a vision that somehow escaped from the shiny pages of one of her magazines. You're beautiful, Shakkra. I'm certain now that one day I'll

430

have to be strict with you and Aayla. I'll keep you both close to me until we find you a man of your own."

"I'm happy, sweetheart, to have felt the softness of her clothes against my skin a few times. I'll never forget Aayla's expression when she saw herself in a real mirror made from glass."

He nodded. "Shakkra, my mother, we can never again go to Tombolina. We've become too casual, too curious. It's too late for us to learn more. We have no more time. We've done all that we can."

Her lips pursed, her taut cheeks quivered and her eyes glazed.

"You're my son. No one will ever do more than you. Your father's proud of you. I'm proud of what you've done for us."

"You don't understand." He paused. "We have no more time."

She nodded, her thin smile failing her.

"No mother. You don't understand me…and you must, now more than ever."

He squeezed her, easing her away to arm's length. He wasn't smiling, his face was devoid of expression and she searched his eyes for what she couldn't see. He turned and walked into his room, neither quickly nor slowly, his shoulders straight, his head held high. Still she wasn't able to define him.

He was a boy, yet a man beyond his years, strong in mind and body, yet what incredible weight each must bear, she thought. She studied his every step coming towards her, his hands clasped behind him.

"Stop your tears and listen to me. Understand me, because we have no more time. Tonight you'll prepare my favourite dinner of goat's meat and yams for me. I want a big platter of fresh fruit from your garden and a bottle of fine wine."

"What are you saying, Cassidy? We have no wine and, now to know the truth, your little heart will cry in my bed until morning."

"Because she'll miss me, Shakkra, and so will you until I return. That's the only truth, and this bottle of wine." He brought the bottle from behind his back. "There's no more time, Shakkra, because I'm ready. I'm leaving Tombola tomorrow. I'm leaving without you, for a short time, and this evening we'll celebrate."

Her beautiful face paled with fear.

"What craziness is this, Cassidy? How do you expect to leave? Where will you go, and how will you return to us?"

"You know where I'll go, Shakkra. You've known for a week, since Aayla told us of his plans. I'm going to Miami. I'm leaving Tombola tomorrow when the tidewater is high; I'm leaving you tonight with my stomach and my heart full."

She was frantic, tears flooding from reddened eyes.

"You can't do this. This isn't what we dreamed. We'll leave together."

"Shakkra, we dream when we sleep and I haven't slept well for so many nights. I'm going. How else will we leave before The Seven Feasts? I don't think he'll take us with him in the helicopter and he won't think well of us once he knows we've played on his yacht and drunk his fine wine."

She wiped her eyes and her nose. "You'll be gone five days. How will you eat? Where will you sleep?"

"I'll eat the sandwiches and fruit you'll wrap in a cloth for me. Prepare nothing to tempt their noses or the flies. I know the yacht as well as I can, Shakkra. I'll hide in a compartment in the engine room that's empty and big enough for me to squeeze into. Beside the engines is a place for the crew to sleep, a crew he doesn't have. We know he stays at a marina. I'll hide each day in the compartment until they're gone, then I'll have fresh air and see what I can," he grinned, "and maybe drink some wine. At night when they sleep, I'll sleep on the floor of the empty cabin."

"What will you do if you're discovered?"

"By someone else, I'll pretend I'm with them. But I won't be seen. If Garrett sees me," he shrugged, "my father will be with me to pluck me from the sea and bring me home to you in your dreams."

At that moment she lost her breath. She wanted to smack his face.

"I'll stop you."

"No, you won't. This is why Zach died. Do you think he couldn't have snapped the old man's neck? Do you think he was afraid of Garrett? He sat at the pole to give us the time he lacked." He pinched her chin. "Five days isn't a long time."

He held her tight, rocking her.

"What will I tell the Chief Counsellor, or anyone who sees that you're gone?"

"Tell them I've gone to the south, to explore the island, to see my father's grave before I couple and join with the fat one. They know me. They've seen me at the gorge. They think I didn't see them, but I did. They'll believe you. They'll think I'm my father's son."

"What will you tell Aayla when she comes for dinner and sees you leave?"

He chortled. "I won't tell her anything. You will. You're better with her than I am. She loves you more. You'll think of something, when your eyes are dry."

"Are you afraid?"

"No, I'm not. I've lived six years for this night. But, Shakkra, I have a second plan in case I don't come back to you, one that won't tell us what we need to know. What we're missing is what Garrett knows, what he thinks and what he plans. That's what I want, to know what's in his head. He'll never write a diary for me to read. I'll hear the words he speaks in private to her, which I hope to do each night. When the water's calm voices travel easily over water and I won't be far from them."

"And when the sea isn't calm?"

"I'll think of you and Aayla."

"I'm afraid. What if they search for you here?"

"You saw the island from the precipice. Where would they start?"

Shakkra inhaled a deep breath.

"The field and my weaving won't miss me for a day. I'm too sick thinking of you wandering alone in the forest." She clasped his head between her palms and kissed him. "Aayla and I will cook a fine meal for you." She took the bottle. "We'll celebrate my brave son who will not make the little girl a widow before she has a chance to marry. Will he?"

"He won't."

"When will you leave us?"

"Before midnight when the tidewater in the gorge is at its lowest." He looked at the wine. "After a glass of this she'll sleep quietly long before I leave. Tell her nothing until morning."

"The truth," Shakkra said.

He nodded. "She trusts you, and she's learned a lot in six months."

"I'll keep her with me the entire week. I'll speak with her mother. I'll tell her I'm teaching Aayla to weave and knit shields."

Neither one had much else to say. Each knew what was in the other's heart.

Cassidy went to the sea to cast his net, returning to Shakkra at noon with his catch gutted and clean, his empty stomach yearning for food. In the afternoon he toiled in the field and when the day was done he went to his tree for his watch and to read his father's letter once more for comfort as much as to strengthen his determination.

When he arrived home Aayla was sitting in her evening tunic with Shakkra. She ran to him, delighted with her new name for him. She wasn't the same girl. She was a woman. She'd transformed from an impish teenager into a demure young woman partly, he believed, because of Shakkra's influence, partly because of what she'd learned.

He'd been right about the wine. By ten Aayla was curled into Shakkra's lap, asleep.

She woke late the next morning in Shakkra's bed. Sunlight filled the room. She remembered the strength of his arms, his kiss, not wanting to open her eyes to spoil her dream. She felt the warm pressure clasping her hands together. She blinked once to clear her eyes, her face beaming. She blinked again and saw the desperation etched into her big sister's face, afraid to ask.

Forty-Two

Shakkra lay in her bed trembling, clasping the girl's small hands. She'd always known the day would come when she would lose Zach and made each moment with him an hour, a day, but a mother should never lose her son.

Aayla's eyes opened. Her face was radiant in the sunlight. She blinked again, her glow fading to fear. She knew, and she would be brave for Shakkra.

Aayla let her cry. She knew Cassidy; she knew he was gone from them.

"He's left Tombola on his own. Hasn't he, Shakkra?"

"He went last night, when he was certain you wouldn't wake. He believed that together we'd make his departure difficult."

"He was right to believe that."

"Nothing would stop him, not The Grand Guardian, not two whimpering women. This is what he wanted."

"To what place did he go?"

"He's going with them to Miami onboard the yacht, to learn more of them. He knows more than he's telling us, little one." Shakkra took a deep breath. "Aayla, what we've done is very dangerous. We possess the Ancestral Tomes, the Twelve Scriptures and the private diary of the old man, Wendell Parkens. We possess the entire history of Tombola." She wiped her eyes. "He's read something that makes him so determined, so certain that we'll leave this place. That's why he's gone, to confirm what he's discovered, what he won't tell us."

"A very strong man once brought the box to the island, Shakkra. Because of Jonathon another strong man will soon take the box away...with us."

"You're not surprised he's gone."

"Who on the island is surprised by him? He's Cassidy. All the girls want him, but he wants to marry me. I see how they look at me with envy in their eyes. He climbed a high cliff to call my name; no other man has done that for any of them." She wiped Shakkra's eyes. "No other man has passed his water in the guardian's fancy toilet, and he brought a bottle of wine from the house to make me sleep. He possesses the history of this place, Shakkra, when even they do not. And now he is on their boat. No, Shakkra, I'm not surprised."

Shakkra kissed her

"He should be here kissing you. He knows we love him."

Aayla giggled. "We do, but sometimes he should not be so certain. Sometimes he should believe that we love each other more. When he comes back to us we should ignore him. He'll be too proud of himself."

"I do love you, little one, like a sister and a perfect daughter. Without you my heart would beat only half the time, and one day soon you will marry my son."

"That's what I mean. A few months ago I didn't know that word. How can I be surprised after all I've learned, after all I've seen and after all we've done you and me while he reads and reads and reads?" She sighed. "Will I ever see his face once we're married? I don't think so. But Shakkra, if he can do such a brave thing, he will return to us. I won't cry for him, and neither should you. He's our man. We share him. We must believe in him. He'll know if we do not. And he must not know that. Today we'll think of him and talk about him. He'll know that we are with him.

That doesn't mean we can't be afraid for him, or punch him when he returns for being a silly man."

Forty-Three

Aayla was partly right. Crouched in the largest of the empty compartments in the engine room of Three Fortunes, with his knees against his chin, Cassidy didn't hear their words, he felt them. They believed in him. What he believed, then, was that he'd never walk upright again.

He couldn't imagine their disappointment to see him return with failure in his eyes and, for that reason, he wouldn't. They would see eyes filled with joy, hear of his travels and hear what until then he'd been too uncertain to tell them.

His trespass onto Tombolina was no more difficult than in past times. The moon shone like a beacon in the speckled sky, the sand beneath his feet was cold and bright, his shadow eerie against a dark wall of trees.

The gorge was calm, the waters receded. He waded past the pole and under the bridge, smirking. He had plans for the pole, plans that would please his mother and Zach, Jacob and Jon. He alone would destroy the pole and the divine Garrett Parkens would bear witness.

On the windward side black boulders dotted the shoreline, ominous, unlit by the moon. None on Tombola except him, his father, Shakkra, Aayla, Jon and Jacob had ever seen the huge rocks. Twenty-one of the largest that he knew well. He pressed a hand across each one, needing to feel each eroding scrawl denoting the days and months of Jonathon's life. No, he wouldn't fail. Nor would he cower in the blackness of the channel.

The air around him was still, heavy with the smell of salt. The water was still. Each ripple, barely audible, was a cacophony resounding in his ears. Then he saw a glimmer, the faintest outlines of the launch and the yacht. He touched the sides of each boat either to allay his apprehension or to fortify his resolve with a sense of pride. He didn't know which.

He set Shakkra's knitted satchel on the wharf, dragging himself from the water onto the floating dock with as much stealth as he could manage. He stripped away his thong, using the scanty leather to wipe his body dry. He knelt by the satchel, reaching in for the empty wine bottle, a fresh thong and shorts. He placed the bottle under the dock between the planks and flotations. Then he dressed and stepped onboard. He went directly to the engine room, hid his gear and returned topside to step out onto the island.

He stood between the dock and the pool, studying the manor. Tombolina was no longer Garrett's private domain. He believed Tombola was nearing the collapse of its modern history. Wendell Parkens once brought simple people to the island for a single purpose and was, Cassidy knew, the father of many more.

The village was peaceful, the villagers content with their lot. They knew nothing beyond the sand, the blue water and the field. They knew nothing of time beyond the sun and the moon, nothing of weeks, months and the seasons. And once each year all but the very old and the very young gave themselves to gaiety and wild abandon, their child-like minds fogged with opium laced rum.

He cared nothing about the villagers. He cared about his mother and Aayla whose parents were neither kind and nor gentle. They were marginally more aware than most, enamoured of their higher position, their finer villa and willingly submissive to the whims and directions of The

Grand Guardian.

He neither liked them, nor disliked them. He regarded them as they regarded Aayla, with complete indifference. More importantly, he couldn't trust them and Aayla fully understood his misgivings.

He stared at the precipice without a sense of time, remembering how easily he and Aayla had scampered up the steep slope. Even his mother matched each of their footholds with one of her own. Yet Wendy Parkens stumbled his way to the top, scraping his knees, terrified and cringing once he arrived at the pinnacle. What would the village think of the exalted Grand Guardian to see him not at the precipice of Tombola, but at the precipice of wetting his panties?

He snorted a burst of air, wondering for the first time how often Dakota had seen the island from the top of the world. He wondered what was said between Dakota and his ancient father that last day, words not written in the journal. He wondered how much he knew that Dakota did not.

Fontaine wasn't given to deep thought. He was easily distracted, never left to his own devices and, since becoming the son of The Grand Guardian, was never allowed to wander Tombola alone. Yet he was sent away to complete his learning. Dakota wasn't, despite his father's wishes.

He glanced at his watch and went to the yacht to sit on the afterdeck and wait. At six the sky was dark. He left the boat and went as far as he dared towards the house where he waited for yellow light to glow from any window.

Not thirty minutes later he drew a deep breath, his adventure had begun.

He was familiar with every inch of the boat. The engine room was dark, though he felt his way easily with outstretched arms to the compartment he'd tried on several occasions, more than once squeezing into the cramped quarters for an entire morning or afternoon. He knew what to expect.

Again he waited, this time for the sounds of footfalls on the dock, the slightest swaying motion and voices. All three happened in unison. He closed the door, depriving his senses of time and space, deciding not to close his eyes. Opened, he was in a black abyss; closed, he wouldn't distinguish between darkness and sleep.

He knew from the ship's log the voyage would last four hours, suddenly realizing he was on the brink of seeing a world theretofore unknown to him, a world Jonathon Clayton once denounced to preserve his freedom, exchanging the hangman's knot for one hundred and one stones.

He'd never heard the constant drone of powerful engines, the twin Cummins humming an even pitch throughout the voyage. Nor had he ever experienced the effect of ocean swells, then nothing.

He didn't know how long to stay locked into blackness and silence before opening the compartment door, a rush of fresh air flooding in when he did. The time was 2:30 PM. By his watch they'd been at the marina for a couple of hours. He heard nothing. His back and his legs ached; his was mind groggy from the stale air.

He stooped to touch his toes, grimacing. He bent at his knees several times, breathing deeply. He arched his back, his arms outstretched, hearing the crunch of his vertebrae realigning, twisting his torso from side to side. Somewhat refreshed, he manoeuvred his way back into his confinement, leaving one leg dangling free, one hand gripping the handle.

He heard the dull thuds of footsteps, one heavy, one light, and a woman's muted laughter. He was pleased. She was in her stateroom near the bow. If he could hear that much from below deck at the stern, he would hear that much more whenever they chose to sit in the afterdeck lounge mere feet above him.

He distinguished another voice, muffled, this one beside him, the heavier footsteps and separate murmurs, each voice too deep for a woman's and too weak to come from onboard. Garrett was on the dock, and suddenly Cassidy remembered he hadn't eaten in twenty hours.

At 5:00 PM he heard her clearly. She was excited. They had reserved a table in Little Havana for a dinner with friends. Then they would dance the night away and, he assumed, that meant they would return late. By 7:00 PM he hadn't heard a sound or vibration for an hour and he crawled out, repeating his callisthenics.

He went first into the crew's quarters, inching from the second door to the bottom of a spiral staircase where he stood five minutes before climbing step by step to the main deck. He was alone, privacy curtains covering the lounge windows, canvas covering the windshield. All he could see clearly was the vessel at dock behind him. The thing was huge, towering over him, and when he stepped out he thought his heart would explode.

All he could do was stand and stare. He didn't believe what he was seeing. How would he ever tell his mother and Aayla what his mind could not conceive?

He saw no one and stepped onto the dock. All that he'd imagined from his reading was now forgotten to him, archaic, obsolete. He walked, every twenty paces glancing over his shoulder.

He passed one yacht that was much larger than Garrett's. The man and woman waved and wished him a pleasant evening. He returned the wave and smiled. They sounded no different than him. He passed two young girls in tiny bikinis. When he thought to turn, to see them from a different perspective, they giggled and waved at him, their arms wrapped around each other's waist.

One had long hair the colour of the ripe oranges, the other girl's hair was white, the colour of a full moon on the darkest night. They wore small bathing suits, not as small as the shields Aayla wore to swim in the sea, and they wore small patches to cover their breasts. He couldn't see their eyes. They wore dark blue and red glasses. He waved back.

At the end of the dock he could turn either left or right and walk a thousand paces or more. He didn't. He sat on the steps and gazed around him at the yachts, people walking past in beautiful clothes like the ones he'd seen on television and in her closet, and planes flying so low he could see each detail and feel the thunderous roar of the engines.

They all waved to him. Some said hello, others said something he didn't comprehend. They smiled as well and he didn't feel afraid. He felt sorrow that Shakkra and Aayla were on Tombola eating their evening meal, worried about him. More than that he felt deep sorrow because he could see what they could not.

He'd seen similar tall buildings inside the television, never imagining the incredible heights.

And then he listened, to the halyards flapping against masts, fenders creaking against the wharf, and automobiles.

He knew about automobiles. He'd read about them, Zach had often told him about Jonathon's automobile and he'd seen them inside the television as well. He climbed the steps and saw hundreds more, all gleaming in the late day sun. He went to one that was missing a roof and looked in.

"I had her delivered yesterday. Like her?"

Cassidy jerked back.

"Sorry, I didn't mean to scare you. She's brand spanking new. What do you think?"

"Her?"

"The car?"

"Yes, I do like it."

"She was a gift, from me to me, sort of a goodbye gift." The woman chuckled. "He never should have married a lawyer. It's not as though I didn't warn him."

"I don't understand."

"Neither did he." The woman looked at her watch, extending her hand. "I'm Brenda Wilson. My boat's the Legality. It's not the biggest, but, hey, it's all mine. He lost that too. Are you a boater, or somebody's guest?"

"I'm a guest. My name's Cassidy. This is my first time to Miami."

"We have a first time for everything." She thought a moment. The kid couldn't take his eyes from the car. "Ever sit in an Aston Martin?"

She patted the edge of the leather seat.

"No."

"So, listen, guest, how about a ride so I can show off a little. The weekend's not over yet and it's kind of a bummer being alone on a fantastic evening."

"You mean in this car?"

"I won't bite."

"Thank you. I must return to the boat. I don't know when we're leaving. They've gone for dinner."

"Here in Miami, dinner. Hey, you're talking all night. So let's do it, once around the block? I'll have you back in thirty minutes. I don't think they'll leave without you."

She was gorgeous, perhaps his mother's age, he thought. She was dressed like the women in the magazines. Her skirt was shorter than Aayla's tunic, her legs bare and golden and she wore shoes like the ones Aayla didn't like. Her blouse was shiny and white, opened from her throat to her below her breasts in a way that made him feel strange. He thought her voice was strange, almost like a man's, but not unpleasant.

"You're staring."

"I'm sorry. I'm not thinking anything bad. I was

445

thinking that you're attractive, like my mother."

"Okay, attractive is good, very attractive would have been a little better, but like your mother is not so good."

"Yes, it's good. She's very attractive, and very young."

"She must be real doll to have made something like you. So, do we ride or not?"

"Yes, Brenda. I would like to ride with you."

She didn't move. She waited, smiling and clearing her throat. Finally he understood and opened her door, mesmerized as she slid in. She smelled like fruit from his mother's garden. She'd painted her lips deep red and her eyes were the colour of the sea in the morning.

"You're staring again. Never seen legs before?"

He had, but never panties as pure white showing at the top of them.

"I'm sorry. I like the way you dressed yourself."

"Yeah," she chortled, "I'm sure you do."

"One day I'll see Aayla and my mother dressed the same way, with their lips painted like yours, the colour of pomegranates."

"Pomegranate."

"Yes."

"You're a poet."

"No, I'm not. But I read and I write."

"That's good. Get in, lover boy, and eyes forward."

They cruised along A1A, Alton and Dade Boulevards in bumper to bumper traffic, thirty minutes turning to sixty. He saw skateboards, motorcycles and women everywhere with skirts and dresses as short as Brenda's. Some wearing tank tops, a recent discovery, others in bras like the fancy ones in the magazines and Forrest's closet.

He asked Brenda whether women always dressed that way in Miami. She said yes, most times, depending what they're after and he didn't understand. He asked about the green, gold and pink high-rises glistening in the sun, and who lived in them. She pointed upward. She did, alone, looking down at her empty boat when she wasn't at the office until midnight billing client-hours. She didn't have much time for friends. Anyway, he took most of them with him when he left, when she kicked him out. She got the better deal.

Cassidy didn't understand.

He asked about restaurants and bars. He asked about those he saw eating on the sidewalks, storefronts, hotels and the frozen man everyone ignored. He was a mime. That's how he made his living, she explained, and all too soon she drove into the marina.

Brenda released her belt, slouching slightly into her seat, facing him.

"Thanks, for letting me show off. I had a good time."

"I did also. Thank you for teaching me what I didn't know."

She smiled. Her face was always happy, he thought, the way he wanted Shakkra to be happy.

"I'm sorry, Brenda."

"What for this time, lover boy?"

"You don't have friends. My mother has no friends either, except Aayla, and I know she feels deep sadness. She wants only Aayla and me. She doesn't want to share affection with others. I know she'd like you. I know she would. You would be good friends with Shakkra, and you'd like Aayla. They're like sisters. Now she reads and writes, like my mother."

"Wow, if that's not enough to make a girl cry."

He nodded. "She cries each night."

"How old are you, Cassidy?"

"I'm seventeen."

Her smile faded. "And, by any chance, are you from Idaho?"

"No, but I know about Idaho."

"So where do you live?"

He thought a moment. "I live on Tombola, a beautiful island. To come here I left my mother with Aayla."

"She's your girlfriend."

"Yes, I suppose."

"Wow, what a fortunate girl. She must be very pretty. Why isn't she with you?"

He shrugged. "It was important for me to come alone."

"Important. What a mysterious young man you are. What boat did you say you're on?"

"I don't know the name. This is my first time onboard." He looked at his watch. "Brenda, I have to go. Thank you for taking me. You're right, very attractive is better and I like your voice very much. I'm anxious now to tell Shakkra and Aayla about you and the car. They'll want me to tell them about your clothes and your smell."

Somehow she wasn't surprised he would say such a thing. Her brow creased ever so slightly. "Cassidy, you came here because you wanted to. Right?"

"I've waited six years to come here."

"But you're okay. You're not in trouble of any kind?"

"No, Brenda. I'm fine. I'm happy to finally see Miami, and you." He touched the gearshift. "I wasn't expecting this, or you. I'm happy that you saw me looking at your car. Thank you."

She studied him. He was peculiar in so many ways she couldn't put her finger on. He wasn't lost or afraid, yet he was worried. He wasn't abused. His skin was clear and, she had to admit, he wasn't hard to look at. Yet she saw a familiar look in his eyes, one she'd seen too many times in court. He wasn't saying all that he could.

"Cassidy, you talk about Shakkra and Aayla. What about your dad?"

"He's dead."

"I'm sorry."

"Thank you, Brenda, for everything."

"You're welcome, Cassidy. I hope I see you again. I wish I had more time with you. Perhaps one day I'll see you with Shakkra and Aayla. They sound so delightful. I bet you I could be good friends with your mom." She watched him climb out. "Cassidy, I don't feel good about something and I don't know why or what. For me that's generally not a good thing. Listen. You need me, you call me. This is my card. I'm a lawyer. Actually I'm the absolute best in Miami." He took the card from her hand. "Don't lose that. If you do, I'm Brenda Wilson. I'm in the book."

"Which book, Brenda?"

She gave him a curious look. "You're a bright kid. You'll figure it out, lover boy."

She tilted her head, blew him a kiss and drove away, watching him watch her in her rear view mirror until she reached the gate. She'd boated off the shores of Miami since she was a young girl and she'd never heard of Tombola. Yet not one word he'd spoken was a lie. The boy was honest, too honest. Even someone from Idaho wouldn't be that wide-eyed and innocent.

Later that night, his eyes too blurred to read the time, the sounds of her heels clacking on the fibreglass deck and the companionway sliding open jolted him awake. He hurried to the compartment and squeezed in, waiting ten, twenty and thirty minutes until all was quiet and he crept into the crew's quarters.

He lay on the carpeted floor, disappointed. He'd learned nothing but what he'd missed in his short life. He thought of Aayla. He thought of Shakkra and how she would look in Brenda's clothes and in her car, driving down crowded roads looking for a place to sit for a glass of wine.

Exhausted, he fell asleep remembering the words Jonathon had written.

Zach, he knew, was the last Clayton to die on Tombola.

Forty-Four

Monday they left at ten and Cassidy stepped onto the wharf not long after to follow them. They weren't dressed as The Grand Guardian and Irene. He wore long blue pants, a pink shirt and a hat. He looked ridiculous, Cassidy thought. She was wearing a short dress, a wider hat and carried her shoes in her hands.

They went into a maze of hundreds of cars and climbed into one that was silver, bigger than most and had five doors. He had no idea how long they'd be gone, believing they wouldn't leave in a car if they meant to return soon.

He committed the number of his dock to memory and strolled amongst the vast maze of boats and yachts tied inertly to their slips. He was looking for Legality, thinking of Brenda, her blonde ponytail, her long legs, short skirt and her open blouse. She was gorgeous, like Shakkra. He thought he'd never stop thinking of her.

Her boat was pristine, smaller than many, imposing to him. He looked around. He was alone. He walked along Brenda's slip counting thirty-five paces. From one side to the other he counted twelve.

He was hungry and began his way back to Three Fortunes. Shakkra had made him two thick sandwiches for each day. Her satchel couldn't hold more.

The girl watched him coming. He watched her. She was the one with orange hair. She was dripping wet, standing on the transom with a hose.

450

She said, "Hey."

"Hi."

"I'm Holly. I totally remember you. The girl with me yesterday is Cindy. She's like my best friend ever. She's like driving her stuck up father to the airport."

"I'm Cassidy."

"Do you want a beer? Her father's gone for like the whole week. What about yours?"

"They're not my parents."

"Are you crewing?"

He didn't know. "Yes, I am."

"So let's have a drink. No one's around. The marina's like totally dead."

He looked at his watch. The girl was cute, her accent difficult to his ears.

"I can stay for one beer. Then I must go to my boat."

"Totally awesome. Give me a sec. I'm like totally drenched."

He didn't understand her, nodding and stepping onto the transom. He followed her onto the deck and watched her saunter through the companionway. Aayla wouldn't like the girl, he thought, or what she was wearing. She'd covered her breasts the way he'd seen them the day before and her bathing suit covered most of her bum, yet he could see through it.

When she came back she was wringing water from her hair. She was wearing a white tank top; a recent discovery while in Brenda's car. The flimsy material covered her breasts, scarcely concealing them. Her thong was the same as the ones he'd taken from Forrest's wardrobe on Tombolina, but red and trimmed with lace. He didn't look away quickly enough.

"We're like totally into freedom when he's gone." She gave him a beer. "Bottoms up," and she clinked her bottle against his.

"Thank you."

She twirled.

"Do you like?"

"Yes, you're pretty. My girlfriend and my mother each have a thong like yours."

"My boyfriend's like so totally gone. I think he was like gay or something."

"Where did he go?" he asked.

"Who cares? He's so totally not into girls. Come on, I'll show you the boat. Our cabin's like really stupendous."

"I'm sorry. I have to stay here to look for them."

She shrugged, straddling the gunwale, making sure she had his full attention.

"One day I'll buy my mother and Aayla many beautiful thongs like yours."

"Your mother? My god, no way."

"Yes, she's very beautiful."

"Mine's a complete bitch." She drained half the bottle. "Hey, Cassidy, he's gone for like the entire week. He won't be back. He's like working on a contract or something." She put the tip of her tongue to the lip of the bottle. "So let's party. We'll have some fun. I like you. So does Cindy. She told me. We're both like totally into guys. We talked about you all night. We're both like so totally bored. Hey, tonight we'll do the club thing. The guys always let us in. We're so totally good for business."

"I like you also, Holly, and Cindy's very pretty." He put his bottle on the table. "But now I must go. I don't want to get into trouble."

"They can't like expect you to crew all the time."

"I don't know when they will go each day."

She ran her tongue over her lips. "We'll be here like all day tomorrow. The beach is so not for us."

"I will try."

"Promise?"

"Yes, I promise to try."

She brought her legs together, sliding onto the deck. She put her bottle beside his, wrapped her arms around his neck and pressed her mouth hard against his.

"You do like to party, don't you, Cassidy?"

He didn't know. "Yes, I do."

"Cindy's so totally hot. She's nineteen and acts like twenty or something. She hasn't paid for a drink for like a hundred years."

He didn't understand. He freed himself and smiled. A sweet taste he didn't know lingered on his lips.

"Goodbye, Holly. I'll try to see you again to party with you and Cindy."

She kissed him again. "And so come as you are."

She watched him cross from the transom to the dock. When he turned to wave goodbye she was walking towards the companionway, stopping to pull her top over her head, disappearing down the steps.

He tasted his lips and wondered what a party would be like. He wondered whether Brenda's red lips would taste the same. He knew the word, curious to discover whether or not he'd like to party. He didn't know.

Garrett and Forrest returned at four. They stayed two hours and left for dinner.

Cassidy spent the evening reading a boating magazine on deck for as long as he dared, his thoughts often interrupted by Holly and Cindy pushing their way into his mind. None of the girls or young women on the island wore their boleros at the beach and most wore their shields when gutting the fish, when they could wash away the blood in the sea. And at home on hot evenings, or in bed, why would anyone think to wear tunics?

Being uncovered was natural for them. Only during The Seven Feasts did the women use their breasts and their painted bare bodies to attract the men.

Holly, he thought, was attracting him. She wasn't natural on the boat. She was trying to share affection with him. Aayla wouldn't like her and he wondered what would happen at the party.

He turned off the light at 9:30 PM and sat in the dark until midnight when Garrett and Forrest returned. He heard not a single murmur and when he'd waited an hour he went into the crew's quarters and spent a fitful night on the floor thinking of the girls and of Brenda sitting in her car.

Forty-Five

Tuesday they left again at ten. Cassidy spent his day at the helm reading the latest entries in the ship's log and the agenda he'd found in Garrett's attaché.

She'd gone shopping. His tee off was at 10:00, the same as Monday, and Cassidy made a mental note to look up the words. Beside 6:00 PM they'd written someone's name with 'marina' in parenthesis. The entire day Wednesday was highlighted, the words 'spa and hair' scrawled across the page. The tee off was at the same time and Wednesday night several people were coming to the boat. Thursday he would go to a tee off again. She would go shopping and Thursday night was blank. Maybe they planned to stay on the boat. He didn't know.

Friday they would depart Miami for Tombola at noon.

He didn't know. He was frustrated with never knowing, never being certain, lying to his mother about being afraid. He was terrified of doing to Shakkra what he'd done to Zach. He'd lied about that too, but she could never know. He would not split Shakkra's skull. He wouldn't. He would split Garrett's first. Nor would Dakota push himself into Aayla when each night he went into the sea to fondle Xandra's breasts under the water.

He didn't know whether Garrett would take the boat to another marina, or use the silver car. He didn't know how safe he'd be the next night in his hideaway with so many others onboard. And he didn't know if he'd ever hear a single word about Dakota. If not, why had he stowed away? So far he'd done nothing except ogle Brenda's panties and breasts in the car, kiss Holly and watch her take off her tank top to attract him. Nothing else he'd learned would help if he learned nothing of Dakota.

At least he knew when they'd be gone and approximately when they'd return. When they did he was squeezed into his cubicle, waiting to hear them leave or to hear the engines come alive. They left at 5:45 PM. At six he crawled out and ate a sandwich. At six-thirty he went to Holly and Cindy.

The marina was virtually deserted.

He stepped onto the transom, calling them. When they didn't answer he stepped onto the afterdeck and called again. He saw Cindy first.

"Hey, Cassidy."

He mimicked her. "Hey, Cindy."

She was wearing a tee shirt.

"Holly's downstairs. We were so wondering if you'd come."

She signalled him to follow, leading him through the galley, the entertainment centre and into her stateroom. Holly was lying on a bed that was bigger than his entire room in the villa. She was wearing a different tank top and another thong. She was watching television, patting the space beside her.

"Hey, Cassidy, come sit beside me."

He didn't.

"I can't party with you and Cindy tonight, Holly, but tomorrow night I can. Tomorrow I won't have to stay on the boat with them."

She looked at Cindy, twisting her lips into a pout. "You're so totally a prisoner."

"Yes, I believe that. That's why I'm here."

Cindy's hand went to his neck, squeezing gently. He scanned the room, seeing objects he'd seen in the old man's library and study. Holly patted the bed.

"Stay for like ten minutes or something." She sipped her drink. "Do you like vodka? It's like totally odourless and so totally the thing to do. Everyone's drinking it."

"I don't know. We are forbidden to drink before our seventeenth year. Then we can drink rum at The Seven Feasts until we are eighteen when we couple and join."

"Come again," Cindy said.

"Yes, I will come tomorrow. I promise."

Holly crawled onto her knees. "This is so totally weird. You couple and you join? Join what?"

"We join with the girls, to become their first-mates."

"I'm so totally into that." Cindy filled her glass with vodka and passed it to him. "Try this."

The taste was cold, yet his mouth and throat burned. He coughed.

"The second one is always smoother. Go ahead. Drink it all, like this."

Cindy filled another shooter, draining the glass without the use of her hands and with a single swallow. He copied her, spitting away the glass, coughing vodka through his mouth and nose.

Holly wriggled from the bed. "We have like so much to teach you. You're like from a different planet or something."

"My mouth is burning."

Cindy grabbed his head in her hands, grinding her mouth against his. Holly poured another drink and watched. When Cindy stepped back, Holly kissed him. Cindy filled his glass.

"Thank you, I can't drink another. I must go back to the boat."

"It's so totally early."

457

"I'll come tomorrow. Perhaps you can teach me what I don't know." He touched the laptop and cell phone. "I've seen these before, and the television. I'm curious to know what they do. Can you teach me?"

The girls exchanged curious glances, giggling. He wasn't real. He couldn't be real. Real or not they liked what they saw.

"You're not like totally serious?"

"I am. These are new to me." He downed his drink, losing and catching his breath, feeling his face infused with deep heat. "But now I must go."

Holly kissed him. Cindy led him to the top deck where she kissed him again. He knew he would turn to wave at her, once on the dock. When he did she was sashaying into the companionway, sweeping her tee shirt around her bare hips.

When Garrett and Forrest returned to the boat he was walking to and fro in the dark, forcing himself to stay awake. He squeezed into his cubicle and waited, hearing faint murmurs. He stayed as he was, his feet dangling over the steel ridge, afraid he'd be found on the crew's floor in the morning.

He fell asleep quickly, thinking of what he would say to Shakkra about Brenda, and to Aayla about Holly and Cindy. Perhaps he wouldn't say anything.

Forty-Six

In the morning he heard them talking about Fontaine and the girl he would soon join with until they could find one more suitable who would adapt quickly to island life, yet not cause them embarrassment in the outside world.

Cassidy knew what would happen to the first girl once the second was found. He wasn't concerned about her. He was worried about his mother, encouraged that he'd finally heard Garrett and Forrest talking, that he began to know their secret thoughts.

They left at nine. Cassidy remained onboard until three consuming all that he could from magazines and researching the words the girls had used the day before. He was anxious. He wanted to know about everything in Cindy's room and he wanted to know about party. He knew why Aayla taunted him without her shield when they'd slept together on the beach. She'd wanted to couple with him, to share affection him. And the day before Cindy hadn't worn hers. Perhaps she didn't have to, but Holly did and so did Brenda. He didn't know.

He went into the main stateroom, curious about what was in the dozens of bags tossed in a corner, what Forrest had brought to the boat from her shopping. He saw bags in bags and boxes of shoes. He looked into all the smaller bags, deciding he would take two. He put them into his satchel, changed his thong, closed the compartment door and left.

459

He stepped onto the transom of Cindy's boat, calling her, calling Holly who sauntered along the starboard walkway between the railing and helm, holding a towel across her chest. She told him to drop his bag and follow her. Cindy was on the foredeck, sunning. When she turned all he could see was a thin string forming a T.

Cindy stood, bringing her towel with her, her thong as small as the ones Shakkra designed for Aayla. She gave him a beer.

"It's so totally hot."

Holly tugged at his shorts. "Do you like wear the same clothes all the time?"

He thought for a moment, letting the beer cool him.

"I wear pants in the afternoon, but in the morning, in the sea, I wear a shield made for swimming."

"You mean like swim trunks."

He shrugged, undoing the cord at his waist, stepping from his shorts.

"Oh, My god, oh my god, you're like wearing a thong. That's so totally weird."

"Yes, it's a thong. All the men wear these where I live, to fish in the sea or to swim when their work's finished. They're called loin-shields. The girls and the women dress like you in thongs when they swim or work at the beach. I've learned that word, but their shields aren't as pretty as yours and they don't cover their breasts with towels or little patches. Only the very old ones wear boleros when their breasts are heavier and lined."

Holly shrieked. "No frigging way! The girls are topless like always. Like all they wear is a thong. No way!"

He nodded. "Yes, it's true."

"He is like so totally awesome." Cindy said. "I need another beer."

She plucked three from the cooler, dropped her towel and stretched herself out on the deck's sun mat, patting the space beside her. He lay where she wanted him, propped onto his elbows; Holly joined them without her towel from his other side, getting up once for another round.

After that beer Cindy climbed onto the small of his back and began rubbing cream into his skin. He liked the feeling of her skin against his, her hands kneading him, and he asked what she was doing. She didn't answer. Instead she shimmied to his ankles and finished that side of him, telling him to roll over. Holly wanted to finish him.

When she did she stretched onto her front and passed him the bottle, telling him not to be too gentle. He didn't know. He did what she'd done to him. He filled his cupped hand with the cream and began at her shoulders, rubbing in small circles to the small of her back. He put more into his hands. Her bum was round and smooth, he thought, softer than Aayla's, much whiter and her legs weren't as muscular.

When she turned she covered her breasts with her fingers and let him work his fingers into her shins, her knees and her thighs. Her belly was flat, softer than Aayla's. She gave him one arm as she reached to cover that breast with the other. When he finished she gave him the other arm.

She was moaning, feeling his full weight rocking against her pelvis. She took a deep breath, raising her arms over her head, telling him not to stop. Her breasts were smaller than Aayla's, her nipples pink, not like any he'd seen before. They were hard, the way Aayla's felt in the ocean.

"Cindy, that was like totally awesome. I feel like totally free. He's so staying tonight." She put her face to Cassidy's, kissing him. "You are like staying the whole night, aren't you?"

"I would like to stay with you, yes. I have much to learn."

Cindy reached for the bottle, signalled him with a finger

and laid her head on her folded arms. He knew to straddle her, studying Holly as she crawled past him to the cooler. She gave them each a beer and lay back against the windshield to watch.

Cindy was darker, her body more tanned by the sun, her titanium hair twisted into a braid. Beyond that they were the same. He saw no difference other than how they moved. Her skin rippled easily under his touch. When he pressed his hands against her bum she squirmed, telling him never to stop. Her legs were straight and, he thought, she didn't swim or walk to strengthen them.

When she turned she didn't cover her breasts. Instead she talked to him. She wanted to hear about the girls where he lived and when he'd finished the front of her legs she drew herself up to meet him, sipped her beer and kissed him before reclining.

Her belly was rounder that Holly's, though not heavy. Her breasts were bigger, fuller, and he noticed a thin white scar under each one. Her nipples weren't hard, barely discernable under her tan, her nostrils flaring with her breathing. He put aside the bottle and sat beside Holly to finish his fourth beer, to watch Cindy roll onto her front and undo her strings.

She said, "That was so totally unreal. You have like so raised the bar."

He didn't understand.

"Holly, we've so got to go downtown tonight."

"We can't. Tarzan's like so underdressed."

Cindy laid her head on the mat, listening to them talk. She'd slept with guys before, duh, but this was totally wild. She was in the marina barely wearing her thong and her best friend was sitting topless talking with a guy who was about to split the seams of his thong. She let her eyes close. Holly reached leaned forward and across Cassidy to take her beer.

"We'll be like totally pissed if we drink more beer,"

Holly said.

"I'd like to piss. My bladder is full from the beer."

"The head's downstairs. Use the one in her room or something. Her father's like a total clean freak."

He nodded and left. When he came topside Holly was as he'd left her with a fresh beer in each hand and her towel draped across her hips. She'd tossed her thong to the side.

"Cindy's sleeping."

"She's totally wiped. We were like so into the vodka before you came."

"She had an accident with her breasts. I saw the scars."

Holly snorted. "Yeah, like a ten grand accident. They were perfect before. I told her that, but guys like big tits and clean girls." She sipped her beer. "And she totally likes guys."

"She is a clean girl. I can see that."

She pinched the edge of the towel, pulling away the fleece enough for him to understand. "That's a clean girl. Guys like us this way." She shrugged. "So do most girls. Who wouldn't? I mean, hello?""

He'd seen Aayla naked. He remembered his mother's bare body painted her favourite dark green from her feet to her chocolate-coloured hair before Zach was killed and the women during the last Seven Feasts lying on the sand in the morning. He'd never seen a girl or woman that way.

"I didn't know."

"Now you do." She looked at Cindy. "Let's leave her. Or she'll fall into the water or something. I need to like really pee and take a shower."

She reached for her thong and top, dropping the empty bottle into the cooler. She took his and did the same. Then she wriggled her way to the forward hatch, raised the cover, dropped in her towel and eased herself onto the steps. He followed, glancing once at Cindy.

Below deck Holly stepped into the head, closing the

door. He waited where he was until he heard a coarse gushing sound and his name He opened the door. She was in the shower, glistening under the steaming water.

"There's like nothing you haven't seen, Cassidy. Come in. All the girls do it. It's like totally okay. But, first, take that off that thong or whatever."

He wasn't certain, but he wanted to. She was cute. He'd never been naked with anyone but Aayla when she was sleeping on the beach and seeing Holly drenched under steaming water he'd never felt on his skin was beyond his imagination.

He pushed his thong to the floor and stepped in beside her. He let her close the door and wrap her arms around him. He'd never felt water as hot, or a woman so smooth with oil and water. She passed him the soap and faced away, telling him to wash her back. She was moaning. She leaned away from him, raising her arms over her head. He watched the rivulets streaming from her shoulders to the soft mounds he was soaping with slow even strokes. He knelt to wash her legs and her feet, bringing his hands nervously to the small of her back, standing to take in every inch of her.

She faced him, putting her shoulders against the acrylic wall, her arms by her side, her legs parted. He was fascinated and curious. He was afraid. His hands had touched all of her except where she was clean. He thought of Aayla's blonde curls, her smooth belly and how hard he'd resisted her until at last he'd touched her one night as she slept.

She'd wanted him to touch her as a man touches the woman he loves, and he'd disappointed her. Now Holly wanted the same, but he didn't love her.

He didn't look at her. He looked at lips he'd never seen so vividly, and might never again. He touched them, tentatively at first, then more freely, pulling away, dropping to his knees to hide himself and wash her from her belly to her feet. When he stood he coated her breasts with soap, letting the water rinse her body clean.

She took the soap and turned him around, guiding his arms over his head. He'd never felt soap as soft on his body, never a woman's touch beyond his mother's or Aayla's as she clung to him in the sea or on the sand.

She washed from his shoulders to his ankles, moaning, her arms wrapped around him, the pressure of her nipples and her pelvis making his breathing erratic. He'd made himself erect many times in his tree and in his bed, and once Aayla witnessed his weakness. This was different. Holly was intent. She made him turn, looking down at him and breathing in deeply.

"We're like so not going out tonight," she whispered, massaging his chest, running her hands across a hard abdomen, sinking to her knees to finish washing him.

He couldn't talk, his shoulders pressed hard against the stall. She was gripping him, doing what he would do. He was helpless, staring at her breasts, reaching for her belly and her lips.

But he didn't know. He was on the verge of blackness. He'd never thought to touch Aayla that way. This wasn't coupling, yet he felt the crescendo surging in his chest and in his loins. Her eyes remained fixed on her hands. She'd placed one over his, teaching him. He was learning. Her pressure more determined each second, her hands moving back and forth faster and faster. He was breathing through his mouth, drowning in steaming water, his body convulsing, hers shuddering, jerking away from him.

She leaned forward, her hands on her knees.

"That was like so frigging fantastic. She'll be so totally freaked out and jealous." She kissed him. "We are so staying in tonight."

Cassidy didn't know what to say. Aayla had seen him in

the tree. She'd told him so. She'd told his mother, but she'd never done that to him and now that he knew she'd be pleased that, at last, he could touch her without fear.

"I feel good. It's different with a girl."

"Get out! You're a frigging virgin?"

"Yes."

He leaned forward to push open the door.

"I didn't mean like get out. I meant like no frigging way."

"Sharing affection, having sex, is forbidden until we're eighteen."

"That's like so archaic. It's like only sex. She'll be so out of her mind."

"What will she do?"

Holly pushed the door open. "She'll like blow you away, that's what."

She took a towel from the rack and dried herself. He watched. Then she tossed him the towel and watched him. She led him into Cindy's stateroom and went to her luggage, choosing panties and a halter top. Then she looked at him, dug deeper and tossed him a pair of purple tap pants.

"They're mine, but I think we like know each other well enough."

She reached into a mini-fridge for the vodka, poured three glasses and sipped from one.

"She's been up there like long enough. Put on my panties and go get her, Cassidy. I can't wait until she like freaks right out."

He nodded, put one leg into the panties then the other, pulling them to his hips. The sensation was strange. He liked what he felt. He sat on the bed sipping his drink, watching her dress.

Cindy was lying as they'd left her. She was naked. He sat beside her, touching her shoulder to wake her. She pushed herself onto her knees, tousling her hair, her thong hidden somewhere between her legs. When she noticed the silk panties her eyes opened wide.

"Holly's downstairs waiting for us."

"You guys showered?"

"Yes. We went together."

"No way. That bitch. What did she do?"

He shrugged. "I washed her with soap. Then she washed me."

Cindy looked around. The sun was beginning to set. She shivered. The cooler could stay until the morning. She squirmed to one side extricating her bikini bottom from between her cheeks, gathered her top and her towel and wriggled her way to the hatch, not concerned by who might see her.

Raising the cover she dropped everything into her father's stateroom below and made her way to the bottom step by step. She waited for him and kissed him as though standing naked was normal for her, making him wonder how Brenda would look on her boat.

Holly was lying on the bed, finishing her drink, watching television, watching Cindy yank the purple tap pants to the floor, leaving Cassidy naked. Without a word she dragged him to the shower and pushed him in. When they finished Cassidy's skin was a deep pink, tingling in a way he'd never known. Cindy was slumped against the wall. This time he hadn't needed a woman's pressure over his hand. He did fine on his own.

They dried, and this time she coated him with moisturizer he'd never known. He coated her and when he was finished she went to her room, slipped into a pair of panties and laid beside Holly to watch him. He was totally magnificent and she whispered to Holly that they would so not let him go before the morning.

Dinner was pizza, ordered in, and wine from her father's bar. The pizza guy must have died and gone to heaven,

Holly told them, when she went unabashedly and carefree to the afterdeck with the money. She was certain, she told Cindy, that the tip wasn't necessary. The poor guy would be awake all night, and Cassidy asked why.

He was learning. He'd never tasted pizza or hundred-dollar wine. He'd never known what Garrett had paid for his, but he knew that he liked it. The girls each ate a slice, he finished what was left, pleased when Cindy pulled away Holly's top. He liked them very much. They were teaching him and when the wine was finished they lay in bed and talked, Cassidy wedged between them in his purple panties.

He'd learned about cell phones, take-out and 30-minute delivery, realizing what the old man had once told Zach was true when Cindy plugged his ears with her IPod's buds. She asked what music he liked. He didn't know. He'd never heard music before discovering the remote to Wendell Parkens' television. Then she dragged him to the stern and let him phone Holly on her cell who told him she was waiting for him, that she was like the horniest ever. And, again, he didn't know.

If all that were true, he wanted to know how letters could be transmitted through the air, and they taught him. Cindy taught him to open her computer and type a message she then sent to Holly, the same message appearing in seconds. They showed him the internet and CDs, photos of them lounging at the marina's pool and dancing in clubs. He asked how. The girls exchanged glances and Cindy dragged Cassidy to the bed. She pushed him down, pulling away his panties, pushing away her own and sprang onto his hips telling him to smile at Holly. He did.

He didn't think he'd ever stop smiling.

Cindy clambered from the bed, pulling him with her. She poured them each a drink and went to the printer. The girls let him stare at himself in awe. They went to bed and swept back the covers. He'd never seen himself in a photograph. The only one he'd ever seen was the faded sepia of Jonathon Clayton.

Holly dimmed the lights and called him. Neither girl wanted total darkness, each one certain neither did he. She was the horniest ever. And they soon discovered that so was he.

In the morning muted light filled the room through double portholes. The girls were sleeping. They were naked. He was naked, flat on his back and the air was stale with a pungent smell he found arousing.

He craned his head from one side to the other, studying the girls, his mind filled with novelty. The pain he felt was new. He'd never hurt himself that way. He squeezed his penis, grimacing, bringing his hand to his nose. He looked toward Cindy lying against him, her hips at his shoulder, her arms wrapped around his left leg, her bare pussy inches from his nose.

He eased gently to one side, bringing up his arm. He slid his hand between her legs, to the soft flesh of her ass, kneading, feeling the dampness and warmth emanating from her cleft, remembering how Aayla looked to him that morning on the beach, her body naked. He pulled her closer, putting his nose to her, inhaling deeply, her scent intoxicating.

Aayla's scent was the same.

Holly was straddled across his right leg, her breasts pressed to his chest, her face touching his. He eased a hand under her, pressing his fingers against her pussy. She was cool to his touch, the thin space between them wet with stickiness. He smelled the moisture.

Holly stirred. She smiled and laid her head onto his shoulder. Cindy was motionless. He eased his other arm under Holly again, bringing her hips slowly over his.

He'd learned so much that he would soon teach Aayla.

"My pussy's so totally sore."

Holly wriggled the rest of the way herself.

"I never knew pussy. Now I do and I like pussy very much. I like ass also, and tits."

"Everyone likes pussy."

It was happening again. He could feel himself against her belly.

"Cindy's sleeping."

She ran a hand along Cindy's back, resting a hand beside his. "She's so gorgeous, and she'll like wake up when she thinks she's missing something. She's so totally into sex. You so wore us out. Are you like certain you were a virgin?"

She stretched over him. He withdrew his arm from between Cindy's legs, holding Holly in place, his fingers kneading her cheeks.

"Yes, after last night I would know the difference."

She looked at the clock. "It's 9:30. We haven't slept more than a few hours." She kissed him, pushing herself onto her elbows. "Is that her or me on your mouth?"

"It's both of us. I'm surprised he didn't like totally suck us dry." Cindy groaned, lifting her head, propping herself up. "I am so totally raw." She pushed herself onto her knees and wriggled her way behind him, his head centred between her legs. She reached over to the night table for what little was left in a wine glass, rinsing her mouth.

He looked up.

"Thank you for teaching me. Now I will teach Aayla. I also enjoyed your sucking, and Holly's."

That was enough for Holly. She wasn't waiting, Cassidy straining his neck to watch her. Cindy replaced the glass, pushing herself back to kiss him, wriggling forward to kiss Holly, something else he'd decided he liked. They had their arms locked around each other's necks, swaying.

His groan erupted from deep inside. Holly's heat was soothing against his raw skin, her tight grip arousing, the wetness between them erotic and Cindy was moving with her. He put a hand between them fondling their breasts, his other hand caressing Cindy from her ass to her shoulders. He was barely able to breath. He didn't care. Neither did she, neither did Holly.

The night and predawn hours were beyond believable; though this would be the morning he'd remember. They weren't finished with him. Or was he the one not finished? He didn't know. He didn't care.

The girls shuddered in unison. Cindy collapsed against the headboard behind her, framing him with her legs. Holly sank into the open space, covering his mouth with hers. All he knew was that he could finally breathe.

He went first to the head. He urinated, staring at himself in the mirror, his body coated with sweat, his and theirs, his face smeared with lip gloss and Cindy's scent, his mouth swollen. He didn't wash his face or hands. He didn't know when he would ever smell that way again and he wondered whether Aayla would like the smell, or if she did already.

Cindy went second, setting up the DVD and plasma screen when Holly couldn't wait a moment longer and scurried from the bed. Cindy brewed the coffee, Holly made the toast and Cassidy watched them. In the stateroom they lay in a row at the foot of the bed, Cassidy on his side stroking Cindy, watching her caress Holly's curves from her knees to her shoulders, stroking her hair. He was no less fascinated by that as by Holly working the remote.

At first he didn't understand. Then he pushed himself to his knees in shock. He was inside the television. He was seeing himself, he was seeing them. The girls rollicked. The time was 11:00. They had four hours and Cindy was down by one.

She moved onto Holly's back, hardly noticed by Cassidy. His eyes were glued to the screen, watching himself on Cindy, watching Holly watch them until suddenly Cindy was watching him on Holly, under her, beside her. Then he was sitting against the pillows on the bed inside the television watching them.

Then he noticed. Cindy was sitting on Holly, her ass planted on Holly's, rocking, massaging her back and her shoulders, playing with her hair. He'd never seen girls share affection, but he liked watching them. They liked each other very much, he thought. He liked them very much.

Cindy raised her hips slightly, letting or telling Holly to roll onto her back. He didn't know. Her face was flushed, the colour of her hair. Cindy's hair was undone, pasted to her shoulders in wet strands. She wiggled backwards, telling Cassidy to do the same. He did, not knowing where to look first. Holly was lying on the bed the way she was inside the television, with her legs over Cindy's shoulders and back. Cindy was kissing her mouth, her breasts and her belly, rocking to and fro, her legs parted, her ass in the air facing him.

She wriggled closer to him, mimicking the television, putting her face between Holly's legs the way he remembered, the way he was watching inside the television. Then he moved, inside the screen, lurching, grabbing her hips, moving with her, rocking, pushing her and being pushed. She was calling him, her painted fingertips signalling him from between her folds. He lunged forward, pushing himself past her fingers, watching her, probing, watching himself probe her inside the television, pushing, being pushed, collapsing.

He couldn't move. He lay watching them, watching the screen, imagining Aayla with Cindy, Aayla with Holly. Maybe she would like Holly. He didn't know.

The girls crawled unashamedly away from each other and into thongs and triangles as though they'd been lovers for years. They pulled him from the bed. They wanted to take him to the pool. And, yes, he was wearing his thong for

472

them because they were wearing thongs for him. Besides, the pool would be like totally empty. Nothing ever happened until Thursday night and he'd be back by three.

Cindy went to her father's bar and half-filled three plastic glasses with soda water and what was left of the vodka. She didn't want him to go. She'd been screwing guys for five years, since her mother died and her father obsessed with work, but Cassidy was different. He was like, she didn't know, Holly. Holly was so totally stupendous. Four years had to mean something. She didn't mind screwing guys, that's what girls did, but she didn't think she could live without Holly.

Holly wanted him to stay longer. She didn't feel like she was cheating on Cindy. He wasn't like other guys. She thought like maybe she and Cindy should talk. They always talked. They'd talked since day one in her room after school when Cindy was like so totally into listening to her, except they never talked about whatever. She would, after the pool. She smiled to herself. She would, after she helped Cindy clean the mess.

He wasn't shy at the pool. He didn't know shyness. He was in awe. He'd thought the pool might be small, like in the picture, like the one on Tombolina. He was wrong, and asked what Olympic-size meant. He spun around, the deck strewn with lounge chair and umbrellas. He pointed to the far end and asked what that was. They couldn't believe him, but they liked him. He was totally different, so not into himself, and they ran with him.

Cindy jumped with him first, Holly stayed on the deck aiming her phone, following them through the water to the chromed ladder. Then Holly climbed the twenty feet with him, holding his hand at the very edge, Cindy freezing the pair in midair. Aayla wouldn't believe him, though his mother might.

He waded in the salted water with them for two hours,

Holly clinging to his front, Cindy to his back, each girl completely forgetting her drink. He told them of the high precipice, too high to leap from, the lush forests, the white sand and blue water, Shakkra and Aayla.

They listened intently. They asked if he regretted all the sex they'd shared and he said no, he didn't. He regretted that Aayla wasn't with them. He thought now that Aayla would like them. They were kind, and they were generous. They'd helped him when he needed help the most.

Holly asked with what, and he dunked her. Cindy maintained her tight hold, clinging to his back. She looked at her watch and asked if he wanted to have more sex with them. He totally rocked, she told him. He said no, and thanked her, telling her that her body was to die for, that she was very pretty. So was Holly when she surfaced, parting her flame-red headdress, her lips squeezed into a pout.

He thanked her as well, but thought he'd like to dry in the sun before returning to the boat.

He told them of The Seven Feasts, not the pole, The Grand Guardian or Garrett. He told them about the tincture, not the opium, and looked at the vodkas. He told them about Shakkra and Zach before his death, about how they loved each other. He told them how each morning they remembered the festive night before when others didn't because of the tincture. He told them how he was mesmerized by their lovemaking, that he could be so close to them, to touch them. He told them what he knew because he saw in their eyes what he saw in Aayla's, what he knew Aayla saw in his. Perhaps that's why they'd crossed paths, he said, so that they would know.

"My father would be so totally freaked out. He's so totally into his business since my mom died. He's so uptight. He's got like the biggest stick up his ass."

Cassidy winced.

"Would he prefer that you leave him alone, without a

daughter to remind him of your mother, to give all your emotion to Holly and not share her with him?" He shook his head. "I don't believe that, Cindy. Perhaps you should be the first to speak with him. Listen to his heart. When Zach was killed I didn't leave Shakkra for one moment. I stayed with her each night. I listened to her cry each night until she slept. It's all I could do for my father. Perhaps you haven't heard your father cry, perhaps you should."

Her lips began quivering. She was holding back, her confused mind racing.

"And my mom's such a total bitch, like ever since my dad walked out she doesn't even see me. She'd like kill me or something if she knew about us."

"Perhaps she's a bitch because she's afraid. Perhaps she must first see you with Cindy to understand you. Where I come from jealousy and envy are not allowed, each is forbidden. We own nothing, therefore we can't desire what other's possess. Perhaps your mother is jealous of Cindy. Perhaps she feels that she no longer possesses your heart, the way she lost your father's. Shakkra and Aayla swim in the ocean each night; they hold hands and they walk with their arms tightly wrapped around each other like wet muslin. They hug and they kiss each other more than me. I'm not jealous of what they share together. This week, while I'm away from them, they're together in my home sharing the emotion they each feel for me. Perhaps your mother will share Cindy's emotion for you." He looked at Cindy, grinning. "Perhaps she will feel emotion for your father."

Cassidy reached for his drink, emptying the glass onto the pool deck.

Cindy's eyes opened wide. "That's so premium."

"I liked being with you," he beamed, "very much in fact. Yes, my head's a little sore, I admit, and my thong could be bigger this morning, but I remember everything that happened between us. Those people, the ones who drink the tincture like water, in the morning they don't remember anything. Why do you want to forget each other, Holly and Cindy, when I want to remember you always?"

The girls looked at each other, lacing their hands together.

"I'll phone my father," Cindy said, "to tell him he's taking us to dinner tomorrow night. He'll freak out," she looked at Cassidy, "but we'll be ourselves."

"This is so totally weird. We meet a guy in a leather thong who likes to wear my panties; he does us like a frigging army and waits until he's ruined our pussies to tell us we're lesbians."

"We are lesbians, totally awesome lesbians. I guess now we have to like get into this darling and honey stuff."

Holly nodded, hanging her head. "I'll phone my mother. I'll invite us for the weekend. I so didn't expect this...honey." She reached for her glass. "Cassidy's right. We don't need this, not all the time."

Cindy did the same. "We'll miss you, Cassidy. And all we thought we'd get out of you is a good lay. Go figure."

He knew not to leave. Holly leaned forward, kissing him. "And we totally did. Talk about like going out with a bang."

He didn't understand.

"Thank you, for all that you've taught me." He shrugged. "Will you keep us in the television?"

"No, we don't have to." Cindy put a hand between her legs. "I'll remember last night for a hundred years."

Holly peeked into her thong, grimacing. "I don't think I'll pee like ever again."

He leaned forward, kissing them, sitting, putting a hand to his thong.

"And I will never again make rain in the forest."

He chuckled. This time they didn't understand.

Forty-Seven

They frolicked in the pool awhile longer, teasing, being teased. Onboard the girls changed into red and silver slingshots and halters, refusing to let him leave in a wet leather thong, choosing bright white tap pants for him, despite his claim that he had extra shields in his satchel.

Holly prepared lunch while Cindy explained how the boat worked. He turned over the engine and went to the dock to see the gurgling water as she explained propulsion. She explained the throttle, forward, reverse and the trim tabs. She explained GPS and radar and the marine radio which she used to call another boat that came through five on five. He paid particular attention to the compass and the cardinal points, asking more questions as they ate.

They'd given up wondering about him. He was so totally a mystery.

Cindy explored his satchel, disgusted. His sandwiches were stale, he had nothing to drink and his one clean thong was tangled amongst the others. She emptied the contents into the garbage, tossing in the satchel, ignoring him.

She put her cheek to Holly's and they whispered, their heads nodding. She disappeared into her stateroom, Holly went to the galley. Not long after she appeared holding a grocery bag filled with fresh sandwiches, sodas and fruit. Cindy came out a few moments later holding bright leather handbags and a small plastic tube.

The tube was for him to open at home, not before. Nor

was he to open the handbags for any reason. They made him promise. The heavier one was for Shakkra, the lighter one was for Aayla.

Holly asked whether they would ever see him again. He scanned the marina and said he would try; he would like them to meet Shakkra and Aayla, if he was not meant to meet with his father first because of what he must do.

They didn't like that. Tears trickled down their cheeks. Not kissing as ex-lovers seemed foolish, inappropriate after what they'd shared. So they did. They would miss him very much. He'd given them so much to talk about, so much to change in their lives. And what had they given him in return except a few abrasions on his totally fantastic body?

They would never know how much more.

He stepped onto the dock, facing away, waiting, inhaling a deep breath. He thought yes. But then he thought no. He turned on his heels to prove himself right or wrong. Either way he was right. How more naked could they be? His face beamed, his teeth shining against his dark skin. Their toothy smiles were as bright as his, their eyes sparkled. Their wet faces pressed cheek to cheek, their bodies fused in a tight embrace, glistening with red and silver threads. He blew them a final kiss, waving as he walked away. Cindy and Holly forever etched in his mind.

Boarding Three Fortunes he moved quickly to unlatch the door lock. He hurried to the engine room, climbed through the deck hatch onto the afterdeck and relocked the latch, sliding back into his hold to wait, stocking his cubicle with the food and the gifts.

Garrett and Forrest boarded ninety minutes later amidst the sounds of golf clubs crashing onto the deck, the dull thuds of shopping bags dropping, her heels clacking against the fibreglass.

More noises ensued. He heard the sound of water running, first for ten minutes, then fifteen. He heard the toilet flushing and the muted jostling of bottles. Then he heard nothing, until dull footsteps and voices just above him, clear voices.

Sitting with one leg dangling from his cubicle he listened, biting into one of the sandwiches Holly had made for him, rinsing his mouth with a dark soda she'd put in the bag, another discovery, forcing the girls from his mind. He could revisit the past twenty hours of his life when the two above him were asleep in their bed. Until then no one was more important to him than Dakota's older brother.

"I spoke with the bank again, and the lawyers. Neither knows of a will or signed letter from the old man, or they're not saying. Either way there's nothing either one will do for us."

"There must be a will. It's an island for Christ sake. We'll search the house again. The old man was nuts. His mind was probably rotten with syphilis. We'll demolish the house. Anyway, I get the creeps sleeping in his room. We'll tear down the place, board by board and build a magnificent mansion."

There was silence.

"Then you'll find his ring. That was the message, Garrett. The ring's with his will. In his sick mind that's what made him The Grand Guardian, that stupid ring and his ridiculous hair. Find the ring and you'll find the will."

"I know that. He knew if he gave it to the kid something would happen. He didn't trust me. I'd kill the kid to read that will."

"And you know I want to be Irene on Tombola as much as I want an exclusive resort on Tombolina for people like us. Right now they still look to Taliah after six months, not me, never me. And they never will. They must know I'm the true Irene. They must acknowledge me. She's old. I'm not. We're young and we should have a finer yacht that we anchor in our own marina for everyone to see, not always hidden in a dark hole. We should care about our future, not those without one. They should see us as we are, beautiful and elegant. If not for us, what would become of them? What do we gain by them seeing us in robes trimmed with cheap braiding? They're not like us. They're happy the way they are. Let them see how different we truly are. We should appear more magnificent to them, so that they feel more humble."

Garrett nodded. Cassidy slipped from his cubicle.

"Dakota's the biggest concern." Garrett said. "He's intelligent, more than my son. Still, he's my brother."

"Get real. He's your enemy. You just said you'd kill him for the will. So is that girl he's always with, that Xandra. I don't like her one bit. She's trouble."

"She's not an issue. I can only imagine one thing about her he can possibly like."

"You don't have to imagine much longer."

"He won't join with the other one easily. And that Cassidy's no better. My father should have dumped him in the sea with his mother years ago."

"We can't let this get away from us. I want that resort, Garrett. We deserve something good after everything we've been through. It's our dream. The grand guardian thing's fine for the village and, let's face it, who doesn't like fucking eighteen-year-olds? That doesn't have to stop. But I want to be Mr. and Mrs. Parkens. I want our friends to see my paradise."

"Nothing will get away from us, but let's not forget balance. That Shakkra's up next in five months. She's a done deal. Then who do we stone the next year? If we take care of her kid, we still have to deal with my brother and, if I stone my brother, we have to deal with Taliah, unless we can arrange to bring them here together for a meeting with the bank. They wouldn't be missed. Then that Aayla girl could screw whoever she wants…after me."

The laughter was raucous.

"We should, Garrett. I'd throw the bitch over myself if you can convince her to come with us, something I seriously doubt. I wouldn't suggest you hold your breath. They met together with the old guy before he died. They know something. They know a lot. I can see it their faces. Your brother's waiting for something. He should be pissed, and he's not. Neither is she since we put her into our old house. She should be outraged, and she's not. I'd rather surprise them before I'm the one surprised."

Cassidy hated the silence, the soft tapping sound inches above his head.

"I'll tell him I've changed my mind about completing his academic and social education. I'll suggest taking him stateside before the fall semester to enrol him and find him a suitable condo. She can go with him to see him off. He'll believe that. He can't wait to get back into his boots and denims. He's no different from us. He wants the good life. Then she can swim home and we'll get rid of Cassidy next year. Anyway, no love's lost between him and Cassidy." He guffawed. "Not since the old man made told the world he was giving his girlfriend to Dakota, albeit for a trial run. What was in the old man's head to think I'd step aside for him? Let a kid rule Tombola with his mother until he's twenty-five?"

"You were right to put him at the pole. He could have lived another ten years. Then your brother would have taken control and you'd be hard pressed to stop him. We did what was right. That doesn't mean we should forget Aayla. She's a deceitful little bitch, always hanging around the kid's mother. Something's not right with her."

"Let them play their little games in the water. They won't join. At worst, if Dakota doesn't leave, he'll join with her and Shakkra's kid can get himself off milking that cow that's waiting for him. Could be he'll stone himself. I sure as hell would."

"Still, I don't trust her. You know what the old man always believed, about the buried chest."

"Even if it's true, we don't need what's been buried for over sixty years. It's a myth. The old man was insane long before I came along. I read the Ancestral Tomes years ago, you haven't. They were all insane. Spend your whole life on an island with zombies, are you kidding?"

Cassidy heard muted steps, and bottles clinking together.

"They're the real dilemma," Garrett continued, waiting for the young girls in shorts and sweaters to pass by. "We don't need them, we don't want them, but what do we do with them. Not a single one could serve a plate or a drink. And the way they talk makes me fucking crazy."

"Blame your father. He got what he wanted: an island full of simple-minded believers. Status quo, we'll give them what they want. They'll work the fields to supply the resort and once each year they'll get a week of love thy neighbour. The last thing we want is zombies freaking out our guests.

"Not all of them are brain-dead. Not all the teaching on this island's been done by him in his lagoon with his flaccid pecker in his hand."

Cassidy heard her chortle.

"You haven't seemed to mind the last few years since you took over the hardest part of the job."

"And you hate watching, I suppose, and painting their little wet bodies. I've seen you with enough pigment on your hands these past few years, red and yellow, pink and blue, or white and green. Any favourites so far?"

"All of them, if you must know. And you know very well, especially the good looking ones."

"But not the next batch, not Aayla, Xandra, or the fat one."

"I'll suffer with the ox. I suppose we both will. Maybe

I'll use a spray gun. But I'll truly enjoy the other two, each for different reasons. I think I'll do them in florescent colours." Her laughter was coarse. "Tell me that wouldn't freak out the village at the pole. And don't tell me you won't like playing with them in the water."

"Paint them whatever colour you want. None of this means a thing, Forrest, unless we get the will, or something concrete signed by him. The old man was at his desk all day after I went to see him, to tell him he was leaving us. He was writing something with his face buried in a book as though he had hours to live, not days. He was doing the same the last day. I doubt very much whether he slept. Then we were too busy getting Taliah and the kid out of the house. When the CC and I went to get him there was no book, just him slumped over the desk blabbering."

"What was he writing?"

"I don't know. Dakota claims to know nothing about it, says he's never seen such a book."

"He's a fucking liar. He'll change his mind when he sees his mother hanging over the gunwale in four-foot seas."

"Let's hope so. No will, no dream, no Isle of Tombola, the most exclusive and refined resort in the Caribbean, Mrs. Parkens."

"That's not acceptable, Garrett."

"No, it's not, but the groundwork's set: first Dakota and Taliah, then Shakkra after you finger paint the girls."

Garrett paused; Cassidy stretched himself a few inches higher.

"You've got a point, Forrest. I think I will enjoy teaching Dakota's little girlfriend and Aayla, for different reason, while you're spray painting the big one for Cassidy. I've seen her up close. He's got first refusal on her whether he wants it or not."

"He'll be a problem, Garrett. His entire family's been a

righteous pain in the ass, the women included. The old man could've been right, about the chest and the books. They're different, as though they believe themselves equal to us."

"He's not a problem. With his mother gone and his girlfriend nursing Dakota's progeny, or mine for that matter, who will he cry with? Not Dakota, and certainly Xandra who can barely speak let alone dissent. Anyway whatever happens to the kid before his time will depend on him." He watched the same girls scurrying in the direction they'd come. "How'd you like to paint that combo in your Sacred Pond?

"Tell me after you wake up. Shit…"

Cassidy heard feet padding quickly across the deck, followed by dull thuds, bottles clinking and the companionway slamming shut. He bolted to his cubicle.

What remained of the evening was a continuum of ear-shattering thunder and deafening reverberation, each raindrop an explosion on the open afterdeck above him, the water coursing through the bilge sounding louder than a raging torrent to his ears.

Cassidy sat cramped in his cubicle, expecting the worst, not knowing.

Forty-Eight

The cacophony ended by daybreak, torrential rain becoming a light drizzle, the early morning sun making the day more miserable with thick humidity.

He'd survived his final night, pleased that Garrett Parkens hadn't discovered him, killed him. That he hadn't been discovered in Holly's panties, counting each second from his first bite into her sandwich until the twin engines came to life.

His joy was short lived. He didn't know what the girls had done. They had suspected and went to the gas dock wanting to feel closer to him, worried for him. Cindy wasn't certain he'd understood. He'd learned so much in so little time. He'd probably forgotten.

Below deck Cassidy's heart was pounding. He was blind in the dark. Hearing sounds he'd never heard, sounds he'd never learned: 1000 gallons of fuel, 400 gallons of water flooding at once into separate tanks, 500 gallons of grey water and black sucked out at the same rate of speed.

Everything stopped but his heart, until blowers began clearing toxic fumes from below the deck, bilge pumps grinding out water left by the rain. He wanted to scream, holding himself in check. He'd gone this far. He was fine. If he died his mother and Aayla would never know of their gifts.

Finally the engines turned over and water churned a mere few feet from his familiar space.

Cassidy would never know that Cindy and Holly sat at the end of the dock holding hands, swinging their feet, watching Three Fortunes glide onto a plane and disappear. They felt afraid for him. They wanted so much to see him one last time, to thank him, to make his face as wet as theirs for what he'd done.

The night before Holly's mother was on the phone with her daughter until midnight, crying. Holly was crying. And Cindy was crying beside her. Her father was coming home early to take them to dinner and they wanted Cassidy to know.

He remained huddled in the dark throughout the voyage, remembering his time with the girls, wondering whether he should feel guilty. He didn't. What he felt was free. He felt Zach's pride. He had understood Cindy. He remembered her exact words and would speak them to Shakkra. One way or another Shakkra and Aayla would leave the island, if not with him, then without him.

He'd told Shakkra of his second plan the night he left, watching Aayla sleep in her lap. She understood his every word, and she'd promised.

He felt Three Fortunes slow, sink lower into the water, the engines somehow louder. He felt a slight nudge, his head jerking to the side. He released the latch, peeking into the darkness beyond the compartment, waiting, his hearing attuned to the faintest sound.

The voices, the clamour came soon. He visualized them doing what he'd seen other boaters doing at the marina, securing the ship to the dock, unloading the boat, carrying away all the bags he'd seen in their stateroom. When quiet engulfed him he stayed where he was. He felt in the dark for a sandwich and ate his dinner of smoked meat and cola. Then he slept. He had nowhere to go.

When he woke he crawled from his space. He palmed his way to the door leading to the crew's quarters and flipped the light switch. He'd slept, he thought, for six or seven hours. His watch was showing eleven o'clock. He darkened the room and stood by his compartment, waiting until he was certain.

He thought of Cindy and her father, imagining how the inside of a restaurant would look. He had a good feeling about Cindy and Holly. He liked the girls. Aayla would like them very much. He flipped the switch again. He left at midnight with their gifts, the grocery bag and his plastic tube.

On the transom he pushed Holly's panties to his ankles and dropped them into the grocery bag with the tube. He didn't want salt water to ruin his keepsake. He sank effortlessly and stealthily into the water, reaching for all the bags and waded away with his arms held high.

At the shoreline he walked naked along the beach, reaching the gorge, peering into the dark, searching for shadows, listening for echoes. He went forward, wading under the bridge, passing the pole, smirking. The pole would soon be the embodiment of his achievement.

At the leeward shore he walked along the water's edge, unhurried, thinking how best to walk through the door, how best to wake them, how they would look to him. He'd never been away from his mother, never far from Aayla since he'd fallen in love with her.

At the grassy path leading to the village he wiped his feet clean, stepped into the tap pants, slung the handbags over his shoulders and made his way to the end of his week-long adventure.

A faint glow outlined the slatted window at the front of the villa. He breathed deeply and walked through the door.

They were huddled together on the daybed in the sitting area, crying, stroking each other's hair. He didn't know what to say. He held his arms open wide.

"Good evening, ladies. Am I too late for dinner?"

They stared, their mouths agape at the sight. He looked terrible, and wonderful. Bright leather straps crisscrossing his chest, a long strange tube gripped in one hand, a strange bag in the other, flimsy white shorts clinging to his hips. He kicked the door shut.

They ran to him, hugging and kissing him, staining his face with tears. Aayla stepped back for space, punching him as hard as she could. She rubbed her fist, and then she kissed his eyes, his nose and his mouth.

"I should not feel emotion for you."

"I don't understand what you're saying. Speak English."

She punched him again. He was getting no help at all from his mother who stood quietly by, wiping her eyes.

"I shouldn't love you for what you've done to us. You're a stupid man. You put me to bed like a little girl."

He grinned widely. "So that one day soon I can put you to bed like a big girl. Besides, I knew you'd spend your time plotting against me, my little witch and her teacher." He hugged them. "Shakkra, Aayla, if you've never believed me before, you won't believe one word of what I will tell you." He led them to the daybed. "First I have gifts for you from new friends." He shrugged away the straps, assigning each bag. "These gifts are from young women like you, girls who saved my life when I was real in danger. Without them I wouldn't be here now. This I know."

Aayla dug into hers first. Shakkra and Cassidy looked on. Inside she found a brand new wallet in a beautiful box, and five dollars, a short belted dress, a panty and bra set wrapped in tissue paper she'd never felt, a slingshot bronze-coloured bikini she had no idea about, a tank top, a powder compact that she held to her nose and a magazine showing young girls on the cover.

Everything was new and she recognized everything from the magazines she'd read with Shakkra except the jumble of bronze-coloured strings.

"Your gifts are from Cindy and Holly, Aayla. You'll see better in the morning when the light is much brighter. It's your turn, Shakkra. I told them everything I could about you and Aayla. They cried because they couldn't know you. Everything comes to you from their hearts."

Shakkra sat by her little friend, wiping her eyes. She reached into the bag, grasping a bottle of wine. She read the label, with no understanding of Château Margaux. Taped to the back of the bottle was a note. She looked at her son who shrugged. Taped to the neck was a corkscrew.

"They wrote my name, Cassidy." Tears formed again in her eyes. "I haven't seen my name written since Zach wrote me letters in the sand. They wish us to drink the wine tonight, Cassidy, as though we're with them in the restaurant. What does she mean?"

"Tonight is very important to Cindy, Shakkra. When I met them her heart was broken because of her father. Tonight she's well, if her father has listened to her and tomorrow Holly will be well with her mother. I know that in my heart. I'll tell you more about them tomorrow."

Aayla hurried for three cups. Shakkra brought each item from her bag in a daze.

"Cassidy, am I dreaming?"

"No, Shakkra, you're not. I told them that one day I would buy you pretty things, but that I could not for a while. I suppose they saw the sadness on my face. They were excited to give me your gifts. Holly and Cindy are thinking of us at this very moment. I know they are, the same way I'm thinking of them."

"What danger were you in, Cassidy, for these girls to save you and give you such wonderful gifts?"

"That's not important, mother. The danger's passed. Open your gifts. I haven't seen them."

A bright green silk scarf wrapped in tissue, a white linen top wrapped together with matching high-waisted and flared shorts and a thin black belt, circa 50s, linen sandals, panties and a bra, and a dark green slingshot and halter. Separately Cindy had added bath oil and shampoo.

She covered her mouth. Each of her gifts was brand new.

"I told them your favourite colour was green. They wanted you to have nice things to wear when we leave this place."

Aayla came in. Cassidy opened the wine, watching the women holding their new clothes against their evening tunics. He filled their cups.

"Cassidy, how will we thank them? Shakkra wanted to know. "We have no gifts for them."

"They know already, Shakkra. They want nothing in return."

Aayla asked, "Are they pretty?"

"Yes, Aayla, they're very pretty. Holly has hair the colour of fire, Cindy's is the colour of the moon. They're two years older than you and know everything about you. They never stopped asking questions, like you."

"I love them, Cassidy."

"How do you know?"

"They helped you, when Shakkra and I couldn't."

"They're the reason I'm here now." He raised his cup. "Bottoms up. That's what Holly would say."

"What does she mean?" Aayla questioned.

"That one day you'll ask her yourself. I have so much to tell you."

Shakkra held her cup to her nose, inhaling deeply. When she drank her mouth dried with flavours she remembered from the night he left.

"Cassidy, this is delicious. Now, tell us about those," her expression was quizzical, "tap pants. They're very lovely on you. Are they from Cindy or Holly?"

He blew frustrated air through his lips.

"They took my satchel and my thongs, mother, after our time in the pool. They're like you and your little friend. I had no say in what I did or said with them. They controlled me. I was a slave. In fact, I was their prisoner."

Shakkra turned to Aayla. "That's good, little heart. This way he'll be easier for you to train once you're married. He already knows his weakness. He won't be difficult."

"I don't think I want a man who wears girls' panties."

"My food was stale, and my shields were damp." He touched the tube. "I believe this is my gift. They told me not to look into yours, or this." He laid the tube aside and put what was in the grocery bag onto the daybed. "This is smoked meat for our lunch tomorrow. These are potato chips and these are soft drinks." He looked to Aayla. "You must drink them as quickly as possible. It's their custom."

"What's in the little bags?" Aayla asked.

"I thought to give them to you and Shakkra as gifts from me. But after what Cindy and Holly have given you, I won't. Tomorrow I'll throw them in the sea. They would ruin what Cindy and Holly have done."

"What's your gift?" Aayla asked.

He opened the tube, slamming the open end against an open palm until the photos slid out. He uncurled them, transported to another world.

"What is it, Cassidy?"

"Yesterday, before Garret and Forrest returned to their boat, I was with Cindy and Holly. I went with them to the pool. These are photographs of the three of us together. I wasn't expecting this. Seeing them again makes me remember."

He gave Shakkra and Aayla the photographs.

Aayla gasped. "They're so pretty, Cassidy," she said. "How are you flying in the air? Never have I seen hair this colour."

"We're not flying. We we're falling, jumping from a

491

diving platform into a cement pool filled with ocean water and big enough for the entire village."

He sank between them on the daybed. "I have so much to tell you, about Brenda and her car, hotels and noises, restaurants and frozen men. I can't begin to explain. I'm so tired."

Shakkra took his cup.

"Then you will sleep, sweetheart. We'll talk more in the morning. We have so many questions to ask."

"Aayla, you must tell me of their next departure, and of the one after that. We aren't the only ones in danger. Somehow we must take them with us. He'll never believe me."

Aayla leaned across and kissed him. He wasn't crying, Shakkra told her. The wetness in his eyes was borne of fatigue, though this time she didn't believe Shakkra. She knew her man was afraid for them, and for someone else. She wondered who wouldn't believe him.

They left him to his dreams, toppled across the daybed, each one patting the back of Holly's panties, giggling. He was too heavy to lift. They covered him with a sheet and went to Shakkra's bedroom to do what all girls do with a new wardrobe, and to cry where they wouldn't wake him.

He'd come back to them as he'd promised, although he was no longer the Cassidy, the son, the boy they once knew. He was a man, their man. The difference was undeniable. He would never again be what he once was to them. They'd lost the one and gained the other.

They were leaving, they knew. They gazed for hours at the photos of the pool and the girls, sitting in bed in their new panties and bras, drinking wine, falling asleep, whispering thanks to girls they'd never met but loved in their hearts.

Forty-Nine

Cassidy woke late. He went into Shakkra's room and saw them lying on her bed in their panties and bras. The empty bottle was on the floor, their gifts laid out neatly on her night table.

Saturday was a workday, he didn't care. He knew that very soon Shakkra and Aayla would spend their Saturdays shopping and going to restaurants in stunning clothes. He would buy a car like Brenda's and drive them wherever they wanted to go. Today he would let them sleep. He'd waited a very long time to see them that way and stood by the door taking them in.

Shakkra stirred first, rubbing sleep from her eyes. She sat, combing her fingers through her hair, putting a finger to the rosettes trimming her bra, tracing another across the front of her embroidered panties, exchanging silent glances with her son. She whispered into Aayla's ears to wake her. But the girl didn't want to wake and snuggled her head deeper into her pillow.

She creased her brow. "My head hurts, sweetheart."

"I see why."

She eased her legs over the edge of her bed. "We thought we'd lost you. Don't ever think to do that to us again."

"I arrived earlier yesterday, but couldn't leave until dark."

She looked at her table. "How will I thank Cindy and

Holly for saving my son?"

"By wearing your gifts when we leave here."

"When, Cassidy? You didn't say when, only that you must know of their next two trips and that others are in danger who must leave with us. Who else can be in danger?" She put a hand on Aayla's hip. "Do they know about this little girl? I would kill them first."

"No, they don't. It's bad enough that they suspect her and don't like her. Her first punishment will be in the pond, her and Xandra with them. They're dangerous, Shakkra. If the old man was insane, and he was, these two are worse. I learned everything that I must know, directly from Garrett and Forrest as though I was sitting with them. I was so close at times I thought they would hear my breathing"

"Who else should be afraid?" He hesitated. "Tell me, sweetheart. This is no time for secrets."

He took a deep breath. "Taliah will be the first, she threatens them, and Dakota with her. You will sit at the pole this July, but you won't be lonely very long. I'll follow you next year."

She wasn't amused.

"It's their plan, Shakkra, not mine. They won't succeed. I will. I know their plans, they don't know mine. No one will harm my mother."

"I know that. But Dakota, they're brothers."

He shrugged. "They're half-brothers. He killed his father because the old man was living too long. They believe Dakota has the ring, and their father's will. They want to build a resort on Tombolina for rich people while Tombola remains a prison for the village. Their problem is Dakota. He's the rightful owner. He has the will, but I have the ring, the key and the letter. I suppose when Dakota's dead the island will become Garrett's, but he has no idea which bank or which box. They know of the journal, but not where to look."

494

"When will I read Zach's letters to me, Cassidy?"

He didn't answer.

"They won't wait long. That's why Aayla must tell me before the next time they leave."

"What will you do?"

"Cindy and Holly taught me about the machines in his office and his library. I know how they work. What the old man told Zach was true. Machines do send words through the air as quickly as we speak them. Others are for printing words and making photographs. I saw them make the ones you saw of me. I saw what I had done the day before, as though I was someone else. I heard my voice and I heard music with a radio attached to my ears. It's all true. Shakkra, I was inside their television, though first I was hidden inside a silver disk, like the ones we saw in the house. I know now how to use them."

"What were you doing inside the television? How did you feel?"

"We were eating pizza, but I couldn't feel myself."

"We must warn Dakota, sweetheart. He's a nice boy. This little girl is the reason you don't like him, but I do. And I like Xandra. He's not responsible for what his father's done."

"You know I wouldn't let him be killed. That doesn't mean I should trust him. I know I have to warn him, as soon as I think of a way. Would you believe that I went to Miami without Cindy's and Holly's gifts as proof?" He smirked. "Or your headache?"

She ignored him, giving Aayla a gentle spanking.

"Wake up, little one."

"He knows not to trust me, Shakkra. He's known since he was born, which doesn't mean he's not in my plan. He is. He'll leave when we do, if he wants to. And he will, or he'll lose the island, not to mention Xandra."

"What proof will you give him?"

He thought for a moment. He went to the night table, chuckling. "You and Aayla," he reached for the Aayla's slingshot and halter, "in these."

Aayla rolled onto her side, curling her body around Shakkra.

"What's it for, Cassidy?" she wanted to know.

"It's a bikini for the ocean." He slipped his feet between the strings and pulled them to his knees. "This part is the shield. Pull the strings to your shoulders."

"Show us."

"No." He stood, tossing strings onto the bed. "Some girls wear the halter to cover their breasts, others don't. That's how he'll know I'm telling the truth."

"What time is it, sweetheart?"

He checked his watch he'd attached to the tap pants. "Ten-thirty, too late for me to cast a net and too late to break your backs in the field. Besides, I want to see you in your bikinis."

He walked out. Five minutes later Shakkra and Aayla walked into the kitchen, mimicking the women in the magazines. Shakkra was wearing her halter, Aayla her tank top. They could be sisters, he thought, and the older one would have no trouble finding a man.

Shakkra said, "You're staring."

He flushed. "That's what Brenda said to me when I was in her car."

"Why did you stare at her?"

"I wasn't. I was looking at her open blouse and what she wore under her skirt because I was thinking of you and how you will dress when we leave. I told her she was beautiful, like you. I saw many women dressed like her when I went with her into the city."

"Is she young, like Cindy and Holly?" Aayla asked.

"She's older, like Shakkra." He paused. "And she'd look as fantastic as Shakkra in a slingshot. Wow. That's what she

496

likes to say."

"What does she mean?"

"She means she'd like a bikini like this very much."

"I feel naked, sweetheart."

He grinned widely, stepping behind her. He patted her bum. "You are, Shakkra. I'll have to carry a big stick when I'm with you at the beach to stop someone from stealing you. I can see you walking with Brenda also."

She smacked him. "Maybe, sweetheart, you're seeing too much."

He pursed his lips, shaking his head. "I would like to see the three of you very much. You'll like her, Shakkra" He became serious. "She wants to help us and I know how to find her again. Perhaps we should let her."

They saw Aayla staring at herself through her new compact.

"We are beautiful, Shakkra, aren't we?"

"Yes, little one, we are. And so is Cassidy in his new panties."

"He must like being a girl, Shakkra. He's worn them since he was with Cindy and Holly."

He threatened with his thumbs hooked to push them down. Shakkra threw out her hip; Aayla threw hers out. Shakkra shrugged, and Aayla shrugged. When he came out from his room in his loin-shield and shorts they were in the kitchen in their beach-shields and boleros, setting the table for lunch, anxious to eat smoked meat. Not quite certain about the mustard or how to open the soda bottles.

Cassidy took over, repeating his instructions to Aayla to drink the soda as quickly as she could. She gulped twice before her cheeks bulged and brown spray exploded from her nose and mouth. Shakkra wasn't amused. Apparently her son wasn't always an adult. He claimed remorse, garnering a punch from the victim and a raised eyebrow from her friend.

Aayla wouldn't drink another drop until Shakkra did. She trusted Shakkra, not her son. Then she ate her sandwich, putting it on her plate after each bite to make it last longer. Her father would be angry with her. She didn't care. Her part of the fields wouldn't rot in a single day, and no one would starve because Cassidy's net was empty. She wanted to read her new magazine. She wanted to try on Shakkra's new outfit and to see herself in her new mirror.

Cassidy agreed, as long as they did so in Shakkra's room while he put his mind to work in the sitting area. At day's end they would go to the beach and he would tell them more about his adventure with Brenda, Cindy and Holly, or about most of it. In the meantime he wanted them not to think of what lay ahead.

He didn't have to think much about Dakota. The boy would believe or he wouldn't. He would help or he wouldn't and Cassidy had to believe that he would. Cassidy had the ring and the keys. He chortled, making Shakkra and Aayla glance over their shoulders. He was, in fact, the true owner of Tombola until Dakota believed him or Garrett killed him.

He didn't care about The Grand Guardian or the Chief Counsellor. Why would he?

He studied Shakkra. Imagining her with Brenda wasn't difficult. Trying to think of her as a mother was. He knew why he'd stared at Brenda, for the same reason he'd stood watching his mother lying on her bed in her new lingerie. They were gorgeous and he was a man. He'd never seen her that way before, and she was a stunning woman. He'd never seen her in a slingshot that covered the tiniest part of her. He enjoyed what he saw, though he'd seen her since his birth wearing only her thongs and her naked body painted green during The Seven Feasts before his father was killed.

He'd never thought of her that way until leaving Tombola, until seeing Brenda. And now not touching Aayla

498

was torturous, thankful she was in the room with his mother.

He opened his mind to Cindy and Holly, remembering their smells and their taste, their clean bodies. He wanted to smell and taste Aayla that way, urgently. He wanted to touch her; he wanted to feel inside her. He wanted to teach her what he'd learned. He wanted her coated with oil in a steaming shower, not a warm ocean. He wanted her in a soft queen size bed, not on the grass, the sand or his bed that was no wider than twice his width.

He was glad Shakkra no longer slept with him. He was a man. He heard them laughing. He was their man, and twice cursed.

Fifty

They swam in the ocean and spoke more about the girls and Brenda.

Cassidy told them about Holly's mother and Cindy's father, making his mother and Aayla sad for the girls and their parents. Aayla listened intently. She was now learning by listening, reading on her own and asking Shakkra for help when she really needed to, or wanted to.

While the sun's warmth was still strong enough to dry them, Shakkra left them and went to the villa. She changed from her beach-shield into her evening tunic and went to Aayla's home to ask her mother if Aayla might stay one more night. Cassidy had finally made his way from the forest, she explained, and Aayla wanted to finish the night-shield she'd begun knitting for herself. She was an excellent student.

Her mother agreed and Shakkra wasn't surprised when Aayla's father came to the door.

He wasn't pleased that Cassidy hadn't cast his net all week, nor that she and his daughter hadn't worked in the field that day.

She shrugged. She explained that she hadn't been well and that Aayla had stayed with her to care for her. Before she turned to leave she asked whether he'd ever explored the island's forests when he was young. He hadn't. Nor did he care enough about his daughter to investigate why she hadn't come to the field, she added. Did he treat his other

500

daughters that way, or only the one who felt emotion for her son, she asked, turning and walking away.

What would the puppet of The Grand Guardian do to a woman condemned? Screw you, she thought, pleased with herself.

She gave the kids time alone.

In the ocean Aayla didn't stop asking questions. She wanted to know about the people, the cars, Cindy's boat and how he hid in The Grand Guardian's yacht. She wanted to know what was in the little bags they hadn't opened. He reached into his shield, showing her before letting them float to the ocean floor.

"When will you marry me, darling?"

"You're spending too much time with my mother...darling."

"Shakkra's nicer than you. If I was a man I would marry her instead of you."

"Maybe you're a lesbian."

"What's lesbian?"

"She's a woman who feels emotion and shares affection with other women."

"I don't believe you."

"Cindy and Holly are lesbians. That's what they must explain to their parents. That's why they're afraid."

Her mind was working. "They will never have children."

"No, I asked them. They might adopt one when they are much older. They might take one that has no mother or father. It's possible."

She was hanging from his neck, letting her body sway in the water. He was striding backwards, doing his best to keep her afloat.

"I don't care. I love them anyway."

"I think you love everyone."

"How do they share affection if they cannot couple?"

He was going to drown, with his head completely dry.

"I asked them. They showed me lesbians in a silver disk on the television. In Miami people like to see others having sex on the television. It's like The Seven Feasts. They told me all girls like what they do, even straight girls."

"What's a straight girl?"

"You're straight. "He grinned. "Unless you want to marry my mother. Then I'll ask Cindy for her silver disk so you can learn to be a good lesbian."

Since she'd begun reading, learning, her mind never stopped.

"If straight girls also like what they do, can straight girls be lesbians?"

"Holly said yes, many of them are."

"And you watched how they share affection, you know how."

"Yes, I do."

"And they will never have children."

"No."

"Then I want you to show me." She pushed him away. "So I can decide if I like girls more than you."

He buried himself in the ocean, grinning, congratulating himself. He was saved. Zach was right. Women didn't need to know everything.

She pushed her way through the water to the shore, letting him walk behind. By the time he caught up she'd put on her bolero.

"Did you like watching?"

"Yes, I did."

"Then you should enjoy teaching me, unless you don't want to."

He kissed her, wrapping his arms around her waist.

"Aayla…"

"Yes, darling."

He wondered whether one day Dakota would be a

friend, someone he could speak reasonably with, or was he to spend his life suffering the female mind, a penance for some terrible wrong he hadn't yet committed.

"Keep pestering me and I'll leave you here for Garrett to mash your berry skins when he takes you to the pond before giving you to his brother."

"Six months ago I would have cried to hear that, now I know you love me. Anyway, Shakkra won't go without me." She stuck out her tongue. "And she won't like you when I tell her what you said."

He let her walk ahead.

At the villa the table was set with his favourite goat's meat and yams, boiled fruits and the last two bottles of cola. One was part of Aayla's place setting; the second was part of Shakkra's. She did tell his mother, he knew, watching her running her tongue across her lips after each sip. He ignored her, content to drink his goat's milk.

When the meal was finished, Shakkra and Aayla washed the dishes. Cassidy went to the enclosure at the back of the villa to bathe, much earlier than usual, knowing full well his mother and Aayla were anxious to wash their hair and coat the bodies with bath oil. They could bathe in the morning he told them.

Shakkra agreed. Telling Aayla that, after all, he was the man and that she would have to learn her place.

When they went out to check on him he was pleased with himself, his arms and legs slung over the tub, until his mother took his thong and his shorts and Aayla took his towel. Everything was thrown inside and they sat on the edge of the tub. Aayla reached in and pulled the stopper.

He asked for his towel. No. He begged for his towel. No. He asked them to look away. No. Aayla peered into the disappearing water, asking what the difference was since they were all girls. He threatened to stand. They crossed their arms and smiled. He did, cupping his hands over his parts, putting one leg over the edge, then the other, almost losing his balance, skipping and hopping to prevent further damage to his pride, looking ridiculous, turning and walking into the house with his head held high, ignoring the gleeful giggles.

When he was inside he burst into laughter. He dressed and went to the kitchen where a pot of boiling water was gurgling on the woodstove. He didn't think his mother would ever grow old, he knew Aayla would never grow up. He hoped not.

He carried the pot to the enclosure, emptying the water into the tub. Shakkra and Aayla stood together in their night-shields and boleros, waiting. He sat on the edge, waiting. Shakkra shook her head, asking him when he would ever learn. They pushed him in, and stepped back.

He splashed to the surface, crawling out, coughing water from his mouth and his nose, sneezing, feeling even more ridiculous stripping away his clinging shorts. Defeated, he went in to boil more hot water; afraid if he didn't he wouldn't have a breakfast to eat in the morning.

When he went out Shakkra was kneeling on the grass behind Aayla, washing her hair, her head a mountain of frothy suds, her shoulders and breasts gleaming with oil. He stood in a trance, remembering his steaming showers with the girls, their touch and the sensation of oil on his body.

Shakkra stood. She went for a towel, placing herself in his line of vision, helping Aayla to stand, wrapping her, helping her out, patting the girl dry, afraid to erase the oil. She pulled away the stopper, filling the tub with more rainwater, telling Cassidy to be useful and to hide his tongue in his mouth.

When he'd poured the steaming water into the tub he was ordered into the house, summarily.

Shakkra stepped from her night-shield and bolero into the water. She hadn't taken hot baths since Zach would clamp a gentle hand over her mouth so that the neighbours wouldn't come to see what was amiss.

She sank in, letting the water flood over her. Aayla sat on the edge, sprinkling oil in the water and on her shoulders. She stepped behind her best friend, filling a cupped hand with shampoo. She'd never dreamed of washing Shakkra's lustrous hair with shampoo. She'd never known shampoo and she asked if they could always wash each other's hair on the nights she stayed over.

"I would like that, little one."

She'd never seen shampoo turn into white froth. She cupped her hands, filling them with weightless suds, blowing them into the air. She wrapped her arms around her friend's shoulders. She knew to whisper. "Will we take baths together when we're gone?"

"Yes, we will. We're girlfriends, aren't we?" Shakkra twisted onto her front, crossing her arms over the rounded edge, her nose close to Aayla's so that no one would overhear. "But one day you'll marry my son, once you're ready."

"I'm ready now. I will marry him the first day we leave."

"No, little one. You won't. You're ready now because we're here on the island. Once we leave we'll have much to do. If he doesn't yet know, he will. For now his mind is full and we should be patient with him. He's doing what men twice his age cannot do. That doesn't mean we can't tease him, to relax his mind." She stretched a little to kiss her friend. "We must go to school. What you've learned from us is nothing to what you will learn. We're going to another world, one we don't know, one that doesn't know us. We'll have to learn to live with them, to understand their ways."

"Cassidy told me that you're my school."

"Yes, for now, but Jonathon went to school in a strange city, a very big school the size of our village. He spent many years doing nothing but reading and writing to learn of the world. You'll do the same, and I'll go with you. Then you'll marry Cassidy and be even lovelier than you are."

"You'll never leave me."

"Not until my time comes to once again be with Zach." She eased herself from Aayla's arms, kneeling, running her palms over the water, cupping her hands and letting the water cascade down her front. She'd never felt oil on her body.

She stood, letting Aayla wrap her and help her onto the grass. They hugged and they kissed. They went inside and ordered him outside, to clean the tub. When he came in they were dressed again in their new panties and bras, sitting together in her bedroom with the door half closed, sending a message, combing each other's hair.

The compact was a matter of some discussion, Shakkra deducing that the creamy powder couldn't be for their eyes or their mouths, so she pressed the pad against the powder, gently patting Aayla's face, smoothing away the excess with her palms. Aayla closed her eyes, paying attention in her mind to what Shakkra was doing.

Satisfied with their work the women went into the sitting area where Cassidy was talking to himself.

"That's a lot of trouble, to read a magazine."

"Sometimes you're such a wonderful boy, and such a strong man. Other times, Cassidy, I wonder why I didn't push you back into me. You say something nice, right now, before I smack you on that thick head with a spoon."

"You look wonderful."

"We know that already. Say something else, or aren't you Zach's son?"

"You glow like the sun and smell like a garden after a rain."

Shakkra grimaced. "That's so sad. Who are you? What did you do to my man's son?" She took him by the arm, pinching him. "You tell this girl she's the brightest star in the universe, too distant for a pitiful boy like you to reach. Tell her that her warm and tender body glows like the ocean at sunset and smells like the most fragrant petals you've ever held to your nose."

He had been thinking of something nice to say. He was seventeen and a simple villager. What did they expect?"

"I'm sorry. I've never seen you in my dreams this...delightful to my eyes, Aayla. You're a vision my poor eyes don't deserve." He looked to his mother. "And, Shakkra, no other woman on the island or in Miami will make me...will make me...not want to close my eyes."

The women looked at each other. Finally they shrugged and walked back into the bedroom satisfied.

When he fell asleep in his room Shakkra's lantern was burned brightly.

Fifty-One

The next morning Cassidy went into his mother's bedroom with cups of cinnamon-spiced water, a small platter of breads and his mother's home-made wild berry jam.

Shakkra was sitting on her bed sleeping, squeezed into the corner. Aayla was framed by her legs, his mother's arms wrapped around her shoulders, the teen magazine open across her lap.

He would marry Aayla one day soon, he also knew he'd never come between them.

He coughed once, twice, three times, waiting for their eyes to open, for their minds to clear.

"Good morning, ladies." He stood erect, unwavering, the tray steady in his hands. "I viewed the morning sun rise from the blue sea, its golden glow dulled by my thoughts of you; its warmth was a bitter cold when I remembered your loving embrace." He swallowed. "I'm nothing without each of you filling my heart, an empty shell on the beach."

Aayla didn't know what to think, despite knowing the words. She twisted onto her knees, straddling Shakkra, whispering. Shakkra nodded, whispering, repeating her words once. Aayla twisted back into her warmth.

"That was very nice, Cassidy. Thank you. We'll join you later, after our perfect breakfast. You can go now."

He left, grinning from ear to ear as he closed the door behind him.

When the women came out dressed in beach-shields and

boleros Cassidy sensed he was forgiven.

"Mother, Aayla, I'll be spending the afternoon away from you once we've eaten our lunch with the other's at the beach. Until we leave we shouldn't appear too distant from the village."

Shakkra nodded her agreement. "Where will you go?" She asked.

"By tonight I'll know whether or not to trust Dakota. If not, I'll win the race to the pole. If so, we'll leave this place very, very soon." He smiled. "And by the way, ladies, sometimes being in the company of such stunning women isn't easy, with or without your make-up. I'm very proud, Zach is very proud."

"You see, little heart, he's learning. He simply needed a little push. They all do from time to time."

"Do we love him?"

"I think we should."

Cassidy added, "Not having both of you here this week will give me time to think. Together you're too much for any man, but, let me tell you, the coming weeks will go by quickly if what I believe is true."

"What's that, Cassidy?" his mother asked.

"That Dakota will join with us for what he knows is right, if not as a friend."

"Once he knows what you're doing, giving him the island, saving his Xandra, he will be a good friend."

He smirked. "Or once he sees what will convince him."

Shakkra rolled her eyes. "Come, little heart. We'll swim in the sea to clean our faces before we help to prepare the midday meal." Her expression was serious, facing her son. "I will gut more than a fish if they hurt you, Cassidy. No one will stop me. No more Claytons will be slaughtered on this island."

He stood stoically until they were gone. He believed his mother.

As he flung his net each time across the water he watched Dakota from afar. Soon Dakota was eyeing him. Cassidy smiled, Dakota didn't as they cast their nets for the better part of the morning.

After lunch Dakota and Xandra spent their afternoon wading in the ocean. Cassidy spent his time watching them, choosing his words. Went the sun began to weaken Shakkra and Aayla went to the villa. Dakota went with Xandra to her hearth before walking the path to his own.

"What do you want, Cassidy? All day you have watched me like a bird of prey."

"I want to speak with you. I did not want to spoil your time with Xandra."

"Talk with me about what? When was the last time we spoke? Did we ever?"

"You are the reason we do not speak. Now we must, about Xandra."

"Do not speak of Xandra. She is nothing to you."

Cassidy looked around. They were alone, not far from the beach.

"Stop speaking like a village idiot, unless you're okay with your brother sticking his dick into her pussy in June, June 30th to be precise. But then, you'll be dead. So who cares what he does to her?"

"I will not go to the pole. Would you like to know who will?"

"Not my mother, friend, and not me a year from now, we'll be in Miami. And yes, you'll be dead. Now come with me. We have to talk. I'll show you that what I'm saying is true."

Cassidy walked onto the sand, away from the gorge, straining his ears to hear Dakota behind him. When he sat, Dakota sat with him at arm's length.

"How would you know about Miami?"

"I was there last week."

Dakota laughed hysterically, ready to stand.

"I saw your brother's silver car. I saw Forrest in her short shirt with half her ass hanging out. Not bad for a woman her age. His tee off time was ten. She went shopping. Oh, yeah, I really liked driving along A1A in Brenda's shiny new Aston Martin, especially seeing all the pretty girls."

"That isn't possible."

"Yeah, it's possible. You already believe me. Your problem is you don't know how." He looked out to sea. "So, do we talk, as friends, or do you want to drown in the ocean with Taliah when he takes you to enrol in college?"

Dakota stared at him, saying nothing.

"On the windward shore, the rocks with markings, you've seen them."

"Yeah, I've seen them. They're from the time of the ancients."

"No, not the Weatherbones, my great-grandfather made those marks as his calendar. Each one is a day of his life. It's because of him I can read and write. I saw them for the first time when I went with my father onto Tombolina through the channel."

"Tombolina's forbidden."

"So is Miami, so is the precipice behind your father's house, yet I've been to all three. I've been to his house, his pond and the pool. I've seen where your brother intends to play with Xandra and Aayla; I know that Forrest is really anxious to cover them with paint. I heard them."

"When your mother told the village you left your work to explore the forest."

He shook his head. "On the last day of The Seven Feasts and until your brother returned. I've seen your father's library and office; I've seen his computers and televisions. I've seen your brother's clothes, and Forrest's." He smirked. "I've tested her bed, Dakota, and her toilet. My bed will never be the same, or the wash tub outside. I've seen your room, your backpack and your laptop. Nice posters."

"If all this is true, you're the dead man."

"No, I'm not, because you're going to save me."

"You think so."

"I know you will. The day your father was killed you spoke with him. He told you things no one else was to know, things I also know. I've known practically since he told you. He wanted you to read his journal, to understand and have proof, but you can't because your brother threw you from your house. You were supposed to live beside him, go to school and be the so-called grand guardian with your mother's help until you're twenty-five. Guess that didn't work out for you."

"Anyone in the village could make up a story like that."

"When you're swimming with Xandra or lying with her in the sand, are you teaching her what you know?"

"Are you teaching Aayla?"

"Yes, except for what I believe is dangerous for her to know," he lied."

"It seems to me that you're dangerous to know."

Cassidy waved to his mother and Aayla walking along the water's edge. Not far from the boys they pulled away their tunics and ran into the water in their tank top and halter.

"I met a couple of girls in Miami. They wanted Shakkra and Aayla to have something nice. They're slingshots."

"I know what they are."

"What gifts have you brought for Xandra?"

"I used to bring her chocolate bars." He followed the women. "I couldn't trust her parents to see anything like that."

"Do you trust me?"

"No."

"My mother likes you. She likes Xandra."

"Joining with Aayla wouldn't be such a bad thing, but I feel no…I don't love her."

"Don't worry about it. You'll be dead and she'll be with me."

"So what can't you tell Aayla? What do you know that's so dangerous?" He snorted, showing real surprise. "You stowed away on my brother's boat."

"In the engine room."

"Somehow I don't think he'll let that happen again. Guess you can kiss off Miami. So you hid on his boat, went through his house and took a leak in his toilet. Big deal."

"I did, you didn't. That's the big deal. Why is that? He was gone for a week."

Dakota pointed to Aayla. "Her father was told to spy on me. He went everywhere I did. He does each time they're gone. They know everything I do."

"Your brother's ready to tear down the house to find what your father wrote before he died, and the letter he left for you. Your brother wants the will."

"There isn't any letter. He told me what I needed to know."

"He told me too, and yeah, there is a letter. I was in his house each night. It's pretty cold in there, though I didn't really know about televisions and computers until I met the girls in Miami. I read every word he wrote. I read the Ancestral Tomes and the Scriptures. I read the letter. I know this island is yours. So does your brother. The boat's yours, so is the helicopter. I know he'll kill you, and he'll kill Taliah. So you might want to think of a reason not to go on his boat in the next few weeks. You're screwed, Dakota, without me."

Dakota sniggered. "He's not that stupid. The journal's in the library."

"No it's not. His handwriting was hard to read. I

suppose because he was old, or nervous about being killed, which is sort of ironic. Did you know your father killed his first wife and stuck her in an oven with her lover? He threw his second into the ocean with half her head missing. Did you know his father was a Weatherbone, that he shot himself after freeing the slaves first brought here by the so-called ancients, old Charlie Weatherbone? But that before he killed himself he came here to drop his silver and ruby ring in your father's crystal pool."

"What's your point?"

"Your father's my point. I've got the journal. I've read each word and I've read the Ancestral Tomes. When I was tired from reading I would bathe in his crystal pool and the pond, you know the sacred one. Xandra's going to like being painted with something called florescent at high tide with Forrest's hands all over her. I've seen two women together. Maybe she'll forget you. And when she's finished with Xandra, he'll take her. She won't weigh a thing in the water. I guess you know that already. She might not even feel the old man fucking her." He paused. "Between us, that's something else I learned in Miami. So I know how much he's going to enjoy her." He stood. "Your brother won't find the journal, Dakota. He won't find the letter and he'll never find the ring or the keys to the boats or the safety deposit box. Now are you beginning to understand? Either way, with or without you, we're leaving the island. He can't get his hands on the will. He's tried, and he won't let you off the island. The funny thing is, he doesn't know about the spare keys. You do. But guess what."

He walked to the shoreline to kiss his mother and Aayla. Aayla waited by the water, his mother went with him to Dakota who stood to greet her.

"Dakota, everything Cassidy's told you is true. We're leaving Tombola with you, Xandra and Taliah. I want Xandra and that little girl by the water to become friends. I like you very much. I want you and this man to be friends, unless you'd rather be killed by your brother. He will kill you, Dakota, and very soon. We know that."

"Her father can't be trusted."

"But we do trust Aayla. Without her, without Cassidy, you'll never own this island. They're very important to you. Listen to him. Believe everything he tells you. Be a friend to him. He needs you to trust him. He needs a good friend. Telling your brother what you've learned won't change what will happen to you or Xandra. You already know not to trust him. Your father told you so. We know what he wrote."

He looked to Cassidy, then to Shakkra

"I've been told since I was a child that I shouldn't trust Cassidy. But I've always liked you, Shakkra. And I've always liked Aayla. So does Xandra. She avoids Aayla because of me. I'm sorry, Shakkra."

Shakkra hugged him. She kissed Cassidy and walked to Aayla. They covered themselves with their tunics and disappeared along the path to the villa.

Dakota extended his hand. "This is difficult, Cassidy. One minute I don't like you, one minute later I do. Really, I don't know what to think."

Cassidy chuckled. "Yeah, it's like totally weird, and you have to make me a solemn promise until our time comes to leave."

"What?"

"Continue not to trust me. Tell Taliah and Xandra nothing about this and keep her away from Aayla. No one must see a difference in us. Keeping our secret will keep you and your mother alive."

"You really have the journal and the Ancestral Tomes?"

"The Ancestral Tomes are diaries written by the Weatherbones. The Scriptures are scribbled on the back cover. William Weatherbone wrote them."

"When will we do all this?"

"The next time they're gone, and don't worry about the Chief Counsellor. By that time it'll be too late. Until then, Dakota, we'll meet like this on the beach at night. No one would believe you coming to our villa. I want to know more about boating and the United States. The books I've taken from your father's library over the past six months have taught me a lot. Now I want to see through your eyes what I've missed. I want to know about schools and education. I want to know everything."

"I can bring you more books."

"Does Xandra read?"

"She was learning secretly to write properly. Now her lessons will be in the sand."

"Not for long. Thank you."

"Cassidy, keys to the boat and the helicopter are hidden with the ring."

"That's right, very well hidden."

Dakota snorted. "I'll have to lie to my mother."

"Only if you tell her something that isn't true. Now I have to go. If I don't walk her home she'll cry for a week and my mother will hate me."

"Cassidy, what if he forces me to his boat before we're ready?"

"We're ready now."

"Still, it's hard to refuse a gun."

"Then we'll have to kill him first."

"Did you take one, a gun?"

"Not yet. We will the next time he's gone."

Dakota grabbed his arm. "There is one other problem, Cassidy, a very big one."

Fifty-Two

Aayla was waiting for him, placing her gifts neatly beside Shakkra's in a dresser drawer. He walked her home and kissed her goodnight far from the stoop where her father was standing. He'd scarcely see her throughout the coming week.

When he returned home Shakkra was lying across her bed, crying. He lay beside her, pulled her close with an arm tucked under her waist and fell asleep. The day or night would soon come when he wouldn't.

When he woke she hadn't moved.

"I saw Zach in my dream. He's watching over us, sweetheart."

"I know he is. Do you think I did this by myself?"

She eased away his arm, turning to sit facing him, her eyes discoloured with a night time of tears.

"I'm glad about Dakota."

"You were right about him."

"Feel my skin, sweetheart." She held out her arm. "I'm as smooth as my new clothes. I've never seen my your little heart so happy."

"When Dakota saw you I thought he eyes would fall from his head. He was doing his best not to believe me, until he saw you. By the way, mom," he winked, "you look great in green."

She smacked him.

"He's a nice boy."

"Xandra can read. When I walked with Dakota to the path he thanked me for giving her to him."

"You'll change many lives, sweetheart, including theirs. We can't leave here and forget the village."

"I have enough on my mind without thinking of them, Shakkra. We won't forget them, once we're gone. We can't do anything with them or for them while we're here. We won't forget them. I promise"

She sighed deeply. "I find myself wondering all the time, Cassidy."

"About what?"

"About him, about the man I'll meet in Miami. Zach told me the day he died that I must find someone. He knew we would leave one day. I saw his belief in his eyes. They shone with happiness for us. When I see you with Aayla I feel lonely when I'm not. When I think of other men like those in the magazines I feel guilty when I shouldn't. When I lay in bed with you I know Aayla should be curled into your arms, not me."

"Why can Aayla curl into your arms, and not me? I need my mother once in a while. Your new man will understand that. He'll understand Aayla's feelings for you, and mine. He'll understand your first guilt. Of course you should have a man of your own and if I weren't your son..."

He scrambled from her bed, shaking his head.

"Where are you going?"

"I'm going to the sea, to clear my mind of drop-dead gorgeous women."

She creased her brow. "What does that mean? Did you learn that from Cindy and Holly?"

He didn't answer. Maybe, he thought, he'd take a gun from the house and shoot himself.

That was the middle of January. By the middle of February Aayla had stayed over three Saturdays for what she now knew was Girls' Night.

Dakota and Cassidy never exchanged glances let alone smile at each other, yet twice each week they met in the shadows of the tall trees at the beach. They spoke about Christmas and Easter, Thanksgiving and New Year's. They spoke about college and careers, girls and strip clubs. Cassidy wondering why someone would pay to see naked women when women were always naked. Even Cindy and Holly were naked on the boat.

Dakota told Cassidy everything he could think of. He told him about Valentine's Day that was in two days. He never forgot and always made the day special for Xandra.

"Why?"

"It's a day for lovers. Actually it's a day for women. They pretty much expect it." He shrugged. "I love her."

"What do you do?"

"I pick flowers from the forest. It's our secret. Nobody here knows about these customs."

"Soon you'll give her chocolate."

"I hope so, Cassidy. And, by the way, I officially like you now."

They gripped hands.

"What time do they leave?" Dakota asked.

Cassidy looked at his watch. "In three hours. I'm too excited to sleep."

"I haven't been inside for seven months. I wish I could bring Xandra. What a gift that would be for Valentines, though I understand Shakkra and Aayla. They deserve to be there after all they've done."

"Once Xandra leaves here, she'll never want to come back. Not unless the resort is yours and your brother is dead or banished."

"He's not my brother. He's dead to me. I feel closer to you."

The boys choked out a laugh and ran into the sea, racing into deeper water and back, neither one winning, sprinting to the trees and back to the water, neither one faster than the other, each one collapsing, their chests heaving.

Cassidy woke with Aayla bouncing on his bum; Dakota woke with Shakkra's fingers tugging at the back of his shield. The sun was barely emerging from under the water. The dim light passing the northern tip of Tombolina was Three Fortunes, their compass heading north by northwest, their destination the marina in Miami for a Valentine's dance. They wouldn't return for five days. Cassidy needed two.

The foursome walked north along the leeward shore, wading across the mouth of the gorge onto Tombolina. At the channel the water was high. The women stripped away their tunics and swam, excited about wearing their slingshots and tops, leaving Cassidy with his hands full to follow behind with Dakota who didn't feel strange having the three with him. He felt empowered; he felt hatred towards the one who wanted him dead for the sake of resort.

He went into the house as though he'd never left.

In the kitchen he showed Shakkra how to make breakfast on the stove top. They ate French toast, crêpes with maple syrup, strawberries and whipped cream. They drank mimosas, after Dakota wished the girls Happy Valentine's and gave them flowers picked from The Grand Guardian's garden. Shakkra kissed him, so did Aayla, snubbing Cassidy with her nose in the air.

The women washed the dishes. Cassidy went first with Dakota upstairs into the study, then into the cellar under the pantry. They came out with white wine, red wine and beer as Shakkra and Aayla were finishing. Aayla asked what was on their hips. She'd seen her first real guns, disappointed that she couldn't hold one.

They went into the living room, the television coming alive. Dakota scrolled through each channel, slowly, without the sound, explaining programmes, stations, networks, movies, adult entertainment and porno, everyone turning to Aayla when she asked if she could see lesbians making love. Shakkra didn't think so.

They went to the second floor. Dakota went into Forrest's closet without the slightest hesitation. He explained that the tickets meant the clothes were never worn, the size and the cost. He gave Aayla a pair of forty-dollar panties, Shakkra's were a few dollars more. They didn't change because what little material made up their slingshots was dry, but he gave them new tee shirts and they twirled together in front of the walk-in's mirror.

Forrest would never know. And what if she did?

They went into the study. He showed them the laptops, a printer and a fax. He showed Aayla and Shakkra an e-reader and the internet. He showed them Miami and the Isle of Tombola. At noon they ate lunch, not caring they'd be missed in the field and the sea. For the first time Shakkra put pizza in an oven and Dakota opened hundred-dollar wine because Cassidy had told him that he liked the taste. They left the house by two.

They walked towards the pool, the women anxious to doff their new tops and jump in, but the men said no. They hadn't come to play, garnering a pout from Aayla and no reaction from Shakkra. She knew her son; she knew something was in store for them and wrapped an arm around her little heart.

At the dock she knew. So did Aayla who refused to step onboard. She wasn't going with them, not until Cassidy swung her over his shoulder and carried her onboard. Until then Dakota hadn't spoken a word about what was in his mind.

He knew about the chest, but not where. He never would. He knew about Jonathon, Jacob and Zach. He'd apologized to Cassidy who didn't see the need. A son should carry his father's pride, he'd told Dakota, not his shame.

He stood at the helm staring into the channel. This was the telling moment, the true test of their new friendship and mutual determination. The passing of the key went unnoticed by the women. Dakota now had a way off the island. Cassidy knew he no longer did, not without Dakota, not until his friend grinned, brought the engines to life and put an arm around his shoulders.

Aayla shrieked, hurrying to Shakkra. She never needed much of a reason. The passage through the channel was eerie, surreal, in stark contrast to the open sea. Dakota ordered them to sit. He cruised one mile at 600 rpm, letting them gaze over the transom at their prison. Once out to sea he opened the throttle, trimmed for maximum revolutions and circled the island.

As much as Cassidy had needed time alone to think, to plan, so did he.

Off the leeward shore he slowed to a stop, floating in the sea, Tombola rising from turquoise water a thousand feet away. He dropped the anchor, then the ladder. He threw over lines attached to cleats at the bow, amidships and stern. Then he plunged into the sea. Not even Cassidy thought himself that brave, following to preserve his status and soon they taunted the women together.

Aayla was the first to yank the tee shirt over her head, sliding carefully onto the gunwale and over the edge until she dropped the remaining several feet. Shakkra put her tee shirt by the ladder, testing the water one rung at a time. And soon she was diving from the transom with Aayla and the men in water deeper than she'd ever seen. They were no longer boys in her eyes. They never would be again.

Then Dakota did something they didn't expect. He climbed onboard, urging them to follow. When they did he threw a fender into the sea. Then he aimed his gun a put a hole in its centre with his first shot, explaining to Cassidy that Garrett wasn't really a problem.

Cassidy emptied his clip, and a second, missing the target completely, possibly killing a few fish he couldn't see. With the third he did more significant damage to the already dead fender and too quickly the time had come to head back.

He had one request of his friend. He wanted to see his mother and Aayla on the front deck, sipping wine and asked Dakota whether he would find sun cream somewhere onboard. Dakota said yes and they enjoyed the view on their slower than expected return to the channel.

At the house Dakota and Cassidy conspired. Cassidy had much more to learn that didn't involve his mother or Aayla. They needed time alone. They prepared a bath for Shakkra, sprinkling the water with oil, however the tub was huge and Shakkra pulled her little friend into the room before closing the door. They were girls.

Dakota laughed. He knew. Cassidy didn't. The women were having their first spa day.

With their skin pink, their faces glowing, they climbed from the tub, patting their bodies dry, slipping into the silk robes Dakota had laid out for them. Forrest wouldn't know the difference.

They ate a dinner of creamed soup, filet mignon and vegetables they'd never seen, cooked to perfection by Shakkra with Dakota's help. He told them he'd always cooked with his friend's mothers when he was away at school and wanted nothing more than to become a world-famous chef.

After dinner, Shakkra and Aayla watched a movie and sipped wine. When they left, the robes hung in the closest. At the path Dakota stayed behind. At the villa Shakkra and Aayla changed into their newest collection. They sat together flipping through Forrest's latest fashion magazine. Cassidy sat at the table reading a novel.

The four met at the ocean at predawn. They spent the morning swimming and diving into deep water, snorkelling and waterskiing. In the afternoon the women lay on the forward deck, coated with lotion, sipping soft drinks, watching the men destroy a fender, watching Cassidy learn to pilot a boat.

When they returned to Tombolina Dakota prepared a lavish meal of rôti de boeuf au jus with creamed potatoes and a twenty-year Château Pétrus. They dined by candlelight, listening to soft music, and for the first time in her life Shakkra danced.

Then Aayla wanted to dance. Cassidy stayed at the table. He'd never known of Spring Break. Now he did. Now his father's dream was real.

Fifty-Three

Four weeks went by like four years, each hour a day. On only one other occasion, when Dakota was told his brother would be gone for a few days, did they trespass onto the island he knew was rightfully his.

He'd needed no more than a minute and he was done. Then he joined them at the pool. He believed Aayla had wanted one more dip with Shakkra.

He came out with four glasses and a bottle of white wine. The women were sitting on the natural bench in water to their shoulders; Cassidy was waiting for him, sitting on the grass beside them.

When he'd poured the wine he sat with them. They'd wondered how to tell him and decided the best way was not to.

Cassidy sipped his wine, jumped into the water without saying a word and disappeared. He stayed under for a few brief moments, Shakkra and Aayla said nothing and Dakota thought his friend was a little peculiar. When he surfaced he put a bar of gold by Dakota's foot and climbed out. He'd been there the day before with his mother and Aayla. The other 199 bars, all stamped with 999.9 were well hidden in the forest near the beach.

The three raised their glasses and wished him happy birthday.

Throughout the days that remained the key to Garrett's SUV sat wedged into the bark of a palm tree inches above the gold. .

By mid-March Aayla wasn't asking Shakkra for help. She was researching words in dictionaries and writing letters to Shakkra to tell her friend what they would do together once in Miami. She was excited about hearing all the noises and seeing all the buildings. She wanted to see all the stores the way Dakota had described them and she thought Xandra should come with them.

She slipped from her bed and looked at her youngest sister. They weren't a close family and Aayla didn't think she would miss them. She knew her father believed himself better than all the villagers. Lately she would wait until they went to bed and sit by their door. She knew that he liked watching over them, his flock, that he liked being seen walking through the door of his bigger villa each morning and evening.

She knew her mother enjoyed sharing affection with younger men once each year. She was older than Shakkra by five years. She was pretty enough, but not on the inside and she wasn't kind like Shakkra because, Aayla believed, she didn't like herself or her first-mate who was much older, losing his hair and fat. He didn't share affection because he couldn't. None of the women wanted him.

And now that The Grand Guardian would be gone with Irene for eight days she thought her father would be too busy to notice she was missing. She kissed her sleeping sister goodbye. She looked in at her older sister and smiled. They seldom spoke. She passed her mother and father in the kitchen, telling them she wasn't hungry. She was going to bathe in the blue water before going to the field.

When she arrived at Shakkra's villa she went into the bedroom to undress, pulling her friend with her. She threw her tunic onto the bed. She slipped into her embroidered panties, letting Shakkra help her with the matching bra and the dress she'd never worn. She put her other gifts in

Cindy's grocery bag along with Shakkra's, accounting for each item.

She was crying. Shakkra was crying, wearing her linen shorts, top sandals and green scarf for the first time. They were leaving. Cassidy had done what he'd promised. He was taking them from Tombola.

He knocked twice, anxious to see them. He stood in the doorway feeling like a beggar before them, wishing he was wearing the designer shorts and sweater Dakota had given him. He was at that moment the happiest beggar in the world.

He knew he looked bedraggled, sleep deprived. He didn't care. He'd never been so happy to see his mother's tears. He'd just come in from the forest where he'd spent the night with Dakota digging Jonathon's strongbox from where it lay hidden for sixty-five years and carrying the gold from the pool. They barely managed to drag the chest to the tree line, causing Dakota to ask how big a man Jonathon had been.

He left the women to cry and placed the single bag by the front door, checking the time, counting each second until precisely 10:00 AM.

Fifty-Four

When they'd finished hauling the chest Cassidy showed him the journal and the Twelve Scriptures written inside the Ancestral Tomes. He gave Dakota his father's ring, shocked when his friend flung the island's one known piece of jewellery into the sea, commenting that he doubted the ocean would ever wash it clean

He gave Dakota the letter and the bank's key, leaving his friend to read his father's last words sitting alone on the chest. As much as he'd once loved his aged father, he now deeply despised the old man for the words that he wrote. He knew he could easily open the chest to read what Cassidy had read of his father's life, he didn't. He realized that what Cassidy had said was true, believing his friend's warning that he would find no joy in his father's life story.

Of greater importance was what Cassidy would do with the books and what Dakota would do with the 200 bars of gold.

Dakota went to Xandra's villa the moment he left Cassidy. He told her to kiss her parents, to say goodbye, to say she was going to the blue water to bathe before her work in the field. And she did. She was always excited to be with Dakota. Then she heard the truth and was afraid. She didn't understand what she was hearing.

She waited for him on the stoop. He walked into his villa as Taliah was preparing his morning meal, not hiding her surprise at seeing him, thinking he'd been in his room

528

ignoring her calls.

He was filthy. But more than that, she saw his eyes. Yet he didn't see her, walking past her to his room, telling her he wasn't hungry, that he'd eaten at Xandra's. He went to his dresser where he brought out gifts for Xandra that he could never give her before. He wrapped them in clothes he would wear later. He put them into a designer backpack already containing his passport and driver's permit, money clip, wallet, jewellery he'd been forbidden to wear, his laptop whose battery was dead, and his cell phone whose battery was dead. He slung the bag over his shoulder and left without saying goodbye. When he closed the door behind them, neither he nor Xandra looked back. She'd never seen such a wonderful and colourful bag.

He never saw Taliah's skin turn cold as he walked out, when she saw the gun strapped to his hip. He never heard her voice calling him through the closed door.

At Shakkra's villa he knew to walk through the doorway without knocking. Xandra was even more afraid at seeing the three standing there looking so peculiar to her. Time didn't allow for explanations. Shakkra swept the girl into her bedroom, closed the door and undressed her.

When Dakota saw her again Xandra was dressed in jean shorts and a V-neck sweater, combing her hands across her body. A silver pendant hung from her neck. And, he thought, she looked fantastic. He could scarcely believe himself what was happening.

Aayla went to her and touched her jeans, peeking under her sweater. Xandra touched her hair, turned her around once and looked under her dress.

When they stepped from the porch, walking along the path, passing villagers who sat on their stoops waiting to begin their day, they waved farewell, bright leather bags hanging from the women's shoulders. All who saw them stopped to gape, some puzzled by what they saw, others afraid. No mention was made of Irene. All but Xandra knew.

At the trees Cassidy gave Shakkra his gun. No one was to touch the box. She understood.

The moment Three Fortunes came into focus at the northern tip the two boys bolted along the beach, passing men preparing their nets. They ran through the water at the gorge and dived into the channel. They swam the full length and hurried across the garden and onto the dock. Dakota purged the bilge of stale air and fumes, Cassidy undid the figure eights wrapped around the cleats and brought in the fenders. What wasn't needed was thrown onto the dock.

The engines groaned, the dock disappeared around the corner and Dakota had the boat skimming the surface before they shot from the channel. Thirty minutes later they'd sped around the northern tip and were beached on the leeward shore. Dozens of men stood in awe, terrified by the sight of boys they knew travelling across the blue water, leaping from the strange machine and rushing to the trees, bewildered by Shakkra and the girls in such strange clothing running to the water and throwing bags onto the machine.

Cassidy and Dakota refused help, preferring to strain their muscles, or show them. Finally the strongbox and wooden crate laden with gold were loaded and secured to the inside wall of the transom. Cassidy swept Aayla to the platform, Dakota carried Xandra, both boys taking a moment to decide who was strongest, best able to lift Shakkra onto the boat. She pushed past them and climbed onboard herself.

Dakota set a course of north northwest and motored into deeper water for what he believed was the last time. Not until the island was a far off blur of greens did he push the throttle close to the red zone. They were free.

Aayla held Shakkra's hand, telling Xandra that her best

friend had another hand and wouldn't mind. The girl moved in quickly. She'd never seen white turbulent water, a boat, or felt such vibration under her feet. She'd never felt her feet in such soft sandals or felt such wind in her face if not in the midst of a hurricane.

Shakkra believed Dakota knew what he was doing, forcing from her mind that all she could see was water. Even though he didn't seem at all worried, and neither did Cassidy, she was happy to have the girls so close to her, hoping neither girl would touch her heart.

The voyage lasted five hours in the smaller boat. After four hours Dakota cut the power to idling speed. Shakkra stood, not letting go of the girls. She looked at Dakota, searching his face. He understood they were terrified by the glistening glass and steel towers rising from the sea, by gigantic cruise ships floating so close to them and the one he called a battleship.

He cruised the rest of the way at half power. When they neared the marina he spoke into the marine radio, pausing, Shakkra and the girls cowering at the roar of jet engines a mere few hundred feet over their heads, believing the jumbo jet was falling from the sky. Neither boy laughed.

Dakota docked the boat with ease, springing over the gunwale to secure his lines to the slip.

When he was done he went to the office to sign in. Aayla had never twirled so many circles in her life. Shakkra wondered what she'd done to the girls by taking them from Tombola. She looked to her son who sat on the strongbox, completely unruffled.

When Dakota returned, he believed champagne was in order. He'd made hotel reservations and dock hands would arrive soon to help carry the chest and wooden box to the SUV. The bank was expecting them.

He'd gone to the parking lot and went close enough to Three Fortunes to see his brother entertaining in his usual outlandish style. He knew his brother's habits. Garrett was the centre of attention, the centre of his own universe. He always was.

The dock hands made easy work of the two boxes, loading the back of Garrett's silver SUV. Shakkra and the girls stood staring at all the cars. She thought she'd never stop staring. She stared at the people, Aayla and Xandra stared with her at other girls in bikinis, dresses and shorts, halter tops and sunglasses.

Aayla asked Dakota and he promised he would and asked what colour. She said red, green and blue.

Shakkra was nervous. She'd never seen traffic, she'd never heard horns blaring, or car radios. Cassidy pointed to the mime, explaining that the man wasn't dead. He pointed out restaurants and stores. Dakota let him talk. He was the man of the hour. Without Cassidy he'd soon be floating in the sea.

Dakota explained parking metres. He let Xandra drop in the coins. Cassidy stayed by the vehicle watching the guards remove Dakota's wooden crate. Dakota followed them into the bank with his entourage of three. He spoke quietly with the receptionist and met privately with the manager while Aayla and Xandra looked into every corner, walking past the man with a gun, wondering why his pants were tucked into his boots, why he was wearing sunglasses when there was no sun. They asked him, their eyes practically exploding when they saw a different man walk past them man with steel legs.

Shakkra sat watching people pulling money from the wall.

When Dakota came towards her he was smiling. He sat to explain that he was the sole legal owner of the Isle of Tombola, no one else. He was also a very wealthy man apart from the gold in the pool. She hugged him, truly happy for him. He knew she was, and he wanted her to smile. He gave a cheque for four million dollars, half the value of what was found in the pool by her son. Then he was doing the hugging, sad that he'd waited so long to know her.

He'd once offered to co-sign the safety box agreement, though once hearing the procedure Shakkra had declined. She had another idea and Dakota understood.

Driving to the hotel Dakota pulled in front of a store window and parked, chuckling, explaining mannequins to the women and why they were dressed. When he came out he gave Cassidy a cell phone and a thousand dollars. He gave Aayla the red sunglasses, Shakkra the green and Xandra the blue.

He drove to the hotel, parked underground and took the elevator to the lobby with the chest on a trolley, explaining that the cars would disappear.

He was right, they did. Four mouths wide open at seeing dozens of people milling around a bright, colourful lobby, hearing the upbeat Latin tempo, not a dank garage, slamming doors and luggage wheeled across a concrete floor.

Dakota went to Reception. He wanted ocean views for both suites. Before they stepped into the elevator he told Shakkra and the girls to close their eyes, warning them not to scream. When they reached the twentieth floor they were holding their stomachs. And they did scream; when they blinked open their eyes to see themselves standing in the sky, tumbling into the corridor gasping.

The suite was larger than their villas, boasting two bedrooms, two bathrooms, one with a spa, a living room, en suite workstation and an exterior patio. Their day was over. The restaurant could wait. Dakota dialled room service once he knew what to order. They would meet for breakfast in the morning. Then he left with Xandra.

Aayla ran into the bedroom. She needed to pee. When

she came out she had chocolates in her hands. She'd found them on the bed with soft white robes. Cassidy tried the phone and the television. He opened the small door and found the minibar. Shakkra sat on the bed. She was not stepping outside, she insisted, telling Cassidy that neither was he, scolding him when he didn't listen.

When he came in he sat beside them with his cell in his hand. He was nervous. He didn't know. He trusted Dakota, but what did he know about banks. And Shakkra was right in what she believed. Zach had given them independence by teaching them to read and write. Jonathon had given them independence with what lay in the box. Why then would they now give up that independence even though Dakota had agreed to let them keep the journal for a short while?

In fact he'd suggest that Cassidy keep the journal. He would need it. His lawyer would need it. The big problem hadn't gone away. They were illegal aliens.

He dialled the one number he knew.

"Hello."

"Hello," he repeated.

"Who's this?"

"This is Cassidy. Are you Brenda?"

"Who are you again?"

"This is Cassidy. You let me ride in your new car at the marina."

"Cassidy, hi. Wow, where are you? Are you in town again?"

"Yes, I'm in town with my mother and my girlfriend. Brenda, you said once that you could help me."

"Yes. What's wrong? Is anyone hurt? Are you okay?"

"No, we're illegal aliens and our friend says a lawyer can help us."

"She coughed. "You're what?"

"We're not supposed to be here."

"Where are you?"

534

"The Skyway Resort, our suite is two zero zero five"

"Wow, not bad for a kid with no shirt. Listen, stay where are. Give me thirty, forty minutes. And don't talk with anyone."

Brenda got there in thirty.

He didn't look the same in slacks and a sweater. She shook hands with Shakkra and Aayla. She went to the balcony and stepped outside, Shakkra and Aayla with their eyes fixed on her, hoping she wouldn't fall over.

Her hair was pulled into a severe bun, red and silver earrings dangling close to her shoulders. She wore a white sleeveless vest closed with black shiny buttons, her linen pants were form-fitting and her shoes were three-inch stilettos. She was one of the women they'd seen on television and in the magazines, Aayla thought. She liked Brenda with her soft, deep voice.

She stepped in. "Wow, nice view. First off, before we get into this, your son has to work a little on his chivalry. He said you were attractive. He should have said you're absolutely gorgeous. And little Aayla here's a complete knockout." She turned to Cassidy. "You really are a lucky man. Now, tell me about this place you come from. Tell me why you're here and who brought you."

As he began room service came to the door. Aayla had ordered a cheeseburger with fries and a Coke, Cassidy a smoke meat platter and a Coke. Shakkra ordered a salad and white wine which she shared with Brenda.

Fifty-Five

Brenda listened for a couple of hours. She heard about The Seven Feasts, the Pole of Tombola, his father, the pond, the pool and first-teaching. She heard about a chest of gold. She heard why and how Cassidy had first come to Miami in January. She heard about Shakkra's pending execution, and his.

"That's some story, Cassidy. But let's get real; no one at immigration will believe you. This is Miami, kid. If I didn't know better I'd be looking for a hidden camera."

Shakkra took her by the hand, with her other she reached into the box for a gold bar.

"My son's telling the truth."

"He's also telling me that you killed your husband."

"I saved my husband, from the pain of a hundred stones. He didn't drink the opium. His mind was clear. His eyes were clear when he saw me for the last time. The son of the man who killed my husband at the pole is in the next room with his girlfriend. We escaped together. This book is the diary of Wendell Parkens; this one is the diary of the Weatherbones who came to Tombola first. Read them."

"These people next door, they're legal."

Cassidy answered. "Dakota's a US citizen, not Xandra."

"Read them, Brenda." Shakkra repeated.

She looked at each of them. She looked at her watch and went to the phone. She booked a room for the night.

"I knew there was something about you that day at the

marina, Cassidy. Do you have any money on you or just a few million in gold?"

"I have a thousand dollars from Dakota, hundred-dollar bills."

"Give me a hundred."

He did.

"Good, you've got yourself a lawyer. Stay in this room and don't talk to a single person that you don't see right now. And don't drink. You're underage. Let's start doing things right. Don't even think of going out. I'll knock on your door at eight for an in-room breakfast, invite your friends."

"You told my son you're the best lawyer in Miami."

"That's right, Shakkra, because it's true...all modesty aside. I'm also the most expensive."

Brenda went to the lobby to register and into the boutiques to buy what she would need to feel fresh the next day. In her suite she ordered a bottle of wine, a cheese plate and sat on the bed.

She finished reading Wendell Parkens' lunacy by two AM, by 7:30 she'd finished the Ancestral Tomes and couldn't believe what she read on the back cover. At 8:00 she knocked on 2005.Cassidy called Dakota in 2007; he'd barely hung up before the young man strolled in with Xandra not appearing the slightest bit out of place in the surroundings.

They ordered in. Three million was too big a tip for any housekeeping staff, she thought.

"The journal and the Weatherbone story will be locked in my office vault. Essentially, lose them and you're screwed. Excepting Dakota, you'd all have a long battle on your hands. If I hadn't read them because your mother was so compelling, if I hadn't seen the gold, I wouldn't have believed what you told me Cassidy. Now tell me why Xandra isn't mentioned anywhere?"

Dakota answered. "She isn't dangerous, which doesn't imply that one day she wouldn't be stoned. Shakkra and Cassidy were dangerous. You read the rest."

"First things first, lose your brother's car."

"It's already done, last night. I took Xandra to a sidewalk café. She has much more to learn than Shakkra and Aayla." He grinned. "I left the keys in the ignition and the windows down."

Brenda understood. No one else did.

"Your father was a frigging hundred years old. You're mother's fifty-five. What the hell's up with that?"

"I can't say more than you've read. Personally, I don't care if I ever read what he wrote. It's enough that I know, that I lived in the house."

"Why isn't Taliah here?" She's a citizen, isn't she?"

"I didn't want her with me. She'll find her own way when her time comes that doesn't include me."

"Meaning what?"

"He provided for her. She has certain proclivities which over the years helped her to stay with a wealthy old man. As Irene she wasn't permitted to mingle with the village. Personally, I wouldn't be surprised to discover that I'm not his son, but officially I am. My birth is documented."

"Boyfriends."

"Until boredom sets in." He smirked. "I know she misses the lagoon. She was a talented painter until my father couldn't get it up or didn't want to. Near the end he was content to sit and watch. That was always a point of contention between her and Forrest."

"That's sick."

"Neither woman could share affection, nor could my father or Garrett without causing jealousy. They knew the women would envy The Seven Feasts, who wouldn't? They knew what they were doing when they brought Taliah and Forrest to the island. That wasn't a random draw either."

"How old is Xandra?"

"She's eighteen, by a few days. We all are." He shrugged. "Remember The Seven Feasts?"

"Does she have proof?"

"Yes, my father kept a ledger of all births and deaths. The records are on the island. We didn't think to bring them. We had a lot on our minds, me and Cassidy."

Brenda looked to Shakkra. "Eighteen or not, she stays with you and Aayla until you leave here. We need to stay focused." She turned to Dakota. "You'll have all the time you want later for playing touch-me-touch-you. In the meantime you don't touch anything without asking me. We don't need unnecessary problems."

"She has her own room."

"The girl stays with you, Shakkra. Understood?"

Shakkra nodded, Dakota didn't.

"What about the gold?" Cassidy asked.

"We'll safeguard it in a bank. In that you'll have to trust me. I'll sign a letter and have it witnessed by the bank manager.

Breakfast came. When they'd eaten Brenda agreed that the four could shop in the hotel boutiques for proper bathing suits and go to the outside pool for an hour or two, suggesting that slingshots weren't the ideal form of discretion. They were to sit as far as possible from others and not do anything foolish. She stayed with Shakkra, making phone calls while Shakkra sat on her bed reading letters written inside Jonathon's books.

When the phone calls were finished they ordered more coffee. Shakkra stood close to the patio doors, her hand pressed over her heart hoping Brenda wouldn't be blown from the balcony into the sea. By the second cup she was sitting on the balcony, but close to the door. In her entire life she'd never sat with or spoken with a woman like Brenda.

Brenda put down her coffee. She took Shakkra's hand and together they stood by the rail, looking down little by little, seeing two guys splashing in the water with two girls, being kids for once.

At noon Aayla burst through the door with Xandra. They ran together to the balcony to tell Shakkra what they'd seen. Cassidy was almost as excited, Dakota wasn't.

"What do you mean she doesn't have more clothes?" Brenda asked.

He was more accustomed to aggressive women. His years at school had diluted his sense of island humility.

"You read the journal. Hello, tunics, shields, lots of bare ass and...."

She looked at Shakkra. "This is all you've got. You left Tombola with nothing?"

"Dakota's right. We owned nothing. We wear a simple tunic in the field and another for the evening. Under them, and for bathing in the ocean, we wear thongs."

"Just a thong."

"Yes."

She turned her attention to Dakota. "We're going shopping. He's your problem and don't bring him back looking like a freak. I don't want purple hair. I don't want baggy pants with his boxers hanging out and no geeky baseball cap. You got money?"

"Yes, a few thousand and more in the bank."

"I want him dressed for an entire week: daytime and night time and I don't go to restaurants with guys wearing shorts and sandals. Understood? Spend what you need. He's on my bill. I'll reimburse you. You're on your own unless you need a lawyer."

"I'd appreciate if you could review a few papers."

She agreed.

"Be here by six and, whatever you do, do not lose him. And stay out of bars. No drinking."

"Yes, mother."

Brenda beamed a toothy smile. She liked the kid. She liked them both.

The phone rang. Brenda answered. Moments later three armed men strode into the room, two with shotguns and one with a trolley. They were gone within fifteen minutes, leaving duplicate copies bearing Brenda's, Cassidy's and Shakkra's signatures. The gold would be delivered to the bank the next morning. Brenda phoned her bank manger to thank him and confirm the pick-up.

Cassidy and Dakota were gone five minutes later.

Brenda had already called the hotel's hair salon, and soon the four women were sitting in a row. Coiffed, with their nails painted, they went out. Brenda held Xandra's hand, Shakkra held Aayla's. At six they were finished and Shakkra looked at her new Rolex. Brenda didn't seem concerned. She could scarcely believe her day. Who'd believe her? She didn't believe herself. Aayla and Xandra were eying all the people lounging with drinks and hors d'oeuvres along the sidewalk.

She had been right about Cassidy and, she thought, he'd been right about Shakkra. She thought they could be good friends.

She said, "The boys can wait. They know I'll hurt them if they screw up. We look too fantastic not to be seen. Right, girls?"

Aayla was the first to agree and pulled Shakkra to the first empty table.

Brenda signalled the waitress. She and Shakkra sipped white wine, the girls had tall lemonades. Girls never went straight home after shopping, Brenda advised, and they certainly never stripped to their panties to try on clothes in the middle of a busy store. That fact was very important to remember. Naked on a balcony or topless on a beach, that was fine, never in a store, never.

What on earth had she taken on, she wondered?

They arrived at the hotel near seven-thirty. They phoned Dakota's room to let the boys know, inviting them for 8:30, expecting to see them properly attired. They would be dining in the hotel's main dining room.

Neither girl liked bras, they decided, even the fancy ones, or shoes. Shakkra liked the look of both, not the feel. Brenda dressed in another pantsuit and new heels. Shakkra wore sandals with a slight heel, a short sleeveless dress and shawl. Aayla was in flat sandals, a sequined tee shirt and designer shorts. Xandra wore the same in different colours. Shakkra and the girls carried their new handbags and their sunglasses as impromptu barrettes, copying Brenda. Aayla had spent her first five dollars on lip gloss for Shakkra; unaware Brenda had made up the forty-dollar difference, choosing less expensive brands for Aayla and Xandra.

The boys were equally elegant in soft-soled shoes, linen pants and polo shirts tucked under belts made from Italian leather. Brenda patted their heads. She approved.

She and Shakkra selected baked salmon with rice and vegetables. The white Bordeaux was crisp and clear. Aayla and Xandra tried fettuccini Alfredo and drank club soda with lemon slices. Cassidy and Dakota went with hamburgers and onion rings, Brenda not disagreeing when Dakota pointed out that Florida's drinking laws were prehistoric, as he drank his ice tea. Cassidy stayed with Coke.

Brenda went home exhausted after reserving a larger vehicle with the hotel concierge for the next morning. At her door Shakkra invited Dakota and her son to spend some alone time with her girls, and maybe have a little wine, not much. She was going to bed. She wanted to read more letters in the books she'd taken from the chest.

She heard the outer door open and close. She heard whispered giggles and soon she saw the light across the bottom of her door go out. She turned out her light and squirmed into the soft mattress and duvet, nestling her head into downy pillows, burying herself to her chin.

She'd just drifted off when the door handle clicked, toes hurried across the carpeted floor, one side of the duvet lifting inch by inch, then the other, two warm bodies soon framing her in place.

Fifty-Six

"Dakota, these papers are legal and binding, all from the State of Florida. You own the island, the helicopter and Three Fortunes. Simply put: Your brother's piloting your boat. You own the house and you own the opium under the kitchen. That's not so good. So this morning I want you to stay here and think about what we can do about that. I don't mean play house. I have some ideas but I want to hear your input. It's your island. Do you know what stay here means?"

She waited.

"Yes, mother."

"Yeah, it means do not go out, or do I have to take Xandra with us."

"No."

"Xandra, you heard me?"

The girl nodded.

"Do you know what play house means?"

She shook her head.

"Good, that's settled. You're coming with us."

She pinched Dakota's cheeks, walking to catch up with her clients and the girls who were too busy chattering to be confused.

By eleven the gold was safeguarded along with a cheque made payable to Shakkra and Cassidy Clayton. Cassidy had more signed documents and a look of amazement on his face he couldn't disguise. Shakkra hadn't told him.

544

By twelve they were doing lunch on the patio by the pool.

"So, Dakota, what's your take on these missing papers? What do we do about them, any ideas?"

"I'm not sure, possibly. One of Cassidy's jackets will be ready in a few hours. I thought I'd discuss my plan with him first. If he doesn't agree, then you won't."

"Is that some sort of Tombolaese for you're taking off for a while?"

"I'm a citizen, remember."

She faced Cassidy. "Be back by four. You keep looking at your daddy's fancy watch. I'm too young and beautiful to die from a heart attack. Don't even think of giving me one."

They went. Outside on the curb Cassidy stopped him.

"Dakota, the four million...why?"

"Xandra, why do you think? I didn't know and you didn't have to tell me. You didn't need me. That Coast Guard plan you had with the EPIRBs..." He put his thumb into the air. "I've been in that pool a hundred times. Anyway you need it more than me. I've only got one woman."

"And a friend."

"Am I going to cry, or what?"

"You lied. There is no jacket."

"We'll get you one later. They don't have to know everything." He reached into his pocket. "She wouldn't understand. Without the documents for the boat, I won't get the ones for the helicopter. He's going back in six days. There's no time, not once he discovers I'm gone and who's with me. I know him. He'd have armed guards posted. Right now he'll be at South Beach soaking up teenage tits and ass, and she'll be right beside him. Believe me." He glanced around. "She said four. I'll meet you here then, with a jacket."

"You're going to the boat?"

"Yeah, I don't have a choice."

"Then you're returning to the island."

"Tomorrow morning and she won't know until I'm gone. I need those papers. I need proof of Xandra's birth. I'll be back before dinner."

"She'll be pissed with us. She and Shakkra aren't good together when we're their victims."

"Cassidy, this is dangerous. Tombola's my problem, so is Garrett. I'll be here at four."

"Three Claytons died on Tombola, and two of their women. The more I defy your brother, the more I revere them. We're wasting time."

The cab ride lasted an hour. Dakota flashed his marina card to the attendant. They were driven to the far end of the parking lot where they climbed out.

Three Fortunes lay along the length of her slip. They watched for almost an hour and saw nothing, Dakota commenting that his brother's memory card must be almost full. They went down the steps, Cassidy hoping not to meet Cindy or Holly. He'd told his friend about the girls in a heated moment, being snide. Perhaps one day he'd tell Dakota the details, though he saw no immediate need.

Three Fortunes was tied with its stern to the dock. They all were, though several nearby slips were vacant. Not a soul was onboard. The boys were inside the cabin within seconds. They found the black corporate document kit in the main stateroom, exiting through the entertainment centre, the galley and up the steps to the afterdeck. Dakota reached into fridge, grabbing a six pack that his brother would notice was missing, stepping from the transom with pride of ownership.

They went to the pool to see what they could see, the female contingent either under ten or over sixty. The others were at the beach. They went to the marina's chandler where Dakota bought foam sleeves for the beers and hailed a cab. They climbed out at South Beach where they stayed until they ran out of beer and time.

At the hotel they stood at the door. They were prepared, fortified by each other's bravado.

Brenda didn't say 'hi guys' or 'glad you're back'. She said "where's the jacket?"

"Cassidy decided he didn't like the style."

"What's that?" Brenda demanded, pointing.

He straightened. The mood in the room quietened. His woman was watching him, Aayla was watching Cassidy. Shakkra was standing by Brenda with her eyes drilling into Cassidy's. He knew not to look at Cassidy, a definite sign of weakness. He gave Brenda his full attention. She wouldn't be easy to go up against.

"Three Fortunes' complete documentation."

She didn't hesitate. "You are a complete idiot."

"Yes, I know."

"And you went with him?"

"Yes, I'm also an idiot," Cassidy answered.

She smelled one boy's breath, then the other's. Shakkra wasn't interfering. Too much was at stake. Nevertheless, Cassidy felt her dark eyes.

"How was South Beach? See anything nicer than what's in this room right now?"

"We wanted to give you quality time together, perhaps to teach them something. We used the afternoon to formulate a plan. And, no, we don't need the company of women any lovelier than what we see here. "

"Puke. Do I look like a frigging teacher?"

"On Tombola there's no word for puke."

"No puke and two idiot kids."

He grinned. "Now there's neither."

"No one saw you, Cassidy?" his mother asked.

"No one did, but Dakota has a good plan that I agree with. Brenda will also."

Brenda said. "Why don't we let Brenda decide whether or not Brenda will?"

They were told to sit on the sofa. They did. The girls were put onto the balcony and told by Shakkra not to look over. They didn't, sitting with their legs crossed under, gazing at the city and ocean through their new sunglass, sipping lemonade through straws.

Thinking she wouldn't, thinking she'd like to give them a sound lecture instead, Brenda did agree with the plan. She just didn't say so. She needed confirmation from someone who knew more than she did about incursion, killing and getting out alive. The one aspect of their blueprint she didn't like at the moment involved the girls who Shakkra hadn't stopped monitoring.

Most of what Dakota said made sense. Coming to Miami they'd been at the mercy of Garrett Parkens' timetable, Spring Break a virtual given. But Dakota couldn't be certain of the will, the island and his father's fortune until he'd made good his escape, which he couldn't do without Cassidy who essentially held the keys for the door through which they did escape.

His father was insane and his brother displayed definite signs of the family trait. So maybe he was a bastard, he joked. He had to be certain. Now he was

He didn't care about Tombola, the boat or the helicopter. He was wealthy, but he did want Xandra. All he ever wanted was Xandra and for that reason he would return to Tombola the next day. He hadn't thought of his father's register. He should have when he'd spoken with Cassidy the first time, however that night the air was either cold or hot depending on one's perspective. What was done was done. And he knew where the register was kept.

Also, just to clarify his and Cassidy's weak position, he insisted, if they hadn't gone to the boat that afternoon he'd have no future opportunity to take the documentation that was rightfully his. Now the helicopter was a simple matter. He would hire a pilot who would go with him to Tombola and fly the thing to Miami.

He'd have all that was his, including proof of Xandra, Aayla, Shakkra and a good friend who hadn't been afraid to be an idiot alongside him. Nor had he forgotten the other six hundred left behind.

His brother would return to Tombola in six days when he would discover the escape, and his ruin. And he would discover much more, including that Three Fortunes had been stolen and that Garret himself was the thief.

He believed there was no danger in his plan, other than for Garrett Parkens and the would-be Irene.

"You believe there's no danger. That's nice."

"Yes, I do."

"Okay, let's get back to the idiot syndrome while it's fresh in your mind. You really think I'm letting these ladies go back to that freak house with you?"

"I didn't say anything about them, or you. That's my boat, that's my island. I'm going. You're their lawyer, not mine."

He slouched to one side. He shoved a hand into a pocket. He brought out a money clip and counted a thousand dollars and stood, placing the bills on the coffee table. Cassidy stood with him, comrades-in-arms.

"Consider yourself paid in full for services rendered."

She took the ten bills.

"Like I said, you're an idiot, albeit a cute one. I wasn't going to charge you. Thanks. Keep blowing your cash like this and you'll be back on that island in a tunic, up to your tight ass in dirt." She turned to Shakkra. "Is he always this temperamental?"

"He's a man, Brenda. Even Zach was an idiot at times. We shouldn't be surprised."

The girls giggled. Girls would be girls.

Brenda pulled him closer by his belt. She pushed the money into pocket and pushed him onto the sofa.

"Sit your ass down, and don't say a word." She thrust out a finger to Cassidy. "You, idiot number two, you sit with him."

She paced the room.

Shakkra said, "I will go with them, if the girls can stay here with you."

"You're not going anywhere, neither are they." She thought for a moment. "Shakkra, stay here with them. I have to make a call. Don't let them talk, not one word. If they do, beat their heads together until they're unconscious."

She went into Shakkra's bedroom with her cell. Xandra and Aayla came in, going to Shakkra who put a finger to her lips. She sat between them, all three appearing superior, Cassidy and Dakota not so much. Half an hour later Brenda emerged. She went to Dakota, leaning over him, smiling.

"Close your eyes." He did. "Now, think real hard about where you left your brain." She grabbed his hair, nodding his head for him. "Have you found it?"

"Yes, I've found it."

"Can you trust it?"

"Yes."

"Good, then take these ladies and your idiot friend downstairs to dinner. Be back in this suite in two hours and don't leave the hotel grounds." She eyed the girls and Shakkra. "Okay, there's a Mariachi band tonight, four hours." She pulled him to his feet. "Don't disappoint me, hombre, four hours."

She left them, talking first with Shakkra in private. She went to her apartment to soak in her tub, to change for dinner and meet a friend. Brenda Wilson never did anything in halves. Everything in her life was all or nothing, with friends and with associates. She was well-placed. When clients met her for the first time they knew not to ask how much, they didn't have to. Brenda didn't know any low-lifes, unless they were filthy rich.

Her work-related list of friends was endless. Outside the office she had one friend: Bill Stone, federal cop and confidant. And, boy, did she have a lot to confide.

Stone didn't get off on flashy gold shields and blue jackets with big yellow letters. He never wore them and didn't particularly like those who did. He wore black leather pants and black tee shirts under a black leather jacket he seldom removed. He was dark, sombre and never smiled. Not since his wife passed away without warning from a gunshot to the head.

He was clean-shaven and big. He carried a chrome-plated Berretta under his arm. He had one on his ankle, another in his car, though what he prized most was the ten-inch pearl handled stiletto: a gift from his once lovely wife.

He knew the worst elements of Miami and lived most days on the worst side. He cared nothing about them, other than shutting them down one by one, getting them off the streets. He had no friends other than whores, pimps and drug dealers who didn't know him beyond his façade. Friends were a liability.

Wilson was an exception. She put the guy who ordered the killing behind bars for life with no chance of parole, after Stone had taken care of the shooter.

He was a man content with loneliness. His voice never changed, not even with her. He was Bill Stone. Take him or leave him. Wilson took him. They met for dinner one night a month, never at Christmas, never on any occasion that brought back memories. He always brought a gift, something small. What could he offer a woman who had the world in her hands?

She chortled. He'd always dreamed of living alone on a sun-filled island with his wife. This, he would not believe.

Stone was already seated at the table to greet her. He stood, stooped over her, hugging her as a bear would and sat down. His shirt was starched and black, his unbuttoned blazer snow white against his tanned face and hands, accented with a black hanky. She knew the Berretta was there.

He drank bourbon straight up; she drank vodka on the rocks. He slid the box across the table, not one for showy presentation. The bracelet was silver, a week before her birthday. Wilson was engraved across the front. She stood from her seat and kissed his cheek. She always kissed him.

For dinner he ordered a glass of Chardonnay for her, ruby red Bordeaux for himself. He never smiled and she wondered whether he ever would. She didn't think so. He didn't have a death wish; she knew that much about him. Neither would he avoid the occasion, she believed.

They sat together for three hours. Stone listened intently. With anyone else he would have laughed and left before finishing his first glass. So many things in life weren't his problem anymore. But this was Wilson.

He signed the chit. She knew not to argue. In return the next meal together would be at her condo. He always brought a rented video, and flowers. They never listened to music. They never danced or sat too close together. He knew the dangers of being close. He pulled out her seat and hugged her. They left the restaurant arm in arm. She knew better than to pout like a spoiled girl used to getting her own way. She wasn't going with them. Deal with it, Wilson.

He nodded, opened the door of her car. She smiled, he didn't. Nothing was left to say.

He went home to change, to grease his hair. A deal was going down. The morning papers would report the names of the two men killed, the one arrested and the one who was seriously wounded, shot by one of his own at close range. That much the reporter didn't know.

Fifty-Seven

Brenda called Shakkra from the lobby, asking for an up-date. The girls were fine. The boys were with them and behaving properly. Could they be trusted alone, Brenda asked. Shakkra said yes and left them to join Brenda for a nightcap.

"Dakota's plan, Shakkra, is absolutely ridiculous. Say the word and Cassidy stays here. I can have him arrested. No problem. He'd be out whenever you want him back."

"I believe his plan will work, Brenda. I know the island. I know Garrett Parkens."

Brenda sipped her vodka. "Yeah, so do I think it's workable. So does my friend. That doesn't mean it's not completely stupid for a couple of teenagers."

"They aren't like other boys you know, Brenda. Who do you know who has lived their lives?"

Brenda agreed. "No one. I just don't want you to lose a son."

"I won't. They're going, Brenda. We can't stop them."

"I know they are, but they're not going alone. Before I let them go I wanted to be certain of you. We're leaving here tonight, you, me and the girls. They boys…the men, are staying. But I'll have to speak with them before we go."

"To what place are we going?"

"To my condo, to where I live. You'll be fine. I'll advise the doorman and security. Hey, we're talking spa, outdoor pool, a killer view from a huge patio for you topless types.

Something I'll have to try sometime. I've been a little me deprived lately, like for all my life since law school." She chuckled. "I must have the whitest breasts in Miami. Someone should enjoy the good life, why not you?"

"Will you stay with us?"

"Apparently so. Some men are just so into this guy stuff. They can be so damned protective."

Shakkra smiled, putting a hand over Brenda's. "We'll enjoy the day together. The girls like you. They will like being at the pool."

"They're adorable."

"Thank you, Brenda." Shakkra paused. "Brenda, I must ask. How much will you cost? My son and Aayla will need money for school and a home. What will remain after you, after all these clothes and our jewellery? He doesn't say so, however he's worried. I share his worry."

She chuckled. "Don't. You've got over seven million and I'm doing you pro bono. My ex married me for all the wrong reasons. Or I married him for all the right reasons. Either way I don't need your money. I need a life."

"I don't understand."

"Then we'll do this again sometime. Somehow I think we'll be doing this a lot. But, right now, let's go talk to your daring duo."

In the suite Brenda spoke straight-talk to Cassidy and Dakota. She wasn't smiling and she wasn't pinching cheeks.

"I did like your plan, guys. I just couldn't say so. I wasn't sure. What I did know was that these women weren't going with you. And now that you are going, if you screw up in anyway, you won't see them again. So don't. To that end you're going to have company. That's right, company, big company who doesn't like children playing hero. He's the hero, not you. So when he says jump that's what you do. His name's Bill Stone and don't piss him off."

"We don't want strangers hanging around. We want to get onto Tombolina and off, fast."

"He's twice your size, twice as limber and when you might be trying to shoot at someone from behind a tree half a mile away, he'll put a bullet in this Garrett's eye. Like I said, don't piss him off. He'll be in the lobby at 8:00. You be there before him."

"What did you say with my mother?" Cassidy asked.

"Why is that your business? We're getting to know each other and if you're asking if she's on my side, she is. Just like you were on Dakota's side on South Beach." She shook her head. "That was so pitiful."

"What are they doing?" Dakota asked, watching the girls and Shakkra busying themselves in the bedroom.

"They're leaving with me. I'm taking a few days of well-deserved vacation." She stood. "We're also taking your luggage with us." She patted her hands together. "So let's not keep the ladies waiting. Go, go. And pack what you've got on. Keep only what you'll wear tomorrow. And make sure you check out before you meet Stone."

Dakota looked to Cassidy. "This guy Stone, he probably wants to get away from her as much as we do." He glanced at Brenda. "Who says any of us will come back...mom?"

She yanked him onto his feet, swinging him around, smacking his ass and pushing him to the door.

"Those gorgeous girls you brought with you, that's who. Not that they'd be lonely for long, not in this town. So do what you're told, and you will come back. By the way, smart guy, Stone, he's ex-marine and an excellent helicopter pilot. He doesn't need this in his life. He doesn't need you. Anything else you want to add?"

He didn't think so, and neither did she.

They were back in twenty minutes, dressed in fleecy robes. If Cassidy thought leaving his mother the first time was difficult with Aayla asleep in his mother's bed, this was near impossible. Xandra was no better. Dakota had thought that she'd want her parents to come back with them. She didn't. She said not a word about them, saying much more with her silence.

The women were packed, dressed as though for a night on the town. Shakkra had never hugged her son as close. Aayla had never loved him as much. Dakota and Xandra held each other in a far corner, exchanging whispers, wiping tears.

Brenda stepped outside, she couldn't take the emotion. She really, really needed a life. She needed a man. She wanted a man, one she already loved.

Most eighteen-year-olds were at South Beach, hammered, having sex with brain-dead girls they didn't know or wouldn't know for much longer. These guys were about to invade and liberate an island. What the hell did she get Stone involved with, she thought? He had enough on his mind. Then the door opened, about as wide as her mouth.

Dakota and Cassidy didn't bother asking Shakkra or the girls. They already understood the arithmetic. Four against two was problematic. They kissed their women goodnight, hugging them. They were confident. This was no time for doubt, misgivings or permission. They yanked away their robes before stepping into the hallway, proudly sporting new, bright red and yellow thongs, the robes draped over their arms.

They each hugged Brenda in turn, squeezing her close and pinching her cheeks before parading the thirty feet to their door. Shakkra and the girls stood at the door, their faces lit with laughter.

Fifty-Eight

The next morning Brenda's kitchen was alive with red, blue, green and mauve silk. The girls wanted to try yogurt, Shakkra was too nervous to eat. She sipped her coffee and shared the morning paper with her hostess.

She asked Brenda about the shooting, the front page reporting two men killed, one arrested and one taken to hospital with serious injuries. She asked why.

Brenda leaned over. She read the first few lines. Her skin crawled with cold. She knew the code name. She couldn't call the hospital. She wasn't supposed to know his dark side. He operated deep undercover. She ran to her phone. She called the hotel, suite 2007. The boys had checked out. Her watch showed 9:00 AM. She had them paged in the lobby and the restaurant. They were gone. She phoned the marina. Legality was gone. She slumped into her chair, staring at the front page. She knew better. She did know better.

If her boat was gone, he must be onboard. The boys would have taken their own, or phoned her. That bastard, she thought aloud, if he didn't call her anytime soon she'd kill him.

Dakota assured Stone that Garrett never walked the docks to see the see the smaller boats, he wanted to be noticed on his. The launch wouldn't be noticed. Even so, Stone wanted to see Three Fortunes and Parkens if he was onboard. He wanted to see what he was up against. He wasn't onboard, the woman was. Stone walked a few feet farther, turning, unsmiling, ignoring the woman's wide smile.

Legality left the pleasure harbour at 8:45. She was bigger and faster than the launch, not as heavy or burdened as Three Fortunes.

Wilson had told him everything he had to know, from her perspective. Now what he wanted was the boys' perspective, the concise version. He listened intently, interrupting to ask a question when he thought he'd missed something. Wilson had also told him their story was way beyond believable, and true.

Dakota asked what was in the bag. Stone kept his eyes on the open sea. He loved the sea. The sea was cleansing.

In the bag were a professional video camera, his Berettas, a semi-automatic, ten spare magazines, five grenades, a kilo of plastique and an ER kit in case either or both of the boys got shot.

He didn't smile then, nor did he smile when Dakota opened his own bag. Stone asked to see the gun, and Cassidy's. They were nice. He liked the pieces, he said. Glocks. He tossed them into ocean and ordered the boys into the cabin. ETA: two hours.

He wanted a schematic of the island. He wanted to know where the channels were situated, the gorge, the house and the chopper. He wanted to know about Tombola, the location of the village, the paths to the beach, the habits of the people, who they would see, who would see them, what was off the leeward shore, what was off the windward. Who had guns, and who didn't? Who was hostile, and who wasn't?

Cassidy responded that no one on the island was hostile. Stone asked them why he'd just tossed their weapons overboard. The boys came up an hour later. Dakota took the helm. Stone sat with Cassidy, expecting specific answers to specific questions. He didn't want conjecture. He wanted facts.

They would take the extra thirty minutes and go in through the channel on the eastern shore, the windward side. He didn't like being the centre of attention. North of the gorge or not, anyone on the leeward beach would see them. He wasn't in the business of being seen. No marine ever went on a mission wearing orange camouflage or holding a spotlight.

Dakota piloted into the channel. Stone was on the forward deck, kneeling, the semi-automatic resting on his leg. Dakota cut the engines at 1220 hours precisely. They would be gone at 1520 hours. They understood he wasn't asking.

Brenda was right. He was big, and he wasn't dressed for a day in the sun.

They went first to the house. Stone did a fast run through, making certain. They took him to the top of the precipice, where he videoed Tombolina and the chopper, the pool and the pond where The Grand Guardians past and present raped innocent island girls. He videoed the length and breadth of Tombola, the village, zooming in on men working in the field. He wasn't done.

In the house they went to the library. Dakota found the registry. Cassidy took back each of Jon Clayton's books. Each man took a ladder, searching the shelves spine by spine for anything that didn't resemble a published work. They found nothing pertinent.

Then Cassidy showed them the cabinets and the albums of girls in the pond, girls being painted by Irenes past and present and photo albums, enlargements of the prettiest of the girls who'd gone to the pond. Cassidy asked a favour of Stone. The man nodded and left the kid alone. Shakkra's son knew exactly where to look.

From the study he and Dakota took the computers. From

the bedroom and living room they took adult magazines, CDs and DVDs, more vivid memories of The Seven Feasts.

Dakota showed him under the pantry floor, and the closet with wall to wall, floor to ceiling weaponry, small calibre and large, eighteen handguns, scoped rifles and semi-automatics. He asked Dakota when the revolt was expected. He videoed the cache. He'd videoed every room and the gaudy façade, everything except the opium room.

The time was 1350 hours. The team was assembled outside. By 1400 hours Legality was loaded with the cargo.

They jogged through the garden, waded into the lagoon and through waist-high water in the channel. They jogged to the gorge onto Tombola, Stone stopping abruptly at seeing the pole.

"That's it, that's the pole?"

"The Pole of Tombola, yes."

"Holy shit."

He ran to the bridge, videoed the arch, the pole and the hundred and one stones.

"Wilson told me. Your old man had guts, kid. You had guts to do what you did, and your mom. Wilson says she quite a lady."

"She'll be a lady very soon, like Brenda. She's beautiful."

"Yeah, so I hear."

"Why do you call her Wilson?"

He didn't respond.

Cassidy looked to the top of the pole. "My dream was to light it like a candle and watch it burn all night. A lot of ghosts are swimming in the gorge, innocent ghosts."

Stone tapped his watch. "Ghosts don't care about timing, kid. You want your old man to see you do something good, you get me to the village."

The time was 1412 hours. One hour, eight minutes remained.

They jogged along the leeward shore, close to the trees. Women were in the ocean cleaning blood from their bodies, naked but for the shields covering their pubes. More were at the tables, others sat in the shade mending nets. They were all naked, all of them terrified.

Dakota spoke with them. Stone stepped back with Cassidy, the video camera recording Dakota talking, the naked bodies, the frightened eyes and the women in the sea, the blood and fish on the tables.

The women followed the three men to the village, from a safe distance. Stone's trigger finger was frozen in place, not missing a single step. Wilson wanted footage, she wanted proof. She had it.

He saw men stooped in the field through one eye and the viewfinder. He saw rows of small villas constructed from a simple design. He saw two that were larger. He saw the man standing on the stoop. He recorded Cassidy speaking with the man.

"Your daughter is safe, if you care to know. Is that what you're looking for from your pedestal?"

"Where is she?"

Stone cleared his throat, loudly.

"She's two places at once. She's with people who love her. And she's away from those who don't."

Cassidy turned his back on the man, pointing to another villa, where Garrett Parkens once lived.

Dakota spoke. He had one request. He asked that Stone not make him beg.

Stone understood. The kid wasn't bad. Neither kid was. They had balls. Anyone who could stand their ground against Wilson had balls. He gave Dakota his gun belt, reminding him that in his other hand he held a semi-automatic, warning him not to get too nervous. He wasn't smiling.

Taliah came onto her porch. She'd heard the ruckus.

"Dakota what is this? Where have you been and who is this man? None are allowed on Tombola."

"We've come for proof, Taliah. Parkens will soon be destroyed. The Isle of Tombola is no longer, not for you anyway. This island is now mine. What Wendell left you is sufficient for you to live well, once you're taken from here. You don't have long to wait. So be ready. You're no longer welcome on my island and if you dare to enter Tombolina before or after my return I won't bother to collect my inheritance from your estate. Do you understand, Taliah?"

He put his hand on the butt of Stone's weapon.

"You would kill your mother?"

"I would kill a fornicating whore and murderer. How many nights did you sit with him to decide who would die? Yes, I would kill you with a single stone flung with all the love I feel for you. Now step aside."

He walked past her, guiding Stone through the villa. They left and went to Cassidy's, videoing the front, the back and the enclosure. He captured the tub and the small bathroom with the coarse wooden seat, he videoed Cassidy's bed, Shakkra's room, the sitting room and the kitchen.

Stone's watch showed 1450 hours. They left, jogging. The entire village had stopped their work to see them. None understood.

At the gorge Stone took back his gun. Dakota was grinning from ear to ear. All that was left for Stone to do was to inspect the helicopter and fly home. A curt order hurled Cassidy into reality. He took a final look at the pole and ran with them.

At the helipad Stone did what he had to do. Everything was in order. The chopper was flight worthy; fuelled and all required documentation was onboard. He shook hands with Cassidy, ordering him to board Legality. He shook hands with Dakota, telling the young man what he expected.

562

When Legality was through the channel, in open water, they saw the helicopter, a speck hovering over the island.

Stone hadn't liked what he'd seen in Taliah's eyes. He knew about deceit and treachery. He knew about venomous hate. The kid would never know to beware of her. Even if he was to believe what Stone would say, he'd believe himself invincible and over time he'd forget. Then he'd be killed. The helicopter landed in front of her villa, the rotors whirring, trees bending, villagers running for their lives.

He went into her house, the semi-automatic in one hand, the Berretta in the other. Taliah was defiant. He had no time for bravado. He shot her once in the forehead and left. His ascent was vertical, high above Tombolina, facing the gorge. He wanted the entire village to see, not to frighten them, to make them wonder. Legality was little more than a white streak on a turquoise canvas.

Dakota beached her, her bow nestled into the sand. Stone landed beside her.

He had equipment in one hand, the camera in the other, the semi-automatic slung over his shoulder. He threw out a finger, pointing directly at Cassidy. Dakota shoved his friend off the boat. Stone was jogging to the pole. Cassidy didn't know. He looked back. Dakota was yelling at him to follow, waving him away. Telling him to frigging hurry. Dakota checked his watch: 1515.

"Kid we can't put a torch to this thing and we can't stay all night to watch. But we can sure as hell blow the shit out of it. This stuff's plastique, more than enough for the job but let's do it right for your old man. This is how it plays out. I do the work, you watch. Then I video you by the pole, as though you've just finished. This is a fuse. It stays lit under water. We don't need it but it'll look cool for your mom. You'll light the fuse then you'll run like hell to the boat with your hands hard against your ears. Don't, and you'll never hear another word in your lifetime. No

563

heroics."

"Stone, thank you. This was my dream."

"Yeah, my dream's to get out of here. Let's kiss each other another time."

Stone wrapped the entire pole at the waterline. He stepped back videoing Cassidy repeating the final step, looking pleased. Stone ran. He inserted the detonator, warning Cassidy to look good, not stupid. Don't touch! He ran to the camera. Cassidy did fine. Stone ran again. He connected the fuse and ran to the helicopter with the camera.

Cassidy lit the fuse. He stood there amazed. Stone emptied a magazine into the air, breaking the kid's trance. Cassidy ran faster than he ever had. Stone recorded every step until the Pole of Tombola launched into the air between the towering precipices, ricocheting from one wall to another, splintering apart, crashing onto the bridge. He recorded Cassidy flying; he recorded Dakota running to haul his sprawled friend from the ground.

The time was 1520. Mission accomplished. Cassidy had the proof in his hands.

Stone hovered to the portside of Legality several miles offshore, counting each weapon held high for him to see, each tossed into the sea. He waved. He doubted he would ever see them again, despite wanting to visit the Isle of Tombola once more.

When Legality cruised to her slip four hours later Brenda's arms were wrapped tightly around Xandra, Shakkra's around Aayla. Stone had called them from the airport three hours earlier. Apparently he was in deep shit for making her wonder all day whether he was alive or dead in some hospital bed.

She had the footage she needed, he told her, including the kid hero who, by himself, took down the Pole of Tombola. His mother should be proud. That said; he did have one small favour. He needed Legality for some personal time. He had to stay off the streets for a few days.

She asked why.

He said, "I need to remember how to smile, Wilson. And, by the way, ask the kid how much he wants for the bird."

Fifty-Nine

That night the boys could do no wrong. They'd come back with the proof Brenda needed.

They were heroes, Aayla and Xandra dressing appropriately with Shakkra's and Brenda's help. Brenda even went so far as to knowingly break the law. She ordered pizza. And what went best with pizza, her best wine."

Stone turned down the invitation. He wasn't much into tears and hugs. Not anymore. However he was with them all the same. The boys didn't stop talking about him, though they didn't say a word about Taliah or the Chief Counsellor. Neither had Stone.

Aayla sat with her man, her hero, Xandra with hers. Shakkra sat quietly with Brenda. They liked each other and Shakkra knew Aayla wasn't jealous. She was Aayla's best friend; Xandra was a new friend. She knew Shakkra needed a woman her own age, a woman who understood more than a teenage girl. And at the moment, so did Brenda. She was afraid.

Stone never took personal time.

The girls slept in her bed that night, the boys crashed in the spare room where the girls had slept the night before. Shakkra and Brenda sat on the sofa sipping wine, talking about Stone. Brenda hoping he wasn't doing anything stupid. She knew he had the key to Three Fortunes.

Shakkra's advice was simple: "Why don't you just tell the foolish man?"

She couldn't.

And he wouldn't. Why? To get her killed one day? Not a chance. Dinner once a month was fine with him. She deserved better, not some guy who slept with a gun strapped to his chest instead of her.

The dock crew knew to allow him. Legality was fuelled, ready for the next morning and docked for the night behind Three Fortunes.

Stone spent much of the evening plugged into his Walkman, the eavesdropping equipment concealed in the cabin. He heard every word they spoke. They were going out to get some later in the evening, just not with each other. Sick fucks.

When they left, so did he. He crossed the dock to Three Fortunes. He wasn't worried. His hand-held device was tracking their rental. He cracked open a beer on the house, went through each drawer, each cubicle, each open space. He didn't find what he was looking for. Good. The kid wouldn't lose his boat to the DEA. He took another beer and left. He didn't need to plant a bug. That technology was archaic. He'd just lie in Wilson's berth and listen.

He was jolted awake at 0300 AM. Parkens was talking about the broad he'd laid this way and that. She was talking about the two girls she'd paid. Stone had seen her up close and personal. Forrest didn't mind strolling her deck in next to nothing. She wasn't bad, if the guy or lesbian wanting to fuck her was over seventy.

He woke again at 0600, ready. They weren't going anywhere. They were blasted, thoroughly pissed when they'd arrived at the boat.

He left the dock at 0610, his compass heading south by southeast. His ETA: 0945.

He went first across the northern tip, accessing the channel to Tombolina. He went to the house and brewed a pot of coffee. Waiting for the first cup he dismantled the

50" plasma screen he could never afford on a cop's salary. Satisfied the unit was properly secured to the boat, he went back.

He emptied Parkens' closet completely, and the woman's into plastic bags. He took them to the boat, not a garter or tie clip remained in the house. He poured a coffee and went through each room, inch by inch, drawer by drawer. He was certain.

Dakota had told him the day before that one day he'd destroy the house, that the house was a bad omen, filled with disease. The kid also had a dry sense of humour. He liked that.

He went to the cellar. He removed the wine and the liquor to the last bottle. He figured he had enough to last five, six years. Then he took the several clear bags of opium. Nothing was left in the house but appliances, books and macabre history.

He placed the twenty kilos evenly into the four corners of the first floor, connected the detonators and went outside. The camera was already running with a new cassette when he pressed his thumb onto the remote.

First the windows blew out. The structure trembled, wobbled, moved from side to side to a slow rhythm, collapsing in a maelstrom of dust and flying debris. He was done.

He dismantled the camera and left. Destination: leeward shore. ETA: 1215.

He went armed to Taliah's house. He slung the corpse over his shoulder and strode out, passing villagers, passing the Chief Counsellor, giving the man the third finger. The gesture was unknown to the Chief Counsellor, yet well understood.

1230. He was three miles offshore. Taliah was in the ocean, Stone was on his way home. ETA: 1600.

He eased Legality into the slip behind Three Fortunes.

There they were. Stone sat on the afterdeck sipping excellent champagne: Parkens'. The least he could do was salute the man, which he did.

Forrest invited him on board. He already knew that Parkens didn't want him, but she did. He declined, asking for a rain check. He had an early morning. Perhaps the next night, he suggested. Then he thought.

"Hey, why the hell not. Listen, you guys look really cool. Tomorrow night, let's say around seven, a bunch of us, we're going to the sandbar. If you're into a good time, a very, very good time, that's the place. Invitation only. Believe me, one chance in a lifetime."

Parkens raised his glass.

He phoned Wilson.

"Hi, Wilson."

"Screw you."

That wasn't good.

"I deserve that. Listen, Wilson, thanks for the boat."

"You're welcome. Who was onboard with you, Bambi?"

That wasn't good either.

"Be here tomorrow at five AM. That means you, the kids and the mother. Call me first from the parking lot."

"What's going on, Stone?"

"Payback."

He disconnected.

"Prick, asshole."

"You don't mean that, Brenda. You love that man, and he loves you. I saw in his eyes that he does."

"He's a jerk."

"They all are," Shakkra assured her, "when they're afraid."

"Afraid of what?"

"Us. You haven't been honest with him. He hasn't been honest with you because he's afraid. Possibly you should be the bravest one."

"He wants us at the boat tomorrow morning at five. He's talking payback."

"I don't know what that means."

She thought a moment, distracted. "Knowing him…something very good, or very bad. What Cassidy did to the pole is payback. But Stone's not a kid, as though I'm not already brain-dead."

"Then you'll sleep."

Shakkra kissed her and laid her down on the sofa. She covered her and remained awake all night sitting on the floor by her side until she woke Brenda at four. Then she woke the girls, and the boys who were such brave men to her.

At 4:55 Brenda called Stone from the parking lot. All was clear. By five AM they were onboard Legality.

At seven he waved to Parkens. The men were alone. At nine he waved goodbye to Forrest as she looked over her shoulder on her way to the car. He smiled at her and blew her a kiss. Her skirt was a foot too short.

Brenda wanted to strangle Stone on the spot. When Parkens ogled her, her skin crawled.

"Can you pilot that thing?"

"What?"

"Can you drive something that big?"

"Stone, make sense."

"Listen up. Don't ask questions. You can or you can't."

Aayla didn't like him and she told him so.

"Yes, I can, with a little space."

He nodded, sipping his coffee. She wanted to smack him so badly.

He told the women to remain on Legality. He told Dakota to bring the launch alongside his other boat. That done, the men removed all traces of Parkens from Three Fortunes. Brenda's eyes glued to the hand held tracking device. They removed all traces of Dakota and Cassidy from the launch. Stone checked once, twice and three times.

The men loaded the launch with what belonged to The Grand Guardian and Irene, taking their time, Dakota enjoying the moment. Then Stone went onboard with the clear bags of opium. He broke a bag. He laced each of the glasses onboard and blew out the excess. Then he made sure the bar was stocked with sufficient quantities of booze.

When they were done nothing of the Parkens remained on Three Fortunes, whatever they had left in life was onboard the launch.

Dakota wanted to leave a note, a final goodbye. Stone said no. Case closed.

Stone phoned the man who'd shot him a couple of days before. That man called another who called another. Stone sat back and cracked open three beers. If they could liberate an island, Wilson didn't have to like it. The three cans came together. Wilson folded her arms and looked to Shakkra, shaking her head.

The Parkens, known to the world as such, arrived at five PM. Three Fortunes was gone. In her place was a boat half the size that they knew. He stepped onboard cautiously. She followed and shrieked at seeing all her clothes, clothes from the other boat and what she'd left in her home. She saw his entire wardrobe and wailed, asking him what was happening.

He didn't know. He went to the helm. He scanned the marina. He knew of only one person. The question was how, which didn't matter. What mattered was Tombola, his house, his island that was his future.

The shithead on Legality shrugged. Yeah, he'd seen their kids. They'd said they needed the bigger boat for Tombola. What was that, a sandbar or something?

Hearing the boat had been stolen he suggested to Parkens that he call the Dade County police. Parkens told the air around him to fuck off and started the engines. He needed a drink. Get me a goddamn drink! She did, and one for herself.

When they were gone, Brenda turned over Legality. They followed at a safe distance, Stone suggesting that Dakota should make the call. Dakota declined. Stone deserved the moment.

Ten miles out the video camera captured the moment. Stone's wasn't the only curious one.

They saw the speedboat come alongside the launch. They saw the guns. They saw the woman's frantic wailing, drug dealers hurling the bags from one boat to the other. They saw the Dade County Police and DEA closing in, sirens screeching, the black and white helicopter hovering over the scene.

The evening papers would report the biggest opium bust in fifty years. What Stone saw were two less pieces of shit for him to step in each night. The kids did good, he told them.

Stone met the cops at the dock, flashing his shield. They didn't know him, and didn't like him. He needed a favour, not the credit, unless they screwed him over.

They didn't.

The men dressed in blue jackets and big yellow letters paraded the prisoners past Three Fortunes. Wilson gave in to him. Shakkra, Aayla, Xandra stood on the afterdeck drinking champagne, looking every bit the part. Mr. and Mrs. Parkens didn't. Their hands were cuffed behind their backs.

Dakota and Cassidy straddled port and starboard gunwales, drinking their champagne, smiling. The cops couldn't care less.

Stone stopped them. He had something to show them, a piece of history to make their day. He wanted them to see Cassidy Clayton blowing the Pole of Tombola to hell.

Sixty

Cassidy needed a favour, not quite certain how to go about what he needed to do. He asked Brenda to help him.

"Pride's Joy, Pride's Joy, Pride's Joy. This is Cassidy. I'm over."

She corrected him. He repeated the call twice more.

Three docks over Cindy's father put down his glass. He was certain he wasn't mistaken. He stood by the second message and was at his helm by the third. Holly's mother was bounding from her seat through the companionway to call the girls through the hatch in her stateroom.

She didn't step aside a moment too soon.

Cindy's father said, "This is Pride's Joy. What's your location, Cassidy? Are you okay, son? Do you need assistance? Over."

"I'm okay. I'm here with my mother and friends. Over"

Cindy and Holly pushed their way into the helm, knocking him onto the seat, giving him questions to ask. He cut to the chase. Cassidy gave him the slip number. The girls sprang from the boat onto the dock and were gone.

"Well you stay right there. Seems you've got company coming your way. Good luck with that. You might want to brace yourself, son. They're a little excited from what I see scurrying down the dock. Now pass me to your captain. Holly's mother and I owe you folks a dinner, and a whole lot more. Over."

Cassidy passed Brenda the mike, Brenda surprised to

discover she knew Cindy's father by reputation.

Cassidy and Dakota stood on the dock, Dakota whistling air through his lips in appreciation.

Cindy and Holly were rounding the corner, flying along the dock, their cover-ups dancing around their thighs, waving hands that weren't held tight, brunette ponytails swinging from side to side. They weren't the same girls, they were the improved version.

The red and titanium hair was gone, the make-up was gone. So were Aayla and Xandra, the four girls colliding midway in a tangle of arms.

Shakkra stepped onto the dock and stood between her men in her own tangle of arms. Her face wet with happy tears and streaked with mascara. Her little one had discovered new friends.

Sixty-One

A week later Cassidy pulled alongside the gas dock at the helm of his own Freedom, his mother standing beside him with Zach. She felt her husband's strength. Aayla and Xandra were seated at the stern. On the dock Immigration Officers waited, assisting with the lines. Beside them were Dakota, Stone, Wilson and Cindy's father who had very good friends in very high places.

Three hours later they were given into Brenda Wilson's custody.

Dakota wouldn't hear of Stone buying the chopper, disregarding the protests when he gave Stone the transfer papers not many nights later at dinner. Stone's smile was payment enough. So was Brenda's wide-eyed shock when Stone showed her the ring, in another envelope along with his letter of resignation from the force.

The weeks passed quickly, dissolving into months and two years later Aayla, Cassidy and his mom had high school leaving certificates.

By the third year Stone owned a touring company and shuttle service based in Miami, operating on Isla Tombola, servicing the first of Dakota and Xandra Dade's upscale clients amongst who were young Mr. Clayton and his wife, Aayla, residents of Miami and first-year university students. Their lives were just beginning, Shakkra insisting she could wait several more years to become a grandmother.

So was her life beginning. She was Dakota's premier

guest throughout the first week following her first-year university finals.

Holly's uncle had lived his life as a confirmed bachelor, until sitting by the most beautiful woman in world one night at his sister's dinner table. When Shakkra wasn't studying towards her commerce degree she was doing lunch with Brenda or designing new lines of swimwear for women favoured by nature, very much in love with the man she was about to marry.

Her son was giving her away. At the altar he stepped back and eyed her not very discreetly from her knees to her eyes. His smirk was telling. Everyone one knew. She knew, and she smacked him. She'd already hugged him a hundred times.

Her dress was simple, deep green silk and A-line, sleeveless and cut to above her knees. She wore nothing on her head, low-heeled pumps on her feet. She wore her single adornment at her neck, her son's wedding gift to her: a jagged splinter of wood he'd taken from a symbol of hell, fashioned into a miniature pole and dipped in Jonathon's gold.

The Feast of Tombola

Other Mystery – Suspense - Thriller Novels
By Doug Booth:

Split Verdict

The 4th Man

The Madam

Family Lies

Mother of Pearl

From Inside Her Bedroom

The Feast of Tombola

Deferred Prejudice

The Hunt for Gilligan Rose

The Fatal Diners' Club

Silent Conviction

A Christmas Killer, Comfort and Joy

Pariah In the Mirror

***

No One to Tell (Creative Non-fiction)

www.ingramcontent.com/pod-product-compliance
Lightning Source LLC
Chambersburg PA
CBHW030536020726
47494CB00005B/1384